"Exciting, sexy, loss high in
Gaelen Foley

author

He caught she *would have retreated.*

~~~ ∞ ~~~

He would have let go of her at once if she had. Instead, he tugged her forward until he could cup his free hand around the smooth, warm nape of her neck. He felt her sharp inhale of breath against his cheek and her fist where it landed against his chest. But he held her anyway, pressing his momentary advantage of surprise.

A tremor shook his body. And then, blissfully, she surrendered. The fingers fisted against him loosened, then dug into his jacket to hold him to her. Nate released her wrist to wind his arm around her waist, and she threw that arm around his neck, clinging as if she would never let go.

Her lips parted beneath his, and Nate felt the earth shift beneath his feet. She kissed him back with hunger and more than a little passion. Her mouth tasted of wine and indeed, he felt half-drunk, upended and swept away.

This wasn't what he had expected; it was something far more dangerous . . .

"Luscious! A brilliant, passionate battle of wits between two smart, dangerous characters. What a riveting read!"
Anna Campbell, author of *Captive of Sin*

Romances by **Caroline Linden**

You Only Love Once
For Your Arms Only
A View to a Kiss

ATTENTION: ORGANIZATIONS AND CORPORATIONS
Most Avon Books paperbacks are available at special quantity
discounts for bulk purchases for sales promotions, premiums,
or fund raising. For information, please call or write:

**Special Markets Department, HarperCollins Publishers,
10 East 53rd Street, New York, New York 10022-5299.
Telephone: (212) 207-7528.   Fax: (212) 207-7222.**

You Only Love Once

CAROLINE LINDEN

A V O N

An Imprint of HarperCollinsPublishers

This is a work of fiction. Names, characters, places, and incidents are products of the author's imagination or are used fictitiously and are not to be construed as real. Any resemblance to actual events, locales, organizations, or persons, living or dead, is entirely coincidental.

AVON BOOKS
An Imprint of HarperCollins*Publishers*
10 East 53rd Street
New York, New York 10022-5299

Copyright © 2010 by P. F. Belsley
ISBN 978-0-06-170648-6
www.avonromance.com

All rights reserved. No part of this book may be used or reproduced in any manner whatsoever without written permission, except in the case of brief quotations embodied in critical articles and reviews. For information, address Avon Books, an Imprint of HarperCollins Publishers.

First Avon Books paperback printing: September 2010

Avon Trademark Reg. U.S. Pat. Off. and in Other Countries, Marca Registrada, Hecho en U.S.A.
HarperCollins® is a registered trademark of HarperCollins Publishers.

Printed in the U.S.A.

10 9 8 7 6 5 4 3 2 1

If you purchased this book without a cover, you should be aware that this book is stolen property. It was reported as "unsold and destroyed" to the publisher, and neither the author nor the publisher has received any payment for this "stripped book."

To John and Nancy,

For all they have given us:
A hunger to learn,
The joy of travel,
The ability to laugh at ourselves, and with each other.
In the house by the lake, and later by the sea
we have gotten a life lesson unmatched in watching
you each grow,
as does your love for each other.

You Only
Love Once

Prologue

Outside Paris, 1793

The soldiers came late in the day, grim and un-wavering. Everyone had expected them, but their appearance, led by a cold-eyed Revolutionary who had once been a neighbor, was still shocking. The master of the house, the Comte d'Orvelon, went out to meet them while his wife frantically made the final arrangements.

"Quickly," the comtesse whispered. Melanie, her trusted maid, was rubbing her hands in the ashes of last night's fire. Soot already smudged her face beneath the turban of the Revolutionists, but now Melanie crouched beside a basket and brushed dirt onto the perfect ivory cheeks of the baby who sat within, trying to pull her tiny foot into her mouth and ignoring Melanie's efforts to dirty her.

"My darling," the comtesse said on a choked sob as she watched. "My baby . . ."

"I will guard her with my life," Melanie promised, dusting off her hands on the plain linen apron she wore. No longer dressed in the comtesse's cast-off silks, she wore a commoner's dress, with dirt under her nails and the sash of the Revolution knotted across her chest. She looked like a common peasant—as she must, if this was to work. "No, Madame!" she cried softly as the comtesse reached for her infant daughter. "You mustn't!"

But her mistress lifted the child, smearing dirt and ashes on her own face and dress. "I will not see her again for a long time," she murmured, holding the child's cheek to hers and stroking the baby-fine hair. "Perhaps never. Let me hold her just a moment . . ."

Melanie glanced at the kitchen door in a panic. Soldiers hadn't made it into the garden yet, but they would. Jacques, the coachman, lurked just outside the door. He caught her eye and made an urgent gesture; they must hurry. She nodded to him and turned back to her mistress, but bit her lip nervously. It wasn't in her to defy her lady, so fair and so generous and now in such danger. The baby giggled and grabbed at her mother's hair, and a tear slid down the comtesse's cheek. Melanie said nothing.

"Marie." The comte had come into the deserted kitchen. He had aged ten years in the last two months, since he had been accused as an enemy of the Republic. White streaked his dark hair, and his skin had taken on a gray pallor like that of a shut-in. Once so urbane and handsome, now he was disheveled and worn. The Revolution had not been gentle. "Marie, they have come. I have told them we will go willingly, to allow more time—" He caught sight of Melanie and inhaled sharply. With three long steps he crossed the kitchen. "Why are you still here?" he hissed. "You should have been gone by now!"

"*Oui*, Monsieur," she murmured, barely remembering not to curtsey to her master. "We are going."

His eyes darted anxiously around, snagging for a moment on Jacques, who again made a gesture to hurry. "Marie, they must go," he said in despair. "You must send them now, or the chance will be lost."

The comtesse sniffled, and dragged her sleeve across her eyes. The part of Melanie that had served her loyally and efficiently cringed at the sight, but she said nothing and put out her arms for the child.

The mother bowed her head over the baby's, whispering something into the tiny ear. Melanie looked away, only to catch sight of the anguish that contorted the comte's face for just a moment. Without a word he laid his hand on his daughter's dusky curls. Two fingers bore the pale stripes of rings that had been worn for years, and were now discarded. Confiscated. Stolen, she thought bitterly. For a moment the parents huddled together over their only child, saying good-bye to her even as the Committee's soldiers waited outside to take them to prison. Fierce hatred burned in Melanie's heart, banishing her tears as she took the little girl into her own arms.

"Here." Madame pressed a small linen bag into her hand with a soft clink. It contained a king's ransom in precious stones, carefully pried from their settings. "Use them carefully, Melanie. They must take you all the way to London. Do you remember the name?"

"*Oui*, Madame."

"Say it!" Madame had made her memorize everything, refusing to commit a single word to paper.

"Lady Simone Carlisle, Grosvenor Square, London," Melanie whispered in a rush. Jacques stuck his head through the door and said her name. "We will wait there for word from you."

"God willing," Lady d'Orvelon murmured. They all knew there was a strong chance word would never come from her or her husband. He had been accused of treason, and judges were sentencing traitors left and right to the guillotine. The comte had tried to send his wife away, but her pregnancy and childbirth had been hard; she had not recovered enough to travel, and now it was too late. They still clung to hope; the comte had renounced his title, ceded most of his lands, wore the Revolutionary cockade. That might sway the judges, but the comte had known from the moment he and his wife were accused that they might die.

But their child . . . The girl cooed and tugged at Melanie's sash, and she held the baby tighter. Jacques had promised to get them safely to the coast, no more. He had his own family to protect. Madame and the comte were trusting her to spirit their only child to safety, to England, to Madame's cousin Lady Carlisle. If God were just, the parents and child would be soon reunited, but if not . . . "Madame," she tried to say, but her voice broke.

"God go with you," murmured the comte.

The comtesse shook herself. "Go," she said quietly. "Go with Jacques. We will do all we can to keep them from following." With visible effort she straightened her shoulders and placed her hand on her husband's arm. "Tell her we love her."

"*Oui*, Madame, every day," Melanie whispered as Jacques, out of patience at last, strode across the kitchen and pulled her by the arm toward the door. Melanie caught one last glimpse of her mistress watching them go, head held regally high despite the tears on her cheeks, before they were in the garden, darting along the row of overgrown hemlocks toward the stables where Jacques had left the pack of supplies they would need for the long walk to the coast.

The little girl struggled in her arms, jabbering in excitement. She wanted to get down and toddle along the path, as she had just learned how to do. Melanie held her closer and murmured lullabies in her ear as Jacques swung the provisions onto his shoulder. The stables were deserted, as was the house. Most of the servants had long since run off, and Melanie's greatest fear was that one of them would be with the soldiers, to see them and identify her and Jacques as loyal servants and the child as Madame's. Melanie didn't know what those cruel Revolutionaries would do to a baby, but she didn't trust them any more than Madame did. Lying, stealing, murdering opportunists, that's all they were. Already Madame's sister and her husband had been sent to the guillotine, and several relatives of Monsieur as well. Melanie said a desperate prayer in her mind that Madame would be spared, for the sake of her daughter if nothing else.

They hurried through the gardens, once elegant and now neglected and shabby, past the statuary and the stagnant ponds, past the little grave that had been dug to give proof to the lie that Madame's baby had died. Jacques urged her on. "We should have gone hours ago," he told her. "Do not look back."

Melanie didn't. If by some chance she should catch sight of her mistress being led away, she might cry out and startle the baby. The child was already fussy, kicking her legs and screwing up her little face to cry. Melanie shifted the baby's weight in her arms and pressed her cheek to the silky mop of curls. She was not a nursemaid, and hadn't much experience with children. If Madame's other babies had survived, perhaps they would have lived distantly in the nursery as proper sons and daughters of a man like Monsieur le Comte. But after so many miscarriages and stillbirths, Madame had kept this beloved child with her, almost every hour of the day. Melanie had grown accustomed to the baby crawling around the floor as she tended Madame. Now it was a blessing, because it made the little girl familiar enough to go quietly with her. Perhaps she wouldn't even have to give the baby laudanum to make her quiet.

At the top of the hill, though, she couldn't help herself. Orvelon had been her home since she was a small child, where she had followed in her mother's footsteps as a maid in the chateau. From this distance it was still beautiful, the pale stone gleaming in the clear light of the day, but to Melanie it now looked like a mausoleum. In a way, it was. All Melanie's notions of French superiority and decency lay entombed in that elegant mansion, which would no doubt soon belong to one of Robespierre's friends. Monsieur le Comte was a good man, a kind master and husband, a philosopher who actually believed in many of the Revolution's goals. The only thing he opposed was the guillotine. Madame was a beloved mistress, compassionate and generous to all, an educated woman and the very model of a proper lady. Melanie could remember a time, not so many years ago, when the comte's kinship to the King was a source of pride. Now it made him an enemy of the state, regardless of what kind of man he was. That was not liberty, fraternity, or equality.

"I hate them," she whispered to the tiny girl in her arms. As small as ants in the distance, the soldiers who had come to lead the comte and comtesse away milled about the chateau, their weapons gleaming dully in the sun. A thin whisper of their coarse laughter drifted across the neglected landscape. The baby's dark eyes peered solemnly up at her, and Melanie made a silent vow. If the worst happened, and the comtesse never reached England, Melanie would devote herself to Madame's child. She would teach Madame's daughter everything— useful things as well as lovely, ladylike things. She would raise her to be strong and fearless and capable of defending herself. This child would never be left sitting helplessly in her home when men turned on her. "Those Revolutionary dogs," she murmured to the child, turning away to follow Jacques. "I despise them, and you must, too."

Chapter 1

London, 1820

Angelique Martand was not particularly proud to be a spy. It was a distasteful job, often dirty and dangerous, and at times it left such a mark on her soul that she feared the stain would never wash away. But it was also a necessary job, and someone must do it, for the good of the entire country. The fact that Angelique was exceptionally good at it merely made for a convenient—and enriching—coincidence.

Still, the envelope on her breakfast tray that fine late summer morning was not particularly welcome. She knew what it meant, that plain envelope addressed in a nondescript hand. Her employer, John Stafford, chief clerk of Bow Street Magistrates Court and Home Office spymaster, had a new assignment for her. That didn't bother her. What bothered her was the prospect of refusing it.

She considered ignoring it, pretending the post had gone astray and she had never received it. She explored this idea while she breakfasted, letting the envelope lie where the maid had left it on the tray.

She did answer these summonses of her own volition, after all, and no one could make her answer this one. The man who had sent it would never dare approach her more directly than this, and if she did not respond, he would have to find someone else. Someone who did not mind being lied to and sent off dangerously ignorant of the true import of her assignment. Someone who did not mind risking her life to conceal a petty bureaucrat's thieving ways, or the disgrace of a well-respected lord plotting to kill the King, or the embarrassment of a high-ranking army officer at the hands of a blackmailer. Someone, in short, who didn't mind being used by those in power to protect themselves.

Still . . .

Angelique pursed her lips and let her eyes wander about her bedchamber. It was a lovely room in a lovely house, if she did say so herself, simple but elegant, and it was all hers—thanks to Stafford. Whatever offenses he had done her, the man paid her very well. If only she hadn't caught him lying to her. If only she hadn't been unpleasantly surprised and unsettled by it. Cursing silently, she opened the envelope and read the single line inside: *Half past eleven, this morning.*

She flung off the coverlet and got out of bed. "Lisette," she called. "The green striped walking dress today."

Her maid bustled into the room a moment later, the green dress over her arm. "*Oui*, Madame. Shall I send for a carriage?"

Angelique walked to the window and pulled back the curtain. The fresh morning breeze blew her nightdress flat against her belly, and she raised her arms over her head, savoring the feel of the fine lawn against her skin. She hadn't worked for over two months, and had become used to lazy days spent on pursuits of her own whim. That must be part of the reason she was so reluctant to go into the city and see Stafford. "I suppose," she said, answering Lisette's query.

"You are not anxious to see him?" Lisette clucked under her breath and answered her own question. "Of course not. Who would be pleased to wait on the devil?"

Angelique smiled. "Pleased? No. Satisfied?" She paused. "Perhaps."

The maid raised her brows but said nothing. Lisette was more than a mere maid; unlike the other servants, she knew precisely what her mistress was. She even accompanied Angelique on many assignments, helping with disguises, cooking when necessary, binding wounds, and even spying a bit herself among other servants. She was invaluable, both as a lady's maid and as a spy's servant.

Angelique washed, then sat before the dressing table. Lisette picked up the brush and began pulling it through her hair. Angelique gazed into the mirror and watched the maid arrange her long dark hair into a fashionable twist. She smiled wryly at the dark humor of dressing like a lady when she was anything but; why, Stafford might be planning to send her out posing as a whore this time. Then she stopped smiling, and leaned closer to the mirror, ignoring Lisette's exclamation as a thick lock of hair fell out of place. Gently she touched the skin at the corners of her eyes and between her brows. The faint lines there didn't go away, and when she frowned, they grew deeper and more pronounced.

"Madame?" asked Lisette curiously.

She sat back. "Wrinkles," she announced. "I am growing old."

"It is better than not growing old." Lisette shrugged, twisting the loose hair back into the heavy mass at the crown of her head. "I speak from experience."

Angelique smiled reluctantly. Lisette was probably old enough to be her mother, and looked it. What she said was true enough, particularly to someone in Angelique's profession. Besides, she *was* getting old. In less than two years' time, she would be thirty. "That does not mean I must enjoy it." Lisette laughed. "He is making me old before my time," she added on a sigh.

"There's no doubt of that, Madame," the maid replied. "'Tis a hard life. You would be well quit of it, and *him*." Lisette never called Stafford by name, just *him*, as if his very name left a bad taste in her mouth.

"Indeed." Hair coifed, Angelique rose from the table. As she dressed, each layer of clothing tugged and smoothed into place by Lisette's capable hands, she studied herself in the mirror with critical eyes. There was a scar on the inside of her arm from one of her first spying missions, small but noticeable. The burn scar on her shin was more prominent, but it lay hidden under stockings and skirts. The little finger of her left hand had been broken once and healed just shy of straight, also in Stafford's service. Her figure was still slim and her muscles still strong—stronger than the average woman's—but Angelique began to feel old and tired. Or rather she sensed it coming, and was suddenly more keenly aware of the passing of time.

She thought about it as the hired carriage drove her into London, to the heart of the city where John Stafford kept his office. She felt no tension, no anxiety, no exhilaration about whatever he might present to her. That was new; once, a summons from him would have made her heart pound and her blood surge. It was terrifying and thrilling to be sent off on a dangerous assignment, although the terror had waned as she grew more skilled and practiced. But now the exhilaration was gone as well. Perhaps more than anything, that meant it was time to consider retirement. A bored or distracted spy was not long for this world, and she preferred to die on her own terms, hopefully in her own bed at a date in the distant future.

The carriage halted near the busy market in Covent Garden. She stepped down and tipped her driver generously, then walked the short distance to Bow Street. Before she reached the Magistrates Court, she turned down an alley, walking around to the back to a plain door that looked like the entrance to the coal bin. But she pulled a key from her reticule and put it in the lock, and the door opened on remarkably well-oiled hinges.

She locked the door behind her and went down the hall, her footsteps echoing off the blank walls. Stafford's office was not back here, in this narrow passage with unmarked doors every few feet. Stafford's deputy, Mr. Phipps, popped out of one of them as she walked past, on her way to the larger, brighter office upstairs.

"He's been expecting you," Phipps said, trotting at her heels.

"Has he?" she said without looking at him. She didn't care for Phipps, who never risked his own neck but fancied himself better than all the agents put together, and most especially better than she. Once he had scolded her for being seen breaking into the home of a suspected French spy, causing an uproar among the neighbors that alerted the man to their interest. Phipps had sneeringly suggested her sex was the reason she had been so careless. Angelique had simply smiled and offered to break into *his* home without being seen, promising that he would know she had been there by the knife she would leave in his throat. Ever since, Phipps had been like a dog growling at her from the shadows, always waiting for her to make another mistake. He hated her for not having done so, and she hated him for watching for it.

"All morning," he informed her maliciously. "Now he's tied up with a foreign visitor."

"And yet I am here when he requested." She climbed the stairs, and Phipps puffed his way up behind her.

"I'll let him know you're waiting."

Angelique stopped in front of Stafford's private office. She made no reply, just gave Phipps a pointed look. Although she wasn't tall, her eyes were on a level with his as he stooped slightly to hold the stitch in his side. His pale gaze held hers a moment, then flickered down over her figure in the stylish walking dress, the palpable contempt in his expression underpinned with unwilling lust. What a pathetic little man he was, sure she was Stafford's favorite agent only because she must be lifting her skirt for him. Angelique thought of the impossible tasks she had completed for Stafford, many without Phipps's knowledge, and wanted to laugh. For a man who thought she was incompetent, Phipps was remarkably chary of her.

She waited until he looked her in the face again. "If he wished to see me earlier or later, he should have said so in his note," she said with acid politeness. "As it is, he will be glad to see me at all, since I do not sit downstairs and await his pleasure." *As you do.*

Phipps's mouth flattened sullenly. He knew she was right, and he hated her for that as well. Without another word he jerked his head and turned on his heel to walk away. She sniffed at his departing back, then rapped twice on the door. A voice inside called out at once to enter, and she let herself into the room.

It was a large office, but furnished as plainly as a clerk's might be. Bookcases lined two walls, and hard wooden chairs a third. Sunlight streamed through the two high windows onto the scuffed floor and cluttered desk, glittering on a small stack of coins and a thin stiletto dagger. There was something very English about Stafford's utter disregard for any concealment of his activities. At her entrance, he rose from his desk and bowed his head. She nodded back and waited. There was another man, also rising from his chair, but she only paid him enough attention to note his presence.

"Good morning," Stafford said with a thin smile. "Thank you for coming." He held out one hand. "May I introduce Mr. Nathaniel Avery. Mr. Avery, this is Madame Martand."

"Good day." She curtsied as the other man bowed. Again she barely glanced at him; he was hardly worthy of note, moderately tall and lanky with untidy brown hair, unexceptional features, and plain, serviceable clothing. She half expected him to excuse himself, or for Stafford to murmur a pardon and escort him out, but neither happened. He must be related to whatever Stafford wanted to present to her, then. Stafford held out one hand toward a chair, and she seated herself.

"I have an assignment for you," her employer said, "of some international delicacy. Mr. Avery"—he inclined his head politely at the other man—"is in England to find a man who has defrauded his government. You are to help him find this man, so that he may recover any funds remaining."

She pursed her lips and said nothing. Stafford gave her a gleaming glance across the desk before turning to Avery. "Madame Martand is most capable."

"No doubt, no doubt," murmured Avery. American, she guessed from his accent, and not pleased to be presented with a woman. She had certainly heard that dry, doubtful tone enough times to recognize it now. She didn't move or change her expression, but instinctively her regard for Mr. Avery dropped the few levels it had achieved to begin with.

Stafford must have heard it, too, for he smiled in his chilly way. She knew he was savoring the joke. No one ever expected her to be any good at what she did. "Perhaps you would relate your information about Mr. Dixon's actions for her benefit."

Avery shifted on his chair. "Er . . . yes." He cleared his throat. "Jacob Dixon served for several years as the deputy to the Collector of the Port of New York, responsible for collecting tariffs on goods arriving from abroad. Mr. Dixon had charge of all the bookkeeping of the port, and therefore of all the funds. Just a few months ago he abruptly gave notice and returned to his native England. Shortly after his departure, a sizable amount of money was discovered missing from the port accounts. An examination of the books left little doubt that Dixon is responsible for its disappearance. I am here on behalf of my government to recover as much money as remains, and to take Mr. Dixon back to New York for trial."

Angelique raised one eyebrow at Stafford. He met her gaze with a placid look, his eyes opaque and calm, just a clerk going about his business. She knew better. Chasing down a common embezzler? He wouldn't send her out for something so tedious and ordinary. There must be something more to this, and it raised the hair on the back of her neck that he wasn't saying anything. She glanced back at the American fellow from the corner of her eye. His expression was unhappy, his posture stiff.

"You are certain this man is in England?"

He started, as if he had not expected her to question him, and turned to her. He had shockingly green eyes, but answered with a hint of indignity. "We most certainly are."

"Then why do you not simply apprehend him?" She widened her eyes innocently. "Send a pair of constables around to his lodging and arrest him, then retrieve your money."

"It's not that simple, Madame," said Avery in the condescending tone she hated. "We are not just after a chest of coins."

"Perhaps it is not that simple, but that is what you are to do, in essence," Stafford broke in. "Locate Mr. Dixon without betraying your true intent. He may well flee the country with his ill-gotten gains, or leave them so well hidden the funds may never be recovered. We hope to take him unawares. Seduce the information from him, if you will, before he suspects he has caught our attention."

Angelique made a noncommittal noise in the back of her throat. This sounded tedious—suspiciously so. The word "no" was poised on her tongue, ready to fall as soon as politely possible. The moment the American left, if not sooner.

"If Mr. Avery's information is correct, Mr. Dixon may be looking to establish himself in English society using his stolen fortune. You and Mr. Avery will work together to find him. He alone knows what Mr. Dixon looks like, and he alone will know the particulars of the misappropriated funds." He nodded politely at the American, although Angelique didn't miss the wry twist of his mouth as he did so. That was interesting; Stafford must have wanted to know more, and been rebuffed. Perhaps this Avery fellow wasn't quite as simple as he appeared.

It wouldn't make her work with him, though.

She clasped her hands in her lap and assumed an expression of pained regret. "I do not think my talents are suited to this task. I am sure—"

"We must act quickly before Mr. Dixon has a chance to disappear into the country," went on Stafford over her words, as if she hadn't spoken. "His family comes originally from Essex, although Mr. Avery believes there are no members remaining there. The sooner he is found, the better." The spymaster's eyes flashed at her. Angelique sat like a stone, her face a smooth mask. He had heard her begin to protest; he knew she would refuse. For some reason he was carrying on as if it were otherwise, which portended nothing good. She sat in tense silence and waited.

"You shall be man and wife. Mr. Avery, a wealthy American looking for investors. You, his discontented wife." Stafford's gaze darted between the two of them. "Between the two of you, one should be able to discover Dixon's location and loosen his tongue."

Angelique loosened her own tongue. "No."

Unperturbed, Stafford rose. "Mr. Avery, would you be so kind as to excuse us? I will contact you in the morning about how we shall proceed."

"Of course," the man muttered, jumping to his feet. "My thanks for your time, sir. Madame." He bowed slightly in her direction and left. The door opened, then closed behind him with a soft click. Angelique didn't even look after him; she didn't care what he thought, the arrogant idiot.

"How dare you," she began coldly. "He is an amateur—and you wish me to go as his wife? No."

Her employer held up one hand as he resumed his seat. "Do you think I just dreamed up this plan? It has been carefully crafted, I assure you. Contain your temper a moment and listen." Angelique raised her eyebrows, unaccustomed to being spoken to in such a manner. Stafford leaned forward and lowered his voice. "This man Dixon is a grave menace. We want him found, and you are the person to do it."

"All this, over money?" she snapped. "Have Ian

snatch him off the street, and tell him not to be gentle. Two hours with Ian and he will desecrate his mother's grave to return the money."

"No, it is not about the money," Stafford said. He leaned back and clasped his hands on his desk. "Avery can find it, or not. I agreed to try to get his government's funds, but if it comes to naught . . ." He shrugged. "I don't care if he never sees a penny of it again."

"So you would send me off like some errand boy, when you do not even care if the funds are returned." She shook her head and started to rise from her chair. "Find someone else. I have no interest."

"Wait," he said sharply. "I need *you* to find Dixon."

"Why?" She tilted her chin in scorn. "There is nothing in this task that someone else could not do. You knew I would not like being sent out with *him*, let alone as his wife. If I must work with someone, I prefer it to be someone who knows what he is doing. I will spend the whole time looking after this American adventurer!"

"Dixon is reputedly a man of expensive tastes. He likes beautiful women. I am quite sure you will be able to use that to your advantage." His tone of voice intimated exactly how she could do it.

"How does that make him different from any other man?" She shrugged. "You have other spies willing to whore for you."

"Not like you."

"Send Ian along with one of them. He is all too willing to play a husband, and he will not look down his nose at a woman doing her job."

"But Avery must be there, and the simplest pose is

as your husband. He alone knows what Dixon looks like, what his habits and tastes are, the details of his recent life and crimes. Without his involvement we would be searching in the dark. If he is there as your husband, he will be able to remain close to you, and offer plenty of opportunity for you to confer. Not," he added dryly, "that I don't appreciate Mr. Wallace's talents as well."

He wouldn't send Ian. Angelique gave it up and changed her attack. "Who is Avery?"

"He is an envoy of President Monroe, properly credentialed. I believe he has connections to a prominent Boston family."

"In other words, he has a patronage post and thinks to play at being a spy." She shook her head. "Who is Dixon, that you jump to find him on the word of such a man? And for such a motive—I see nothing in this for the Crown, nothing." Stafford just looked at her. She knew that smooth opaque expression, though, and was having none of it. "You have lied to me before," she reminded him. "And I will not tolerate it again."

He drummed his fingers on the desk, then surged to his feet and paced to the window. "I take issue with your use of the word 'lie,'" he said over his shoulder. "But no matter. I never swore to reveal all; you agreed to that. I need someone who will follow my orders, not question every facet of them, and you knew that years ago."

"It almost cost two men their lives," she retorted. "I never agreed to that. How am I to know I am not the next agent to be sacrificed?"

He stood a moment more at the window, hands tightly clasped behind him. "All right," he growled, turning abruptly. "This is what I can tell you: You are to find Dixon as soon as humanly possible. Do what you must to keep Avery in line, but once he has his money, dispatch him on his way at once."

"And then?" she prodded when he hesitated.

"And then . . ." Stafford paused again. "You must kill Jacob Dixon."

Chapter 2

Angelique was so surprised she spoke without thinking. "Why?"

Her employer's eyebrows went up, way up. She was not paid to ask why, and normally she didn't. She had always been convinced of the necessity of drastic acts by the nature of the people on whom he asked her spy. Men plotting to assassinate the King were one thing, though; a common embezzler was another. And this time Stafford was coercing her into a mission she didn't like, in a role she flatly refused to play, with an ignorant, bumbling American to watch over. She lifted her chin under Stafford's regard and waited for his reply.

For a moment he looked annoyed, and then his expression smoothed into its usual imperturbable lines. "The Crown does not wish him to linger. The Crown wishes for him to simply . . . disappear."

Angelique frowned. This mission grew less and less appealing by the minute. "I do not like it. It always makes things difficult."

"You have done it before."

"Not with pleasure," she snapped. "Such a mess. And what am I to do with Avery if he should protest? He declared his intention to take this man back to America with him."

"You will manage."

She scoffed. "If I agree."

"Are you threatening not to agree?"

She met his level stare with her own for a long moment. "More than threatening," she said at last. "You have given me very little reason to agree, particularly with this added"—she flicked her fingers in distaste—"complication."

"I did not think I needed to. Beyond the usual inducement, that is."

Angelique made a face. He meant her payment. She was always paid treble if he required her to kill anyone. She didn't quibble at cutting a throat now and then, not when the throats belonged to men with every sort of sin on their souls already and more contemplated, but taking a life was not something to be done lightly. If she didn't demand a premium, Stafford would have her hands permanently covered in blood. And now an embezzler? When even his victim didn't wish him dead? "I am not so desperate for money as that."

He frowned. It was just a pair of lines between his brows, but she was not used to seeing anything like it on his face. Stafford was ever sure of himself. Perhaps it was because he was suddenly not sure of her, after all these years working together. How many had it been now—nine? Ten? It brought back her morning disquiet about her own advancing age, and made her just want to leave. She put up one hand when he started to speak. "I will think about it," she said. "But I do not like it."

"I tried to persuade Mr. Avery that his participation was not needed." It was a peace offering, or as close as John Stafford ever came to one. She dipped her head in acknowledgment.

"You will have my answer in two days. I trust that will not be a problem."

He, in turn, accepted her delay without argument. "Not at all."

Angelique thought through the strange conversation as she walked out of the building. Stafford wanted her, specifically, to go with the American, when it would be so much easier to have Ian handle it. He didn't want anyone to know what happened to Dixon; he wanted Dixon to simply disappear. Embezzling—from the Americans, no less, not even from the English—wasn't worth killing a man over, let alone so secretively. Stafford must want him dead for other reasons, reasons that must have either just come to his attention, or existed for some time but been negated by the simple fact that Stafford obviously didn't know where or how to find Dixon. Avery said the man had been in America for several years.

Her dark mood soured more at the thought of Avery. A prominent Boston family, a personal letter from the president of his country. This did not sound like a man capable of the deceit, discretion, and daring necessary. And he did not look pleased to hear Stafford wanted her to go with him, which meant she might as well consider him in the same category as Dixon, unpredictable and untrustworthy. Angelique wished it were Ian instead. Ian respected her abilities and did what she told him to do. They got on well together and trusted each other—as well as any two people in their profession could trust each other. Avery, on the other hand . . .

She shook her head in irritation as she emerged into the bustle of Bow Street. With any luck, Mr. Avery would decide he couldn't bear to work with a woman and quit before they even began. With even greater luck, Stafford would call off the entire episode when he did so.

Nate Avery almost missed the Frenchwoman when she finally emerged from the Bow Street offices. She came not out the front door but from an alley some distance away. She walked briskly, without looking around her, her head held high. Nate tossed aside the newspaper he'd been reading as he waited, and followed her.

Had he not known to look for her, she wouldn't have particularly caught his eye. Once he had seen her move, though, he couldn't recall why not. Her posture radiated poise and command. "Command" might not be the usual thing to attribute to a woman, but this one had it. Nate recalled how she had dealt with Stafford and what the man had said about her: *She is exceedingly capable.* Just looking at the back of her bonnet and the set of her shoulders made him think it might be true. Still, she wasn't at all what he had expected, and that bothered him.

Already things were not going as anticipated. Nate had approached Stafford because he needed to; that part had all gone according to plan. There was little to no chance the English would be pleased if he tracked down one of their own and spirited the man back to New York without so much as a courtesy visit. He had expected to be sent along with an Englishman at his side, some pinched-faced fellow meant to watch over him as much as help him. He had not expected the Englishman to be a French-woman, let alone a young, petite one who looked barely old enough to be without her governess but walked with the confidence of a warrior. She was a beauty, to be sure, and that alone would probably be enough to seduce Jacob Dixon, as Stafford had suggested. But Dixon was as slippery as an otter, and had talked and charmed his way past dozens of people who ought to have known better. There was little chance he'd reveal the details of his crimes in exchange for a tumble with any woman, not even that one. Nate was torn between amazement that Stafford wanted to send her, and frustration that he would have to puzzle her out at the same time he tried to pin down Dixon.

At the corner she stepped off the pavement and raised one hand at a passing hackney. By length-ening his step, Nate was able to catch the edge of the door just as she reached out to shut it behind her. Without waiting for an invitation, he swung himself into the carriage, pulling the door closed behind him.

"This carriage is taken," she said. Her voice was calm, but he caught the spark of irritation in her dark eyes.

"I know." He settled into the seat opposite her, not making any effort to hide his scrutiny.

She gave a faint shrug and shook her head. "Then go ahead. Ask your questions."

"You aren't surprised that I want some answers?"

"I never promised answers," she said. "But ask and be done with it. It is not a long ride."

"Oh? How far are we going?" He leaned back and

stretched out his legs, as much as he could in the narrow hackney. His boot collided with her foot, beneath the edge of her skirt. Her expression didn't change, but she lifted that foot, placed it on top of his boot, and pushed down until he thought she was trying to break his ankle. He braced his toes and flexed his foot, resisting. His boots weren't the thin leather ones Englishmen were wearing now, but tougher, waterproof ones meant for a seafaring man. He just sat and waited, smiling until she let up.

"I am not going far," she said. "I don't know where you are going."

"Apparently I'm not going anywhere without you, if your Mr. Stafford has his way."

"He may not," she replied gently, as if breaking bad news. "You may still hope."

Nate raised his eyebrows. "He didn't seem the type to take disappointment well."

"But he will, if he has no choice." She glanced out the window.

Nate hadn't heard the direction she gave the driver, but he didn't know distances in London anyway. He might have only another minute or so to take her measure. "He might accept it, but I won't. I intend to find Jacob Dixon and return him to New York to stand trial, no matter what you or Stafford have to say about it."

"I never suggested you do otherwise," she said, the faintest bit of scorn shading her tone. Unflappable, but annoyed.

He grinned. It was obvious from her expression she'd like to tell him what to do, and not just in regard to Dixon. "I only want us to understand each other. Should you decide to agree, that is."

Her eyes gleamed at him. "Yes, I can see you are concerned."

He was running out of time. She was fending him off with this cool condescension, delaying until the hackney reached her destination and she could escape. As foreign as it was to think of a woman as a cold-blooded spy, he could see it in her; it wasn't enough to assure him of her competence, but he was willing to reserve judgment. He wanted to know what she was made of, and he couldn't while she remained settled in this distant, controlled manner. He leaned forward, not making any effort to hide his interest.

"You're not at all what I expected," he said, and it was true. Her eyes were as dark as a moonless night, her skin as fair as fresh honeysuckle blossoms. She looked like a New Orleans belle, with a hint of foreign blood. Up close she wasn't quite as young as he had first thought, but she still didn't look anything like the bloodless clerk he had expected to be given.

Her only reply was a faint, indulgent smile, as if she were listening to a child—and not all that attentively. "I thought he'd send someone more imposing," he went on, trying to provoke her. "Someone older, perhaps, or more . . . seasoned. You may think Dixon is just some common thief, but he's much worse, clever and charming and utterly without morals. Stafford assures me you're competent, but I confess, I would have preferred someone else." Someone more predictable.

She gave a small sigh, that infuriating smile still fixed on her lips. Her eyes wandered to the window as if his every word bored her to tears. "I just hope I don't have to spend the entire time saving your pretty little neck," he muttered, more as a jibe at her silence than a real concern. He didn't intend to spend his time looking out for her, not when he had more pressing matters. If she couldn't take care of herself, so much the worse for her.

Finally he seemed to have pierced her demeanor. She leaned forward, looking directly at him. She crooked her finger at him, and he, too, leaned forward. Up close she was almost exotically beautiful, he thought, with slightly slanted eyes and a pert, full mouth that was now pursed up almost in a kiss. He edged a little closer, unconsciously breathing deeply to catch the scent of her skin.

"I don't care what you expected or what you would prefer," she whispered in her French-flavored voice. "I will do my part, and you can do yours. Or not; I do not care a great deal what you do. But if you chatter so indiscreetly in public again, I'll cut your throat myself." With a pleasant smile, she sat back and turned her face to the window once more.

In spite of himself, he found a slow smile forming on his lips. He liked her much better already. "Ah," he said. "Then we understand each other better than I thought."

"As if that is a concern." The carriage had stopped. She gathered her skirt in one hand and reached for the door. Feeling more cordial now, Nate opened it himself and jumped down, offering her his hand. She took it and let him help her down. He caught a glimpse of slender ankles and calves as she swished her skirts back into place. Very nice, he thought; a spy with lovely legs and plump, pretty breasts. If he was to be saddled with her, at least there would be some compensation.

She turned and walked up the steps of the neat little house without a backward glance at him. *"Au revoir*, Madame," he called after her, grinning at the way she completely ignored him. She let herself in and closed the door without looking back, but he knew she'd heard him just the same. He could tell by the set of her shoulders that she was refusing to turn back and glare at him. Instinctively Nate glanced at the window nearest the door, wondering if she would peep out at him once she was safely inside. He couldn't tell—was that a shadow just beyond the curtain swaying so gently in the breeze? He touched the brim of his hat and smiled, just in case.

"Two shillings, guv," said the cabdriver then, interrupting his thoughts. Nate started, then laughed at himself. What a clever girl, sticking him with the fare. But what was the cost of the hackney, when it had shown him where she lived?

"Limehouse docks," he told the man, then stepped back into the carriage, taking one last assessing look at the neat little house.

Somehow he found himself looking forward to his next meeting with the mysterious Madame Martand.

"Has he gone?" Angelique kept her eyes on the back of the hall as she unbuttoned her pelisse. Lisette's eyebrows shot up, but she moved quickly to the window, staying just behind the fluttering curtain.

"Oui, Madame. He got into the hackney and it is leaving."

She let out her breath in a sigh of aggravation and yanked loose the ribbon of her bonnet. What a boorish man! So brash, so impolitic, so reckless! Had he even listened to a word Stafford said? Anyone might have seen him follow her—right to her own doorstep! She wrenched off the pelisse and handed it to Lisette with the bonnet, muttering slurs on the American's head as she strode into her small library.

She hadn't been eager to take on this commission before; now she was so annoyed she was tempted to refuse immediately, and announce her retirement as well. How dare Stafford try to impose that imbecile upon her? The American had seemed stiff and condescending, which was bad enough. Then he followed her in broad day, forcing his company upon her and questioning her competence. For a moment she wondered how upset Stafford would be if she were forced to cut Mr. Avery's throat as well as Dixon's, because she wasn't sure she could stand much more of his company.

Of course she could not do that. The American came from his president, and it would cause trouble for Lord Sidmouth if she harmed Avery. Lord Sidmouth, the Home Secretary, was Stafford's master. Angelique knew very well that Stafford ran his little band of agents at Sidmouth's pleasure, and for his service. Making trouble for his lordship would cause immense trouble for Stafford, and therefore for her. She couldn't kill Mr. Avery, no matter how tempting it might be or how she might threaten him. Unless, of course, Stafford gave her leave to do so.

At least, she conceded, he looked the part of a brash American trying to bully his way into English society. From his drab, untailored clothing to his tousled hair and bold gaze, no one would ever mistake him for a proper gentleman. And his voice! It was a nice enough voice, rich and mellow with a hint of rasp, but it rang with the flat drawl of America—Boston, or perhaps New York. Angelique had an ear for languages and had quite a mental catalog of accents. But even if he could play his superficial part well enough, she had grave fears he could handle the clandestine parts of it. How did he intend to persuade Jacob Dixon to hand over the stolen funds? Angelique wasn't about to bed the man just so Mr. Avery could get his money, no matter what Stafford suggested.

She shook her head in disgust. On one hand, Stafford was set on her carrying out his mission, and his plan was much the same as the other assignments he had given her over the years. On the other hand, she didn't feel like taking the job. It sounded tedious and distasteful, potentially messy—disposing of bodies always was—and aggravating to boot, thanks to Mr. Avery. For a moment she stood tapping her fingers on the desk, staring blindly out the window at her small garden. Like the rest of the house, it was small but lovely, and all hers. A peaceful retreat from the violent realities she faced when working. More than ever she felt the pull of retirement, the longing to enjoy what she had earned while she still could. What to do? She even asked the question out loud, trying to squeeze a rational decision from the unhappy choices before her.

No answer came to her, of course. She had no one to talk things over with. The agents she had befriended best, the more decent men, were dropping off Stafford's service left and right, done in by love and resurgent senses of honor. Most of Stafford's people were rabble, common spies motivated by money and, sometimes, personal vendettas. She knew those agents had cost him some prosecutions, but he still used them. Perhaps that was why he wanted her in particular to do this. Perhaps his other agents would be too tempted to keep Dixon's money after they killed him, whereas Stafford knew she could be counted on to do it properly.

Again she wondered why he didn't want Ian involved. Ian Wallace was a big Scot, always ready for trouble and eager to meet it. He had some honor and decency as well, and wouldn't forget who employed him. But he would stand out, she acknowledged; if Stafford was bent on doing this subtly, Ian would be the wrong choice. Still, he was one of the few agents left in Stafford's employ she actually trusted, and it would have made her infinitely more comfortable to have him at hand. At least she knew what to expect from Ian.

She walked back into the hall. "Lisette," she called, retrieving her pelisse from the hook behind the door. "I am going back out."

"*Oui*, Madame." Her maid appeared almost instantly, supremely helpful. "Will you take luncheon when you return?"

"Yes. In the garden." She tied the bonnet ribbons under her chin and went out, setting off on foot this time toward the reaches of Westminster.

His lodging was on the top floor of a tall, narrow building, not far from the bustle of Whitehall. The first floor was a boot maker, the second the boot maker's lodging, and above them all lived Ian. She walked up the back stairs and rapped at the door. She had come here before, though rarely, and knew Ian had told people she was his sister—an amus-

ing conceit, given how he flirted with her so outrageously whenever they worked together. Indeed,
when he pulled open the door, he was nearly naked,
wearing only knee breeches and dripping wet.

"A fine sight for a man's eyes!" he said, his blue eyes
lighting up. "And here I'm lathered up already."

She laughed, stepping past him as he held the
door. "That had more to do with the river than with
me. You reek of dead fish."

He shrugged, closing the door firmly behind her.
"Cold and uncaring, you are. Can you not see I'm
developing a cough?" He cleared his throat twice,
then forced a weak cough.

Angelique ignored him, removing her bonnet and
gloves as she moved toward the tiny sitting room.
A garish yellow sofa sat right behind the door, and
she laid down her bonnet before seating herself. The
only other furniture in the room was a musty old
leather armchair with worn spots on every horizon-
tal surface, and an octagonal table, minus one leg.
Ian must have furnished the entire flat from the
castoffs of some merchant household. "Why were
you in the river?"

He followed her into the sitting room, now with
a length of toweling in his hands. Unabashedly he
draped the linen over his head, vigorously drying
his hair. "I dropped something." She arched a brow.
He grinned. "Someone. 'Tis over. I can't even remember what it was about, now that there's a beautiful woman in my lodging."

She laughed. "I have come for sage advice."

"Sage advice? You break my heart. I thought it
would be more interesting, given your lovely frock."

Angelique didn't smile back, and Ian's grin vanished. He tossed the towel aside, finally serious. "What is it, then?"

"I saw Stafford this morning. He sent for me about a new assignment." There was nothing odd about that. She chose her next words carefully, though. "There is something curious about what he asks." Again she hesitated, but Ian just raised his eyebrow and waited. "An American was in his office. He seeks a man who stole from the American government. Stafford agreed to help him find the thief so he can get the money back."

"Is that all?" Ian flipped one hand dismissively. "Can't take more than a week, if the fellow's in London."

"Perhaps," she said sourly, "if the American can be persuaded to listen to me."

"Ah." Already Ian was smirking at her predicament. "Not the type, eh?"

"It does not appear so. I asked Stafford to send someone else, and he refused."

This time Ian laughed out loud. "Of course he did! You're his particular favorite, love; he doesn't trust the rest of us half as much as he trusts you."

"Be serious, Ian," she snapped. "I do not like this job."

"Well, who would? He doesn't send us out to smell the roses, though." Ian cocked his head and squinted at her. "What's so upsetting about this one? Is the American chap that bad?"

Angelique smoothed her skirt. Stafford's private charge to her was not to be mentioned to anyone, not even to Ian. Ian knew that she did things like this from time to time, but he never asked specifically and she never told him. Not because Ian would hold it against her; he himself had had a hand in some "disappearances" at Stafford's request. But Stafford turned to her when he didn't want anyone to suspect his involvement; he turned to Ian when he didn't care who knew. "He is a rash fellow," she said in response to Ian's question about Mr. Avery. "I do not think he trusts me any more than I trust him. He will not subject his will to mine, even if he knows nothing."

He thought about that, then shrugged, his face relaxing. "Well," he said. "It's not much different from usual, is it? Stafford orders, we do. Some matter of British security or similar excuse from the lawyers up in Whitehall."

She hadn't expected him to say that. It was true, but Ian appeared not to care that it bothered her this time. Angelique, who had a healthy respect for her own intuitions, was annoyed by his indifference to them. "It *is* different. He wants me to go alone with this American."

"He sent Brandon off alone last time," Ian pointed out at once. "Then sent us after him to tidy things up. I'll be expecting the old fox's note in a fortnight, sending me after you, eh?" He grinned.

"He sent Alec *home*," she retorted. "Alec could hardly go back to his family with a string of people in tow, even if his family hadn't thought him dead for five years."

Ian swiped a trail of water from the side of his face and pushed back his still-wet red hair. "So you don't like the American. You hardly need to rely on him."

"Of course not," she snapped. "He is an amateur."

"Everyone must seem so, love, after you've worked with me." He gave her an outrageous wink.

Angelique hesitated. Here was the last line she had never crossed with Ian. They had worked together for a few years, and she liked him a great deal. He was a smart agent, tough and efficient, and there was no one she'd rather have at her back in a tight spot. He was also a flirt of the highest order, constantly making innuendo and suggestive comments. Angelique knew she was hardly the only one he flirted with, and that while he hadn't actually attempted to seduce her, he hadn't hesitated with a whole host of other women. If she'd had to choose a man to propose to, Ian was hardly the perfect candidate.

But he alone knew her for what she was—a spy, an imposter, a thief, a hired assassin. With him alone she could be herself and not be forced to lie and pretend to a decent, honorable past she didn't possess. Ian's soul might be as dark and blemished as hers, but it made them equals. She would never live in fear of him discovering what she had done because he already knew. And if she didn't want to spend the rest of her life alone, Ian might be her only choice.

But it wasn't an easy question to ask. She gathered her composure, not wanting to seem too eager. "I was thinking of retiring," she said a low voice. "I have been at this too long."

"Retire? You?" He seemed amused. "What would you do with yourself—decapitate the daisies while your harpy of a maid gets fat and lazy?"

"Perhaps." She tilted her head back and watched

him through her eyelashes. "Or perhaps I shall find myself a husband and spend my days making love to him."

"Don't forget the nights," he said with his usual rakish leer.

She smiled. "Never. He shall make love to me at nights. We must be equals, you see."

Ian cast his eyes upward, clapping one hand to his heart. "You're a terrible tease, Angelique. Breaking my heart, you are, talking about this lucky fellow. A pox on him, whoever he is."

Angelique smiled, disgusted to realize her pulse was beating hard. "Perhaps he will be someone you know. Perhaps it will be you."

For the merest moment he froze. If she hadn't known him so well, she would have missed it. Instead she saw it, and the message it sent. He was shocked, horrified, and looking for a way out. Then he threw back his head and burst out laughing. "Oh, bloody hell. What a corker! I deserve that; should have known you were just trying to have a little fun with me." He finally grabbed a shirt from the back of his chair and pulled it over his head. "You're twisting my tail about Staff, too. He's a crafty old fox to be sure, but this doesn't sound unlike his usual sneaking and lying."

"You think I should take the job." Her heart still thudded hard, but slower now; betrayed.

Ian shrugged, his attention on buttoning the cuffs of his sleeves. "Why not? You know you'd find it more satisfying than marriage."

Why not. She let out her breath carefully, not wanting him to hear it. Ian saw nothing wrong with Stafford's request, nothing in her instinctive reluctance, and nothing in her hints that they might suit each other—at least, nothing that interested him. Unexpected humiliation fizzed in her veins for a moment, and she held herself very tightly together to hide it. "Yes," she said, when she could speak coolly again. "Why not?"

"Of course, if you don't want to do it, tell him to go bugger himself," Ian added quickly. He might have even sounded relieved. "Although if you do, let me come along. I'd pay ten quid to see his face then."

"No, no." She tugged at her glove, ignoring his jokes. "As you say, there is no reason not to accept."

He jumped up to follow her from the room. "I'll watch for that note, sending me after you to make sure all is well." He reached around her to open the door.

She raised her eyes to his, once more calm and self-possessed. "I am sure that will not be necessary. I can handle one American, no matter how amateur or bellicose."

He grinned and winked at her. "Aye, but if you need a hand with the embezzler—"

Angelique gave him a brief, dismissive smile. "You know I won't. Thank you, Ian. You have been most helpful." She left, feeling his eyes on her back until she rounded the newel post and went down the stairs.

On the street once more, she walked briskly, scourging herself with the sting of his disinterest. Ian Wallace wasn't the only man in the world, and she was far from a dried-up crone. But how dare he flirt with her so outrageously and so often, if he had no interest in actually having her? Surely he couldn't have been alarmed by that word "husband"; surely Ian had bigger ballocks than that. She certainly hadn't expected him to fall upon her with a declaration of love and desire, but a spark of interest or acknowledgment would have been agreeable. He couldn't even give weight to her suspicion that Stafford wasn't playing fairly with her, but laughed it off and then offered to step in and *help*. As if she needed help, let alone *his* help.

She realized she was quivering with fury and forcibly reined in her emotions. Very well. Ian had persuaded her, for good or for ill: she would take Stafford's vile little job, but this was the last one. A fortnight's work, no more, and then she would walk away from all this ugliness. And woe betide Nathaniel Avery if he got in her way.

Chapter 3

Nate returned to the ship in a thoughtful mood. Angelique Martand was not at all what he had expected, and he still wasn't sure what to make of her. There were a dozen ways she could complicate his true purpose, but perhaps she could also serve it. Still, it would be like holding a copperhead snake in his fist, terrifying to have near but too deadly to let go. He couldn't keep from wondering just what her bite would be like.

When he went into his cabin, his traveling companion was pounding something in the stone mortar with a pestle. Now that they were in port and not as subject to the roll of the ocean, Prince had set up his chemistry equipment again. The table was covered with a collection of pots and jars, some with lids, some with glass tubes sticking out the top, and one with smoke wafting from it. Nate had little idea what he was brewing, but it would probably come in handy, whatever it was. That, and the fact that he didn't trust anyone more than he trusted Prince, was why Nate had wanted him to come to England. "Well?" Prince asked without looking up.

Nate stripped off the overlarge brown coat and

let it fall on a chair. "I saw him," he replied. "As much a viper as I expected. Selwyn obviously wrote to him, warning him of what I would say; he was prepared for everything I asked." He paused. "A little too prepared. He wants Dixon found even more than we do."

Prince frowned at the contents of the mortar. "He said that?"

"He didn't have to," Nate said. He tossed aside the ill-fitting waistcoat as well, stretching his arms overhead in relief. He much preferred the more comfortable clothing of the frontier or the sea, but looking like a country buffoon with airs had suited his purpose today. "It was in everything he did and said. Not only was he waiting for me, he had already sent for an agent of his to accompany me."

"Very efficient," muttered Prince.

"Not even the English are that efficient."

A deep frown crossed Prince's face. "Will this agent be a problem?"

Nate dropped into the chair opposite his companion, tugging off his heavy boots. "I don't know yet. She might be."

"She?" Prince had leaned over to peer into the smoking jar, but now he glanced up, a sly smile splitting his dark face. "Don't tell me he gave you a *woman*? A female spy. Did he pat you on the head, too, and tell you to run home to your mammy?"

Nate laughed. "Not in so many words, although I think he would have, if he thought he could get Dixon on his own. I told you, he wants Dixon very badly."

"You said that before. Why would that be? The man hasn't set foot in England for a decade at least."

This time Nate gazed out the small window, thinking before he answered. Already the smells and sounds of London had permeated the ship. He could see masts and rigging, dotted with seabirds, and hear the calls of boatmen and sailors as they worked, loading and unloading cargo. "I've no idea," he finally admitted. "I could make a guess; Dixon probably had his thieving ways well established before he left for New York. He might still be wanted here. Of course, if that were the case, it would seem best to mount a determined search without delay, and Stafford agreed completely with my request for stealth and secrecy. In fact, he agreed with almost everything I asked. Somehow I doubt the Crown would be so eager to hand him over to us if they had a prior claim on him."

"Then what?" Prince shrugged. "They send a woman to charm the breeches off him? Odd way to punish a man, if you ask me."

Nate just shook his head. He didn't know, but he was quite sure he was right about Stafford being just as anxious, if not more so, to find Jacob Dixon. But why? That was a mystery, and the choice of agent selected to assist him didn't make things any clearer.

"So, what is she like, this lady spy? What is the plan now?"

What was she like? He had no idea, not really. "She's a beauty," he replied. "French. Slim and petite, the sort of woman who can appear as helpless as a spring lamb." Prince snorted in disgust. "I said *appear*; she's not helpless at all. She offered to cut my throat personally, and there's something in the way she moves that radiates . . . power." He was a little surprised to hear himself say that last word, but it was true. In that carriage ride, she had been hiding nothing from him. Whatever else she might be, Angelique Martand was nobody's fool, and nothing like a weakling.

Prince snorted again, then put back his head and laughed. "A beautiful French lady," he said, grinning wickedly. "Full of power. You rolled snake eyes on this one, eh, Nathaniel? She will keep your eyes open, and perhaps not where they should be."

"You'd better have your eyes open, too," Nate told him. "I don't know much about her except that she's a mystery. Don't let yourself be taken in by her appearance, whatever that appearance is. She's Stafford's agent, and I don't trust him—or her—not to have other motives beyond serving Lord Selwyn's directive."

"Of course not. Never trust the English devils." Prince pointed the pestle at him. "So what are you to do, while she is off charming her way into Dixon's confidence? That is what this Englishman intends for her to do, isn't it?"

Slowly Nate nodded. "But she didn't seem happy about that. In fact, she doesn't want to do this at all. I wonder how Stafford plans to persuade her . . . ?"

Prince watched him for a few minutes. "Bugger the lot of them," he said finally. "We do not need them. One hundred dollars will hire a brace of investigators who can track the thief down. We can snatch him ourselves, exercise a little tender persuasion"—he tapped the variety of weapons spread on the table in front of him—"and be off."

"Monroe didn't want that," Nate said dryly. "You know I was willing enough, but when the president says no . . ." He shrugged. "Besides, we're committed now; Selwyn and Stafford know all about our presence and purpose, to say nothing of this Martand woman. It's the diplomatic way or no way, and I'm not going home without Jacob Dixon chained to the mast."

The other man cursed him good-naturedly. "I hardly know you anymore. When did rules and diplomacy matter to you?" He pointed his finger in accusation. "You want to work with this pretty French girl. Corrupted into propriety by a skirt!"

Nate caught up one of his discarded boots and chucked it at Prince. "For Ben? Anything."

Prince ducked the flying boot. "Ah. Blame it on the general." He shook his head and began sprinkling the dust from the mortar into the smoking pot.

It all came down to Ben, who was the real victim here. General Benjamin Davies had been a hero of the American Revolution, leading his New England militiamen, including Nate's father, through the woods and over mountains to fight the British. Ben lost his right arm at Saratoga but taught himself to swing the sword with his left arm, and was back in the saddle within a couple of months. After the war he had gone into business and politics, privately saying each would balance the deleterious effects of the other on his constitution, but age and infirmity finally caught up to the general. In thanks for his war service, Ben had been appointed Collector of the Port of New York, collecting tax duties on shipments through the harbor, a rather plum post of some standing. Since the loss of his arm, Ben had employed a secretary who handled much of his correspondence, and as collector he had needed even more assistance. Jacob Dixon had appeared the perfect candidate—capable, conscientious, modest. Before long Ben had left much of the actual collection to Dixon, until one day Dixon said he had inherited a fortune from an aunt in England and was returning home at once. The day after his ship sailed, a gaping discrepancy was discovered in the accounts of the port.

A close examination of the books revealed Dixon's deceit, and the theft of over four hundred and fifty thousand dollars. Ben was devastated. As collector, he was responsible; he pledged his every possession to the government to repay the debt. It was a terrible blow to a man who had already lost an arm in service to his country, especially now that he was old and in declining health. Nate, Ben's godson, had been only one of the men who called upon President Monroe to ask for clemency for an old soldier.

Monroe willingly believed that Ben had not stolen the money, but he was caught. The young country needed those funds desperately, and Ben *had* been responsible for their collection. The best the president could do was agree to let Nate go after Jacob Dixon in an attempt to recover as much of the money as possible, and bring Dixon back for trial so that at least Ben's name would be cleared. Nate, who wouldn't have even been born if Ben hadn't saved his father's life at the battle of Brandywine, refused to go home without Jacob Dixon—with or without the money—and he'd work with Lucifer's spies if that's what it took. If he failed, Ben would lose everything, not only his lands and modest fortune but his good name as well.

And Nate was determined not to fail, no matter what was required of him. President Monroe had sent him along with an introduction to the Foreign Office to smooth the way. Lord Selwyn had been appropriately shocked by the account of Dixon's crime, but also disinclined to simply hand over a British citizen to American justice. He was sympathetic enough to send Nate on to John Stafford, indicating that Stafford was the man to see in cases of such political delicacy. Now Nate had Stafford's cooperation—or interference—and a Frenchwoman to watch his every move. As long as he ended up in possession of at least some of the stolen funds, and Jacob Dixon's person, he was fine with all that.

But if either Stafford or Madame Martand got in his way . . . he was just as willing to take matters into his own hands.

A note arrived early the next day from Stafford that he would need two days to make arrangements, and to expect further word within that time. Madame Martand must have accepted after all, Nate thought, since the note made no mention of a change in plans. For some reason this didn't annoy him at all; quite the contrary.

"I'm going to have another look at Madame Martand," he said, pulling on a long gray coat and taking up a plain black hat. It was a cool, cloudy day, so he also grabbed an umbrella for extra concealment. Prince gave him a long, speaking look, a wicked grin curling his mouth, but went back to his experiments without a word. Nate ignored the look and left.

He found his way back to her house in good time. Retracing a path through a city, with so many more fixed landmarks to note, was always easier than retracing a path through the forest, and Nate was rather good at doing that. Fortunately for him, she lived in a quiet area opposite a small park, where he could linger out of sight for hours, if necessary. Not that he hoped to; staring at her house wouldn't give him much idea of what kind of person she was or what she would be like to work with. He tied up his horse at a nearby shop and went to scout the area.

But she helped him out by leaving the house. Nate had barely taken a turn around the street when a hired carriage rattled up and stopped in front of her house. Almost at once the front door opened, and the lady herself walked down the steps, demure and prim in a gray traveling dress and black bonnet. She stepped lightly into the carriage, pausing only to speak to the sturdy-looking maid who followed her out to the street. The maid nodded, the carriage started off, and on impulse Nate slipped quickly back to his horse and followed.

He didn't know what he expected to gain by doing so. He'd been too far away to hear what she told the driver. Perhaps she was going to have tea with a friend or going shopping for new gloves, and he would waste an entire day that could be better spent tracking Jacob Dixon's movements. But too much depended on his knowing her, this odd French spy who worked for the English and seemed perfectly at ease offering to cut his throat. His entire enterprise now rested on how well he could manage her, and she was a complete enigma. He had rather be safe than sorry, he told himself as he drifted into the swelling stream of traffic and kept one eye on her carriage.

They headed out of the city, around the wide expanse of Hyde Park and then west on the turnpike.

With his rudimentary knowledge of London geography, Nate was reduced to reading signposts as they passed through villages and toll gates, and still traveled on. Where the devil was she going—and why? He hadn't seen any luggage, so hadn't thought she would go far or stay long. But as he rode on, hanging back to avoid being seen, he began to think this had been a damned foolish idea. He should have stayed in London and taken advantage of her absence to knock on her door and chat up the servants. Servants always knew pretty well what sort of person employed them.

After almost two hours, the carriage finally turned into an inn yard at one end of a small town. Nate reined in his horse at once, dismounting and pretending to tighten the saddle girth as he watched from the corner of his eye. After a few moments Madame Martand walked out of the yard and headed down the dusty lane on foot.

Curiosity had long since overtaken Nate's mind, so he walked his horse to the inn and stabled it. He noticed the carriage driver had retired to the taproom, presumably waiting for his passenger to return from whatever her errand was. He didn't feel too conspicuous, leaving the horse there—no one would recognize it as his—but he did school his voice into clipped British tones just in case, silently thanking his Hertfordshire mother for raising him to speak "proper English," as she called it.

Madame Martand had vanished from sight by the time he walked back out of the stable yard, but it was a straight road that followed the dip and rise of the land. He strode briskly along until her slight figure came into view, and then moderated his pace to stay far behind her. With every step his curiosity grew by leaps and bounds.

After a while she turned and went south, climbing a stile over the rock wall into a meadow with a thin dirt track through the middle. A local shortcut, he thought; she'd been here before. He left the road, moving into a small wood that ran alongside the meadow. He hung back behind the trees, staying close to the shadows and stepping soundlessly through the thicket. He flexed the muscles of his abdomen, controlling his breathing until it was long, deep, and silent, as he had learned to do in the forests of New England. Giving oneself away there could be fatal, and given her threat the other day, it might well be the same here with this woman.

But Madame Martand evidently had no idea he was there. For a while she strolled through the meadow, picking wildflowers as if she had not a care in the world. Nate wondered what she was thinking about as she wandered aimlessly through the tall grass, reaching out from time to time to run her gloved hand over the rustling tips. Nate began to feel foolish again, and then puzzled, as she let herself into the graveyard behind the small church at the top of the hill.

She wound her way through the graves and then seated herself on a stone bench. She made a lonely figure in a sea of wild heartsease, her dark bonnet and gray dress stark against the sun-bleached grasses and the colorful little flowers that swayed and bobbed against her skirt. Nate shifted through the woods until he was only a hundred yards or so away; the trees grew thin, and he inched dangerously close to exposure, but still couldn't see her face. The bonnet shielded her expression, and he wondered why she was there. Despite the location and the quiet air of her pose, there wasn't much of mourning in it. There was something very . . . still, but so alert, about her; he had the impression she had come to think instead of to pay respects.

After a while a woman came out of the rectory at the side of the church. She was short and plump and simply dressed, with a basket over one arm. The rector's wife, he guessed. She made her way to the woman on the bench, whom she greeted with a smile and a bob of her head. They chatted for a few minutes, and the rector's wife gestured toward the rectory with one hand. Madame Martand stood up with a nod. She scattered the meadow flowers she had picked atop a grave in front of her, and went with the plump woman around the church into the rectory.

In the shadow of the rustling trees, Nate narrowed his eyes. She came to visit a grave? Everyone was entitled to sentimentality, he supposed, even the most capable spies. Part of him felt a bit ashamed, that he had followed her on such a somber mission, but part of him also wondered how somber it was. And by far the largest part of him was curious enough to wait it out and see what she did next.

Chapter 4

Angelique lifted her teacup to her face and breathed deeply. No one prepared tea quite like Melanie, with a hint of lemon and mint in it. Angelique always associated the scent with her childhood. Lemon and mint made her think of Melanie's arm around her, rocking her to sleep or consoling her for some hurt. It had been a long time since she needed Melanie's shoulder to cry on, but the scent of lemon and mint tea always brought back a bit of that comfort and security.

"Sugar?" Melanie Carswell smiled at her. "Unless you have lost your taste for sweet?"

Angelique shook her head as she reached for the sugar. "Never. You know I would swim in honey, if it were not so sticky."

"I remember." Melanie's voice was as fond as any mother's could be. "But you have not come all this way for sweetened tea."

She took a long sip of the tea before she answered, letting the familiar flavors swirl over her tongue. "But I have indeed," she said. "No one makes tea like you, not even Lisette. I have tried everything to teach her, but she refuses to learn. Not even when I threaten to beat her can she do it; instead she sniffs at me and says she shall pour brandy into the tea until I cease complaining."

Melanie laughed. "She must crush the leaves just a little, and add them to the steeping water. Then it will be the same."

"It will never be the same, and we both acknowledge it," Angelique replied. "So I must come all the way to Whitton or do without."

"Yes, *that* is why you come to see me." Melanie paused, waiting.

Angelique said nothing and sipped her tea. She ought to come see Melanie more often, and not just when she was preparing to go off on one of Stafford's assignments. Melanie was the closest thing to family she had, practically her mother. Angelique did not remember her own mother, a French countess who had gone to the guillotine when Angelique was only an infant. She remembered only Melanie, her mother's maid who had smuggled her out of France and brought her to England, and safety. Melanie deserved more than this sort of visit, with the shadow of death hanging over it, as if she were a priest and Angelique had come to purge her conscience and seek absolution for the sins she was about to commit. The trouble was, she needed that absolution, since she never knew just which additional sins would be required in the course of her assignment. And Melanie was the only person on earth who truly knew everything about her—the only person Angelique loved and trusted enough to tell.

"Where is he sending you this time?" Melanie finally asked.

The gentle question stung. She added more sugar to her tea and stirred it carefully. "Nowhere," she said, watching the steam curl up from the liquid. "It is in London, for now."

"Hmmph." Melanie's low opinion of Stafford was clear in her tone. "I hope it is not too dangerous."

That made her smile wryly. Everything Stafford had her do was dangerous. Of course, he only sent her because she had made herself equal to it, and capable of deadly response. She never told Melanie any of that, but she suspected Melanie knew it anyway. And Melanie certainly hadn't raised her to be a soft, weak female. "It is not a typical job," she said, then stopped. The American's shocking green eyes flashed through her mind, and she shifted uneasily at just how odd this assignment was.

"He wishes you to merely follow someone? Steal something?" Melanie guessed. "Nothing that involves knives or garrotes or playing the courtesan?"

"I do not know what it will involve; perhaps all that, perhaps none. It may be simple, but I suspect . . . I suspect it will be more trouble than anyone knows."

Melanie's plump face tightened, her expression almost fierce. Angelique glanced at her, and for a moment thought she saw how Melanie had lied and bribed her way out of France. Melanie had never told her exactly what she'd had to do to escape the bloody Revolution, but Angelique guessed that experience was what made Melanie so understanding, if still not quite approving, of her profession now.

"I don't know that it will," she went on, choosing her words carefully even as she wondered why it was so difficult to tell Melanie. Normally she had no trouble; she never revealed names or exact destinations, and never a hint of what Stafford hoped to achieve, but she wanted Melanie to have an idea, in case something disastrous should ever happen in the course of her work. No one else but Melanie would care or notice if Angelique Martand simply vanished off the face of the earth. That was why she had come, as usual, and yet for some reason she felt at a loss. "I am not working with the usual people. It is an American who will be with me, and I am not sure of him. He is . . ." *An enigma*, she thought. "He keeps his own counsel," she finished. "But the main objective is his; he brought the job to Stafford, and I am sent to keep an eye on him as well as fulfill my own task for Stafford." She wondered how this Avery would react when she cut the villain's throat. She must confirm with Stafford how she should proceed if he objected.

"But what interest does Stafford have in American affairs?" Melanie exclaimed. She looked as unpleasantly surprised as Angelique had been by this introduction of a foreigner. That was mildly comforting in some way, especially after Ian's careless disregard.

"None he has told me. We are to find someone the American is pursuing. I hope it will not be too difficult, or take too long. The person is believed to be in London, and we must merely run him to ground." *Then kill him.* "Monsieur Dexter will notify you, as usual, when it is over," she added. Angelique always came in person before a job, but only on the pretext of visiting a grave. Afterward, once she was safely home, she had her solicitor send word to Melanie that all was well. Ever since she became Stafford's spy, she had kept this veil between her and Melanie. It was better for both of them if no one knew of their connection.

"You should leave this," Melanie urged her. "Resign. Tell him you do not wish to do something so . . ." She fluttered her fingers in frustration, searching for the word. "So *méprisable*."

Angelique flicked one hand. "Everything he asks me to do is despicable. I have made my peace with it."

"But you are not at peace with it this time. I can see it in your face and hear it in your voice." She paused. "I thought . . . I suspected you were tiring of this life."

Of course Melanie knew. Wordlessly she nodded. Just once.

"Every time you come to see me, I always hope it is to tell me you are done with it," Melanie said quietly. "Every time I see you in the graveyard waiting for me, I pray you have come to tell me you have fallen in love, or have decided to open a millinery shop, or to travel the world—anything but this. I live in fear, *chérie*, that your every visit might be the last I ever see or hear of you. I shall have betrayed your honored mama if I saved you from the madness in Paris only to let you give your life for some English clerk's scheme."

"You have never betrayed my mother," Angelique snapped. "Never. And whatever I bring upon myself . . ." She reined in her temper and spoke more evenly. "You of all people must understand why I do this."

Melanie's mouth pinched. "You cannot avenge what happened to your parents."

"I don't try," she said testily. "But I do know that when they needed a savior, none was there. Perhaps if someone had taken Marat's life when he was still a dirty rebel in the streets, my parents would not have been killed for a piece of land. Perhaps if the ministers and King had fought the anarchy instead of hiding away in their palaces, they would not have lost their heads, along with the heads of so many other decent people. I do not pretend the English government is a beacon of beneficence, but they keep order."

"*Oui*, I realize that," said Melanie, retreating at once, lowering her eyes like a servant. "I am the one who taught you to hate the Revolutionaries, after all."

Angelique's anger faded, as it always did at that expression. Once Melanie had said Angelique looked so much like her mother when in a temper, it was impossible for her not to yield. Melanie's loyalty to the late countess ran deep and absolute, and it reminded Angelique how much Melanie had done for her. She leaned forward and clasped the older woman's hand. "I know you speak from concern," she said softly. "I am sorry to disappoint you time after time."

"You are not a disappointment to me."

Angelique smiled. "This time I am not. Because . . ." She hesitated. "This assignment will be my last." Hope and cautious joy sprang into Melanie's eyes. "I am still not even certain I will do all he wants. He asks a great deal of me, and I do not look forward to it."

"What does he want?" Melanie demanded.

"He asks me to pose as a bored wife." Angelique pulled a face. "With an American nabob who wishes to play spy. Can you imagine? But we shall see how things begin. It may not be so bad." Melanie didn't look convinced, but she said nothing. Even if she asked, Angelique would not tell her more, and they both knew it.

To change the subject, Angelique opened her reticule and took out a plump packet. "This is for you."

"For the poor," said Melanie firmly as she accepted it. Angelique lifted one shoulder; if it pleased Melanie to give the money to the poor, so be it. She knew her foster mother wouldn't spend the money on herself, but they had reached an agreement. Angelique gave the money freely, and Melanie didn't protest how she earned it.

She rose to her feet. "I should go." Melanie put aside the package of money and walked her to the door. Angelique took another look around the comfortable rectory. "Mr. Carswell is out, I presume."

"He will be sorry to have missed you," Melanie said. "Someday you will come for a real visit, I hope, and stay with us. You are always welcome."

Angelique felt almost wistful. She sometimes thought of visiting Melanie openly, without the artifice of visiting the graveyard. Mr. Carswell, Melanie's husband, was a generous, decent man and never condemned her—although, one must admit, it was highly unlikely Melanie had told him the precise truth about Angelique and her occupation. "Perhaps," she said softly. "I think of it often."

Melanie beamed. "You must. Finish this job, and come to me. Spend the winter with us."

"It is possible . . ." She paused; perhaps it was better to say nothing. "Do give Mr. Carswell my regards."

"Of course. I will look for Mr. Dexter's letter every day." Melanie embraced her. Angelique caught a whiff of lemon and mint again and felt another pang. More than ever before, she had a wild urge to accept Melanie's invitation to stay. Hang Stafford and his messy assassinations. Let him send someone else with that mysterious American with the watchful green eyes, and she would just remain in Whitton with Melanie, tending the quiet graveyard and sipping lemon-mint tea.

Instead she kissed Melanie's cheek and turned to the door. "*Au revoir*, Mellie," she murmured. Melanie rallied a smile, then opened the door and bid her good-bye as politely as if they had been strangers. Angelique walked out, heading for the road back into Whitton where she had told her driver to wait. The die was cast now. She would see her solicitor when she returned to London, and tell Lisette to pack.

Nate watched her leave. Her visit had been less than an hour, and the rector's wife showed her to the door with a kind smile. He'd managed to creep closer to the church and had a better view. She went through the graveyard again, but straight to the road this time. He followed until she reached the road back into the small town and headed down it.

What a puzzle. Had she come all this way just to lay flowers on a grave? Whose grave would that be? He couldn't see what this could have to do with his business, but he had come all this way and now the curiosity was overshadowing even his desire to follow her. There was little she could do on that road except return to town and her hired carriage, and he could catch her again before long on the way back to London. For now he wanted to know what had brought her out here.

He turned back toward the church, this time taking the road instead of the thicket path. It was a quiet English chapel, weathered gray stone with a bell atop the tower. Trying not to look too focused, he let himself into the graveyard by the gate and walked the paths, studying each grave. The one she had sat over was near the back, a good twenty feet from the rear fence. He paced himself, working his way back.

Just before he reached that grave scattered with wilting wildflowers, the rector's wife came out of her house again. She shaded her eyes to look at him, then came briskly toward him. As she drew near, Nate doffed his hat and bowed. "Good day."

"Good day, sir." He caught the lilt of French in her voice. How interesting. A coincidence—or not? "Are you seeking a particular grave?"

He glanced around, affecting a look of apology. "Yes, although I am not sure it will be here. My mother asked me to look for her grandparents, and see that the site is well tended." Hopefully that was ancient enough.

"What are their names?" she asked politely. "My husband has been the rector here for almost ten years. I am Mrs. Carswell." Up close she was a pleasant-looking woman, plump and gray-haired. Her long thin nose and high forehead spoke of her

Gallic ancestry, and there was a touch of aristocratic reserve in her manner.

"Delighted to make your acquaintance. Nathaniel Avery, at your service." He bowed his head. "My great-grandparents were Mary and Edward Owens," he said, truthfully. If he ever got caught following Madame Martand, let him have a solid excuse. "They lived for a time near Richmond." That part wasn't true, but it was the only town name he could recall from the journey here.

Her brow wrinkled. "Hmm. I do not think so . . ."

"I've been trying to make out some of the carvings," he said, gesturing toward the grave in front of him, a moss-covered stone listing slightly to one side. "There must be a dozen generations here."

She smiled. "Indeed, there are! Some families have been here for centuries."

"So I see." Nate leaned forward and squinted at the nearest marker. "Two hundred years, in this gentleman's case."

"I would be glad to walk with you and look. Perhaps along the fence."

"Thank you, ma'am." They walked along, Nate studying each stone with a thoughtful frown. The graveyard was neatly tended, although time and weather had taken a toll. When they passed the flower-strewn grave, he hid his interest; there was no need to peer closely at it. It was obviously old, perhaps as old as the two-centuries-old grave a few feet away. The names were weathered into near-oblivion, although he made out the surname Wilkins and a date in the 1600s in his quick glance at the stone. So Madame wasn't mourning a close relative or friend. He wondered again why she had come all the way out here, just to leave flowers on an ancient grave.

As they walked Mrs. Carswell chatted politely. He answered obligingly, again sticking closely to the truth. His great-grandparents had died about forty years ago, give or take, well before he was born. His mother had gone to America shortly before they died, and met his father there. No, he didn't think his mother had ever come home to England. His grandparents were also dead, buried in Hertfordshire where his grandfather had been an attorney. He wasn't quite sure where his great-grandparents were buried, and his mother had forgotten; the only thing she could recall was that they had lived near Richmond. That last bit was false, unless one counted anywhere in England as "near Richmond," but overall Nate felt fairly honest. And he said a silent apology to his keen-witted mother for implying, even to a stranger who would never know better, that she had grown forgetful in her old age.

"I've visited at least a dozen graveyards between here and Richmond," he said with an apologetic smile. "I shall know half the curates in England before I return home, it seems."

Mrs. Carswell smiled. "Such dedication! You must love your mother very much, to honor her wishes so."

"Indeed, ma'am, I do." By careful maneuvering he had managed to end where they had begun, right at the grave in question. Nate glanced at it. "I should have liked to leave such a token, but it seems not to be. At least not today."

She followed his gaze. "Yes. Perhaps you will have better luck in Ealing, or Twickenham."

"I hope I might." He bowed again. "Thank you again for your courtesy and kindness, Mrs. Carswell."

"Of course." She smiled and bobbed a polite curtsey, but Nate felt her sharp eyes on his back all the way down the road. And he still didn't know why Madame Martand had come.

Chapter 5

Nate had to admit Stafford kept his word on moving swiftly. By the time he returned to London, a message had arrived laying out a plan. Nate and Madame Martand were to be man and wife, newly arrived from America. A house had been let in their name and they were to take possession the next day. He and Madame Martand were to work out the details of their masquerade, but under the general guise of a wealthy couple come to acquire some London polish and sample the delights of town, with some business on the side. It was Nate's duty to figure out how to locate Jacob Dixon and run him to ground; Madame, Stafford wrote, would be as helpful as she could.

He read the letter twice, then sat thinking. Only when Prince growled at him did he realize he was tapping the letter on the table, and put it aside.

"How bad is it?" his friend asked with a sly grin. "Are we not to have the pretty French lady after all?"

Nate bared his teeth in an answering smile. "Not only are we to have her, she's to be my wife." Prince snorted in disgusted amusement, and Nate laughed. "Wait until you meet her. I shall have to sleep with one eye open and a pistol in my hand."

"It is where your other hand will be that concerns me." Prince laughed. "I suppose that will be for the general's benefit as well, eh?"

Nate threw an empty powder horn at him. Prince caught it and gave him a severe look. "The best thing it will do is get us off this ship," Nate said. They had reached London a week ago, but he'd stayed on board the *Water Asp* because he didn't want to announce himself in any way. The *Water Asp* belonged to his father's shipping company and was here on a routine trading run. Nate's parents had sent him with their blessings to capture Ben Davies's thieving secretary, but no one else save President Monroe knew he was here. Everyone had been told Nate was going back out west, exploring the wilderness beyond the Mississippi. His name wasn't on the *Water Asp*'s manifest, and he had routed every expense through the ship's captain, who had been with Boudin Shipping for years and was sworn to secrecy.

Now he and Prince were snapping at each other from too much time in too close quarters. A house would allow them to spread out—although how he would explain Prince's work was something Nate hadn't figured out. There would be the servants who were on Stafford's coin and couldn't be entirely trusted, much like his new, temporary, wife. Nate allowed himself a little smile at the thought of how that first meeting would go. He might as well find some enjoyment in this venture.

And then, of course, he had to set a trap to catch a thief.

* * *

She had already arrived by the time he reached the house in Varden Street the next morning. Nate paused on the threshold of the wide-open door, listening to the voices abovestairs. The house was furnished, but very simply, and sound echoed off the bare walls and floors. She was speaking French, with another woman—perhaps her maid, he thought, recalling the servant he'd seen when he followed her the other day. He glanced at Prince, coming up the steps behind him with a large crate of equipment in his arms, and unconsciously squared his shoulders before stepping into the house.

Servants were cleaning the dining room, sweeping briskly. Holland covers still shrouded the furniture in the drawing room while a maid cleaned the windows. By the time he reached the second floor, he could make out some of the conversation. His French, learned from the fur traders of Quebec, wasn't quite on par with Madame's, but he understood enough. He leaned against the doorway. "*Bonjour.*"

She looked up from folding stockings into a drawer. "Good morning," she replied evenly.

Nate grinned. That hadn't been what she was saying to her maid, who was the sturdy-looking woman he had seen the other day. Madame Martand might have agreed to this plan, but apparently not with much enthusiasm. That would have to change, at least nominally, because failure was utterly unacceptable to him. "A very good morning it is, since it brings me the sight of you, dear wife."

Her expression grew severe at the endearment. She nodded at the other woman. "My maid, Lisette, will help you unpack, if you have no man with you."

Prince had tromped up the stairs behind him and chose that moment to peer into the room, no doubt wanting a look at the French lady. Nate had the pleasure, and chagrin, of seeing Madame's eyes widen and blink at the sight of him. They were going to have a very difficult time if she objected to Prince, and yet anything that discomposed her gave him some satisfaction.

"No need," he said easily in reply to her remark. "I can unpack my trunk myself. Prince will see to the other things; he'll need a workshop. The next floor up, do you think? It must be a bright room."

Her dark eyes moved back to him. "*Oui*," she murmured. "There is a nursery, large and bright."

Prince nodded and carried his crate to the turn of the stairs, pausing just out of her view to flash Nate an absolutely gleeful grin. "Make sure you get all the trunks up there," Nate called after him. "Especially the red one." The red one held the weapons and lead shot, and weighed a ton. It had taken two men to carry it off the ship. Prince just laughed, the sound booming back down the stairs and hall. Cheeky scoundrel.

Nate turned his attention to the women, who had gone back to unpacking and were ignoring him. Feminine clothing was strewn all over the bed and chaise, in froths of ribbons and lace in every color imaginable. The wardrobe doors stood open, as did every drawer on the bureau and dressing table. He ambled into the room, taking everything in. It looked utterly mundane, just an ordinary, though well-dressed, woman's bedroom. It was somewhat disappointing; he'd expected to see knives and pistols inside the hatboxes. He brushed aside a striped green dress and sat on the edge of the bed, bouncing a little on the thick mattress. "I'll sleep on this side, if you don't mind."

Her lip curled. "You shall sleep on *that* side—of the door." She waved one hand toward the connecting room.

Nate, who had deliberately ignored that door, made a face of disappointment. "What sort of way is this to start our marriage? I'm heartbroken already."

"Better your heart than something else."

"I had hoped we might be closer than all that."

"But we are much too fashionable for anything so vulgar." She crossed the room and opened the door in question, revealing another bedroom. "Your quarters, sir."

"Fashion is a cold and wretched bedfellow," he told her as he reluctantly rose from her bed.

She smiled coldly. "So am I."

Nate didn't make any attempt to hide his open perusal as he approached. By God she was beautiful, even with that sharp, dangerous smile on her face. From the top of her dark curls to the tips of her kid slippers, peeping out below her blue skirt, there wasn't a single thing wrong with her figure that he could see. He stopped in front of her and looked her up and down once more. "Maybe I'd be willing to chance it," he said mildly. "Maybe you've just never learned how to be warm and inviting in bed."

She laughed. "You'll never know what I've learned in bed."

A flash of erotic possibilities blurred through his

mind at her tone. Nate had to grind his teeth behind his smile to quell his body's reaction to them. He folded his arms and leaned closer, watching the way her eyes changed as he did so. They were as dark as sin, and sparkling with amusement. "Here I never thought to hear you admit any deficiency. Come, darling, for the sake of our marriage, I can overlook it."

"Ah, but for the sake of your object, I cannot," she purred.

"Right," he murmured, letting his gaze linger on her lips until she flattened them in irritation. Then he straightened and walked into his chamber, throwing open the door to the corridor. "Prince!" he bellowed. "Help me get the trunks!"

He closed the door on the good-natured grumbling that came from upstairs, and turned to survey his room more critically. It was large and bright, with windows on two sides. The house was on the end of a long row of town houses, and he'd seen the high fence running around the small garden out back, with a gate—he opened a window and looked out—right underneath his window. That could be convenient later. He opened the other windows as well, drawing in a deep breath of air that was blissfully almost free of the ocean. Lord, it would feel good to sleep in a proper bed again, in a room that didn't rock and sway with the tide.

Madame still stood in the doorway between their bedrooms, arms folded. He gave her his most charming smile. "Have you reconsidered banishing me to my own chamber?"

"He is your slave?" she asked, nodding her head slightly in the direction of the stairs.

"No," said Nate, still grinning.

"Your servant?"

"No."

She gave him a sharp look. "You will have to have a suitable explanation for his presence."

"Don't worry," said Nate. "We'll come up with something."

Prince opened the door then and stuck his head in. "Did you mean to fetch those trunks now, or later, Nathaniel?"

"Now." Nate turned to Madame. "My good friend, Prince Chesterfield. Prince, Madame Martand."

Prince's teeth gleamed in a wide smile. "A delightful pleasure, Madame." He gave her a courtly bow. "Mr. Avery tells me you will be an invaluable part of our efforts."

"I shall do my best," she replied.

"I'll be right down," Nate told Prince, who nodded and left, his footfalls thumping down the stairs.

Madame turned on him, eyes flashing fury. "That man is a slave," she hissed. "There is a brand on his arm."

"That man *was* a slave," Nate corrected her. "Not any longer. If his presence causes you pain—"

"It is not my feelings you should consider," she said with a slash of one hand. "He will have to stay here in this house. You cannot send him about London, even with the brand covered. If he were detained and the brand discovered, it would make things very difficult for us. Slaves are uncommon in London."

"Don't worry, he won't be going out with us. He's a freedman, but he can pose as a servant."

She didn't look pleased with this idea. "He does not act like the average servant."

Nate was quiet for a moment. "Fine. I shall warn him to keep out of sight."

She hesitated. Her eyes veered away, to the room behind her where her own maid still worked. She stepped closer and lowered her voice even more. "Mr. Avery, if this enterprise is to succeed, you must be honest with me. If you had told Mr. Stafford you had a black man with you—"

"It wouldn't have made a damned bit of difference. Prince has other talents which render him invaluable, even to Stafford's way of thinking."

"Such as?"

Nate smiled and waved one hand. "This and that. You'll have to trust me."

She gave him a look that said trusting him was the last thing she wanted to do. "Very well—for now. We must arrange our story as soon as possible. So far I have acted rather remote and temperamental, and had Lisette manage the servants. You might do the same."

"They're not Stafford's people, then?" he asked, wondering if she would even know.

"No," she said. "He is too tightfisted for that. They will clean the house, then go. We shall talk over luncheon." Without waiting for approval, she turned and walked back into her room, pulling closed the door between them.

Chapter 6

Angelique ignored Lisette's raised eyebrows and went back to work, unpacking her things. Stafford still hadn't given her a clear idea of how she was to play her part, so she had brought enough clothing to last a year. If anything about Stafford could be called endearing, it would be his willingness to pay for such an extensive wardrobe, all of which she got to keep—whatever wasn't ruined in the course of the job, at any rate. But she had better learn soon how fashionable she was supposed to be, so Lisette could retrim some bonnets and adjust the gowns.

At least Avery looked more presentable today. No more shapeless brown coats and lumpy boots; he looked quite English in a well-fitted green coat and gray trousers, his boots shined to a gleam. He cleaned up very well, she had to admit. It had given her a moment's pause when she looked up to see him leaning so elegantly against her door. Then he opened his mouth and dispelled whatever fleeting impression she'd had that this might be easier than expected. *Dear wife*, he called her in his rolling American voice. *Darling*. As if he was enjoying this charade far too much. She had a sense of humor, and certainly had nothing against flirting, but only when the work was taken very seriously. They were hunting a man, tracking him like an animal, and when they found him, she was supposed to kill him. She reminded herself that Avery didn't know that last bit, but he was an utter fool if he expected Dixon to be easily caught and subdued. No doubt chatting about politics in some well-appointed salon hadn't shown him how deadly a man could be when cornered.

There was some commotion in the corridor outside her door, and she looked up in time to see Avery's companion stagger past, holding up one end of an enormous trunk. He was talking to Avery decidedly as an equal, and not as servant to master. Even though she'd seen him already, the black man was startling in appearance, with skin the color of dark mahogany and an exotic accent she would wager came from the sugar plantations in the French Indies. He had exquisite manners and carried himself like no other servant, let alone slave, she had ever seen. They would have to have a good explanation for him, or they would be conspicuous in this neighborhood before breakfast tomorrow simply through the servants' chatter.

Avery himself went by then, holding up the other end of the trunk. He had discarded his coat and rolled up his sleeves, exposing muscular forearms tanned to a rich bronze. His hair was tied back today, and somehow it made him look leaner, stronger, and more dangerous. In Stafford's office she had dismissed him as a rumpled, naive colonial, but something about him had changed since then, more than just his clothes. Angelique crossed the room and closed the door, not needing to see him parade up and down the corridor again.

"He bothers you, Madame," said Lisette.

She lifted one shoulder. "He is but one of many things that bother me." There was a loud thump from the bedroom next door, most likely the trunk hitting the floor, followed by the sound of cursing. She couldn't make out the exact words, but Avery's tone and inflection were clear even through the closed door. He was annoyed but not angry, and then he laughed. It was a nice sound, rich and carefree and honest.

"Americans are noisy," sniffed Lisette, snapping Angelique out of her daze. She scowled as she realized she was standing stock-still, listening for the sound of his laughter. There was nothing funny about this. If only he wouldn't be so lackadaisical about everything. As disgusted with herself as she was with Avery, she stuffed the remaining clothing into the wardrobe and opened the last trunk. She lifted out her small writing desk, then the layer of books a lady of quality might read, and finally pulled up the false bottom. Underneath were her weapons, and somehow sliding her daggers out of their sheaths restored her composure. All her knives were weighted for throwing, since she was too small to win a fight at close quarters against a man, and holding the hard, cold hilts made her feel clearheaded. It was deadly to be otherwise, with knives like these. She tested the edges of every one before replacing them in the leather sheaths, uncoiled her garrote and examined the rope, and finally checked the pistol, her least favorite item. Let Avery laugh and flirt his way through London; one of them had to be prepared for trouble.

When all was unpacked and the weapons safely stowed, she sent Lisette to arrange some luncheon, then knocked on the door to Avery's bedchamber.

He opened it himself, still in his shirtsleeves. "At last," he said with a grin.

She ignored his words and the dimple in his cheek that only sprang into sight when he smiled. "I have sent my maid for something to eat," she said. "If you are not otherwise occupied, we have things to discuss."

"I am never otherwise occupied when my wife needs me," he said. "Where shall we eat?"

"The dining room is the usual place, I believe."

"Ah, but don't we need some measure of privacy?" His voice dropped on the last word, becoming just a shade rougher and darker. Something inside her quivered at the sensual undertone even as her irritation spiked that he persisted in flirting with her.

"Unless you are recommending the privy, I shall see you in the dining room."

He laughed, that same rumble that had caught her attention before. "The dining room it is, if I can't persuade you to something more interesting."

Angelique raised one brow. "What could be more interesting to a man than luncheon, after a morning of moving house?"

"We have a lot to learn about each other," he told her.

She gave him a sardonic smile. "Indeed we do, and we shall. In the dining room."

* * *

Downstairs, Lisette had laid out a spread of cold meats, some bread, fresh strawberries, and a plate of small cakes. A pitcher of water sat beside the strawberries, beaded with cool condensation. Angelique waited until the maid had left, closing the door behind her, before taking out her list.

"First we must decide how we are to be known," she said.

He was filling a plate. "Mr. and Mrs. Avery should be sufficient."

"There is nothing in that name that would alert Mr. Dixon of your interest in him?"

"Nothing more than usual; I've met him precisely twice, for a few moments. If he should happen to remember either occasion, I shall affect not to."

"Twice!" She stared at him. "On this you have crossed an ocean and presented yourself as the only man who can apprehend him?"

"I have a good memory." He winked at her, setting the plate in front of her. "Water?"

She pursed her lips, but nodded briefly. He filled her glass, and caught sight of her list. "Good Lord. Ought I to make notes, too?"

"You most certainly ought not. A man with a good memory will be able to recall everything, yes?"

This time he laughed as he heaped a plate for himself. "You'll be there to remind me." Before she could stop him, he had plucked the list off the table. "Cards," he read aloud. "Introductions. Dressmaker." He looked warily at her over the paper. "We need to discuss dressmakers?"

Angelique rolled her eyes and put out her hand. "We must order cards. We must get introductions. In short, we must announce ourselves to London if we are to be invited anywhere this fellow may be. Finding the proper dressmaker will be part of that."

"I'll find him," Avery said, still reading her list as he ate. Angelique sighed and picked at her own plate. "That's my task, isn't it? The only reason I'm permitted to be here at all?" He glanced up at her. "But I'm not so certain of *your* job."

She met his sharp green gaze for a long moment. "If you did not want Stafford's help, why did you apply to him?" she asked, very softly. Lisette was under orders to keep the other servants away from the door, but one could never be too careful. "Did you really think he would just grant you leave to run about the country by yourself, abducting British citizens? He does not work thus, sir."

He rested his arms on the table, leaning forward until their faces were mere inches apart. She noticed the lines that fanned out from the corners of his eyes, little wrinkles of laughter in his sun-worn face. He was a bit younger than she had thought, just more weathered than most Englishmen. "I applied to him because I was under orders not to simply snatch the thieving bastard off the street and drag him back to New York in chains—which," he added with a significant look, "I was more than willing to do. Still am, if it comes to it." He shrugged. "But if I can avoid causing a diplomatic uproar, it will make things easier at home. And that doesn't answer my question about what you will be doing."

She smiled slightly. "Helping you, of course."

His lips quirked. He knew she was lying. "And mighty glad I am to have your help, my love."

"Stop calling me that."

"We are supposed to be married." He grinned and handed back her list.

"*Unhappily* married," she reminded him.

"Now, why is that?" he asked in reproach. "What came between us? Was it your cold and secretive manner, or all the women who throw themselves at me?"

"It is because you do not please me in bed." She smiled sweetly at his startled expression. "It will explain why I must seek solace elsewhere."

"Ah, yes, of course." His eyes gleamed with mirth again. He was enjoying this tremendously, she realized—as was she, oddly enough. Perhaps it was the way he said, *I'll find him* when she mentioned Dixon, as if he had no doubt of his ability to do so. Perhaps it was the carelessly ruthless way he expressed his intention to drag Dixon home in chains. Perhaps it was just the way he was different today than he had been in Stafford's office, sharper, harder, more focused. Somehow he didn't seem quite so amateur now, despite the flirting and joking. In fact, he put her in mind of Ian, who had always been her favorite agent to work with, despite these little attempts at discerning her role—although she had to admit, in his place she would do much the same.

"You believed I was incompetent," he said. Angelique blinked in surprise that he had read her thoughts, and he grinned wickedly. "In bed. Perhaps you thought I was . . . inexperienced. Unskilled. Naive, even. Ah, my poor wife; no wonder you've been so cold and reserved with me. It's made us almost strangers to each other, hasn't it? Such a pity." He caught her hand from the table and lifted it to his lips. "Rest assured I shall do everything in my power to convince you of my . . . true talents. In bed and elsewhere."

She let him fondle her hand. "Talent cannot replace experience. Even a prodigy needs persistent practice to become a master."

He chuckled, tracing one fingertip down the sensitive side of her palm. "And it's too late for me, eh? All my life until now has been a waste, if I cannot please you. I would only beg you to consider that we don't know everything about each other. I may yet surprise you."

Not if she were any good at her job. Angelique was always willing to believe people more capable than they appeared; indeed, it would be fatal to underestimate anyone in her line of work. Today Avery had proved himself more than the stuffy dilettante he had appeared in Bow Street, but he was not a professional. Even a motivated amateur would be more cautious. He left himself too open, too unguarded. He was approaching this with far too much amusement, and far too much interest in her. Spying was often boring, with long hours spent waiting and watching. There was plenty of time for teasing and fun, but later, once the hard work of setting up the job was done.

Still, it was his commission they were on. If they failed, it would not matter much to her, except for the sake of professional pride.

When he tugged on her hand, she allowed him to pull her toward him. "But you do not have to surprise me," she said gently. "I am quite used to pleasing myself. I would beg of *you*, husband, to let me take you in hand, and let me guide you. Because you see, I know very well what I am doing."

"I do so *respect* a woman with experience," he murmured. "You may take me in your hands any time."

"Good. We shall get on splendidly then." He was doing lovely things to her hand, she had to admit. Angelique watched him feather his lips over the pulse in her wrist and tried to hide how that made her stomach flutter in spite of herself. Perhaps he should be the one sent out to seduce. Not her, of course; his seductions would not work on her. But on another, unsuspecting woman . . . Too bad it was a man they sought.

He flashed a lazy, sensuous smile, and pressed a tender kiss to her now-throbbing pulse. "I am delighted to hear that. And we didn't have to say one word of dressmakers."

She laughed, pulling her hand free. She had let him hold it far too long already. "No, now that we are in agreement, there is no need for that." She laid down her napkin and rose, folding her list into the pocket of her skirt. "I will see to these details, and leave you to your task, as you wished."

He surged to his feet. "You've not finished eating."

Angelique glanced at her barely touched plate. He had filled it for her, with more food than she could eat in two meals. But of course it only proved that he knew nothing about her. "I am not very hungry at the moment. Lisette will bring something later."

Nate debated a moment. He'd rather liked how things were going, and felt it was far more important that they understand and trust each other than that they speak the same sterile lies. But then she turned toward the door and he scrambled to catch her before she put the final touch on her condescending dismissal and left. "We have to be able to trust each other," he said, just managing to get one hand against the door in time.

Two thin lines appeared between her brows. "No, we must be able to work together. That is all."

"More than that," he exclaimed. "We're supposed to act as man and wife. You say the servants know nothing of this, so we must persuade them at home, too."

"We will act the same way as we act in public." She, too, lowered her voice. "The English are more reserved; they do not expect to see emotion on display, in affection or in argument. And the servants will be gone by tomorrow at the latest."

He searched her face for a moment. Her expression was as cool as ever, but there was a bloom of color in her cheeks—put there, he hoped, by their cautious flirting. Prince would give him no end of torment about it, but Nate was in danger of being utterly fascinated by his dangerous, beautiful new "wife." He knew she was trying to control him and remain in charge. He was aware that she still hadn't told him anything about Stafford's true motives in sending her, or what exactly she planned to do to help capture Jacob Dixon. But he was stuck with her, and she with him—less than happily, perhaps, but stuck nonetheless. He would have to discover how to ingratiate himself with her, or risk the whole enterprise collapsing.

"We know nothing about each other," he said instead. "Stafford said I was to be a wealthy American merchant with a bored wife—that leaves a great deal to the imagination. You said yourself we must talk, and better now than later. There's no way we can think of a story that explains everything; we'll have to invent as we go along, and that will be much easier if we share a certain perception of the situation."

"You proved you did not care to be bothered by the tedium of that," she retorted. "Instead you wish to tease and make fun and kiss my hand, as if that will do any good."

"I enjoyed it," he said. "And you did, too, no matter how much you glare at me now."

Her mouth pinched, but the pink in her cheeks didn't fade. Interesting. "It means nothing, and accomplishes even less."

"What plans do we need to make?" Nate was determined not to be shut out of this. "Besides the dressmaker, of course; I refuse to have anything to do with dressmakers."

She glared a moment longer, then her expression eased. "I see now. You are not one who prepares; you are one who prefers to improvise."

Nate considered. "That's half right. But I must warn you, I'm very good at improvising."

"Indeed," she murmured. "How long have we been married?"

"Two years," he said without hesitation.

"How did we meet?"

"You were shopping at the market when a runaway horse almost ran you over. I whisked you out of harm's way, and you fell helplessly, instantly, deeply in love with me."

"No doubt," she said dryly. "Why are we estranged?"

"We are not estranged, we have simply drifted

apart. I devoted myself to business and making money; you, to shopping for ever more expensive clothing and jewels." Nate suspected she wouldn't like that—she hardly seemed like the society women he knew who would spend every waking moment shopping if they could—so he added, on impulse, "It's nothing a trip abroad to England, where we must spend so much time alone together, won't repair."

"You are very sure of your charm. What is your business?"

"Shipping," he replied. This was too easy. Besides, it was true—or would be, as soon as he satisfied his thirst for adventure and dutifully returned to the family business. Nate thought he had a few years left before his father persuaded him to take up running things at Boudin. He'd grown up knowing it was his future.

"How dull," she said with a trace of disdain.

"How profitable," he countered. "If I have a spendthrift wife, I'd better have a fortune for her to spend."

"How American. The English care nothing for earning, only for spending."

Nate shrugged that off. "What else?"

"How long do we plan to stay in London?"

"A month or two. I expect to have won my wife's heart back by then, and will need to return to my offices."

"But you plan to conduct business while you are here."

"Of course. I might want to open a London office. I always welcome new custom. I could even take on a new investor or two, or invest my funds in some promising venture here. Not that I intend to let business overtake the pleasures of this holiday."

Her eyes narrowed at the last bit, but Nate kept his expression open and guileless. It was the first time he had made her pause in the rapid stream of questions she flung at him. "What if someone should make inquiries about your business?"

"My father founded it, right after the war with England. We run between Boston, New York, and Liverpool most regularly."

"There is such a business, then." He nodded, and that vaguely superior look came over her face again, as if she had caught him in some mistake. "Perhaps that is best; the less you lie, the easier it will be to maintain our pose."

Nate laughed. "I'll lie when I need to. There's no reason to hide what could be verified with some small effort, especially not when the truth will work to my advantage."

She paused. "Yes, you are right," she said, rather grudgingly. "It will save time."

"Indeed," he agreed. "Shall we make attempts at our reconciliation, then? I am perfectly willing, Madame."

"That, Mr. Avery, does not surprise me at all."

"Nate," he said. "My name is Nate. A wife should know her husband's name."

"'Mr. Avery' will be sufficient, given our estrangement."

"You might at least try to sound a little regretful we're not on better terms with each other."

"I regret that you regard this as a joke," she snapped. "Stop flirting!"

"Then deal honestly with me," he growled back.

Then he sighed. "I apologize. It was my hope to make things easier between us, since we must work together with some measure of trust. Don't mistake me for anything other than determined to see this through, no matter what."

She studied him in silence, doubt written on her face. "Are you truly prepared for what you may have to do?"

"Without exception."

"Hmm. We shall see."

"You think I'm not equal to the task."

Her eyebrow arched. "I think you have no idea what the task will require."

Nate smiled, rather sardonically. "And you do? My dear, I have made a full study of Dixon's habits and interests. He fled New York in a hurry, but he left his fingerprints all over the city. The reason he has a month's lead on me is because I took my time examining each and every one of those fingerprints to get a full view of his character. Every man has his weak spot, and he'll be much easier to catch if I can place my thumb directly on his, and squeeze until he breaks. I'm not about to run through London shouting my interest on every street corner and spurring him into running off again."

For the first time a glimmer of interest and respect sparked in her eyes. "A careful hunter," she said thoughtfully.

He dipped his head in unabashed acknowledgment. "A determined one. I understand you're following Stafford's orders, not mine, and that you won't tell me what his true interest is. Frankly, as long as I end up with Jacob Dixon in my custody, I don't care why you're helping me or what you do to ensure I get him. But I will take it very much amiss if you think to use me and then brush me aside."

"I do not answer to you."

"You will," he murmured. "Stafford might be sitting in his office across town waiting to hear how things go, with the whole British navy ready to chase me out of the country if he tires of my cooperation. But you're the one here, dealing with me now, sleeping on the other side of the door from me." He opened his hands expansively. "Come, my dear, I want only to make this as pleasant as possible."

"Pleasant?" She gave a little huff of a laugh. "It does not need to be pleasant to be successful."

"Can't we at least try to achieve both?"

"Ah, but if we should fail at one, it would be much better to fail at being pleasant." She stepped closer, tipping up her chin to inspect him closely. "It does not need to be dreadful. But you would do well to remember that we are employed by different people."

Nate couldn't stop himself from leaning down to her. "What does Stafford want?" he whispered. "I don't trust in the goodness of his heart."

Her mouth curved wryly. "Nor should you. He has no heart."

"You're not going to tell me, are you?" He gave her a coaxing smile as he said it.

She sighed, as if she did almost regret refusing him. "You do not wish to know. Believe me. You should concentrate on finding Dixon and getting your money, and do not think of what Stafford might want."

"So I should trust you—after such a statement—and you won't do the same for me." Her eyes narrowed, and Nate shrugged. "That seems terribly unfair."

She arched one eyebrow. "Oh? You ask me to trust you to improvise. I do not improvise more than absolutely necessary. I prefer a well-thought plan, with all possibilities addressed. Just how do you propose to begin, Mr. Avery?"

"My name is Nate," he interrupted to say.

"How shall you find this man you have crossed an ocean to seek?" she went on, ignoring it. "You are so certain it will all work out; you are so certain you will find him and persuade him to lead you to your money. How, sir? You say you have met him only twice. You have no plan and no idea where to find him. You say you will gallivant about London and improvise your way, as if Mr. Dixon will not have made some efforts to hide himself. Give me one reason to believe you have not come to London with nothing but confidence and a charming smile."

"Charming?" He smiled widely. "I'm flattered, Madame." Her expression grew, not thunderous with fury, but stony calm, and Nate dropped his teasing tone at once. "The jewels."

"Jewels," she repeated in a flat tone.

Slowly Nate nodded, keeping his eyes on her face. "The jewels Jacob Dixon will need to sell. He hid his stolen funds in diamonds and emeralds before he left New York. Jewels are more compact than coin, universally desired, and easily converted into ready money. Sooner or later he'll have to sell some pieces, and when he does, I'll be waiting for him."

"Well." Her posture eased. "I suppose that is somewhere to start."

"It's a damned good place to start," he replied. "A rich American with a spoiled wife will want to buy jewels, and I happen to be very particular. Any jeweler who can acquire certain pieces for me—or direct me to someone selling those pieces—will be handsomely rewarded."

"I see." Another amused look. "You are willing to spend freely then, to capture your quarry. Your president has a great deal of confidence in you."

He had told no one about his connection to Ben Davies, and thus to Dixon. Stafford believed him sent by President Monroe on behalf of the United States, and he was; the fact that he was willing to spend not only his government's money but his own changed nothing. There was no reason to correct Madame Martand's assumptions. His personal motives were perfectly in accord with his official mission, after all; what did it matter to her whose money he spent, or why? "I have my instructions."

Her expression turned faintly mocking. "Very good, sir. I suggest you concentrate on following them."

Nate kept his weight against the door as she reached for the doorknob. "I am also not about to expose our 'marriage' for the fraud that it is just because you don't like me."

Her luscious mouth curled into a wicked smile. "It doesn't matter whether I like you or not, Mr. Avery."

It does to me, he thought, *cursed fool that I am*. But he certainly wasn't about to tell her that. Without a word he bowed his head politely and stepped out of her way, letting her sweep past him with a rustle of skirts, out the door and away without a backward glance. For a long moment after she had gone he stood there still, illogically aware of the lingering scent of lavender. That was no ordinary woman. Like a witless lunatic, Nate was falling into a mad swirl of fascination, already in danger of losing some of his focus. As she said, he did prefer to improvise; in his experience, relying too much on plans only left one vulnerable to disaster when some part of the plan failed—as it almost always did. By keeping his goal fixed and letting everything else bend with the circumstances, he kept his options as varied as possible.

And with Madame Martand, he would need to keep every possible option open.

Chapter 7

The house was settled by mid-morning the day after next. The servants who had been hired to clean and set all to rights were dismissed; Lisette would be responsible for stoking the fires, and for the laundry. Angelique had found it easier to have her own maid deal with bloodstains and other alarming insults on her clothing than to risk another servant asking questions or spreading rumors. Lisette was well accustomed to doing more when they were working, and Angelique didn't anticipate living in Varden Street long enough to care much about any housekeeping Lisette couldn't handle. She would have food and drink sent in every day, and Avery and his man were welcome to that; otherwise, they were on their own.

She had spent some time thinking over his plan to find Dixon. It was a good one, assuming Dixon didn't have a shady jeweler pry the stones out of the settings and sell them individually; distinctive jewels were easy to trace as long as they remained distinctive. But it was an avenue to pursue, and with far less trouble than trying to guess which kind of society Dixon might move in and have to join it.

Avery had indicated he would be ready to begin the search as soon as possible, but when she went looking for him, he was not in his room. She knocked twice on the connecting door, then opened it when there was no answer. The room looked much as it had the first day, clean and empty. There were a few personal effects on top of the bureau, and a pair of boots stood by the door, no doubt waiting to be polished. She lingered a moment, considering searching his things to discover more about him, but decided against it. Unless she knew where he was and when he was expected back, it was unwise. Stafford had not told her to view Mr. Avery with suspicion, so there was no pressing reason to do it anyway.

He was not downstairs, either in the dining room or the parlor. He was not in the house at all, to judge from the quiet. Already she had become accustomed to hearing his laughter as he worked with his man, Mr. Chesterfield, and the rumble of his voice echoing down the stairs. After their luncheon the first day, he had stayed busy with matters of his own and left her to hers, but the sound of his voice seemed to follow her everywhere. Now that she wanted to find him, of course, he was nowhere to be seen.

She went to the attic to look for him. He and his man had gone up and down the stairs all day yesterday, setting up some sort of laboratory in the large room under the eaves, and she hadn't ventured up here yet. Lisette had seen it and reported it looked like the den of some crazed scientist. Angelique admitted some mild curiosity about what they were doing. It seemed an odd way to track their man, even though it did have the effect of easing her worries about Mr. Chesterfield's presence; he rarely left the house, to her knowledge.

She tapped at the door, and when there was no answer, she turned the knob. It was unlocked, and swung open without a sound. Angelique stepped into the room and then stopped.

Lisette had been right. Every piece of furniture had been converted into table space; chairs held up wide boards, a mirror had been laid between the old settee and the bed frame, and an old table with a broken leg was propped up by what looked like a powder keg. All that space was filled with scientific equipment: mortars, strange-looking tools, bottles of liquids, and a wide variety of weapons. Even the mantel had been pressed into use, covered with a variety of small jars. A fire roared in the hearth, but the windows were wide open. And there was no sign of Mr. Avery, just Mr. Chesterfield, his close-cropped head barely visible behind a large bottle with steam pouring out the top. He was hunkered down on a stool, attention fixed on an iron pot that sat below the suspended bottle.

"Yes, ma'am?" he asked, eyes still trained on his bottle.

"I am looking for Mr. Avery," she said, raising her voice as a log broke in the fireplace and the flames shot higher. It would be unbearably hot in here, but for the open windows.

"He is out, ma'am."

"Yes, I see," she murmured. Now that she had seen it for herself, she thought Lisette understated the matter. It looked like the den of a madman, scientist or not. "Will he return soon?"

Mr. Chesterfield's teeth flashed in his dark face.

"He did not tell me. But I expect he will. Is there something I may do for you?"

He still hadn't moved from his position crouched over the iron pot. She walked around one of the makeshift tables to see what he was doing. There was a small fire crackling in the iron pot, she realized, and he was feeding splinters of wood into it to keep it burning. Up close, the steam coming from the bottle had a greenish cast to it. "What is in the bottle?" she asked with some trepidation. If Avery had him up here brewing poisonous potions . . .

"Nothing, yet. It is an experiment. I hope it will distill into a liquid capable of producing great quantities of smoke, such as this, when a salt is dropped into it." He waved his hand over the bottle, dispersing the vapor in a thick swirl toward her. It had a slightly mossy scent, but was relatively cool and hung in the air far longer than she would have expected.

"How curious," she said. He just grinned at her again, then went back to feeding his fire. He was a young man, younger than Avery, she guessed, his cheeks smooth and unlined. She thought again of the brand on his arm; Mr. Avery had admitted the man had been a slave, and he had the accent of the West Indies. "*Quel âge avez-vous?*" she asked on impulse.

"*Vingt-quatre ans,*" he replied without looking up. Only twenty-four. "I was born in Saint-Domingue, before the revolution there. Mr. Avery plucked me from a group of slaves to be executed. He persuaded the army captain charged with killing the slaves that he would like the joy of killing a Negro himself. When the captain turned his back,

Mr. Avery nailed me into a barrel and put me on his ship."

"How daring," she said shortly. And how rash. If Avery attempted anything like that on this assignment . . .

"Your pardon—that was Nathaniel's father I spoke of," Mr. Chesterfield said. "Nathaniel is but a few years older than I am."

It was evident from his voice that the young black man revered the Avery family—perhaps with good reason. She looked around at the contents of the room. There could be poisons in the bottles and gunpowder in the kegs. What on earth was Avery planning to do with it all? Or was he just ready to "improvise" some sort of explosion? "And is the son so daring as the father?" she asked evenly.

This time he laughed, a rich, rolling sound of pure amusement. "More so. He is still here, is he not?"

Angelique raised her brow at him. "Do I understand *I* am what he must brave?"

"No," he said somberly, although his eyes twinkled. "It is Mademoiselle Lisette one must fear."

She had to smother a smile at the unexpected reply. "Have you crossed her, then?"

"Not deliberately. She is too delicate a lady to stand my experiments, though."

Lisette had stitched up wounds, served as a watch while Angelique broke into houses, and spied among other servants. She knew how to engineer a dress so it would accommodate all manner of weapons without destroying the line, and she was willing to undertake any job Angelique asked of her. Lisette was no more a delicate lady than Angelique was. "What are you making?"

"Smoke."

"I believe you have succeeded." A breeze from the window had blown more of the bottle's emission toward her, and she waved her hand to dispel it.

He grinned again. "Partly."

Angelique realized he wasn't going to tell her, and that it didn't much matter to her. "As long as you are not going to cause an explosion or poison any of us, neither Lisette nor I have any objection," she said aloud. "If Mr. Avery returns, please tell him I would like to speak to him."

"I will, Madame." He sprang to his feet and bowed very properly. "It was a pleasure to see you."

She left the attic and went downstairs. In her room she rang the bell, and Lisette appeared a few moments later. "What is Mr. Chesterfield doing upstairs?" she asked her maid without preamble.

Lisette rolled her eyes. "Making a large mess and a new horrible smell every day."

"Has he told you what anything is?"

"No, Madame, he just laughs and tries to make me smile." Lisette sniffed. "He has been around his master too long, I think."

That did sound like Avery. "That is not too disagreeable."

"I wish him to stop," said Lisette bluntly. "Is it safe to have him here? My cousin was part of the army sent to put down the slave rebellion in the Indies, Madame; the Negroes committed terrible atrocities against the French . . ."

"He told me the French army executed slaves. There is no shortage of atrocity in any race." Angelique sighed. "Do you fear him?"

Lisette hesitated. "No, Madame."

"Then do not act like it." She went and opened her wardrobe. "Mr. Avery told me he would be ready to go out today, but he is away with no word of where he has gone or when he is expected back. If Mr. Chesterfield wishes to poison someone, he should practice on his friend."

Nate jogged up the stairs to the attic Prince had made into his workshop. He rapped twice on the door and went in.

Prince glanced up. "At last."

He snorted. "It's not like you sent me out to fetch some eggs. I had to visit three chemists to find what you wanted." He handed over his parcels to Prince, who set about opening them at once. "Quicklime isn't on every London tradesman's shelf."

Prince waved one hand. "Excuses! And I have been regaling Madame Martand with legends of your daring."

"Oh?" Nate dropped into a chair, repressing any show of interest in what Madame Martand might have said or done or wanted to know about him. "She was looking for me? I may hide up here for an hour or two."

Prince was not fooled. "Yes, she was looking for you. What a difficulty it must be, to work with such a woman. I commend your fortitude, Nathaniel. You are a brave and noble man, enduring such a trial with so little complaint."

"Yes, it is a cruel imposition," he agreed gravely, "but someone must do it."

"Any time you wish to change places, I will be glad to eat luncheon with her."

Nate hadn't been able to tell what she thought of Prince, aside from her warning about his slave brand. When he'd brought Prince with him, he had thought primarily of Prince's skills and how they might be useful to his objective. Prince could keep him well supplied with poisons, acids, and various other concoctions that might prove useful in his search, with no one the wiser where he'd gotten them. But he hadn't predicted being paired with Madame, let alone how she would react to Prince's presence. Perhaps he should have projected more indifference between the two of them to keep from raising her suspicions. "You must be all done with your work, then," he said.

"Don't touch it," snapped Prince as he reached for the bottle. Nate smirked, and Prince gave him a warning frown as he carefully removed the bottle from the stand that held it above the fire. He blew away the vapor curling around the lip of the bottle. "Hand me a pinch of those crystals."

Nate obliged, sprinkling the crystals carefully into Prince's palm. Eyes fixed on the bottle, Prince poured the crystals in and swirled the bottle. The liquid fizzed, then thick white smoke began pouring forth, billowing around Prince's head like a cloud.

"How long does it last?" Nate asked.

"Wait and see." Prince's face shone with satisfaction as he put down the bottle and turned to his notes, scribbling several lines. Nate flipped out his watch and they waited as the bottle smoked.

"Ten minutes," he announced. The bottle was nearly empty now, the liquid almost gone. A dark green residue coated the inside of the bottle.

"Ten!" Prince beamed and waved one hand about to get rid of the last of the smoke. "Better. That's almost long enough for you to disorient Madame enough to steal a kiss or two."

"Perish the thought," said Nate, getting to his feet. "You'd need a healing potion if I ever attempted such a thing."

"Oh, Nathaniel." His friend was shaking his head. "Perish the thought? Are you telling me or yourself?"

He paused at the door. "Both. You know I never did have the sense to pass up a challenge."

Prince was still laughing at him as he closed the door. Nate went downstairs and knocked on Madame's door. "You wanted me?" he drawled when she opened it.

She coolly looked him up and down. "Where did you go?"

"Out."

"Where?"

"Out," he repeated evenly. "I had some errands to do."

Madame closed her eyes, and her chest filled, doing lovely things to her bosom, but then she opened her eyes and glared at him. "When you go out, tell me," she snapped. "Tell me when you will return. I do not wish to sit about waiting for you to wander back into the house, wondering if you have gotten yourself lost or in trouble."

"You were worried," he said sympathetically. "How kind of you to take such a concern for my well-being."

Her expression smoothed into something almost frightening. "Do not do it again," she said in a low voice. "Are we still to go out today in search of these jewels, or have you already visited every jeweler and fence in town?"

"Not at all. I wouldn't dream of taking action without your oversight—forgive me, without your assistance. When do you wish to begin?"

"This afternoon," she said. "The sooner we begin, the sooner we will find your man."

He leaned one shoulder against the door. "Yes. And then what, exactly?"

Her eyes were clear and innocent. "Then we will achieve your goal, yes? Find the man, reclaim the funds, and you can return home victorious."

Nate narrowed his eyes thoughtfully. She always phrased it like that, glossing over any details. It hardly fit with her declared preference for precise planning, and her comment yesterday, that he didn't really want to know what Stafford's interest was, had kept him awake last night. He might not want to know, but damn it all, he needed to know. "And you are under instructions to help me retrieve the funds as well as find Dixon?"

"No," she said with a little smile. "Are you not relieved to hear I shall leave that to you alone?"

Perhaps. Perhaps not. "I am only trying to learn from your advice yesterday," he said, "and make appropriate plans. So you are only going to help locate him; I presume it will also be my task to secure his person for the trip to New York."

"I am under no explicit instruction to help you do that, either," she agreed.

But there was nothing left, except the simple act of finding the man. Nate still thought his plan was sensible, and it was certainly one he could carry out without her presence. If he was also supposed to capture Dixon, get him safely on the *Water Asp*, and then find the missing funds on his own . . . What was her purpose? This was doing nothing to settle his unease about Stafford's true interests.

"So," he said, drawing out the word suggestively, "you won't be much help at all. I could visit jewel shops on my own."

"I shall do my best to be as helpful as possible."

"Just not as enlightening as possible," he muttered. She simply smiled, acknowledging the point without yielding an inch.

This could be a problem. He couldn't trust her, not as long as he didn't know what she really intended to do, but he could keep only so much to himself. In fact, so far he'd kept very little to himself; his goals and plans had been laid before her almost in their entirety. He had gone through the appropriate channels, as directed, and she was operating as an agent of the British government, which had given him assurances they would do all they could to help him . . . find the man. Finally Nate realized that point: they had never promised anything else. Selwyn had expressed shock at the amount of the missing funds and agreed that of course he must do all he could to retrieve it. Stafford had brought him to Madame Martand, saying she was most capable. But all they had done was agree that Dixon must be caught at all costs. Again he wondered just what motivated the British government so strongly to leap to his assistance. Perhaps it was President Monroe's letter, and perhaps it was something else. But what? Dixon had been in America for at least a decade. He was English by birth, it was true, but

Nate doubted that was any motivating factor. Now that he thought carefully, he wasn't sure he'd even mentioned it to Lord Selwyn. The only thing Nate could think of was that Selwyn, and by extension Stafford, didn't trust him; that Madame was here to ensure he merely apprehended Dixon and reclaimed only the funds stolen from New York, no more. That was plausible . . . perhaps.

"Then we shall begin this afternoon," he said.

"Very well." Without another word she closed the door in his face.

Slowly Nate walked into his own room, still thinking. It was beginning to fester in his mind. What was her real purpose? And why?

Chapter 8

～～～〇〇～～～

No answer had occurred to him when they went out that afternoon, but Madame played her part beautifully. He was impressed by her ability to maintain such a bored facade for so long. Even when they stopped to take tea, she kept it up, listening to him with a slightly vacant expression. To disguise their interest in jewels, they stopped in several other shops as well, and again Madame gave a good show, deliberating over ribbons and having the mercer bring out bolt after bolt of silk before deciding she didn't like any of them after all. Anyone following them would form a strong view of her as a woman difficult to please. For his part, Nate didn't have to feign his impatience with it all; not only did it delay any actual progress they might be making, but her attitude, no matter how feigned, was driving him mad. And there were moments, when he caught a flash of amusement in her expressive dark eyes, that he knew she was laughing at him.

His reaction, of course, was to embrace it. Provoked by her disinterested air, straining at the bit to accomplish something, and furious at himself for finding her so fascinating in spite of her clear lack of interest in being friendly, Nate flirted with her at every turn, making a great show of doting on his "wife." He called her his love, his darling, his beloved; he repaid every disinterested glance with a lavish compliment. He never missed a chance to touch her, whether on the elbow or the hand or, once, on the cheek as he brushed a stray lock of hair from her face. He rather thought he should be dead from the freezing glances she gave him, but she never gave in and engaged him.

It took several days of visiting shops, talking loudly and rather gauchely about what jewels he wished to purchase, before Nate's plan to track Dixon bore fruit. It was at a smaller shop, one he had added to his list as time wore on and they found no trace of the jewels they sought. Tucked at the far end of Bond Street, it had a surprisingly large selection. The proprietor, Mr. Smythe, brought out necklace after necklace for their inspection. Madame was brilliant, as she had been all along, as a bored, vain wife, turning up her nose at every tasteful piece and always asking for something bigger. When the man was ready to tear out his hair, Nate leaned back in his chair and described what they would really like, one of the flashier pieces Dixon had bought.

"I saw just such a pendant in New York a few months ago," he finished, "but by the time I went back to buy it, someone else had snatched it up."

"An emerald pendant, heart-shaped, surrounded by small diamonds," murmured the jeweler. "I do not have such a piece myself, sir, but something very similar was offered to me less than a week ago."

"Indeed?" Nate let his acute interest show. "By whom? I had my eye on that necklace and was most disappointed to lose it." He smiled at Madame. "There, my dear, who knew something like it would turn up in London?"

"If you'll excuse me but a moment, I shall look it up." Looking happier now himself, Mr. Smythe excused himself from the small private room where they sat.

"Could it be the same one you saw in New York?" asked Madame idly, smoothing her gloves.

Nate also kept up his persona. "Oh, likely not, my pet. Still, it's a distinctive pendant, and would look splendid at your lovely bosom. I have regretted letting it go ever since I saw it."

She narrowed her eyes at him, but the jeweler had returned. "Yes, I made a note of it, as I always do when offered especially fine pieces," Mr. Smythe said with a courtly smile. "Naturally I cannot purchase every piece that is offered to me, unless I have a buyer already in mind, particularly a piece of that quality and value. But a gentleman offered me a pendant as you describe, as well as some matching bracelets, barely four days ago."

"But that's excellent news," exclaimed Nate. He couldn't resist turning to his "wife." "We shall have it by the end of the week, love." She gave him a simpering smile even as her eyes reflected her acknowledgment of his victory. He looked at the jeweler. "How shall I contact this fellow?"

"Er . . . he is a discreet gentleman who often assists families who have fallen on hard times, sir," murmured the jeweler. "He does not like to be approached directly."

"Come now," objected Nate. "I don't like that. An honest man is willing to meet me face-to-face to conduct business. I don't want to buy a necklace from someone who hides his face and name; the next thing I know, some wealthy old woman will have the authorities at my door, insisting her nephew stole her necklace and sold it without her knowledge. Tell me his name."

Mr. Smythe hesitated, his interest in his commission warring against the logic of Nate's argument. "He is Mr. Davis Hurst," he said at last, quietly. "You may make inquiries if you like, but I believe he offers his assistance only to those of unquestionable integrity. Shall I contact him and make arrangements to purchase the necklace, sir?"

"I shall want proof of the pendant's provenance," he warned.

"Of course," said the jeweler at once.

"And the bracelets—you did say there are bracelets?"

"Yes, indeed, two perfectly matched bracelets of hammered gold, set with emeralds."

Nate nodded once. "Excellent. Get the set." He scribbled the number of the house on Varden Street on the back of one of the new cards Madame had ordered, and handed it to the jeweler. "Our London establishment."

"Very good, sir." The jeweler took the card and showed them out with a smile.

In the street, Nate waited a moment as Madame fussed with her bonnet before offering her his arm. "Well, my dear, I shall have those emeralds around your throat before the end of the week."

"So you say," she replied. "We shall see if your word means anything."

He laughed, pulling her closer to him. Unprepared, she swayed into him, her breast pressing against his arm before she jerked back with a frosty look. "I always keep my word," he told her. "I told you this approach would work, didn't I?"

"That was not a promise you made, that was your arrogant overconfidence speaking."

He raised his eyebrows. "Arrogant overconfidence? I thought you wanted a man who knows what he's doing."

"Yes, *knows*," she returned. "You did not know this would work; you assumed. And as of yet, there is no proof that it has worked."

Nate thought it had been a pretty logical assumption, and a proven good one since it had paid off within such a short time. Madame was irked at him for being right. "Let it not come between us," he said magnanimously.

"There is plenty of room for that, and a great many other things. But enough arguing. I will learn where we can find this Mr. Hurst, and we shall see for ourselves whether your fanciful scheme has succeeded or not." She tilted her head and regarded him thoughtfully. "I will leave you to deal with the question of the actual necklace."

Nate bowed his head. "Thank you, my love."

She sighed and shook her head. "No more endearments, please."

"But how else shall I address you?" He feigned bewilderment. "I cannot call you Madame Martand. Do you prefer Mrs. Avery?"

"If you wish."

"And yet we Americans are not so formal as the British," he went on thoughtfully. "My father calls my mother Bess, not Mrs. Avery or Elizabeth. I rather fancied such close affection in my own marriage."

"You might yet find it, when you are married."

The streets were bustling with people. They had joined the flow of pedestrians and kept their voices low, so no one would overhear, even if anyone could see what they did. So far Madame had strolled along with an expression as serene as if they discussed the weather. Nate felt somewhat free to bedevil her, since she could do little to respond at the moment. He bent his head until he could smell the lavender scent of her hair. "I'm happy enough at the moment," he murmured. "And there is only one solution to my quandary: I shall call you Angelique."

She pinched his arm in warning, but only smiled. "If you wish."

There. He'd made one small inroad. Content to savor that victory, Nate patted her hand, and they walked the rest of the way in silence.

Chapter 9

Nate had to admit, whatever resources she called upon, Angelique was able to discover quite a lot about Davis Hurst in a very short time. Hurst lived in a modest house off Broad Street; he was a bachelor of middle years; he wore a distinctive wolf's head signet ring on one hand; and he spent much of his time, including dinner most nights, at his club in St. James's Street. For entertainment, he preferred the Vauxhall Gardens, although he was also known to frequent the theater during the Season.

There was one more thing. "For all that Mr. Smythe said, Hurst is little more than a fence," Angelique told him the next day. "He has quite a reputation for selling things for young men who have gambling debts, and he does not take care to establish that the item being sold is a true possession of the person who engages him. Most times it is within a family, and the family does not wish to kick up a row over the missing silver teapot or Mama's pearls. Monsieur Hurst has encountered a bit of trouble from time to time, but always manages to wiggle out from under it. He is a clever one."

Nate was reading the summary of her information about Hurst. "Vauxhall," he said. "A public pleasure garden?" When she nodded, he tapped the paper. "That's our best bet to encounter him."

"I thought you wished to call on him."

He shook his head. "Why draw that much attention to ourselves? A chance encounter at a public garden won't raise any suspicions that might cause him to warn Dixon."

"If he is even the man who can lead us to Dixon," she reminded him. "We must not presume he is the answer."

"Of course not. We should keep visiting shops in search of the jewels. Part of my purpose is to recover them as well as Dixon's miserable person." Nate put aside her list and studied her. He still couldn't tell when she was mocking him or teasing, and when she was completely serious. He decided this time she had made a good point, which must be acknowledged seriously, but that she also liked needling him, just a little, every chance she got. "I shall be very well educated, should I ever need to purchase jewels in truth."

A little smile crossed her face. "Perhaps for your affectionate marriage."

"Ah, yes. Unlike the one I enjoy now."

"Enjoy?" She was amused. "Endure, perhaps."

"Now, darling, you mustn't think you're that great a trial to me," he replied.

She sighed. She leaned forward, her dark eyes soft and bright, no trace of anger on her face. Nate felt himself listing toward her, as if pulled by some invisible force. "You must stop flirting," she said evenly. "Or I shall be forced to retaliate."

He thought about that for a moment. "How?"

She stretched out her neck, almost as if she meant to kiss him. Her lips curved in a smile of pure sin, and her eyes half closed in sensual invitation. Nate's breath stuck in his throat and he stared in suspenseful anticipation. "I shall start flirting back," she whispered.

She might have just shown him Medusa's head. Nate wasn't sure if he should try to provoke her into doing it, just to see . . . or if he should ward her off like the devil come to steal his soul. As he sat like a statue, dumbstruck and aroused by the threat, her smile changed to one more kindly.

"Do not be overly alarmed," she said, getting to her feet. "I will remember you are an unsophisticated colonial, and be gentle with you." And then she was gone, sweeping past him and out of the room.

Angelique hadn't been to Vauxhall in over a year, but it had not changed as far as she could see. It was still as dark and merry as she remembered, filled with people in every mode of dress from elegant to working-class best. The orchestra was better this year, she thought, but the punch was worse.

"What if he's not here tonight?" Avery said, his expression easy even though his eyes roved constantly over the crowd. They had been at the gardens for over an hour with no sign of anyone who could be Davis Hurst.

"We return tomorrow."

He shot her a sideways glance. "Will that interfere with your plans?"

She pressed her lips together. "My plans, Mr. Avery, are to find our man, whether here, in Newgate, or in the halls of Parliament."

"My name is Nate," he said under his breath. "My dearest Angelique."

She tried to ignore it; he was trying to provoke her. He had said he would call her by name yesterday, but this was the first time he had done so. Being called by name didn't bother her, but the rest did, too much. "If I call you by name, will you relent on the endearments?"

He gave her one of those wary sideways glances he seemed prone to. Mr. Avery was still trying to puzzle her out, it seemed. Much luck to him, she thought, keeping her face serene. "Yes," he said, drawing out the word as if he would qualify it but didn't.

She smiled coolly, lifting her fan to wave it languidly in front of her face. Calling him by name didn't bother her, either. "Then we have an agreement, Nate."

He beamed in response, a wide, delighted grin. They walked some more, making desultory conversation from time to time. They certainly attracted some attention, by design. She had dressed in a provocative dress and smiled boldly back at everyone who nodded to them. Her information about Hurst had indicated he let himself be guided by his privy parts, and engaged in numerous clandestine encounters. Most were with prostitutes, but reports were that he wasn't above taking advantage of women he considered beneath him, particularly if they left themselves vulnerable. Angelique saw this as a fatal weakness on Hurst's part, and one she could exploit. She had agreed with Nate that at the first sign of the man, he would walk away and leave Hurst to her manipulations.

But in order to seduce him into revealing his secrets, she first had to locate him, and no one fitting Hurst's description was anywhere to be seen in the pleasure gardens. By the time Nate pulled out his watch to check the time, she was beginning to think tonight would be a waste after all.

"Shall we go soon?" he asked. "Surely it's getting late for a man to arrive for the evening."

She fanned herself some more. "Before the fireworks?" He cocked his head, and she smiled faintly, admitting her joke. "Soon. Fashionable London is out late into the night."

"Very well." He put away his watch. "Would you like some wine?"

Angelique nodded. "Thank you."

He left her in a quiet spot and headed toward the Grand Pavilion. Angelique drifted a little more into the shadows. Part of the reason she hadn't been to Vauxhall in so long was the density and variety of people here. There was safety in the masses, but also loss of control. Just as she could become anyone and anything in the crowd, so could others, and it was much harder to track them when throngs of people were in the way. She preferred to work in the background, where she was less likely to be noticed. When she did call attention to herself, as she had done tonight, it was deliberate and carefully done, but it was also not without risk.

"I say," said a voice behind her, as if to punctuate her thoughts. "Don't I know you?"

Angelique didn't turn, as if she hadn't realized he addressed her. She had noticed a man watching her some time ago. That alone didn't trouble her; it was the expression on his face as he watched her, rather puzzled and determined, as if he recognized her but couldn't quite put his finger on why. It was an ever-present risk in her line of work, and the most she could do about it was try to keep her distance, and keep her back to him at all costs. Nate's constant motion had helped in that regard, and no doubt his presence had deterred the man approaching her— until now. Not for the first time, she cursed Stafford for sending her out on this assignment.

But this fellow must have remembered where he had seen her, or become too curious to ignore it, because he persisted even as she ignored his question. He touched her shoulder, letting his fingers linger a moment too long. She turned, arranging her face in offended surprise, and saw him smiling at her, a little coldly. Suddenly she remembered all too well where he had seen her before, and who he was; there was no doubt it had been on another of Stafford's assignments. She breathed deep to calm the fluttering in her stomach, and prepared to lie.

"Good evening, madam," he said. He had the upper-class drawl she had come to associate with the self-indulgent sort of nobleman who gambled too much, whored too frequently, and was too easily tempted by troublemakers. Fortunately, they weren't often that clever, although this one unfortunately had enough wit to remember her face.

"Good evening, sir," she said, dipping a shallow curtsey. She needed to hold him off only a few moments, surely, until Nate returned. It couldn't take long to fetch a glass of wine.

He leaned closer, inspecting her face. He was a viscount, Angelique remembered suddenly, who liked French brandy and young girls. He was a companion of the Marquis of Bethwell, whom she had been assigned to spy on while posing as his private nurse, just a few months past. He and the marquis were evenly matched in their depravity. She suspected the viscount had the French pox, by the rash she had once seen on his hands, but she couldn't remember his name. "I remember you," he announced.

"*Remember* me?" She blinked, widening her eyes in astonishment. "I don't believe we have met, sir." Deliberately she repressed all but a trace of her accent, mimicking Nate's flat American tones. When she worked for Bethwell, she had spoken crisp King's English. Hopefully, it would be enough . . .

The viscount tilted his head, studying her. He didn't look fooled. "Not formally. I always wondered . . . No nurse ever looked like you. And I see you've given it up, along with those drab gray dresses."

Angelique silently cursed even as her heart kicked against her ribs. God above, he did remember her. He must have seen her a handful of times at Bethwell's mansion, tending to the marquis's hypochondria. She had always wondered why a man so obsessed with his own health could tolerate being around such an obviously pox-ridden friend; now the friend turned out to have an alarming memory as well. And where the devil was Nathaniel Avery when she would finally have welcomed his presence? Had he gone all the way to Mayfair for the damned wine? She pasted a confused look on her face. "Nurse? I don't understand. I'm not a nurse."

Now the viscount's expression turned calculating, hard and unpleasant. "Not anymore? Bethwell tossed you out, I know; he told me," he said as she continued to look at him with bewilderment, despite her thundering pulse. "He said you grew too temperamental."

"You have confused me with someone else," she said. "Excuse me, I must find my husband."

"He couldn't get you in bed, could he?" He followed her as she turned and walked away. "I knew he'd never hire a fine piece of quim like you and not try to get between her legs."

"Sir!" She whirled around, hoping the heat in her face would be mistaken for outraged modesty instead of the killing urge it was. If he hadn't approached her in full view of dozens of people, she could have dealt with him easily. Unfortunately, some of those people were sure to notice if she pulled her knife from beneath her skirt, so she was reduced to escaping. "That is indecent and insulting! How dare you?"

He laughed. "Insult a woman who makes her living on her back? I don't think that's possible."

Her fingers twitched, aching to feel the hilt of her dagger. Or the stock of a pistol. Even if she hadn't known him to be twisted and depraved, she would hate him and want to hurt him for the offensive way he looked at her, as if she were an animal he could buy and abuse and leave to whatever suffering he had inflicted. Fury burned in her blood that a man like this could freely roam the finest parts of London and be respected and admired. A little of her control slipped. "I believe," she said evenly, "you have made a mistake."

"I don't think so," he said, smiling again. "But if you don't want to be exposed, I'm sure we can come to an . . . agreement."

"What sort of agreement?" asked a deadly quiet

voice behind Angelique. Like a bird released from a cage, her heart soared and she gasped in a full breath for the first time in minutes.

The viscount hadn't noticed Nate approaching, either, from the way he started at the question. "A private arrangement," he replied, drawing himself up stiffly.

"Private?" Nate cocked one eyebrow and looked at Angelique, slipping his arm around her waist in a gesture of familiar possession. "Anything you say to my wife is my concern, sir. What sort of agreement?"

The viscount hesitated. Angelique leaped in. "He said I had no morals, and made my living on my back," she said, inching closer to Nate's comforting bulk. "He claimed I have been a *nurse*."

"Indeed," said Nate in surprise. "And we've only been in London a few days."

The viscount had recovered from his surprise. Nate's accent marked him as an American, and to an English nobleman, that meant he was nobody. His physical presence wasn't especially fearsome; he was no taller than the viscount, and was of leaner build. The viscount didn't see him as much threat. "A misunderstanding," he said with a trace of condescension. His pale, glittering gaze drifted once more over Angelique's face. "My mistake."

Nate smiled. "Ah, of course." He released Angelique and took a step forward to clap one hand on the viscount's shoulder, as if they were old friends. "I'm sure it won't happen again." The viscount stiffened. His shoulders hunched and he let out a gulping squeak. Angelique dared a glance around Nate, who was almost chest to chest with the viscount, and realized his other hand had gone to the man's groin. He was holding the viscount by the ballocks, unless she missed her guess, and very firmly so. "But if you even look at my wife again, I'll tear them off," Nate added in a silky murmur she barely heard.

"No," gasped the viscount, his face turning purple. Nate nodded, still smiling, and released him. The viscount staggered back, looking as though he would be sick all over the grass.

"Very good. Are you ready to go home, darling?" Nate offered his arm.

She let him draw her close, tucking her hand securely into the crook of his elbow. "Yes."

"An old friend of yours, I presume," he said when they were several yards away, walking as briskly as they dared toward the exit. Neither one looked back, although it seemed to Angelique she could still hear the viscount's heaving breath.

"Not quite."

"He seemed interested in renewing whatever the acquaintance was."

She hated to tell him, after all she had said and implied about his abilities and preparation for this job. "He recognized me. From another assignment."

He didn't say anything for a few minutes. They walked past the orchestra and the supper boxes, back toward the street where they could hail a hackney. "Should I go back and kill him?" he finally asked. "I'd rather do it now, if it must be done, before he has a chance to ruin things."

"No," she said on a sigh. She could feel the blood pounding through her veins, now in relief but still hard enough to make her hands tremble. "But we must be more careful. He is a disgusting *bête* who likes to abuse women, to feel he is master and owner of them." Again she felt old and tired of her job. She must be slipping, if the viscount had recognized her so easily and she had done such a poor job of eluding him. She was normally quite careful to change her appearance on each assignment; only on this one had she gone more or less as herself, because she was tired of the wigs and cosmetics and padded clothing. Now her own face had betrayed her.

Nate stopped. They had almost reached the entrance of the gardens, and she looked toward it with yearning. Even without the cursed viscount's presence, they had no reason to linger. There was no sign of Hurst, and it was too late to reasonably expect him to arrive; they would stand out if they stayed and kept circling the gardens all night. At the moment, nothing sounded more appealing than leaving Vauxhall and going home to a hot cup of tea. How she wished it were Melanie's lemon and mint tea, but Lisette's English tea with a spike of brandy would do almost as well. She looked at her companion with a trace of impatience.

"What did he do to you?" There was no inflection of any kind in his voice. She had never heard him sound so utterly chilling, and perversely it annoyed her.

"Nothing," she snapped. His face didn't change. "He stared at me, touched my arm, nothing more. If he had tried anything else, I would have gutted him already and he would not have troubled us. Now, shall we go? I have had my fill of Vauxhall, and do not think we will find Hurst tonight."

"How did he know you?"

She hesitated. "Let us go home. I will tell you there."

He pulled her into the shadows nearby, enfolding her in a loose embrace. He brushed a lock of hair back from her temple, and murmured in her ear, "I am not letting that man walk out of this damned pleasure garden and unmask you to the world. Tell me how he knew you, and what he might do that could endanger either of us."

Angelique sighed. She was so tired of this. She let him draw her to him, resting her hands on his chest. It would reinforce the appearance that they were lovers stealing a kiss in the darkness. That it also felt comforting and right to lean on him was just a figment of her imagination, a trick of her fancy—nothing more. It was just part of the job. The fact that he was warm and solid under her hands and so very male meant nothing. "I was a private nurse to a marquis who fancied himself afflicted with every trifling illness known to man. That man, back there, was a friend of his. They are arrogant, rich men, who think women exist for their pleasure, no matter how twisted their pleasures are. They both preferred young girls, whether bought and paid for or unwillingly taken. I believe they routinely abused each other's servants." She couldn't hide her disgust. "The day after I arrived in the marquis's home, a laundry maid, barely fifteen, was dismissed, cast out of the house into the street with nothing but her clothes. She was small and thin, and simply sat weeping on the pavement until the marquis had a footman chase her off. Later the governess told me the marquis had used her—forced himself on her—until she became with child. That was when he turned her out."

Nate said nothing, but his arms closed tighter around her. Angelique laid her cheek against his shoulder. He might not make the most imposing figure, but he was the perfect height for her. She felt oddly at peace here in his embrace, not to mention safe.

She raised her head after a moment. "Let us go. I do not want to see him again."

"What's his name?" he asked.

"I don't remember, nor do I care to."

"If he sees either of us again, he'll remember."

"Grabbing his ballocks did nothing to erase the memory."

"No," he agreed. "But I squeezed them hard enough that he'll remember what I said." She gave a reluctant little snort of laughter. Men like Barings deserved to have their ballocks torn off; it was more fitting than a quick and painless pistol shot to the head.

But it didn't change the truth of what Nate said: the man would remember them both, with crystal clarity this time. She sighed, fighting the urge to rest against him again. "Barings," she murmured. "Lord Barings is his name. I just remembered it."

"We'd better keep an eye on him." He turned toward the gates again and began leading her there, more sedately than before. "But not tonight."

She made herself disengage his arm even though it felt warm and comforting around her waist. It would not do, to become too accustomed to leaning on him. Nate gave her a quick glance, but let her go, keeping only her hand on his arm, his fingers resting lightly on top of hers. She kept her head down, more mindful than ever of the dangers of her profession and current situation. She had never been recognized before; people were usually fooled by a wig, some cosmetics, and most of all by different clothing. She could be one woman sauntering along in a tight scarlet gown, her head thrown back and her eyes boldly raised, and another one entirely in a bedraggled gray dress with her eyes downcast and her cheeks padded out.

But when she was a woman tucked safely in Nathaniel Avery's arm, she didn't even recognize herself. He had upended too much already in her carefully controlled life. She would do well to remember that this was an adventure for him. Once they found his man, he would sail back to his life in America, and she would begin creating her new life here. She still had no idea what that life would look like, and tonight only added to her worries. She couldn't go to Mellie if there was a risk she would be recognized again. She would never forgive herself if she introduced filth like Barings into Mellie's life. She had done most of her work in London; perhaps Whitton was too near to chance it. Perhaps she should look farther afield . . . to some lonely corner of England where she would be a complete stranger to everyone. It didn't sound very appealing, even to someone who wished to remain unknown.

In the street Nate hailed a hackney and handed her into it, with more care than usual. She didn't like that. Or rather, she liked it too much for her own comfort. Their goal tonight had been compromised because of her, and he hadn't said a word of blame. Perhaps she should have thought more carefully before leaving her wigs behind. She couldn't be dressed more differently tonight than she had dressed at Bethwell's home, but it hadn't been enough, and the fault was hers.

By now Nate had told the driver where to go and taken the seat beside her. Still he said nothing, just took her hand. She turned her eyes to the window and looked blindly out, conscious of the strength in his fingers around hers. If their positions had been reversed, and he had been responsible for some near-disaster like this, she didn't know how she would have responded. If he were another agent of Stafford's, she would have flayed him alive and turned him off the assignment. Both he and Stafford would have expected no less. If he had been another of Stafford's men, though, he would be blistering her ears right now. Instead his hand was warm and heavy and comforting on hers.

Curse Stafford, she thought in despair. She was starting to like Nathaniel Avery in spite of herself.

When they reached the house, he jumped down from the hackney and helped her out before she could energize herself. Somehow his tender care had made her sluggish, as if she needed his arm to walk up the steps. That was wrong, of course, but she didn't shake him off. She still didn't need him, but tonight she was glad he was with her just the same.

Inside the narrow hall, he took her cloak and hung it up. "Thank you," she murmured. "Good night."

"Wait."

She had been about to start up the stairs, her hand already on the newel post. At his command she paused and turned back. Nate modulated his tone.

"Please," he said, then stopped. What did he expect her to do? Tell him more about how Barings and that marquis might have imposed on her? Break down and weep over the terrible things she must have seen in her work? "Are you well?" he settled for asking.

Her chin went up. "Well enough." She paused, too; it seemed neither of them knew what to say. "Thank you for your assistance tonight."

"Assistance," he repeated. It was dark in the hall; the maid had left a small lamp burning, but there was no other light. The house was quiet, save for the occasional rattle of a carriage passing in the street outside. But even in the dim light he could see Angelique's expression stiffen.

"Yes. Assistance." She raised an eyebrow. "What else should I call it?"

He crossed the hall to stand in front of her. "I don't give a damn what you call it," he said. In the lamplight her skin was like pale gold, her eyes as dark as onyx. She looked delicate and beautiful and strangely vulnerable, despite the somewhat scornful arch of her brow. "We are in this together. I expect you would have done the same for me."

"Of course," she said evenly. "I am responsible for your safety."

"That's not what I meant," Nate said, incredulous. "Responsible?"

"*Oui.* If anything were to happen to you, I should have to explain myself to a wide variety of people."

"And those same people wouldn't care if you were the one injured or assaulted."

She gave a very Gallic shrug. "Not much. They would be annoyed that they must find someone else to do my work, perhaps."

And Nate knew she was right, even if it made him want to punch someone. No doubt Stafford cared for her much the way he would a horse—no matter how valuable or well trained or useful, it was still just a horse. Perhaps that's the way the man had to think, to be able to send her out posing as a servant among men who routinely abused their servants, knowing what those men would do to her if they discovered her true intent. Nate would never ask one of his sailors to do what he was unwilling to risk himself, and the thought of a man like Stafford expecting Angelique to risk her slender neck to save *Nate*, should he be endangered . . .

As he stood there mastering his outrage, she turned to the stairs again. "Good night, Mr. Avery."

"Nate," he said shortly. "And should you wish to know, I had no thought of responsibility or inconvenience when I acted. Whatever else you may think of me, rest assured I do not view you as nothing more than a useful tool to achieve my purpose."

She stopped. Her shoulders, nearly bared by her gown, hunched a little, almost defensively. Again she turned back. "I know," she said softly. Hesitantly she reached out and laid her fingers along his jaw, so lightly he barely felt the contact. "Thank you, Nate."

He caught her wrist when she would have retreated. The softness in her face abruptly vanished, but she didn't tense or pull away. He would have let go of her at once if she had. Instead he tugged her forward until he could cup his free hand around the smooth, warm nape of her neck. He hadn't intended to kiss her tonight, but he'd certainly thought about kissing her, even before she looked at him with those shadowed eyes and touched his face. So he kissed her.

He felt her sharp inhale of breath against his cheek, and her fist where it landed against his chest. But he held her anyway, pressing his momentary advantage of surprise. A tremor shook her body. And then, blissfully, she surrendered. The fingers fisted against him loosened, then dug into his jacket to hold him to her. Nate released her wrist to wind his arm around her waist, and she threw that arm around his neck, clinging as if she would never let go. Her lips parted beneath his, and Nate felt the earth shift beneath his feet. She kissed him back with hunger and more than a little passion. Her mouth tasted of wine, and indeed he felt half drunk, upended and swept away. This wasn't what he had expected; it was something far more dangerous . . .

He pulled himself back from the brink and lifted his head. In the split second before her eyes opened, he caught a fleeting glimpse of wonder on her face, as if something had taken her by surprise, but happily. Her lips were soft and slightly parted, her eyelashes long on her smooth cheek, and entrancing color stained her cheeks. He could only think he must look as awestruck as she did, and maybe even more so.

She recoiled at once, and touched one finger to her lower lip. "Why did you do that?" she asked in a low voice.

She might be able to freeze a man with one look or cutting word, but she kissed like a temptress, like a woman who craved him as much as he craved her. "You know why," he murmured, and reached for her again.

This time she braced her hands against his chest. Nate stopped trying to pull her back to him, but he didn't release her.

"This is not a good idea," she said. "It is, in fact, a very poor idea."

"Kiss me again, and then you can explain why."

"Stop," she said sharply, even though he hadn't done anything. The lace at the neckline of her gown fluttered with every breath she took. "I cannot— You cannot—"

Nate made no reply. She meant *she* should not, which might be true, given her employer, and that *he* should not, which he didn't believe at all. Shouldn't kiss a woman who dazzled and amazed him, who could mesmerize him with nothing more than a quirk of her lips, who drew him like a moth to the flame? Perhaps he *shouldn't*, but that didn't mean he wouldn't. He'd willingly risk incineration. "Then tell me you didn't like it," he said instead. "Tell me it disgusted you, and I'll keep an honorable distance."

Her rosy lips parted. Desire rose up, hot and sweet, inside him, and Nate realized too late he had just handed her a weapon to keep him at arm's length forever. She would say it disgusted her, even if they both knew it hadn't, and he would have to keep his word. "I should not even have to ask. Don't do it again."

He wanted to growl in primitive satisfaction. She didn't want to say it—she didn't want to keep him away, at least not permanently. But at the same time she was afraid he'd kiss her again, and that her reaction would be even more revealing. Nate, on the other hand, knew without a shadow of a doubt that he wouldn't be able to hide how it affected him.

Even knowing how much it would leave him in her power, he didn't think he would be able to step away twice. "I won't," he agreed, then added recklessly, "Unless we both need it."

She went rigid for a split second, then raised her head to a regal angle. "Your needs, Mr. Avery, are your concern. And my needs . . . are mine. Only mine."

She turned with a swish of her skirt and climbed the stairs. Nate stood and watched her go until she was swallowed by the Stygian darkness above. It was late and he had just been thoroughly rebuffed, but . . . Good God in heaven. She wasn't immune to him after all. A hot tingle of satisfaction rushed through his veins, even as he reminded himself not to be dazzled. Or at least not blinded. Or at the very, very least, not stupid about it.

Chapter 10

The next night Angelique made plans to return to Vauxhall Gardens. Nate said nothing, just looked at her for a long moment before nodding. She kept her own feelings to herself. Their best link to Dixon was Davis Hurst; they knew he liked Vauxhall; and they had almost nothing else to go on. They visited more jewel shops that day, but learned nothing more. No matter that Barings could be at Vauxhall again, or that if he had recognized her, someone else might as well. She knew they had to go back, and go they would, but this time she would be ready for anything.

Anything, that was, except another kiss.

"Remember what we have planned," she said in the hackney. "Do not take it on yourself to confront him."

He shot her an unreadable glance in the dark carriage. "Of course not."

"Even if someone should recognize either of us," she said, as coldly and bluntly as she felt. It could be disaster if Barings were there again, but she reminded herself that it was her lapse, not Nate's.

If it happened again, she would deal with it more appropriately.

Just as she would deal with any other kisses more appropriately, should they occur.

He looked out the window for a while. "I don't think I proved myself useless here last night."

He hadn't. She had thought her heart would explode in joy when he appeared beside her. "No, I did not say so," she said gently. "But we agreed this was the best way to flush Hurst out, and nothing has changed that."

"Nothing," he echoed in a flat tone. She kept her expression neutral despite his probing gaze. It had been only a kiss, after all. "Clear enough." He took a deep breath as the hackney drew to a halt, then turned to her with an urbane smile. "Are you ready, my dear?"

As long as you don't kiss me again.

She rolled her shoulders back and gave him a smile as false as the one he gave her. Her dagger was hard and reassuring against her thigh. "Of course."

They separated almost immediately. Walking the grounds together last night hadn't helped, and tonight she wanted to operate alone, as usual. As planned, Nate headed for the largest group of people. He really could talk to anyone, anywhere, she thought, watching him strike up a conversation with one man, and within minutes become part of a circle of men. Affecting complete boredom, she wandered around, looking at the paintings, refusing a few murmured propositions, and finally ending across the pavilion from Nate. There she settled with a glass of wine, keeping the bored expression fixed on her face even as she let her eyes move around the room.

From this distance she could catch an occasional glimpse of Nate without being near enough to betray herself. Why oh why had he kissed her last night? She could almost hate him for it, except for the sheer beauty and breathless pleasure of it. She had lain awake last night, insisting to herself that she felt so shaken by it because of what had happened with Barings; it was relief and gratitude, she told herself, to say nothing of mere acknowledgment of his un-expected skill. Most men kissed as if they wished to eat a woman in big, sloppy bites. Nate kissed her like a man tasting a rare delicacy, as if he would savor every morsel she fed him instead of falling on her in a frenzy of hunger. She wondered what he would be like as a lover, in bed, and then reminded herself she had told him there would be no more kisses, let alone kisses in bed. Her needs were her own, she had said, not his. As long as she remembered that, perhaps she could escape this unscathed. The last thing she needed was to have her head turned by that man, with his pleasant laugh and his merry smile and his wicked, tempting mouth that kissed her so dangerously sweetly.

Thankfully, after a while she caught sight of a man who fit Hurst's description. It was a relief to focus her thoughts on her work again. Medium height, lean and dapper, he was a dandy, from the top of his graying hair to the polished toes of his shoes. She wandered through the crowd a bit more, passing directly by him at one point and managing to catch a glimpse of the carved wolf's head ring he wore on his little finger. It must be their man, she thought, and let her elbow brush his. He glanced over his shoulder, but his irritation melted away when he saw her.

For a cagey man, he was shockingly easy to lure out. Within twenty minutes she had gotten him to introduce himself, offer his escort, and fetch her some more wine punch, and at the same time thoroughly convinced him she was looking for some adventure to escape her dull marriage to an American buffoon, whom she duly pointed out. That seemed to intrigue him the most, which worked well enough for her purposes.

"America is utterly savage, I've been told," he said to her. She had managed to lead him on a meandering stroll through the pavilion toward a quieter area, all the better to give him the right impression of her intentions. "The politics are all corrupt, the country is brimming with barbarians, and even the best society wouldn't pass in a Cheapside pub."

She laughed. "You have been well-informed—I would even say you had been there yourself."

"No, no," he said indulgently. "It is all learned from someone who lived there for some time before returning to England. I certainly never thought to venture in that direction."

Dixon, Angelique thought. "The contrast is more pronounced when one has become accustomed to American ways."

"No doubt. Americans are different, aren't they?" He turned to study Nate again, who was still talking with the men across the room. "Quite . . . savage, in some instances."

Angelique followed his gaze, silently agreeing with his statement, although for very different reasons. Nate chanced to look up then and caught her eye. Politely he inclined his head in her direction, and she smiled back rather vacantly and took a sip of punch. The candlelight shone on his sun-bleached hair and darkened his skin to an almost olive hue. He did look like a savage here among the pale Englishmen, no matter how elegantly attired he was—but it was far from repulsive. And it was immensely reassuring to know that Nate was close at hand, with whatever hidden savagery he possessed, should she need him again. "Goodness, yes," she said, pulling her mind back to Mr. Hurst. "I had almost forgotten how refined Europeans are in comparison."

He turned back to her. His was the terrifyingly tender smile of a predator about to strike an unsuspecting victim. "I wonder that you have endured so long."

She pasted the limpid smile back on her face and laughed lightly. "I have no choice now." She gestured with her glass and leaned toward him until his gaze dipped to her cleavage. "At least he is rich!" She gave a tiny hiccup and pressed her fingers to her lips. When he looked at her again, she swayed on her feet and giggled. "Forgive me, I think the wine has overcome me ..." She spun around and walked away, taking care to make her steps slow and too careful. Her glass dangled from her fingertips, and she headed for the punch table, conveniently next to the entrance to the Grand Walk. A dark part of the garden would do nicely, she thought, affecting a small stumble as she reached the table and set down her glass.

"Might I escort you?" Hurst asked, taking her arm.

Angelique blinked up at him, still playing tipsy,

and then laughed as if embarrassed. "Oh, please do. Some quiet would be most welcome. I feel flushed and . . . very unlike myself. That wine punch is stronger than it looks."

He had already steered her out of the pavilion. "Your husband won't miss you?"

She waved one arm expansively. "Miss me? He won't notice I'm gone! When there is money to be made, I do not exist, sir." She was slurring her words a little now, hanging on his arm.

Hurst chuckled, slipping his arm around her waist and pulling her indecently tight against him. She could almost feel the excitement quivering inside him and had to steel herself against the urge to slide her dagger between his ribs. Lecherous scum; he deserved to be cut for leading—pulling, even—an apparently intoxicated woman out into the secluded garden. She knew very well what he planned, and it made her stomach knot in fury that if she were as she seemed, he would get away with raping her.

"A man who ignores a woman like you deserves to lose her," he murmured in her ear, his breath hot on her cheek. "Someone else will be tempted to sweep her away . . ."

Angelique giggled again and ducked her head. "Only if he is also rich! I should hate to be poor."

He chuckled again. "So that's Mr. Avery's attraction? I wondered how he could have ensnared such a lovely dove as you."

"Oh, he's Midas himself." She shortened her breath and leaned more of her weight on him. As expected, he was leading her away from the pavilion and toward the darkest part of the garden.

"And always looking to make more. Do you know, he came here tonight to meet more investors?" She hiccupped again. "He's mad for some new"—she fluttered her hand in the air, trying to think of a plausible, yet enormous, figure—"some new scheme to make another million. As if one is not enough!" she finished with another tipsy laugh.

"So much?" Like a hungry fish, Hurst snapped up the bait. He stopped on the path, looking down at her with more calculating eyes. "A million dollars?"

She shook her head and made a face. "Pounds! He keeps most of his money in England, after the last crisis in America with the money. It was dreadful, we had to sell our second carriage . . ."

"Yes," he murmured. "It must be a risky venture."

"Lord, no." She pulled out of his arm and staggered toward a bench a short distance ahead. It was deep in shadow under the trees and remarkably quiet; perfect. "He doesn't chance the risky ones now. Or maybe he does have a magical touch. I only know he makes money when everyone else is ruined. Why?" She turned to bat her eyelashes at him. "*You* don't want to invest in his madness, do you?"

He followed her more leisurely. "Perhaps."

Angelique laughed. She swished her hips from side to side with each slow step. "Is that why you have lured me out here?"

"No," he said, that rapacious smile on his face again. "But if one could combine pleasures . . ." He caught her arms and hauled her up against him, studying her face through shrewd eyes. "How do you know so much about your husband's investments?"

She heaved a sigh, letting her head roll back on her

shoulders. "He talks of nothing else. Can a man not think of anything to say to a woman in bed, except 'this was profitable,' and 'that will make a mint'?" She shook her head, stroking her fingers across the points of his shirt collar. Hurst wore his cravat fashionably high, and her fingers just trailed along the edge of his jaw. "But he would be very pleased if I told him someone else wanted to give him money," she added. "If you do."

He paused. She waited, still smiling blankly. Hurst was not a rich man, but he had rich tastes. Silently she willed him to say something, anything, that would give her the opportunity to ask about Dixon. He had already helped Dixon convert some jewels into funds; he must be thinking of the man now. He thought she was drunk; he wouldn't attach much weight to it, but she couldn't say the name herself . . .

"I might be able to bring him an investor," he finally said. "A man I know is looking for rewarding places to invest an inheritance. Discreetly, of course."

"My husband is very good with secrets," she said. "I daresay he must be, given whose money he handles!"

His eyes glittered. "Whose?"

"Oh, I . . ." She lowered her eyes and laughed nervously. "I shouldn't say. I don't want him to be arrested . . . Not that *he* is a criminal— Oh dear!" She laughed again, covering her mouth with her fingertips.

"I see," Hurst muttered. He was quiet for a moment. "Perhaps I shall call on him, to see if my friend might wish to invest."

"He won't tell you anything, unless it is your money," she said, thinking quickly. "Just bring your friend."

He smiled thinly. "My friend is something of a recluse."

"Mr. Avery would be willing to come to him." She ran her fingers up and down the lapel of his evening jacket. "For his investors, he is always willing." Another artful sigh. "For his wife, less so. Who is your friend? Have I met him?" She gave him a coy smile. "Is he as charming as you are?"

The avarice faded from his face. "You're a bored little strumpet, aren't you?" he said with amusement. "You're out here with me so I'll invest with your husband, and now you'll set your sights on Dixon, too."

There it was. Angelique ignored the thrill of triumph, and gave him a delighted smile. "William Dixon? Why, I met him the other night! Such a gentleman . . ."

Hurst chuckled. "No, Jacob Dixon. You'll not have met him, I wager."

She raised one eyebrow. "Why? Is he dull, like my husband? Spare me any more dull men."

"He's a charming fellow," Hurst said. "You'll like him. He just returned to England after a long absence—like you, my dear."

Definitely their man. "He must be so pleased to be back in the civilized world." She rolled her shoulders as if stretching, letting one tiny sleeve slip down her arm. This gown was tight and low in the bodice, and only the small, wispy sleeves held it up. "I certainly am."

"I can see that." He could see the edge of her

corset, too, judging from the way his gaze fixed on her bosom. Angelique was suddenly tired of dancing around him and his leering eyes. She didn't think he would tell her more about Dixon anyway. It was time to finish this conversation.

"Everything is better here . . ." She drifted toward the bench, her steps wobbling. "Especially the wine. It makes me a little"—she waved one hand in the air, letting it carry her off-balance—"dizzy! Oh!" She put one hand to her head. "Perhaps I should sit down," she mumbled.

"Of course." He guided her to the bench, and sat far too close to her.

She sank down, sliding one finger inside the neckline of her gown, dislodging it even more. "I cannot breathe," she said fretfully. "My corset, it is too tight . . ."

"Let's see about that." His hands were at her back, loosening her bodice. Then he was bearing her down onto her back, quietly shushing her murmured protest, easing down the front of her dress. Angelique closed her eyes as cool air wafted over her breasts, and let her arm fall limply to one side. She made herself lie motionless as he breathed heavily over her. Hurst made a crude noise in his throat, guttural with victory. He squeezed her breast with one hand and caught a handful of her skirt with the other.

Then he slumped heavily across her, unconscious from the blow she had struck with a rock on the side of his head.

Chapter 11

The bad thing about being agreeable was that it sometimes left one in a very disagreeable position.

Nate had seen Angelique with a man who must be Davis Hurst and he played his part, merely nodding to her. He knew she meant to flirt and cajole information from Hurst, and he knew that Hurst would probably fall for her ruse without a thought. Really, what man would be able to resist her when she looked like she did tonight, in a rich purple gown that barely contained her breasts and somehow managed to cling to her slim waist and hips. Her dark curls spilled from the knot on top of her head to fall around her shoulders, a startling contrast to her fair skin. She seemed to glow with a gauzy, sensual aura that caught the attention of more men than just Hurst.

A ripple had gone through the circle around him when Nate nodded to her. "Your wife, Avery?" asked one man, awe apparent in his tone.

"Yes," he said carelessly. "How delightful that she seems to be enjoying herself." He made himself look away from her as a shocked hiss went through his companions. Angelique didn't look like she was enjoying herself, she looked tipsy and receptive to whatever Hurst was saying to her. She was acting, of course. She didn't need his help. His job was to stand here and let her lure the man out of the ballroom to see if she could tease Dixon's name or location from Hurst. His job was not to charge across the room and break several bones in Davis Hurst's body, even though his hand curled into a fist where it rested on his hip. His job was to be a bloody fool, as she had so pointedly reminded him in the hackney, and he hated it. If anyone should be tracking down Dixon by quizzing slime like Hurst, it ought to be Nate. Instead he was left to stand here and wait while Angelique did it, by God knew what means.

But after a while he quit caring about his part in this masquerade and what he had promised to do. She left the pavilion with Hurst—all according to plan—and then she didn't return. Neither did Hurst. Nate resisted the urge to pull out his watch and see how long they had been gone, but the minutes ticked by and still there was no sign of either. Hurst wasn't an exceptionally large fellow, but he still outweighed Angelique by a few stone. No matter how she assured him she could take care of herself, Nate couldn't root out the last bit of chivalry in his mind; after all, if something should happen to her while he stood idly drinking wine and discussing the finer points of horseracing, he would never forgive himself. Nor did he fancy telling Stafford.

He excused himself from his companions and strolled through the well-lit pavilion. At the punch table he paused to help himself to a glass of the nasty stuff, then walked out into the Grand Walk as if he had no more pressing interest than getting some air. A few couples stood chatting nearby, and not far away a woman sat on a bench, fluttering her fan at a pair of men who looked bewitched. Nate went past them, nodding politely as he passed the trio, and sipped his punch without tasting it. His eyes scanned from side to side as he walked. Where was she?

Instinctively he headed for the darker part of the garden, the shadowy recesses where no lanterns glowed. There was no sign of Angelique or Hurst. He glanced down the wider, better lit path and saw nothing there, either—not that he had expected to. His hand was stiff and tense from not folding into a fist at his side. The moment he turned a corner and was out of sight of the other guests, he gave in to the urgency roaring inside him. The punch glass landed with a faint thump on the grass. Without a sound Nate melted into the shadows and went in search of Angelique.

It took his eyes a moment to adjust to the darkness away from the lanterns, but there was a sliver of moon in the sky, and soon he could see well enough to move silently but still quickly. The gardens were a maze of twisting paths, and every now and then he passed a couple engaged in various private activities. The soft sounds of passion and seduction made his gut twist; God help him if he came upon Hurst and Angelique in such a position. If she was willing to seduce Hurst, even fake a passionate response to the man, Nate didn't want to know about it, let alone witness it. Just the thought made his muscles tense with fury—and even worse, jealousy.

His vision sharpened and caught a glimpse of

white, and he heard a quiet moan, then a thud. He paused, listening, then turned in that direction and ran. No longer wary of being quiet, Nate tore through the shrubbery with his hand on his dagger hilt, expecting to see Hurst holding Angelique's unconscious body under him, his hands—or worse—under her clothing. Raw rage burned his every nerve. If the bastard had touched her, even without harming her, he would be dead before he ever saw Nate coming—

Instead he saw Angelique on her knees, calmly searching Hurst's waistcoat pockets as the man lay sprawled on his side on the grass. Disconcerted, he froze, checking what he saw. Hurst was out cold. She was fine.

Thank God.

He shoved the knife, already pulled out an inch, back into the sheath and scowled. Now pain burst forth in earnest in his calves and side, and he inhaled a deep, raspy breath. Thank God she was unhurt. And she apparently hadn't needed his help in the slightest. He rested his hands on his hips and glared at her. "You should have waited for my help."

For the first time she glanced up at him. Her eyes, those deadly calm dark eyes, flicked from his face to his just-replaced knife. "I did not need it."

That only inflamed his temper, not only that she would say it but that it appeared to be absolutely true. "You should have waited anyway, damn it."

"Why?" With that carelessly cutting word she turned back to her task, rifling the contents of Hurst's pocket. "He does not seem to have anything of interest. Imbecile!"

"I presume you learned something to warrant . . .

this." He put his foot on Hurst's shoulder and shoved the man over onto his back. A fist-sized rock lay near Hurst's head, and Nate guessed it was the felling weapon.

"Of course," she said evenly, turning out the rest of Davis Hurst's pocket. "He knows Dixon, and helps him invest his money. I told him you were anxious for new investors and tried to persuade him to bring Dixon to you for advice."

"You did what?" Shock immobilized him. For a moment he felt as though she had clubbed him in the head, as well as Hurst.

"It might encourage him to bring Dixon to us. How much easier it would be, if the man would come to us instead of hiding like a rat afraid of sunlight."

"He won't," said Nate grimly. "Dixon *is* a rat. He won't come out."

She shrugged. "I don't expect him to. I merely said it would make things easier, and thought it worth trying. I have learned never to trust in that happening, though."

He stepped over Hurst's supine figure and leaned down to take hold of the man's shoulders. "What did you plan to do with him, after you knocked him out?"

"What you are doing," she said, sorting through the various things she had taken from Hurst's pockets. "Take him over there, onto the grass."

Nate closed his mouth into a thin line, but did as she said, although none too gently. Angelique followed, slipping something from Hurst's things into the valley between her breasts. "What did you find?" he asked.

"His latchkey." She went down on one knee over

her victim and unbuttoned his trousers, then tugged them down a few inches. She pulled Hurst's shirt out and undid the lower buttons of his waistcoat. Nate caught on to what she was doing and helped, roughing up Hurst's clothing in a few efficient moves, grinding dirt onto the knees of his trousers and slipping one shoe off. Angelique returned some of Hurst's pocket contents to their places, then just scattered the rest on the ground.

"He knows your name," Nate said as he dusted off his hands. "You invited him to call on us. How will you explain this?"

She just gave him a look as she hiked up her skirt. To Nate's astonishment, she had quite a large dagger strapped to the side of one thigh. He had expected there was a weapon on her body somewhere, but he hadn't expected to see it on her slim leg, the leather sheath buckled right over the lace of her garter. She drew the dagger with a soft hiss, and pulled up a section of her skirt hem. The dagger made a clean rent, slicing through the magenta silk with hardly a whisper of resistance. She tore it the rest of the way, then stuffed the long strip of cloth into Hurst's lax hand, closing his fingers around it.

Nate watched her in mingled awe and alarm. This was the woman he had thought incapable of doing what was required. He had feared he would have to look out for her. He had suspected . . . But now he realized that he had fallen for her appearance just as Hurst had—not so literally, but just as completely. For all that he had seen the steely determination in her, he had also felt her tremble in his arms after Barings accosted her in these very same gardens just one night before. That had spooked her and exposed a deep vulnerability within her, and he had been filled with protective rage on her behalf, ready to cut out Barings's liver. He had told himself that she might be a spy, but she was still a woman at heart.

Then tonight she had coldly lured Hurst out here, discovered what she wanted to know, knocked him out, and was now setting him up to wake with a blinding headache and no memory of the debauchery he appeared to have enjoyed. Nate was surprised, unnerved, and deeply, deeply impressed.

"Will that do?" she murmured as he watched in silence. She circled the unconscious man, pausing to pick up the rock and place it strategically near his head. "What will make him believe . . . ? Ah." She ran one finger across her lips, then smeared the lip paint across one side of Hurst's mouth. She gave Nate a glance simmering with mischief. "Pull down his trousers some more."

Nate's eyes narrowed, but he knelt and did it. She leaned down and rubbed another bit of lip color across Hurst's lower abdomen, just inches from the man's groin.

Nate sat frozen on his haunches, staring at the pink streak across Davis Hurst's skin. In the normal course of things, there was one principal way a woman's lip color would end up there on a man's belly. It was brilliant, though devious, and it sent all the blood in his body flooding to his own groin. God almighty—just the thought of her deep pink lips closing around his flesh was making him hard, while she was calmly wiping the color from her fingers with the hem of her ruined gown.

Carefully he climbed to his feet. He should be

glad they had learned something useful; he should be glad they had confirmed a link to Jacob Dixon. He should be relieved that Angelique hadn't been injured, and that they were about to walk away from Hurst with no outcry and little chance he would seek them out again. But all he could see was that pink streak, moist and warm from her lips.

"Let's go," she said quietly. She saw him staring down at Hurst. "He will be fine," she added with a trace of impatience.

Hurst would wake thinking he'd had her luscious lips around him. Nate swallowed. His pulse beat like a drum in his ears. Hurst would be more than fine, aside from a brutal headache. He, on the other hand . . .

"Right," he muttered, and turned on his heel to follow her out of Vauxhall.

Chapter 12

Nate said little on the carriage ride home. Angelique could feel the tension humming off him, though, and wondered what had set him off. Surely his manly pride couldn't be that offended, that she hadn't needed his help; he was the one who had said he wouldn't be saving her pretty little neck, as she recalled. She stole a glance at him, tempted to remind him of that, but changed her mind when she saw his face, hard and set in the waxing and waning light from streetlamps they passed.

She turned to look out her window. Dealing with Davis Hurst, no matter how unpleasant, had restored her equilibrium after the disastrous other night with Barings. That caught her unaware, unsettled her and upset her. Tonight she had regained her composure, never dropped her guard, and succeeded as much as was possible. Nate was probably right that Dixon would never come to them under any pretext, but she knew where Hurst lived and she had his key. A discreet search of his home would probably provide all the information they needed to find Dixon. If Nate were in a better mood, she would do it tonight, while Hurst was still lying unconscious in Vauxhall.

Perhaps she still could, if Nate closed himself in his room to sulk. She darted another glance at him. He didn't seem like he would sulk, but one never knew with gentlemen.

"What would you have done," he said suddenly, when they were only a street or two away from the house, "if he hadn't gone down so easily?"

"Easily?" She snorted. No sulking, but a patronizing scolding. Men and their pride. "You think I do not know where to strike a man to make him fall?"

"I didn't say that," he said, staring straight ahead. His hand, resting on his thigh, was curled into a white-knuckled fist. "I asked what you would have *done* if he hadn't fallen senseless at once?"

"I would have hit him again."

Slowly he turned to face her. Something hot and dangerous burned in his eyes. "He outweighed you by five stone. Don't even tell me you would have had time to get your knife out if he suspected you were trying to kill him—which is not an unreasonable assumption for a man to make, when struck in the head with a large rock."

Angelique sighed. "I know what I am doing. Did the plan not work?"

"It might not have!"

"But it did!" she lashed out scornfully. "You appear to think I have never done anything dangerous before. This is not the first time I have been charged with getting something from a man like Hurst. Unlike you, I am not on this adventure for revenge or gallantry. This is my *profession*, sir."

He seemed to be having difficulty mastering his breathing. "Then you are accustomed to fucking men to achieve your purpose."

"I did no such thing," she snapped, then realization dawned. He was furious with her, but also unbearably aroused. And now that she knew it, she seemed unable to let it slip away unnoticed. "Does that offend you? That I wanted him to think he had enjoyed every sinful pleasure I can give with my mouth, instead of that I hit him before he could do more than squeeze my breast?"

His gaze veered to her bosom. Angelique looked down. Her gown had slipped again, only a little, but enough to show the swells of her breasts almost to her nipples—which were tightening as he watched, growing hard and aching. She was horrified at her own reaction, but didn't pull up the bodice, even as he continued to stare. And then was equally alarmed by that omission. It was one thing to notice he was aroused, and another to heap fuel on that fire because it aroused *her*.

"I knew that gown was trouble," he said in a harsh growl. "Thank God it's ruined."

"Oh?" She smoothed one hand down her stomach, drawing the silk taut enough to slip another fraction of an inch down her bosom. Her nipples would pop out above her low-cut corset in a moment. "I thought I would have Lisette repair it." Nate's face was hard, his flush visible even in the darkness, and his eyes were fixed on her like a starving animal's on his prey. She was flaunting herself before a man in the grip of ravenous desire, and instead of turning her back on him, she only wanted to taunt him more. To provoke him. To let his desire meet her own, flowing hot and fast beneath her skin . . .

The hackney stopped before their rented town house with a jerk. Angelique flinched, realizing where she was, who she was, and most importantly who he was. She must have lost her mind. "I'm going inside," she said in a rush, and threw open the door to leap out before he could stop her. She hurried up the steps, leaving him to pay the driver. Lisette had left the door unlocked for them, and she was at the top of the stairs before Nate appeared in the doorway.

"Don't run from me," he warned, closing the door and shooting the bolt with a crack. "I have more to say to you."

"Don't you tell me what to do!" she fired back, leaning over the railing to glare at him.

"You are not in this alone, goddamn it," he replied furiously, coming up the stairs after her. "Don't you dare do anything like that again!"

She made a rude gesture with one hand, and then stalked to her room, twitching her ripped skirt behind her. If she didn't walk away, she might do something far worse. Nate had flirted with her, but always in a laughing way that made it easy to dismiss; he would have said the same thing to any woman, she told herself. He had kissed her, but sweetly, as if to let her lead him. This was different. There was a feral, possessive hunger in his gaze tonight, not for any woman, not for the tipsy wife of easy virtue she had pretended to be with Hurst, but for *her*. He had worried about her. He had run through the garden looking for her, ready to draw his knife in her defense. Then he had listened to her instructions and done what she asked of him to conclude the business, and only after that had he turned to her with unchecked desire in his face and anger for the danger she'd been in. Even after what she'd said. A tiny voice inside her mind whispered that he was answering every criteria she had wanted in a man, and that little voice scared her most of all.

He followed her, even though she ignored him. He pushed the door back open when she tried to close it in his face. He barged into her room when she tried to bar it with her arm. She backed away from him as he closed the door and turned the key in the lock behind him. Lisette had left a pair of lamps burning, and she could see the controlled focus in his expression.

"Go away," she spat, turning her back to him and walking away. "I am very tired."

"Then you should go to bed," he said, following her. She whirled to tell him to get out, and he put his hands on her shoulders and shoved her onto the bed. Off balance, Angelique sprawled on her back, then fell again when he grabbed her foot as she tried to scramble backward away from him.

"Tsk, tsk. You must undress first." He pulled off her slipper and tossed it over his shoulder. She kicked at him, but he just smiled, his eyes lit with a frightening expression as he easily caught her ankle before she could injure his sensitive areas.

Her stomach clenched, not at his expression, but at her reaction to it. The white-hot desire in his face reflected an answering desire in her belly. Oh God, she wasn't supposed to want him. He took advantage of her distraction to flip off her other shoe and throw it aside, then climb onto the bed atop her. "Still tired?"

Angelique bucked, trying to get enough leverage to drive her knee into his stomach. "I am certainly tired of your company!"

He caught one arm, then the other, as she slapped him full across the face. He balanced his weight just over her, not enough to crush her at all but enough to hold her in place. It had been a long time since Angelique felt the weight of a man above her, felt the shimmering heat of his desire for *her*, not for whatever part she played. It had been a long time since she had wanted a man so badly. Heat pooled between her legs, and hunger surged through her veins. God, yes, just a quick tumble to get over this insane urge, this weakness . . . But she was afraid; a quick tumble might not be the antidote she wanted. It might be the first taste of addiction.

"Are you really?" he murmured, looking down on her.

"Yes!" But her body betrayed her. Her knees rose alongside his hips, and when she tried to twist free of his grip, she only managed to rub her breasts against his chest. The friction made her tremble and want to writhe against him again.

"Indeed." His eyelids dropped as his gaze turned hot and speculative. He lowered his head, his lips whispering down the side of her neck. Once, twice, he moved his hips, slowly grinding his erection against her. Oh God, he wanted her as much as she wanted him. She could feel the swollen length of him pressing against her; he would probably be inside her already if not for the layers of cloth between them. Angelique inhaled sharply and arched her neck as she imagined his trousers gone, her dress gone, his flesh sliding hard inside her, her flesh wet and ready for him . . .

"Then good night." Abruptly he was gone, rising to his feet and leaving her there, trembling with lust. Angelique raised her head in astonishment as he turned toward the door as if he hadn't nearly had her right there on her own bed without so much as a gentle word. She struggled to sit up and then threw the first thing her fingers touched.

The knife made a dull thunk as it embedded in the door, mere inches from his head. He paused, his hand still on the key in the lock, then turned. "You might have taken off my ear."

"If I had wanted to do that, it would be on the floor right now," she hissed. He was coming back toward her. The pulsing between her legs grew harder.

"You play a dangerous game." He stripped off his coat and let it fall to the floor.

"I never play," she taunted him. A strange sort of smile crossed his face as he tossed aside his waistcoat, and she somersaulted off the other side of the bed, rolling to her feet and facing him across the mattress. Slowly he paced around the bed, still watching her with that odd expression.

"You should," he whispered a second before he lunged at her. Angelique was ready but he was faster, and he dragged her back when she tried to leap over the bed. He pulled her closer, into his arms, holding her despite her attempts to push him away. "No more weapons," he murmured against her neck. "Just this."

Angelique's hands, braced on his shoulders to shove, tightened and gripped as his lips sucked at her skin. Her nails dug into his flesh and in reply his teeth sank into the tender skin at the curve of her neck, just hard enough to make her shudder. His hands flexed and squeezed around her bottom, pulling her tightly into him as he rocked his hips.

Angelique's shudders only grew harder. Dear God, she had been too long without a man if her body reacted this way to him.

He tipped up her face to his and brushed his lips against hers. It was an oddly tender kiss. She rebelled against the wave of feeling it caused, not even wanting to name that feeling. She wasn't a naive little virgin, ready to lose her heart to the first man who kissed her with such tenderness, as if he cared for her as a woman. He was just as much a liar and imposter as she was. Angelique knew how this game was played; she was a master at playing it herself, and the heart was the one card she never played. People went all to pieces when they thought their hearts were at stake. They became stupid, careless, and rash, which could easily lead to far worse. She wasn't about to risk it, not for a quick tumble, not for him, and not for herself.

She turned away from his kiss and sucked in deep, steadying breaths as his mouth moved down her jaw, onto her neck. She tried to turn her thoughts coldly inward, away from the burning pleasure his lips were leaving on her skin, away from the desire that raged through her blood. Not him. Not now. Not like this. She couldn't give in to this madness, this unguarded lunacy. And if she didn't break the spell now, he would have her completely bewitched, no matter what her good sense said.

Her palm struck him across the cheek with a loud crack. Unprepared, he recoiled, his eyes flying to hers in shock, but when he spoke his voice was even. "That's three times you've struck me tonight."

Angelique clenched her teeth, glaring back. She would much rather hate him than want him, at least for this moment. "Make it an even four." And she swung her other hand.

He caught her wrist, and when she tried to pull free he twisted her arm, bending it behind her until she gasped. The shape of her hand was printed on his face, dull red against his tanned skin. "Not tonight."

Still holding her arm behind her, he bent his head and pressed his lips to the back of her jaw, right below her ear. Angelique choked on her moan of desire. This was wrong, all wrong, she thought wildly as his kisses wandered over her neck and face, even as she tilted her head to let him. So very, very wrong . . . but so very, very good.

His hand pulled the neckline of her gown from her shoulder a moment before his mouth moved there. She shuddered again, unprepared for the fierce need that roared to life inside her. When he bore her down onto her back, onto her bed, she didn't have the strength of body or will to stop him.

In a matter of minutes he had stripped her bodice down from her shoulders as far as it would go, just low enough to free her breasts. His hands circled her breasts, cupping their weight in his palms, and he groaned in unmistakable male appreciation as his thumbs swirled over her tight nipples. Angelique acknowledged the battle was lost, if only because her body had already surrendered to his touch.

Without a word she grasped the back of his shirt and pulled, sliding her hands beneath to his solid flesh, hot and firm under her palms. He reached over one shoulder and yanked the shirt over his head, pulling his arms free even as she twined herself around him. Her skin seemed to burn where it touched him, and she squirmed closer, wanting it to consume her and burn away every last trace of rational thought. He was helping considerably with that wish. His hands were everywhere on her, one sliding up her thigh to curve around her bottom, squeezing her hip and holding her against him. She raised her leg, hooking her knee around his waist so she could raise her hips into his, rolling her spine to rub herself shamelessly against the erection straining at his trousers. His breath hissed between his teeth, and his eyes glowed like jade as he loomed over her, braced on one elbow, and yanked up the tattered hem of her gown. He ran his fingers between her legs, through the folds of her sex, pausing to swirl over that spot where all her longing was knotted, then sliding lower. She caught her breath at the first pass of his fingers, gasped in giddy shock as his finger pressed hard and deep inside her, and all but screamed as he laid his thumb against that aching spot and stroked.

"Christ," he said between gritted teeth. His hair fell forward, tumbling over his brow. The muscles of his arm under her neck flexed and hardened. Angelique dug her toes into the bed, straining against the unspeakable pleasure of his touch inside her. She ran her hand down his bare chest to his waist, letting her nails bite into his skin. With two quick twists she popped the trouser buttons free and then she had him in her hands. From the guttural curse he whispered in her ear, he was as much in her thrall as she was in his. She raised her face, welcoming his ravishing kiss as she curled her fingers around him. He was thick and hard and so alive, burning hot. She gripped and squeezed, imagining him driving inside her, and felt her own inner muscles quiver and melt in anticipation.

He tensed and jerked in her hands, then shoved himself off the bed. "Take off the dress," he growled, kicking off his shoes and peeling off his trousers and undergarments. "Now."

Angelique sat up and reached for the buttons at her back, but obviously not fast enough. Nate was naked in front of her, and her eyes were drawn to the sight. How much the clothing had concealed, she thought; he was neither skinny nor gangly, but lean and hard with muscle. While she was still staring, he caught her hand and pulled her to her feet. "Never mind," he whispered as he turned her around and pushed her forward until she braced her arms on the edge of the bed. "I'll do it."

He undid the first few buttons in a rush, then paused. The bodice loosened and sagged forward, and his arms came around her, his hands slipping inside the dress to cup her breasts again. Lightly, leisurely he stroked her, his long fingers circling and pinching her nipples until they stood up tight and hard. Angelique gripped fistfuls of the coverlet to hold herself up as he played with her—there was no other word for it. He had his hands on her bare breasts and he was playing with her body. She felt the heat of his breath at her nape, and shivered as his lips whispered over her neck. She squeezed her eyes shut and curled her toes into the carpet. She didn't want this; it was only to be a quick tupping, to take the edge off her body's needs. She didn't want him to spend an hour exploring her skin. She didn't want it, but somehow she seemed unable to stop him.

At last he slid his hands out of her bodice, leaving her breasts heavy and aching. He opened a few more buttons, pulling apart the edges and running one fingertip down the ridge of her spine to the lace-trimmed edge of her corset. Her back arched instinctively, but then his mouth was there, his tongue swirling over her skin until she melted again. With agonizing slowness he pushed the dress down her arms and then over her hips until it was a pile of fabric around her legs. With one tug he untied her petticoats, and shoved them down with the dress. The cool air on her bare thighs made her skin tingle and burn, as if she could feel his gaze moving over her. Angelique still stood bent over, palms flat on her bed, paralyzed with desire. He was doing this to torture her. She gathered her wits and stood upright, desperate to recapture some control of the moment, but he pushed her back. He took her hands and placed them back flat on the bed, holding them there a moment with his arms braced around her, his chest pressed to her back.

"Not tonight," he breathed. "Tomorrow you can take me, dominate me, and do with me what you will. Tonight I take you." His words rippled across her skin, dark and seductive. Her breath came out in a faint moan at the thought of all he might do to her, and what she could do to him tomorrow.

With quick, sure movement he pulled at her shift, hanging down her thighs below the corset. There was a rip, and the next thing she knew it was gone; he spread his palms over her buttocks, now bare. "You tore my chemise," she gasped, scrabbling for thought as he stroked his hands over her bottom and down her thighs, then back up, shaping and molding her flesh.

He laughed, rough and low. With short, quick movements he unbuckled the sheath strapped around her leg and tossed it away. "Sweetheart, I'll buy you a new one. Blessed saints, you're beautiful like this."

"Faceless?" she flung back, twisting to peer at him over her shoulder.

His face was dark and taut in the lamplight. At her question he grinned, a savage expression that only made her shiver again. "You want to see my face? You want me to know who it is I'm making love to?" Without waiting for a reply, he flipped her over, pressing her down onto the bed. He loomed over her, his hair falling forward in a rumpled wave to shadow his face. "Did you think I would forget?" He swooped down to kiss her. "Did you fear I don't know?"

"You don't know me," she managed to say. "Not really." He kissed her again, his arms flexing as he lowered himself on top of her. Despite her words, Angelique was reaching for him, clutching at him.

"Not for lack of trying." He settled his weight between her legs and spread her knees wide. Again he stroked her, smiling his wicked smile at the way she inhaled and how her body arched at his touch. When she reached for him again, he caught her wrist and pinned it to the bed. In frustration she swiped at him with her free hand; he was holding her motionless when she burned to move, to slide and rock and push her hips into the mindless ecstasy of his fingers inside her. He laughed, then caught her second hand and held it, too. Now she was helpless, her arms spread wide and his hips lodged between her thighs. She could feel his sex nudging against hers, not driving inside her the way she wanted. She lifted her hips in silent pleading as a tear leaked from her closed eyes. He was a wicked scoundrel for naming tomorrow her turn. It meant there would be more of this addictive pleasure tomorrow. She could no longer deny she wanted it—him—voraciously.

"Open your eyes," he whispered, his lips brushing hers. "Angel, look at me." She forced open her eyes, and saw his face tighten as he finally thrust inside her.

She gasped at the invasion. He seemed to fill her completely and her muscles tightened around him in reflex. That made him shudder and drop his head for a moment. With a leisurely movement he pulled back, then thrust again, so hard and fast her hips rocked off the bed. A slow withdrawal, a hard thrust. Her legs were wrapped around his waist, her arms still pinned flat to the bed by his hands. She writhed under him but couldn't escape his grip or speed his movements. He was destroying her, scraping away at her control and reducing her to a mass of nerves, defenseless and vulnerable to everything he did. She tossed her head, trying to wriggle free, and he chuckled in her ear, although it was a strained sound.

"Don't fight me," he said through his teeth. "Tonight is mine." Every time he surged into her, he seemed to hit something raw and vital that sent jolts of intense pleasure through her. When she felt her climax gather and break inside her, as swift and stunning as if she had fallen off a cliff, Angelique almost wept from the relief and exquisite bliss of it.

Nate felt her spasm around him and instinctively caught his breath; the sensation was similar to being thrown headfirst into the ocean, deep and dark and suffocating. He buried himself inside her once more, letting the contractions of her climax pull him under, and came with a gasp not unlike that of a drowning man finally surfacing for air.

He stayed where he was until the last aftershock had faded away, holding her. Angelique was limp and trembling beneath him, her dark hair tangled about her bare shoulders. One curl lay across her cheek, and he brushed his lips over it, smiling at the silky feel of it against his skin. Wearing little more than her corset, her hair wild and disheveled, she was an intoxicating, seductive sight—but what Nate loved best was her face, soft and peaceful. Now she wasn't the sharply beautiful spy with the hard eyes of a courtesan, but just a woman, well sated and flushed beautifully pink with satisfaction. A woman who wanted him in spite of everything between them. A woman who couldn't deny her own needs and wants anymore. A woman he was in mortal danger of completely losing his head over . . . if he hadn't already.

"I thought you would kill me," she said faintly. She hadn't opened her eyes yet.

Nate laughed, even though his heart still thundered and his chest ached with each breath. "You can take your revenge tomorrow night."

"If I can move." She sighed, stretching languorously. She ran one stocking-clad foot down the back of his calf, and Nate's stomach jumped at the soft tickle of her toes on his skin. "I may not leave this bed for a week."

"An excellent idea." He felt his eyelids weighing down upon his eyes. "I don't think I can walk to my own."

For a moment she didn't respond. She might have gone to sleep; her breathing had grown soft and deep. Nate sighed inwardly, knowing he was an idiot to have hoped she might want him to stay, especially after what he had said to her earlier. Accusing a woman of playing a whore was rarely the best way to win her heart. In all his life, Nate had never felt the debilitating combination of fear and anger and desire he'd experienced tonight. He wanted to shake her and hold her and then make love to her again and again, until she swore on her mother's grave that she would never put him through that again. He'd completely lost his control, been crude and offensive, and unlike every other lady of his acquaintance, Angelique had replied in kind. There wasn't another woman in the world like her, and he'd be damned if he'd lose her now.

But going back to his own bed wasn't the end of things between them, and he of all people knew it was sometimes best to beat a tactical retreat in order to regroup for another attack on the stronghold. Things had changed between them now—not everything, but enough. She wanted him, and that was all he needed to know, for now. Gently he shifted, thinking to leave without disturbing her too much.

She stirred as he started to rise from the bed. Her hand reached out for his. "Stay," she said quietly, looking up at him with heavy-lidded eyes. "Unless you wish your night to be over so soon."

And Nate smiled slowly back at her.

This was more than enough, for now.

Chapter 13

He left her room in the gray hour before dawn the next morning, with a soft touch on her cheek and the flash of a smile at her wistful sigh as he slipped out of bed. She listened to him gather his clothing from the floor where he had thrown it the night before, and then the empty silence when he had gone. His night was over.

She rolled into the depression left by his body, and stared at the ceiling. His warmth and scent still clung to the sheets, surrounding her with the reminder of how much trouble she was in. Deep inside her heart, Angelique admitted she didn't want it to be over. Last night would be seared into her memory until the day she drew her last breath. If she'd had any sense of self-preservation, she would have let him leave after that first, explosive, time. She probably could have survived it well enough, armored herself against any foolish sentimentality, and gone on with her physical desires sated. But instead she told him to stay, and he had.

As a rule, she didn't go to bed with other agents. It was bad practice; lovers grew careless if affection was involved, and ruthless if it was not. Even

Ian, who had flirted with her furiously at times and hinted he wouldn't let an affair interfere with their work, had been easy to keep at a distance. She knew most men were frightened of her in some way or another, even the ones who were willing to risk it for a chance to get beneath her skirts. Nathaniel Avery, though . . . Nate refused to believe her angry denials that she wanted him as much as he wanted her. Nate held her down and made her let him please her until she stopped fighting it. And after he dominated and controlled her, after he had all but forced her into unspeakable pleasure, he offered himself up to her mercy tonight.

But what was she to do, now that she had crossed that line? It was too late to pretend she had been seeking only a physical release. When she had invited him to stay, he had tucked them both between the sheets and simply held her for a while, stroking her back lightly until she dozed off. When she woke in the full dark of night, he had been still holding her, still stroking her, and then he made love to her leisurely, stretching out the sinuous pleasure for what seemed like hours until she almost broke under the sheer rapture of it. And then he did it again, just before he left. Another night like that, and she would never recover.

Angelique stretched her arms over her head, wishing she could just stay in bed for the rest of the day, dreaming away the hours before tonight. *Her* night. How was she to match what he had done?

She should have been exhausted. Her muscles ached even through the residual glow of contentment, and she would feel him between her legs with every step she took. Nate had kept her awake much of the night, and she should close her eyes and get another hour of sleep before Lisette came to stir the fire and bring her breakfast. But instead, her eyes were open and her mind ran onward. They must be discreet. Lisette was her maid and loyal to her, and even if she disapproved of Angelique's actions she would never voice that disapproval to anyone, especially not to someone who might report back to John Stafford. Angelique had no idea about Nate's man, Prince, but it certainly wouldn't be in his best interest to cause trouble now. If anyone else was watching them, though, it could reach the wrong person's ear. And she wouldn't at all doubt the possibility that Stafford might send someone to see how she was faring.

So today she must act as if nothing had happened between them. She must be as bored and dismissive of Nate as she had been before she had held his head to her breast and smiled at the touch of his lips. Before he had run his wicked, clever hands over her bare skin and brought her to the pinnacle of ecstasy. Before she had felt a small, lonely part of her heart warm to his smile. And most of all, she must push the thought of tonight from her mind.

She rose from the bed and dressed. The magenta gown with the shredded hem lay in a pool of silk beneath her petticoats, on the floor where Nate had left them when he stripped her. She shook the petticoats out and draped them over the chaise, then inspected the dress. It was a dangerous dress, as Nate said, and certainly had its uses, but it was fairly well ruined. Still, she smiled a little as she laid it across the petticoats. Perhaps Lisette could replace the skirt.

Lisette knew at once. Her maid came in with a

tray while Angelique was doing her morning exercises, and stopped when she saw the bed. An arrested expression stole across her face, and then she looked at Angelique with such maternal concern it made her hackles rise.

"What?" she snapped.

"Nothing," murmured Lisette, hurrying to set the tray down. "Nothing at all, Madame."

Angelique scowled and tried to concentrate on her exercise. It was hard to stay as strong as she needed to be in order to make up for her petite stature. Being slim and flexible could take one only so far. She raised the heavy iron bar above her head and swung it in slow, controlled circles as if fighting an imaginary swordsman. Ian had taught her some of these motions, and she had added to them. The exertion required her to bathe every morning after she finished, but the taut power in her muscles was worth it. She knew she looked dainty and delicate, and being even a little bit stronger than expected was an invaluable advantage.

"You will be going out today?" Lisette asked. She took up the laundry without batting an eye at the ripped and crumpled gown.

"Later. And then again tonight, after dark." Angelique held the iron bar above her head and slowly lowered it behind her until the muscles at the backs of her arms ached. With a grateful sigh, she set the bar aside and wiped her face with the fresh towel her maid held out. "Today I will be at leisure."

Lisette raised one eyebrow, but said nothing. She went in and out of the room as Angelique ate breakfast, preparing the bath and laying out an old, comfortable dress. By the time Angelique finished bathing and dressing, and Lisette was pinning up her damp hair, it was barely past ten. "Has Mr. Avery risen yet?" she asked idly, watching her maid's deft fingers twirl her hair into a neat twist.

"Risen, and gone, along with that man of his," said Lisette. She poked in the last pin as Angelique started in surprise. "I only heard them leave when they closed the door. Like ghosts, Madame, they move without a sound."

Indeed. Angelique hadn't heard a single sound herself, even though she'd been awake since Nate left her room. She had just assumed he had crawled into his own bed and gone back to sleep. Not even a squeaking stair had betrayed them. What could they be doing? she wondered, and then she shoved aside the thought. She had work to do today, and if Nate stayed away and lessened her distraction, so much the better.

But what was he doing? For a man who tried so hard to wheedle her intentions out of her, he hadn't mentioned anything of his own plans. Perhaps he had none, and was merely improvising again. Or perhaps he had lied to her about improvising, and had carefully planned every last moment of last night . . .

She sprang to her feet with an impatient huff. She would make herself mad if she thought about him all day. This was what she had feared last night; this was what she could not allow, even given her tacit acknowledgment that he would be back in her bed tonight, and perhaps the night after. It was an affair, nothing lasting. When they had caught their man, Nathaniel Avery would go back to America and she would retire to a quiet life in the country. Or perhaps travel abroad for a while. A quiet life in the country sounded very . . . quiet; perhaps too quiet at the moment. She could see Italy, Russia, even France. Perhaps Melanie would go with her.

"Find the market basket, Lisette," she called out. "I shall go for a walk." She had planned to go later, but suddenly wished to be out of the house. She got out her plainest bonnet and draped a drab gray shawl around her shoulders. The dress she wore was simple and plain, a soft beige color; completely unremarkable. Her maid hurried in with the basket. "What would you like from the market?" she asked, letting her dimple show impishly as she hooked the basket over one arm.

"Fresh berries, *s'il vous plait*," said Lisette with a smile. "And no more ripped skirts."

Angelique hesitated. "Can it be repaired? Can the skirt be replaced?" Lisette made a dour face. "Well, toss it out if not. I liked the color."

Lisette smirked. "*Oui*, Madame. It is a lovely color."

She gave the woman a severe look as she went to the door. "Do not begin."

"No, Madame." Lisette waited until she put her hand on the doorknob to ask, "And what shall I say to Monsieur Avery, if he should return while you are out?"

Angelique froze. She was accustomed to Lisette's impertinence, but this touched her too closely. Slowly she turned. For a long moment she fixed a rather haughty stare on her maid, who just stared boldly back. "You may tell him," she said quietly, "that I have gone *out*." And she closed the door behind her.

* * *

Davis Hurst lived on a bustling street where the houses were small and tightly packed but neatly kept. She walked past it on the opposite side of the street, studying the house from beneath her eyelashes. It looked no different from any of its neighbors, and no less difficult to enter. At the end of the street, she turned and went down until she found the alley that led behind the row of houses, to see the rear entrance. Then, her errand complete, she walked on to the market in Covent Garden.

It was convenient that the street in front of Hurst's home was so busy; she could walk up and down all day without drawing much notice. A small house like that, with only a bachelor living in it, couldn't have many servants, and likely some of them went home at the end of the day. He didn't have a cook, she knew; they had learned he dined most nights at his club. A valet, perhaps a footman, would be the only people at home tonight if Hurst held to his usual pattern. With a key in her possession, it wouldn't be hard to get inside.

The trickier part would be finding anything helpful. Just by nature of what he did, Hurst would probably have taken some pains to secure his papers. On the other hand, he appeared to have a great deal of arrogance, and arrogant men were usually careless. She must be sure to check the obvious places first.

When she walked past the house on her way home, fresh blackberries in her basket, she studied the windows. Even at this hour, the shades were still drawn. She wondered how Mr. Hurst was feeling this morning, if the lump on his head ached fiercely enough, and smiled to herself. It served him right for thinking he could take advantage of any woman.

She went around to the back of the house in Varden Street and let herself in. She left the blackberries in the scullery for Lisette, and went up the stairs to her room. It should be a simple job tonight—or perhaps a very boring one, if Hurst decided to stay home— but one must still be careful. It would be easiest if she went alone, but Nate would most likely insist on coming, especially after last night at Vauxhall. She kept her mind resolutely away from what happened after Vauxhall. That would only muddle the issue and be a significant drain on her concentration. She slipped the shawl from her shoulders and opened her door.

Nate was waiting there, sitting on a chair turned toward the window. Angelique stopped abruptly in the doorway, and he cast only the barest glance her way. "How was your walk?" he asked.

"Refreshing." She closed the door and went to the wardrobe to put away her shawl. "And yours?"

"The same," he said, watching her with idle interest.

Angelique waited, but he didn't ask where she had gone. Nor did he volunteer where he had gone, but she accepted that. It was only fair that she not make demands on him, if he did not make demands on her. He just sat there watching her with those cool green eyes and an unreadable expression. She crossed the room to the window and drew the draperies more fully open. "It's a lovely day," she said, looking out at the street. The sun was bright and the sky was clear, even if the air had a chill in it. Autumn was coming.

"Indeed," he agreed.

Angelique kept looking out the window even though there was nothing to see. It kept her back to him, and meant she didn't have to face him. It galled her that she was unsettled about facing him at all, after what had happened between them last night. This morning. Just a few hours ago, just a few feet away from where she now stood, staring blindly out the window. Angelique was not accustomed to feeling this way. How wretched that she was the one who felt awkward and unsure, while he sat there cool and composed. She should turn and go on as if nothing had happened. She should carry on as if things were exactly as they had been. They were still working for different people, with different goals in mind. Going to bed with Nate didn't change any of that; it couldn't. She had resolved to carry on as if nothing had changed, but now that he was here, his gaze almost a physical touch on her back, she found it was not as simple as she had expected.

"When are we paying Mr. Hurst a visit?" he asked.

"Tonight." Angelique pushed all her jumbled emotions aside and turned to face him. "I am perfectly content to go alone."

"No doubt." He was a man of few words today, it seemed. So much the better, she told herself in aggravation.

"I saw the house this morning," she went on. "It will be no trouble to break in. One presumes he keeps his documents close at hand. Men like him do not usually trust others."

"Nor should they. Men like him do not inspire trust." He tilted back his head to look up at her as she approached. "I expect you have it all planned."

"I have the key," she reminded him. "That makes things considerably easier."

"What if Hurst does not go out this evening? His head may still ache from the very large rock that struck him last night."

"If I could have found a larger one, I would have used it," she said coolly. "As it was, I was defending my virtue and had no time to search."

"My dear, I make no objection to you bashing in his head, whether your virtue was at stake or not."

"Good. Then we do not need to argue about it."

He raised one eyebrow. "Were we arguing? I thought I was being agreeable."

He was, damn him. "If he does not go out this evening, we will simply go later. And before you ask," she added as he looked about to speak, "I will be armed with more than a rock tonight."

A faint smile crossed his mouth. "No doubt," he said again.

"Is that all you can say?" she snarled. "Have you no helpful suggestions? I have already been out to see the house and plan how we will get inside. What have you done today?"

As soon as she said it, Angelique wished it back. It was ill-tempered, rude, and unfair; she had no idea what he had been up to this morning, but not in her worst mood could she accuse Nate of being unhelpful. He had treated her far better than she had just treated him, and even now that she had snapped at him, he still didn't snap back at her. She drew a deep breath and let it out. "Forgive me," she said more calmly. "That was wrong of me."

Nate rose. "Apology accepted. You must be tired today, and that is my fault." He walked toward her, and she felt her face warm as his clear green eyes met hers, deep and pure and knowing. "Prince will be returning to the ship. His work here is just about completed, and it will be more convenient to have his laboratory already stowed aboard when we locate Mr. Dixon. We notified the captain this morning; a cart and some men will come this afternoon for his equipment. And . . . I went to get you a gift." He put his hand into his coat pocket and took it out.

Angelique blushed—deeply. It was a knife he held out to her, with a dark carved handle and a sheath of some fine leather embroidered with pale beads and threads. She slid the blade from the sheath; it was slightly curved, made of finely honed steel. The hilt was as smooth as satin under her palm, and perfectly balanced. It was a beautiful, deadly, weapon, but not like any knife she had ever seen before.

"It's a Wyandot knife," he said when she looked up in wonder. "From the frontier of America."

"How exotic." She didn't know what else to say.

"I thought you might like it," he said. "Should you need to protect yourself against men like Hurst again."

"It is beautiful." She tested the blade, razor sharp against her thumb.

He grinned. "It's not meant to be an object of art. Mind you don't cut yourself."

"I do know how to use a knife." But she slid it back into the ornate sheath. "Thank you."

"Thank me tonight," he replied in a low voice. "In any way you like."

She met his gaze, and awareness crackled in the air between them. "I will," she whispered.

His slow smile made her stomach flutter. He

caught her hand and raised it to his lips, kissing the tip of her index finger. "I look forward to it." Then he turned to go.

"What is a Wyandot?" she asked on impulse. He stopped at the door to his bedroom and glanced back at her.

"A tribe of native people," he said. "They live in the Ohio Territory. They are known for their ferocity, especially to their captives." She turned the knife over, looking at it in renewed amazement. "It's a warrior's blade," he added. "A scalping knife."

Chapter 14

It was as dark and silent as a tomb inside Davis Hurst's house. Getting in had been no trouble at all, thanks to the purloined key, and now they stood in the narrow hallway listening to the faint ticking of a clock. Any servants must have retired for the evening after Hurst left for his club, sporting a bandage just visible under his hat. Angelique had quietly relished the sight of that bandage.

With a soft touch on Nate's arm, she led the way up the stairs. She winced as one step gave a soft squeak, but behind her Nate was utterly soundless, and the house remained as still as before. Upstairs, they found Hurst's study and slipped inside, and Angelique drew her first full breath in some time when Nate closed the door behind them.

"I shall start on the desk," she murmured. "Will you do the cabinet?" He nodded once and moved to the ornately carved cabinet by the window. Angelique knelt on the hearth and poked at the fire until she got an ember to light her small lantern. Nate lit a candle from the mantel and they turned to their respective tasks.

Hurst was a careful bookkeeper. His desk drawers were locked, but she was able to open them with only a few minutes' work with her lock picks. Hurst had ledgers coded in colored inks, detailing his transactions. He was nothing more than a glorified fence, she realized, but a clever enough fence to identify his clients only by numbers. She paged through all the ledgers and searched the other drawers, but couldn't locate a key listing names and directions. By the dates, they could make a guess which transactions might be connected to Jacob Dixon, but that would still tell them nothing about where the man or his stolen money were now. Angelique was just cursing eloquently in her mind as she replaced the ledgers where they had been when an unexpected sound stopped her cold.

Someone was at the door.

She froze, her gaze flying to Nate. There was no escape from the room; the one tall window looked out on the street, and there was no other door. Nate made a motion urging her to get down, and blew out his candle. Angelique followed suit with her lantern, then dropped to the floor behind the desk and held her breath.

Metal rasped against metal as the doorknob turned, until the latch released with a soft click. She could hear rapid, heavy breathing, then an extended creak as the door opened. A slice of light fanned across the floor, less than a foot away from where she huddled. Slowly her fingers inched toward the dagger strapped at her waist, the scalping knife Nate had given her. She wasn't going to kill a servant simply doing his job, but if he had a pistol, she wasn't going to wait to be shot, either.

With terrible precision, there came a footstep,

then another. The light spilled over the desk now, and Angelique had to dig her fingernails into her palm to keep herself from flinching away. Staying completely motionless was far better than instinctively jerking out of sight; the movement itself, the rustle of cloth, a change in breathing would give her away. She remained still as a stone and waited. Where was Nate? she wondered. Her fingers tightened on the knife hilt as she imagined him being slowly revealed by that approaching light. He had been exposed on the other side of the room by the window, with no large furniture to hide behind.

The next thing she heard, over the pounding of her heart, was a startled intake of air, followed by a thump and a wheeze. Something pinged softly, like a fork tapping on a wineglass, and then there was a rushed choking, gargling sound. It sounded like someone being strangled.

Angelique scrambled to the corner of the desk away from the light, no longer silent but ready to spring to Nate's aid. Her fingers touched her garrote, coiled at her waist by the knife, and she rocked onto the balls of her feet. She slid around the heavy mahogany desk with deadly intent, then stopped in surprise.

Nate held a stocky older man with one arm around his neck, the other around his forehead covering the man's eyes. In his hand was a small glass bottle, pressed to his captive's nose and gasping mouth. Hurst's servant was clutching at Nate's imprisoning forearm with one hand and flailing rather aimlessly about with the other, which clutched a stout walking stick. As Angelique watched, his arms relaxed and then flopped to his side. The walking stick thumped on the floor and rolled under the cabinet. The servant's head lolled unconscious on his neck. Only then did Nate ease his grip. The man in his grasp slumped forward.

Nate glanced at her. "I found a box of correspondence," he said, his voice barely audible. "Look—there on the table. I'll take care of him." He set down the small bottle, then hefted the unconscious man over his shoulder with a strength greater than his lean frame indicated. Moving slowly and carefully, he went out the open door, and a moment later she heard his footsteps descending the stairs.

Angelique snatched up the bottle and took a cautious sniff. The sickly sweet scent of ether made her wrinkle her nose and put it down. A small bit of liquid sloshed in the bottom. Ether fumes could make one feel faint, and she kept her distance from the bottle, even opening the window to get rid of the smell. She got the lamp that the servant had left burning on the table by the door and went back to work, making much faster progress with better light.

Nate returned several minutes later, less quietly than before. "There's no one else in the house," he reported. "Did you find anything?"

"He is an organized rogue," she said, digging through Hurst's correspondence. "These, perhaps. I cannot read it all."

Nate took the letters she held out, scanning through them. After a moment he made a quiet hiss of triumph. "Here's Dixon," he muttered. "He's being called Chartley now, and staying at the Pulteney Hotel in London."

"Are you sure?" Angelique asked even as she

began placing the other letters back in the box.

He tilted the letter toward the light. "He lists the jewels here. The necklace with the teardrop emerald pendant is quite distinctive—as Dixon knows, from the way he mentions its unique design and high value."

"Do we need anything else here?"

Nate looked down to flip through the other letters, then shook his head. "His last letter is just a day ago from the Pulteney, and makes no mention of moving. We're done here."

"Good." Angelique replaced the letters, then let Nate return the box to where he had found it. She closed the window and checked once more to see if they had left any trace of their presence. "What are you doing?" Nate was on his knees by the desk, running one hand over the carpet.

"Looking for the seal," he whispered back, wiggling the bottle at her before tucking it into his pocket. She joined him on the floor, and moments later found the hard wax wafer that had sealed his bottle of ether. With one last look around the room, they blew out the lamp and left, hurrying quietly down the stairs.

In the hall below, they had just reached the bottom of the stairs, ready to go out the back, when a key rattled in the lock of the front door. Angelique's heart leaped halfway to her throat; there was no place to hide in the hall. Almost before she had formed the thought, Nate had seized her arm and hustled her down the hall and around the corner to the back of the stairs, where the servants' door to the lower level was. The front door was opening. Nate shoved her against the wall right behind the baize door, and then flattened himself against her as light from the streetlamp in front of the house seeped into the hall.

"Puddlestone," called Davis Hurst. "Puddlestone! Where are you?"

Angelique barely breathed. She was squeezed tight between Nate in front of her and the wall at her back, and breathing would have been difficult even if she weren't trying to hold herself utterly motionless. She could feel the faint puffs of Nate's breath on her temple, and knew he was doing the same. As soon as Hurst went upstairs, they could slip out, but for now the man was in his front hall stamping about, waiting for his servant to attend him. Slowly she tipped back her head, meeting Nate's eyes. Although his body was tensed, he was grinning broadly and there was a wild, excited glint in his eyes. He wiggled his eyebrows, then leered downward at her bosom, flattened against his chest, as if this had all been a ploy to press up against her, and in spite of her thundering pulse, Angelique had to bite her lip hard to keep from smiling back at him. What a daredevil he was, to find it amusing that they were literally inches away from being discovered breaking and entering.

"Puddlestone!" Hurst barked again. He muttered under his breath, and Angelique caught the words "lazy" and "idiot."

With a creak, the baize door next to them slowly opened. The man Nate had knocked unconscious stumbled out, rubbing his forehead. His gray hair stood up in a ruff around his bald crown, and he moved like a man just roused from a deep sleep.

"Coming, sir," he mumbled. He shuffled toward

the front of the hall, not noticing the two of them plastered to the wall barely inches away from him on the other side of the door. The door had shielded them from view this time, but if he came back toward them, there would be no escape. "You're home early, sir," Puddlestone said to his master.

"And you took the opportunity to drink, I see," snapped Hurst. Silently, Nate reached out and caught the edge of the door before it closed. He eased away from her and motioned her to go through.

"No, sir," Puddlestone protested plaintively. He was around the corner now, his lamplight illuminating the front of the hall. "Just a drop of sherry, no more. I have such a headache, though."

"I'm sure it's nothing to mine. Bring some of that headache powder and some wine, and be quick about it," Hurst ordered. Angelique slid around the door under Nate's arm, then dashed as quietly as she could through the scullery, Nate right behind her. Once the baize door to the hall had closed, she felt safe enough to slide back the bolt and open the door to the back stoop. Hesitating just long enough to take a quick glance out to be sure there was no one about, they were outside the house. Nate closed the door behind them, then caught her face in his hands and pressed a hard kiss on her mouth. In spite of everything, her knees started to soften, and she had to grab his arms to keep her balance when he released her. Still grinning like a madman, he took her hand and they ran through the garden into the alley and back to the street.

"*Mon Dieu!*" she said, sucking in a deep breath. "*Incroyable!* What brought him home so early? He was not gone above an hour!"

"Perhaps his splitting headache of last night caught up to him."

She laughed, a little giddy with relief. "Perhaps! And his servant also, I think."

Nate shrugged modestly, his stride long and easy. "Ether can give a man a hangover as powerful as one from brandy."

"Where did you get it?" She had not known he had it, and it was an oddity; if Hurst and his man pieced together what it was, they could chance upon the chemist who sold it. She had tried so hard to eliminate any trail that led to them, even dropping Hurst's latchkey into the area below the front steps where he would find it eventually and never suspect he had lost it in Vauxhall. She couldn't deny the ether had come in handy, but she also couldn't deny being a little irked Nate hadn't told her about it.

"Prince made it for me," he said. "An extra potent mixture; he warned me not to breathe it myself or I'd be staggering around like a drunk."

"Oh," she said. "Did the man see you, before you seized him?"

"I doubt it," he replied, giving her an aggrieved look. "And he'll likely have some very fanciful notions of what happened; ether gives men strange dreams."

She said nothing, but Nate caught the flash of pique on her face. He thought it had been a very successful night; they now knew where Jacob Dixon was staying, and they hadn't been caught. Now they were on their way home, and his blood was already running hot and fast from their close escape. Just the thought of the pleasures she might inflict on him was making him hard and ready. Or maybe it was the way he had pressed her against the wall, sparking all sorts of images in his mind as he inhaled the soft scent of her hair and felt her lithe body shift against his. Or maybe it was the spark of irritation in her face that made him tense in expectation of the unknown. Maybe he'd breathed in too much of the ether after all, for his fantasies were taking reckless turns.

"You can exact whatever revenge you wish when we get home," he said to her in a low voice.

Her eyes flashed at him. "You may depend on that," she replied. "I trust you remember your promise last night?"

He'd said he would be hers to do with as she wished. Nate had to forcibly control his breathing. "I do."

By the time they made it home, both were almost running. All thought of what they had learned vanished from Nate's mind; all he could see was Angelique stripping off her dark, fitted jacket, and the way she watched him with a fierce fascination that must be mirrored in his own face. Desire made him hasty and clumsy. At least one button burst off his coat as he struggled out of it. He barely got it off, let alone back on the peg behind the door, before she grabbed the front of his shirt and pulled, sealing her mouth to his in a blazing kiss.

It wasn't the ether. He felt as wild and drunk with anticipation as a sailor stepping on shore for the first time in months. She was a living bonfire in his arms, tempting him toward immolation, and God help him, he was already ablaze. He wrapped both arms around her and lifted, striding toward the stairs.

"No," she breathed, wriggling free.

Nate set her down without releasing her. "Upstairs now, or here on the stairs."

"You said it would be my night to command," she whispered, twining her fingers through his hair as he kissed her bare throat. She tipped her head back and moaned, and the vibration under her skin, against his lips, made Nate shudder. He wasn't going to survive this woman. She would drive him mad, one way or another.

"Then command quickly," he growled. He had undone the buttons of her bodice and now pulled it down with a sharp yank. Without taking his eyes from hers, he slid his hands beneath the fabric and cupped her breasts.

For a moment she let him; she braced one hand on the wall beside her and gripped the banister with the other, spread like a sacrifice to his desire. Nate all but choked. He gave up; he surrendered. He was wholly, completely, utterly conquered, hers to command in any way she wanted. He wrapped his hands around her waist and kissed the exposed line of her throat down to the swell of her breast. Urgency and hunger roared inside him, and he started to bear her down onto the stairs. Making love on the stairs was hardly what he had planned, but who cared for plans at a time like this?

With a visible effort she gathered herself. She put her palms against his chest and pushed until Nate had to step back or fall. Her hair was coming down from the tight knot she had secured at the nape of her neck, and her eyes glittered in the dimly lit hall. Her chest heaved, the edge of her white corset rising and falling behind the loosened bodice. Her skin glowed like a pearl against the black of her clothing.

"My command," she said, her voice husky but controlled. Standing two steps above him, she was just his height. She laid her fingers along his jaw, leaning close enough that he could see how dark and dilated her eyes were. "Tonight you are mine," she added.

More than tonight, he thought. But when he moved toward her, she stopped him again. "Come," she whispered in that bewitching velvety voice that made his stomach knot on itself with lust. She crooked her finger at him and led the way upstairs, and Nate followed because he couldn't not follow her.

Chapter 15

~~~~⚬⚬~~~~

In the bedroom she closed the door behind him, then turned to him, studying him. Nate's very skin seemed to stretch and prickle under her gaze, and the throbbing in his groin grew harder. "What would you have me do?" he asked, because he didn't think he could stand there much longer doing nothing.

"I find it so interesting where a man keeps his weapons," she murmured instead. Running one hand along his shoulder, she sauntered around him, her hips rolling. As they had been last night, two lamps were left burning in her room but turned down low, and a good fire crackled in the hearth. With a soft hiss, she pulled the knife from the sheath strapped at the back of his waist. "A good blade," she said. He cast his eyes over his shoulder to see the gleam of his hunting knife in her hand as she turned it from side to side.

"A knife is no good without a sharp blade," he said.

She smiled darkly. "No." She laid the knife on the dressing table behind her. "What else? Apparently you have weapons I know nothing about."

She meant the ether, which had been in his coat pocket along with a pistol. He didn't have any more weapons on his person now. Nate gave her a slow, predatory smile. "Find them yourself."

Somehow he stood motionless as she continued to circle him, first pulling away the dark kerchief around his neck with a sensual swish of silk, then unfastening his shirt. She gathered it up and slid her hands beneath it, up his back until she could push it over his head, and Nate had to grit his teeth to keep from coming in his trousers as her body pressed against his, from her breasts to her belly, even though she was still clothed. His breath was rasping in his throat by the time she let him remove his boots, and then his trousers.

Angelique knew she was playing with fire as she made him stand naked in front of her, his erection stiff and ready. His face was drawn taut, and his eyes never wavered from her as she moved about the room. She liked this. She liked having him await her pleasure. She liked having *him*, and by now her own body was hot and pulsing in anticipation. "Sit down," she said.

Slowly he lowered himself onto the chair she indicated. The muscles of his shoulder tensed in hard lines as he laid his palms flat on his thighs, but still he waited for her instruction. She whisked the thin black cord from around her waist. "You held me down last night," she murmured. "Give me your hand." His jaw tightened as if he knew what she would do, but he put out his hand.

She knotted the rope around one wrist, then took both his arms behind the straight-backed chair and bound the wrists together, looping the rope through the slats of the chair. His chest filled with air, and his exhalations were harsh and loud in the dim, quiet room. By the time she came around in front of him again, his head had fallen forward. His hair hung loose around his face, shadowing but not hiding the fierce control in his expression. "If you mean to kill me, do it now," he said through his teeth.

Angelique smiled. Languidly she pulled her arms free of her bodice and untied the loose trousers she wore. She let both articles drop to the floor and stepped out of them, then kicked off her shoes. Nate's eyes devoured her as she stood in her shortened chemise, the hem just covering her hips. As she plucked at the string of her corset, she angled her head to watch him watching her. "As you can see," she whispered, "I am completely unarmed."

"But far more dangerous," he growled. "My God, Angelique . . ."

She unlaced the corset and tossed it aside, and peeled off the chemise. With deliberate slowness she cradled his jaw in her hands, tilting his chin up as she bent down to kiss him lightly, her lips lingering on his, and for a moment the intense heat in his eyes faded to something almost yearning. He surged up against her, straining to prolong the kiss even as her rope held him to the chair. Angelique stared at him, her heart pounding. "What should I do with you?" she asked aloud, both of herself and of him. She had been right to be afraid last night; this was not a passing attraction. Something inside her responded to Nate in a deep, elemental way, and she didn't know how to control it.

"Kiss me," he whispered. "Just . . . kiss me."

She touched her lips to his again, letting herself

be pulled along by that force for a moment. His kiss lured her, tempted her to surrender to it. How could something she knew to be dangerous feel so sublime, she wondered hazily as Nate seduced her with nothing but his mouth. She had stripped him and tied him to a chair, and yet somehow she felt as though he held her captive, enslaved by that connection between them that she was helpless to deny.

She turned away, trying to recover herself. He made a low murmur of protest, but simply transferred his attentions to her neck, sucking lightly at the sensitive skin below her jaw. Angelique shivered, and pushed herself away. He would own her body and soul if she allowed that sort of thing to continue. There wasn't just lust or seduction in his kiss; there was longing, rich and sweet. That, she could not allow. Lust and seduction were all she could offer, and all she could accept.

"You called me ferocious," she murmured, sinking to her knees. "When you gave me that knife."

"I said the Wyandot are ferocious," he rasped. She spread her hands over his shoulders and then raked her fingernails down his chest, and he shuddered.

"But you gave me their knife, as if I were just as cruel." She swept her palms across his stomach and down his thighs to his knees. His muscles tensed into iron-hard readiness under her touch. "I think I must torment my captive to deserve such a gift."

"I thought you would like it," he said swiftly. "Not that you would—should—torment— Ahh . . ." His voice faded into a ragged groan as she flicked her tongue over the head of his cock and circled her hand around the shaft. Angelique looked up at him, her lips poised above his erection. "Do you wish to beg for mercy?"

He grinned, although it was strained and feral and he didn't open his eyes. His head had fallen back against the wall behind him and the pulse beat hard in his exposed throat. Veins stood out on his arms, flexed behind the chair. "Never."

She smiled and closed her lips around him, taking him deep in her mouth on one stroke. Nate made an otherwordly sound, half rapture, half anguish. He dug his toes into the floor and pushed, and the chair rocked back until it hit the wall. Angelique simply shifted her weight and swirled her tongue around him. Just the sound of his breathing, hard and uneven, was arousing. For tonight at least he was her captive. She meant to repay the devastation he had wrought on her body last night. She meant to exact a price for the tangle he had made of her logical, coldly pragmatic life since the day he appeared at Bow Street. By dawn, Nathaniel Avery would feel as stripped and vulnerable as she had felt this morning, when his absence seemed a thing of pain.

When she tasted the first salty drop welling up from the head of his erection, she licked him once more and released him with a last lingering stroke of her hand. Nate's eyes popped open, wild and fever-bright. "Witch," he croaked.

"Captive," she countered softly. "Don't you like it?" She ran the tip of her tongue around the head of his member, and his entire body spasmed in ecstasy. The chair tipped forward, the legs hitting the floor with a thud.

"No, it's . . . good," he said, his breath almost panting. "God, is it good. Too good. Untie me."

She just smiled, running the tip of her tongue over her lower lip. His eyes fixed on it, and his erection bobbed. "I like having you at my pleasure. I may not untie you until tomorrow."

His jaw hardened. Angelique got to her feet and circled him, running her fingertips up his biceps and over his shoulder. At the nape of his neck she dug her fingers into his hair and pulled, tugging his head back until she could see his face. He met her gaze evenly. "Let me touch you."

"No," she replied. "But I shall touch you."

"Then do it." It was almost a plea—almost, but not quite. She took her time strolling around to stand in front of him once more. This really was intoxicating. She stepped up and straddled his lap, curling her toes around the rungs of the chair to keep her weight balanced above him and bracing her hands on his shoulders. Slowly she lowered herself until his erection brushed the dark curls between her legs. In spite of her desire to remain in control, that contact sent sparks across her skin. She rocked back and forth, rubbing her sex against his; his shoulders tensed and strained beneath her hands as she clung to him, sliding up and down him, losing a little bit more of her composure with every pass of his erection against her center. Nate whispered dark, guttural encouragement, daring her to move faster, taunting her to tilt her hips just a little and ride him properly, promising to pay her back for this exquisite torture.

Abruptly she abandoned her desire to drive him mad. His words, his expression, the heat of his skin against hers . . . it was too much for a woman to withstand. She was torturing herself at least as much as she was him. She slipped one hand down her belly to touch herself, just once, then let her legs fall open wider. She sank down on a slow slide, taking him inside her.

With a harsh exhalation, he swept his hands up her back to cup her shoulders and pull her down, hard, at the same moment his hips bucked upward. The unexpected pressure caught her off guard; she cried out as he filled her completely. Before she had recovered, he was lifting her to do it again, and this time she could barely breathe as he thrust into her. The next time she was ready, though, and moved with him. The chair legs banged on the floor as the chair rocked back and forth under their urgency. Angelique had been on edge already, and this was too much. Without much warning her inner muscles clenched and she came with a shuddering sob. Nate growled, gripping her shoulders almost painfully hard as his hips jerked up twice more before he stiffened in his own completion.

Not until she was draped over him, feeling boneless and tingling with warmth, did she realize something. "I tied your hands," she muttered.

Nate's arms were still locked around her. He turned his head and kissed her forehead where it lay on his shoulder. His skin was dewed with perspiration and his heart thundered beneath her cheek. "Someday I'll show you how to tie a sailor so he can't get free . . . but not tonight." Her rope, still knotted around one of his wrists, trailed down her spine as he stroked her hair, and Angelique smiled in spite of herself.

"You were not at my mercy, then. We must start all over again."

"Christ, no," Nate said with feeling. "I was completely helpless. Powerless to resist you; like clay in your hands. If you start over, I shall lose consciousness on the spot. I didn't promise to allow that."

"You said I could do what I wished with you."

"Oh dear." His breath warmed her cheek; he was laughing at her, the scoundrel. "Was that not what you wished to happen?"

"No," she said tranquilly. Now was not a moment to argue. "But it was near enough."

He chuckled, then rose to his feet, holding her bottom securely in his hands even when she squeaked in alarm and threw her arms around his neck. The chair clattered to the floor behind him as he strode toward the bed. "I shall try to do better, Madame," he told her, pressing her back onto the mattress while keeping her legs around his hips. "But not tied to a chair. You may guide my hands as you wish"—he cupped her breast with a suggestive look, flicking her nipple with his thumb—"but I'll be damned if you're going to tie me up again."

He was still inside her. She could feel him growing hard again. Angelique squeezed her intimate muscles around him, meeting his gaze with pure challenge, and he caught his breath. His eyes half closed as she did it again, and then he focused on her face.

"You minx," he muttered. "As if you need a rope to hold me prisoner." He began moving his hips, just a gentle movement, but enough to make her gasp and squirm as he slid through her still-swollen flesh.

He held her there, moving in her with maddening lack of urgency. His hands covered every inch of her, with skill and devotion until she was almost sobbing from the sensations. As the tension knotted tighter in her belly and she writhed toward release, she found herself begging. "Please," she gasped, trying to raise her hips to meet his harder and faster. "Please, Nate . . ."

"Command me," he rasped, maintaining his infuriatingly slow rhythm.

"Harder," she gasped. Obligingly he drove into her harder, making her back arch off the bed. Angelique threw back her head and cupped her own breasts, her breath burning her throat. "Touch me," she said, her voice almost drowned by the squeak of the bed ropes. His fingers plunged into the slick, wet folds at the top of her thighs, circling and pressing on that brilliantly sensitive nub of flesh, and she almost expired; if she'd had any breath at all left in her body, she would have screamed.

"Do you cede to me?" Agonizingly, he slowed almost to a stop. Her eyes flew open and she cursed violently in French, that he could do this to her, bring her to this razor-sharp edge of pleasure and then *stop*— "Do you cede?" he demanded again.

Mutely, she nodded. Anything, to make him continue. His teeth flashed for a second in a primitive grin, then he pulled away. With a quick yank, he flipped her over onto her stomach, leaving her half on the bed, her bottom in the air and her toes touching the floor. He pressed first one foot, then the other, between her feet, sliding them apart. He splayed one hand across her lower back, and with the other guided himself back into her. With her hips angled down, he drove hard into her, seeming to rake across something raw inside her, behind her belly. At the same time he reached beneath her and stroked her hard, in time with his increasingly powerful strokes. She gave in at once; there was no denying his mastery of her body. She bowed her head and let the climax overtake her, rolling through her in waves that made her writhe and shake. Nate's fingers dug into her hips, holding her to him as she convulsed, and then he gave a low growling cry and pulsed within her.

Afterward it was the sound of the fire crackling that first penetrated the daze into which she'd fallen. It was a muted, comforting sound, reminding her of quiet days spent sewing by the hearth, with Melanie bringing her cups of lemon-mint tea. Which was a very odd thing to think of as she lay slumped over her bed with cool air drifting over her bare back and a confounding, infuriating, irresistible man between her legs, still inside her. In her right mind she would be disgusted with herself for letting things get this far out of hand with him; she hadn't wanted to let him affect her this way. It was dangerous, not just to their work but to her own peace. She couldn't afford to start daydreaming of any future beyond the next few days with him.

Unfortunately she was far from her right mind tonight. Nothing seemed more right than being where she was at this moment, and so she lay there letting her thoughts roam, while a silly smile curved her mouth.

Nate was glad she didn't move or say anything. That last climax had drained the life from him, it seemed; he had to blink to see straight when he finally opened his eyes. She was still and quiet beneath him, her hips gently curved under his palms, her slim waist rising to her rib cage, where he could just make out the swell of her breast as she lay sprawled facedown on the bed, her arms thrown wide to clutch at the covers. Her dark curls ran riot over her pale back and the side of her face. All he could see was her profile, serene and perfect, with a blissful smile on her lips.

He was doomed.

Nate had never been a romantic, sighing over a succession of ladies. Enough women liked him as he was that he saw no reason to change his ways, to court, to pursue. If any woman he'd dallied with ever expected more from him . . . he was sorry for her, because he never intended more. His mother had scolded him more than once about his ability to collect hearts without giving his own, and Nate had just laughed; he wasn't that sort, he told her. Tonight he realized it hadn't been him, it had been the women. None of them had ever drawn him the way Angelique did. None of them had ever fascinated him as she did, and none of them had ever been so hard to hold. He was quite sure that in the morning, she would try to be her normal cool, efficient self. There was a hard shell around her, and he wasn't such a fool to think that two nights together—even two nights of such scorching passion as they'd shared—would be enough to melt her resistance. That meant it would be up to him to convince her they were meant to be together, not just for however many days he had left in England but for the rest of their lives. Without her, he'd end up one of those sad old men, alone and unhappy, who whiled away his life at the local tavern. He would have to win her, by stealth, by charm, by force of the raw physical attraction that drew them to each other like magnets. Tomorrow he would think more of how to do it. Tonight he just wanted to fall asleep with her in his arms and not think at all.

He eased back, shuddering a little as he slipped from the tight grip of her body. She moaned and stretched, arching her back again, and his cock twitched instinctively in response. She really was a witch, if she could stir a response from him now, when his legs felt as though they'd been at sea a month and aftershocks of pleasure still crackled through his bones. He rolled his palm across the smooth globe of her bottom, feeling the firm muscle beneath her skin. She wasn't soft and round like other ladies; she was almost thin, at first glance, but that delicate-looking exterior hid a lithe, well-toned creature who was neither weak nor soft. He shook his head, amused at himself for even comparing her to other women.

He braced his hands on the mattress on either side of her and leaned down. "And now to bed," he murmured, blowing a gentle puff of air across her cheek. Her nose wrinkled, and he had to laugh at the innocent sweetness of it. He raised her to her feet, slipping his arm about her waist when she swayed. "Don't worry," he said in amusement as he reached out to flip back the covers on the bed. "I won't let you fall."

She turned in his grip, draping one arm over his shoulder. "How kind of you," she purred. Nate had barely a second to register alarm before she hooked her foot around his calf and jerked, shoving with that arm placed, not so lovingly after all, around his neck. He toppled onto the mattress, caught so off guard he couldn't even brace himself. Like a cat she was on him, her knee on his back and her hands beside his head. "I command tonight," she whispered against his ear. Then she laughed and sank down on top of him. "And I say we go to bed now," she finished in an easy, slumberous voice.

Against the cool sheets of her bed, with her warm weight covering his back, Nate grinned. Oh yes, he was doomed—and God save his wicked soul, he exulted in it.

Chapter 16

It was raining when she woke. The steady patter against the windows sounded almost like a command to stay in bed where it was cozy and warm. Although perhaps that was due more to Nate's presence in her bed than to the rain. He hadn't left last night, but still slept behind her, one arm draped over her waist. Without opening her eyes Angelique sighed in bliss and relaxed into him. Let the world go hang, for one morning at least.

The door creaked as Lisette opened it, coming in to stir the fire and lay out her clothes for the day. Normally Angelique would already be awake and dressed by now, ready to do her exercises. Today she should be especially awake and alert, planning their next step. They had a strong clue where to find Jacob Dixon, and it would be best to act on it as soon as possible. If she or Nate had slipped and left any sign that they'd read Dixon's letters, Hurst might hasten to warn the man, and Dixon could vanish again. If she had any sense at all, Angelique would roust Nate from her bed at once and tell him to be ready to leave for the Pulteney in half an hour.

Instead she lifted her head an inch and waved one hand in dismissal at her maid, who had stopped short. Not only was Nate still in her bed, their clothing was scattered all over the room. Lisette looked shocked, and no wonder; it looked rather like a whirlwind had gone through.

Lisette met her gaze, her expression dubious. "When shall I come back?" she whispered.

"When breakfast is ready," said Nate in a sleep-roughened voice. Angelique started at the sound. He'd woken without any movement or change in breathing.

Lisette drew herself up. "When shall I return, Madame?" she asked again, pointedly stressing the last word.

"When I ring," Angelique told her. Lisette's mouth pinched, but she turned and left without a word.

Nate rolled over and stretched his arms above his head. "Ring and tell her to bring breakfast."

"How romantic you are," she replied, sitting up and swinging her feet over the side of the bed. "It is time to get up."

"Not quite." He caught her around the waist and pulled her back beneath the blankets, then beneath him. "It's damned cold in this room," he said, kissing her after every few words. "Let me stir the fire first."

"I am used to rising in the cold," she said, even though her arms had gone around his neck and she lifted her face unabashedly for his kisses.

"So am I. But let me spoil you this morning." Without warning he threw back the blankets and jumped out of bed. Angelique just had time to register the rush of cold air before he tossed the blankets back over her. "Don't move," he said with a grin. "Keep the bed warm for me."

She laughed, and obediently snuggled into the sheets again. Nate strode across the room to the hearth, seemingly unbothered by the chill in the air even though he was completely bare. She watched as he knelt down to stir up the fire, coaxing a small flame from the embers, then building it into a merry blaze. By the time he returned to the bed, she could feel warmth streaming across the room. It would be nice to rise to a warm room.

"Where was I?" he muttered, sliding beneath the sheets again and tucking her against him. "Ahhhhh . . ."

"You do not seem overly chilled," she said. He was still as warm as the well-stocked fire behind her. Even his feet were warm. The cold hadn't done anything to dampen his morning erection, either, to judge from the hard length pressing against her belly.

"You warmed me so thoroughly last night, I'll be hot for days," he murmured.

"But still hungry."

"Bloody right," he growled, biting her earlobe lightly.

"Hmm," she said thoughtfully. "Then let me"— she shoved his shoulder and rolled on top of him, sitting up to straddle his hips—"satisfy you."

"Be gentle," he rasped as she took his member in her hands. She just raised an eyebrow as she ran the pad of her thumb down his length to his ballocks, and he bared his teeth in a grimace of pleasure. "Or not . . . I'll repay you tonight, though . . ."

But she had given up torturing him, just as she

had abandoned hope of keeping some part of herself removed from their affair. She told herself, as she sheathed him inside her body, that she could withstand this intimacy; it was only her body being pleasured, and she would be a liar to deny that Nate pleasured her exceedingly well, especially now as his clever fingers found their way between her legs, to where his body joined hers, and stroked with unerring skill while she rode him. There was no reason this lovemaking had to result in love, she thought, even as Nate's gaze grew fixed and fierce, and she knew he was fighting back his own release, waiting for her to find hers. The pleasure she found in his arms, in his bed, was a fleeting thing—but oh *God*, was it powerful. Her climax rolled through her in strong waves, leaving her spent and gasping as Nate seized her hips and then came with a shout of his own.

Yes, she thought weakly; she could withstand it. If she wanted to.

Nate opened his eyes and looked up at her with the dazed expression of a lost man, as if he had come as unmoored from his carefully built persona as she felt from hers. She had known he wanted her from the very first day they met, when he stared at her with such frank interest in the carriage outside Bow Street. She was used to that, and dismissed it as the same passing desire she'd seen in other men's faces. It had given her some callous comfort to think he only wanted her for an affair, that he would leave for America in a few days or weeks and never think of her again. It was the way men were, and she was well aware of it. She knew how to use that fever of desire for her own purposes, whatever they were, and then walk away when it was over. Her affections remained safely locked away at all times.

But in Nate's expression there was far more than just desire. With shaking hands he tugged her down to lie atop him, her head cradled against his shoulder. His lips touched hers in a gentle kiss. The longing in his kiss wasn't just to seduce her. Without warning that kiss slipped right under her guard and straight to her heart. Whatever she told herself about his intentions, Nate cared for her. In spite of everything he had seen and heard from her, he felt more than lust. For the first time in a very long time, Angelique felt wanted for *herself*.

In that light, maybe she couldn't withstand this after all.

Unnerved, she cast about for something to say. "Where did you get a scalping knife?"

"From a woman," he murmured.

Her eyes opened wide. Angelique fought off the unreasonable spike of jealousy. "What an odd gift to get from a woman," she said evenly. "I wonder what you did to deserve it."

His laugh was low and knowing. "Do you wonder? No doubt you also wonder what you did to merit such a gift from me."

She stiffened. "Let me test the blade to see if it is good enough for my purposes—"

He dragged her back when she started to slither away from him. "Calm yourself," he said in the same lazy tone as before. "No need to see if it's sharp enough. You've no need of it anyway."

She said nothing, but her rigid posture said volumes. Nate grinned. "A settler's family was kidnapped by the Indians and held captive during the last war. The man managed to ransom his wife and daughters, but the Indians kept the son. The man had known my father, years ago; he wrote asking for any help possible in retrieving his son before it was too late."

"They would kill a child?" she asked, her opinion of that practice clear.

"Likely not," Nate told her. "They would raise the boy as their own. The Wyandot were decimated, losing many of their young warriors to the wars and their women and children to raids. They needed men, and they often made captives part of their tribe. Once the boy was grown, he could be married to a Wyandot girl, with Wyandot children. Sometimes captives forget their old lives; they do not want to return to their parents.

"My father wanted to help. The man had once worked for my family, before he went west, and my father had seen what could happen to captives of the Indians during the wars. The next time a ship of ours went down the St. Lawrence, he sent me with it to see what could be done. Through some lucky chance, we located the boy—a monumental task in itself—and I bought him."

"Bought him?" she said sharply. "Like a slave?"

"Exactly like a slave," Nate confirmed. "He was a wild thing by then, but I got him home to Boston, and in time he was reunited with his parents. His mother, who had somehow kept the knife from her captivity, gave it to me in gratitude."

She was quiet for a moment. "You do not approve of slavery."

"No," said Nate flatly. "It's a vile and immoral practice."

"Your man Mr. Chesterfield said your father plucked him from a revolution in his country. He was a slave there, was he not?"

He looked at her in surprise. "Prince told you that? Well, you knew he was a slave. My father used to trade with a few planters on Saint-Domingue . . . not perhaps entirely legally, you understand . . . but he didn't realize he was sailing into a slaughter that time."

She gazed up at him, endearingly solemn. "Mr. Chesterfield said they were killing the slaves, and your father nailed him into a barrel."

Nate laughed. "I'd forgotten that part! I remember now. Prince popped out of that barrel as skinny as a stick and as black as coal. And as loud as a ship's bell; for an uneducated slave child, he knew an impressive amount of French and English, and all of it profane. My father weighed anchor at once and we didn't go back to Saint-Domingue for years. I'd never seen him drive the crew so hard as he did to get away from there, as if he felt the brimstone breath of the devil on his back."

"You said you were a sailor, last night," she said, a line forming between her brows. "You must have been a child when that occurred."

"My father was a sailor, and he took me to sea with him as soon as my mother allowed it. I was a twelve-year-old cabin boy when we snatched Prince."

"Snatched," she echoed.

Nate's mouth flattened. "They weren't selling those slaves. They were burying them alive." She frowned. "To quell the rebellion," he added. "There were some rebels fighting the French, natives and escaped slaves, mostly. The French commander wished to make a point."

"By burying them *alive*?"

"Prince's mother was one of them," he said quietly. "She all but threw her child at my father, screaming for help. Only by luck did she choose a white man who cared enough to do something."

"And she herself was buried alive." Angelique's face might have been carved from stone.

"As far as I know. It was hard enough to smuggle one small boy out; we couldn't stay to know what became of her. Just taking Prince could have gotten all of us thrown in jail or executed." He watched her curiously. Something about this story had touched her deeply, he could tell, but she gave no clue what. Slowly Nate went on. "We took Prince home with us. By the time we reached Boston Harbor, he was nearly fluent in English and had started drawing rough star charts on old pieces of sail. My father said he'd never seen such voracious intelligence in a child so young, and he deserved an education."

"Your parents raised him," she murmured. "He treats you as a brother."

Nate shrugged. "He practically is."

Her face softened, saddened. "How fortunate for him."

"He's earned his keep, I would say. Prince's passion is chemistry. He mixes gunpowder for us, and various other potions that have been invaluable. Some solution of his keeps moss from growing on the decks."

"And he makes ether."

"He's a scientist," Nate said with a grin. "He makes what he wants to make. But your maid can rest easy now; he's moved his laboratory back to the ship."

"Ah." Some reserve crept into her voice, and she avoided meeting his eyes. "We should get up—there are plans to be made. We must begin monitoring the Pulteney—"

"Let it wait." Nate didn't give a damn about Dixon right now. This was the most open he'd ever seen Angelique, and it was entrancing. He wanted to prolong it, to discover who she really was. "Now that I've told you all about my life, what of yours?"

"You have not told all about your life."

"What would you like to know?" he asked, stubbornly keeping his arms around her even as she began squirming to get up.

"Nothing," she snapped. "We have spent too much of the day lying in bed."

"Answer one question first," he parried. "What would you do if you weren't Stafford's agent?"

She stopped trying to wriggle out of his arms and looked up at him with surprise. "If I had never been, or when I am no longer?"

"When you no longer are." The other choice was impossible anyway.

"I don't know yet," she said softly. "I always thought I would go to Mellie, but now that does not seem wise, given what happened in Vauxhall."

"Who is Mellie?" he asked.

She smiled, her face luminous with affection. "Mellie was my mother's servant. My parents were killed in the Terror in France, and she carried me to England in her valise. She told the soldiers I was hers, the child of a French partisan. She raised me as if I were her own. I owe everything to Mellie; she is my only family. I only see her a few times a year, before I take new assignments from Stafford. If only I could visit her more . . ."

Abruptly Nate recalled a quiet graveyard, where she sat pensive and still, as if waiting . . . waiting for the rector's wife. The warmth of her smile hadn't been mere politeness but familiarity. She knew Mrs. Carswell, even loved her, unless Nate missed his guess very badly. "Mellie is Mrs. Carswell," he guessed aloud.

She paused, her eyebrows arching slightly, then shrugged. "Yes. You need not have followed me there."

"Doubtless not," Nate murmured. She went to the rectory before beginning new assignments, which meant she must have mentioned something to Mrs. Carswell. Most likely Mrs. Carswell had known, or suspected, who he was the moment he opened his mouth and spoke to her in his American accent. "Who lies in the grave you visited?"

"An Englishman and his wife," she answered, although he could see the spark of warning in her eyes.

"Ancestors?"

"Of someone, I am sure."

"But not yours." For some reason, he felt sorry for that.

"No."

"So you pretend to mourn them?"

"I cannot visit my own parents' grave," she said coldly. "I mourn them, and all the rest of my family, and at the end I say a little prayer for the Englishman and his wife, too. Does that satisfy you?"

"No," he said, staring at her thoughtfully. "Not nearly."

She sniffed. "Pity. It is more than you deserve to know."

"I meant," he said in a low voice, "that I want to know more. You are a riddle to me—one I find myself unable to resist."

His words acted as a killing dose on her prickly manner. The anger faded from her dark eyes, leaving them shadowed with something wistful and a little sad. "You do not want to know more," she replied at last, even more quietly. "Believe me, Nate. I keep my secrets for good reason."

Chapter 17

Nate spent the whole of that day regretting pushing her to talk about her family; it had chilled Angelique's mood ever since. She hadn't been cold to him, as she had been before, but the warmer, tender side she'd shown last night and early this morning had vanished. By the time he'd gone back to his room to wash and get dressed, she had directed her attention to finding Dixon, and nothing of their scorching night together, not to mention the more intimate morning, was mentioned. She was clear-eyed and focused, a professional spy operating at her most efficient. It was time to get down to work.

For the first time Nate felt his determination wavering. He still wanted to find Jacob Dixon, but more and more of his attention was wandering to Angelique. How had she become a spy? What was she really up to? And how could he draw out that sympathetic, tender creature who visited the maid who raised her and said a prayer for long-dead strangers? As fascinated as he was by the beautiful, dangerous temptress, that other woman could bring him to his knees. To tell the truth, she might have already done so.

But there was no way to bring that up. As she outlined plans for luring Dixon into the open where they could abduct him, other plans for sneaking into the hotel and spiriting Dixon away from his own room, and still other plans for waiting it out until Dixon chose to leave, Nate could barely keep up with her. No matter how hard he tried, part of his mind kept returning to her—how her skin glowed in the sunlight, and the way her eyes could sparkle at him even when she caught him not paying attention. It was the closest she came to evidence of affection, until they went to bed that night and she was once again his unrestrained lover, with no talk of plans or Dixon. Perhaps it was the dark, he thought, holding her as she slept. At night she was his, while in the day she remembered she was Stafford's. Or perhaps it was all a fancy of his, a waking dream he never wanted to end.

They went to the Pulteney the next day, when the rain had stopped. The Pulteney Hotel was in Piccadilly across from Green Park, where they could stroll unremarked as they studied the hotel. It was reputed to be one of the finest in London, famous for the czar of Russia's visit a few years past. To Nate's eyes it was a large, though rather unremarkable, mansion, although Angelique did point out the balcony where Czar Alexander had waved to the crowd some years before. He wondered if Dixon, who had an affinity for fine things and powerful people, had contrived to stand on that balcony.

"Tell me more about Mr. Dixon," Angelique said, as if she could hear his thoughts. "What sort of man is he?"

"He likes luxury," Nate replied, turning his gaze

away from the pillared hotel. "I suppose that's why he stole such an enormous sum. At first glance he is clever and capable, quiet mannered and unprepossessing. He appeared the perfect head clerk, in other words."

"And that is how he embezzled from your government?"

"Yes. The man who was appointed Collector of New York—responsible for collecting all the duties due at the biggest port in the country—lost an arm in the War for Independence. He needed a capable clerk, a secretary, to assist with the running of the port."

"The War for Independence," she repeated. "That was decades ago."

"Yes, he's an old man," Nate conceded. Ben Davies *was* old, nearly eighty years or so. That was no excuse for leaving so much of the port duties to Dixon, not to mention overlooking the absence of almost half a million dollars from the accounts, but General Davies was an honorable man. His fault was one of trusting too much, not one of duplicity or corruption. "He thought he was doing the right thing by hiring Dixon, and for years it seemed to be true. Jacob Dixon is an able administrator, a quick thinker, and adept with numbers."

"He will have secreted the money away, then."

"He's also a thief who must know he's not going to just walk away with a stolen fortune. He's clever enough to know he might have to flee at any time. I'll wager he's got most of the jewels close by, ready to be snatched up at a moment's notice. He'd be a fool to sell them all at once and call attention to himself; it's a truly impressive collection he bought."

"It must have taken him some time to commit such a fraud."

"At least five years," Nate admitted. The fault for that was also General Davies's. Ben had stopped even cursory examinations of the books after a few years of Dixon's demonstrated competence. "I didn't examine all the books, but it seems Dixon must have started siphoning off small amounts within the first few years of his employment."

She turned to him thoughtfully. "That was very lax on someone's part."

"It was."

Her perceptive eyes saw past his curt reply. "You are motivated by more than duty to your country, aren't you?"

Nate drew in a deep breath. "Dixon's theft ruined a good man—a man who risked his life, and lost his arm, for his country. Yes, he was responsible; but he was not complicit. He was horrified by his clerk's actions, and pledged his every possession to repaying the debt. It will never be enough, of course. If I can recover even part of the money, it will go some way toward restoring his peace of mind, and save him from living the rest of his days in disgraced poverty."

"You respect him."

"I do," he replied. "Even though he was lax in overseeing Dixon for years."

She was quiet for a moment. "It takes a great deal of respect to overlook that lapse."

"It didn't happen because he was lazy or indolent or incompetent. He's a soldier, not a businessman. I admit he wasn't well suited to the post, but it was what the president offered him, and he tried to do it well."

They crossed the street and turned into the park. Even if Jacob Dixon walked right out the door, there was nothing else they could do at the moment, and truthfully, Nate would rather walk in endless circuits of the park with her than sit and watch for Dixon. He knew they were living on stolen time already. The sooner he got Dixon and the money, the sooner he would have to leave; his first duty was to keep his vow to his country, to his president, to his parents, to Ben. It would take weeks to return to New York, and even if he got on the next ship to London that same day, it would be months before he could see Angelique again, without any unpleasant business dividing them. She said she was quitting Stafford's service after this, but that could change; Stafford might persuade her otherwise. And there was always the risk that someone like Viscount Barings would recognize her and retaliate for some long-ago action of hers. He was caught between promises he had made before he knew her, and the bone-deep determination to stay with her.

"How did Melanie escape France?" he asked, turning his thoughts to something more appealing.

"Smugglers," she said briefly.

"I thought it might be instructional," Nate said, thinking quickly. "One can never know too many tricks for avoiding trouble. It was quite a feat, slipping out during the Terror with a small child."

Her hand flinched on his arm. "I suppose it was." She was quiet a moment, then sighed. "My parents gave her a fortune in jewels to bribe her way out.

She must have told a great many lies as well. She has never said much about it, just the bare details."

"She must have been devoted to you."

She smiled. "Not to me. I was only an infant then. Melanie was devoted to my mother. She still is; she worries over me as a hen might over her chick, fretting that she will have betrayed my mother's memory if she lets something happen to me."

"That sounds like devotion to you, not just to your mother," Nate murmured.

"We had no one but each other. I cannot even remember my mother's face, and Melanie lived many years in fear that her flight would be punished by those still loyal to the Revolution. She saw Napoleon as a great savior, come to restore order to France."

"Does she know what you do?"

"Yes." Nate glanced at her, surprised. She looked back, her lips curved with faint amusement. "Does your mother know what you are doing now?"

"She does, as a matter of fact, and she approved." He grinned. "She insisted Prince come along, thinking we could help each other. I've no idea what she'll think when she hears what really happened."

Again her eyes flickered toward him, and he knew what she was thinking: What would he tell people about her?

Nate had no idea. Maybe nothing, for her own protection. But saying nothing of her would leave a large hole in his explanation for why he must return to London without even seeing Jacob Dixon stand trial, not to mention leave people under the impression he had found Dixon on his own. And that wasn't even the most important thing about Angelique he wanted to tell his mother. He thought his parents would be quite taken with her. "She'll not be surprised to hear a woman had to step in and help us both, of course," he added lightly.

"No woman is." But she smiled at him—her true smile, nothing false at all. Her eyes lit up and her nose crinkled just a little, and she looked so lively and happy he could almost forget the other sides of her. Of course, there was no side of her that didn't fascinate him. Even when he didn't understand her moods, they were all part of her, and he loved them all.

He loved *her*.

God help him, he was in love with her, a dangerous woman who spied for a living. Who probably had a dagger hidden somewhere on her body right now; he had noticed she preferred knives to pistols or other weapons. He was in love with a woman who could be cold and calculating, sensual and dominant, clever and practical, and then tender and thoughtful. He was mad—and as evidence, he wanted to shout for glee and throw his hat in the air.

That would be the wrong thing to do, naturally. He had already reflected on how he could win her, and now he realized of course it was her heart, not just her mind, he wanted aligned with his. Which meant he had no time at all to lose.

"Tell me more about what you will do once you're done with this work," he said. "You'll visit Melanie more."

"Yes." She smiled again. "I will. I shall take a small cottage somewhere quiet, where I can lie in bed all day if I wish. Read a great many books. Learn to play a violin. Perhaps I shall get a dog, and spend my days wandering about the countryside taking the air."

"Hmm. That sounds . . ." He glanced at her, his eyes dancing. "Dull."

"Do you not read, sir? How uncivilized Americans are." She was teasing him again.

"Oh, I read," he said. "And enjoy it greatly. But after this life? Reading will seem tame and sedate. Wandering the fields with your dog? All alone?"

"You sound as if it is a bad thing, to be alone."

"Not always," he said, choosing his words carefully. "But do you wish to be alone for the rest of your life?"

She tilted her head in reflection. "No. But I am used to it. My life has not admitted much in the way of society."

"Just Mellie."

"Mellie is my family."

Nate seized on the word. "Do you wish to have a family of your own, though? Wouldn't Mellie wish that for you?"

"Mellie would wish a great many things for me," she said. "To marry a Frenchman. To return home and reclaim my father's lands. To raise a pack of children for her to fuss over, since she had no children of her own. But Mellie also still wishes, after all these years, to see Marat's body unearthed from his grave and dragged through the streets before it is fed to rabid dogs. She is bound for disappointments."

"But what do *you* want?" he asked again. "Do you not wish to marry?"

She stopped walking and faced him with a slight smile. "No one has ever asked me."

"Perhaps no man ever thought you would say yes."

She paused, then inhaled a deep breath. "They would have been right," she said lightly.

Nate hesitated, too. Did that mean she still would say no to any proposal of marriage? Or just that she never would have married any man she met before? Some women, he knew, did not want to be married; to be married meant they belonged to their husbands, with no property of their own, always subject to another's decree. If any woman would chafe under being subordinated to a man, it would be Angelique Martand. And the truth was, if she were opposed to marriage, Nate would go without it. He wanted her, any way she would have him.

"Shall we walk on?" she said, and he realized he had hesitated too long. She was already strolling down the path again, and he hurried to keep up. What he wouldn't give to know what she was thinking. Her expression was serene, and she might have been any lady out for a walk. In her crisp, pale green dress she was lovelier than any other woman he'd ever seen; her hand was so dainty and light on his sleeve in her white kid glove. He cursed his hesitation. If he'd been just a moment quicker, he might have prolonged the conversation along the vein he was growing unbearably interested in, but now the moment had passed.

They came to the Mall and turned back toward the City. Angelique's parasol snagged a tree root and clattered to the ground. With a muffled sigh, she stooped to retrieve it before Nate could move, and they walked on as before.

Or rather, almost as before. Nate felt as if the wind had suddenly switched directions. She had been relaxed and easy a moment ago, and now she wasn't. He could feel the change in her, even though her hand never flinched on his arm, and when he glanced at her from the corner of his eye, her expression hadn't altered an iota.

"What did you see?" he asked on impulse.

She raised her eyebrows at him. "What do you mean?"

"You changed," he said evenly. "You saw something, or someone, who made you drop your parasol. Or else you dropped it on purpose to take a closer look at something that caught your attention."

She looked at him for a long moment, although not a flicker of surprise or alarm crossed her face. Finally she turned her head, looking forward again. "Ian is here."

It took him a moment to place the name. Unexpected dislike stirred in his belly. "Sent by Stafford, I suppose."

She smiled, and answered as lightly as if he had said it was a lovely day. "*Oui.*"

Nate didn't let himself look back. He had no idea what Ian looked like, after all. But he did remember her telling Stafford to send the man after Dixon originally, that first day in the Bow Street offices. She had implied Ian was rough and dangerous, not the sort of fellow to be sent on a mission of subtlety. At the time, Stafford had disagreed with her and refused to send Ian. So what did it mean that he was now here?

Stafford could be getting impatient with their

progress. He might have sent the man to spur things along, or to keep an eye on them. Nate felt the light pressure of Angelique's hand on his arm, and a whisper of alarm went through him. Somehow he doubted the English spymaster would be pleased by what was happening between the two of them. Could Ian have been sent to remind Angelique of her true loyalty?

"I don't suppose he could simply be enjoying the fine day, and we passed him by coincidence."

"I wouldn't think so, no; not from the way he winked at me."

The dislike in Nate's belly congealed into animosity and dread. "We'll be seeing him soon, then."

"Too soon," she agreed, very quietly.

That, more than anything, set off alarm bells in his head. "Why too soon?" he murmured, barely moving his lips.

She hesitated. "We have not found our man yet."

The alarm bells rang louder. That hadn't been her only reason. But he looked at her placid face, and suddenly didn't want to know. The very fact that Angelique was worried was unsettling enough. The added fact that she was lying to him about it terrified him.

It took all of Angelique's discipline to remain calm and composed during the walk home. Nate sensed her disquiet—she could hardly hide anything from him, it seemed—and lapsed into silence as they walked. That was disquieting, too, but at least it gave her a moment to address her own rioting thoughts. Like a fool, she had let herself ignore the looming conflict between her intentions and Nate's for too long, and now she must confront it quickly.

Ian was here. That meant Stafford was here, effectively. Normally it would be just an irritant, smoothed over by sending a report to Bow Street and getting on with the work. But in this instance, it unnerved her. They had hardly been dragging their feet; that first meeting in Stafford's office was barely a fortnight ago. What was his haste? There was still nothing to report, or she would have done so.

Of course, something *had* happened. She told herself it was none of Stafford's concern whom she went to bed with. She told herself it hadn't interfered in their work in any way. She told herself their affair was too new, too discreet to have come to Stafford's notice . . . yet. Lisette, and perhaps Mr. Chesterfield, were the only souls who knew, and Lisette in particular would sooner cut out her own tongue than tell Stafford. Angelique was quite sure her employer wouldn't care much even if he did know, because hadn't he himself told her to seduce Nate if that's what it took to keep him quiescent? Stafford didn't need to know there were any other reasons involved, certainly not any that might signal her allegiance was wavering.

More and more she regretted taking this job, even as she came to crave being with Nate. If she had simply refused to appear when Stafford's note first came, she wouldn't be caught in this dilemma between following her orders and betraying a man she was coming to care for a great deal. Nate still thought he would be carrying Dixon back to New York; Stafford still thought Angelique was going to prevent that by slicing Dixon's throat. But nothing had happened to reassure her that killing him was the right thing to do, and everything Nate did made her want to see him succeed, even though his success would still mean he left. At least if he left with his goal accomplished, she could say good-bye knowing she hadn't lied to him and stolen the prize he sought.

She glanced at his profile from beneath her eyelashes. His clear, level gaze was fixed forward, taking in everything around them. No doubt part of him was watching for Dixon, never realizing that the greatest threat to completing his mission was Angelique herself. She looked away before he could catch her staring, and blinked back an unexpected rush of feeling. She didn't know how she would untangle this knot, but she couldn't pity herself for facing it, just as she couldn't truly regret accepting Stafford's assignment. If she hadn't, she would have never known Nate, and that would have been the greatest loss of all. He was worth whatever struggle she had to face.

After he first made love to her, she'd said he almost killed her, but that was wrong; he wasn't killing *her*, just the hard, cold part of herself that protected the rest of her. Every kiss, every tender gesture, every bit of rapture he wrung from her body with his wicked, talented hands chipped away a little more of that protection. Everything she did to cling to that shell, he managed to undo. And instead of being furious that he was making her feel things she most emphatically did not want to feel—for him, of all people—she felt rather like a girl, silly in love but so happy she didn't mind being silly. Angelique, who was never silly, was baffled to find she liked being silly with him.

That would all come to a crashing halt when she put her knife into Jacob Dixon, though. Nate would be shocked and furious at her betrayal, and she would have no reasonable explanation to give him. Damn Stafford. If he'd explained himself—to her or to Nate—at least she could be honest about her true intent. The secret was festering inside her like a parasite; she could almost feel it eating at her.

Perhaps she wouldn't do it. John Stafford wasn't standing behind her, compelling her to act. Angelique thought about that for a while. She didn't think Dixon deserved to die. All she had heard about him had been from Nate, and she still thought fraud and embezzlement deserved what Nate planned: a lengthy stay in prison. All she had to do was . . . nothing. Continue as before, until they could spirit Dixon away, then let Nate sail away with him as planned.

But that would leave her behind to face John Stafford. This job was very important to him. Not only had he pressed her to take it in the first place, now he had sent Ian to see why she hadn't completed it yet. Perhaps she should go resign immediately, tell him she had had no luck finding Dixon and quit on the spot. She discarded that idea at once, as it would leave Nate to deal with an angry spymaster, and no Dixon to show for it. Above all, she didn't want to bring trouble on Nate. He might think Stafford was just a clerk, assigning spies to carry out orders from above, but she knew better. John Stafford was a dangerous man, especially when crossed.

The last option, she supposed, was to tell Nate

what Stafford had ordered. It would be the fairest thing to Nate, and it would ease her growing discomfort over keeping it from him. But it would expose her for what she really was—a hired killer—and she couldn't bear to see the look on his face when he realized it. He would recoil from her in disgust, sorry he had ever flirted and teased and laughed his way into her heart and her bed. He would know in a few days, most likely, when they finally got Dixon. She was a coward and a thief, keeping that ugly secret, but she was also too selfish to stop. Let her enjoy these last few days of happiness. They might well be all she had left.

Chapter 18

When they reached the house in Varden Street, Angelique silently hung up her bonnet and pelisse and started up the stairs. Ian would arrive soon, if he weren't already down in the kitchen trying to wheedle some ale and a piece of kidney pie from Lisette. Perhaps Ian would know something, or have some further instruction from Stafford. If the fates were kind, Ian would have come to tell her that Stafford no longer wanted Dixon dead, that she was free to help Nate fully in every way. But fate had never been that kind to Angelique, and it was more a wish than a hope.

Nate followed her upstairs. "Shall I have Lisette set out some luncheon?" she asked when they had reached the landing outside the bedchambers.

He was staring at her door with a slight frown. "No," he murmured absently. "Not yet. Are you tired?"

She nodded. "A little. Perhaps I shall lie down."

He opened his mouth, then closed it and gave a nod. Without a word he turned and went into his room, closing the door.

Already she felt bereft when he left, and she was merely standing in the hall alone. How much worse would it be when she knew he was gone, not just on the other side of a door but on the other side of an ocean? She sighed and went into her room. The afternoon sunlight slanted through the windows, drawing two dazzlingly bright squares on the polished floor and leaving the rest of the room in shadow. It was warm in the room, and she went to open the window.

She heard the barest whisper of sound before the man spoke. "Nice to see you again, lass."

Angelique smiled and shook her head. Thank goodness he'd given himself away. Ian would never let her hear the end of it if he'd managed to catch her off guard. "Must you persist in trying to sneak up on me, Ian? It is not necessary."

Ian grinned. He was leaning against the wardrobe, cloaked in shadows. "No, but it's fun."

"The words of a man whose life is a drudgery." She paused, pulling off her gloves and laying them in a drawer of her dressing table. "Why are you here?"

He came to stand beside her. The Indian knife Nate had given her lay on the dressing table. Ian picked it up and drew it, a thin frown knitting his brows. "You know why. The usual reason."

"Explain it to us all," said a quiet voice. Angelique started. It seemed to have come from nowhere. She hadn't heard the door, or a footstep, or seen a flutter of movement in the mirror she faced. Ian froze; the knife sheath fell from his hand, but not the knife.

"Easy, mate," said Ian quietly. His fingers curled tightly about the knife hilt.

"Stop," said Angelique at the same moment. "He is my friend."

"Then he should put down the knife he just drew."

Ian darted her a shocked glance, but she reached out and took the knife from him. "Nate, you have heard me speak of Ian Wallace. Ian, this is Nathaniel Avery." She gestured behind him.

With a little jerk forward Ian turned. Nate lowered the small, pointed dirk he had held to the back of Ian's neck. Neither man smiled. "A pleasure to meet you at last," Nate said after a moment.

"Aye," growled Ian. His face was flushed dark red. He looked enormous, towering over Nate by a good eight inches, all brawny muscle and Scottish temper. And yet Nate had stolen up behind him so quietly that neither one of them had heard him. Angelique had heard Ian shifting his weight before he spoke. She would have to ask how Nate had managed that . . . some other time.

"It is a Wyandot knife," she said, holding up the blade for Ian's inspection. "They are a native people in America, very fierce fighters. Nate gave it to me as a gift."

"Hmmph," said Ian, still eyeing Nate with dislike. "An odd gift to give."

"And unique. I have never seen the like in England." She slid the knife back into the sheath and put it down. "I presume you have not come to take tea and discuss exotic gifts, Ian."

"The usual way to call for that purpose is to knock at the door," said Nate calmly.

Ian swelled in indignation. "How do you know I didn't?"

"He knocked; Lisette would never feed him if he

did not." Angelique glared at Ian. "I told you it was foolish to attempt to sneak up on me, and pointless as well. I heard you shuffling your feet."

"Not much, I should think," he muttered.

She sighed. Stealth was not Ian's strength; strength was. Still, he worked at it. "Not much," she agreed diplomatically.

"It sounded like a herd of cattle," said Nate. "I heard you while walking up the stairs."

"You did not," Ian retorted.

Nate shrugged. "Just because I didn't run into the room and cry, 'I heard you'? Try it without the boots next time."

Automatically Angelique and Ian both looked down. Ian wore boots, while Nate stood in stocking feet.

"I'll keep it in mind." Still glowering, Ian dropped into a chair. "No need to stick a man in the back of the neck, though."

"I didn't, until you pulled out the knife." Nate glanced at Angelique. "I didn't know if he had your affection for blades."

"No, Ian prefers to hit people with his fists." Again Nate had been looking out for her, trying to protect her. That little blaze of happiness flared inside her chest again. She kept it buried behind a serene face; her instinct was to keep that feeling hidden, even though the glow of it warmed her still. "But he has not come to hit anyone today," she said, turning to Ian.

"Of course not. I've only come to have a chat."

The ember of warmth went out. "He grows restless already?"

"Curious," Ian replied in the same careless tone,

a tone that didn't match the close way he watched Nate. "He bade me inquire after your progress and see if you need any assistance." Ian smiled broadly. "Which I would be pleased to offer."

"Curious, perhaps, but impatient." Angelique pressed her lips together in pique. "What sort of assistance do you propose to provide? We have done all the work so far, taking care to be unnoticed, and now you will kidnap our man off the street?"

Ian leaned back and draped one arm over the back of the chair. It was the same chair where she and Nate had made love just a few nights ago, and Angelique had to school her expression very strictly as Ian pushed it back onto two legs, just as Nate had done when she— "I am at your command, Angelique, ready to offer any assistance you desire." He flashed a wide grin at her, and winked.

A thin smile crossed Nate's face. He still just stood in silence, arms crossed and feet apart, watching Ian. At least he had put away the dirk. He glanced at her, mischief simmering in his eyes, and she had to look away to keep from blushing. *At her command* . . . Ian could have chosen any words but those . . .

"Thank you, Ian, I do not think that will be necessary," she said. "We are making good progress, and expect to have our man soon. You may tell Stafford I will report to him when there is anything of interest to report."

"I could wait about for a few days," he replied, not moving from his seat. "Another pair of hands to ensure everything is completed."

She felt a chill. *Everything* meant killing Dixon. "Oh?" she said, hiding her sudden turmoil. "Are there additional instructions?"

Ian shrugged. "Not that I know of. I expect he told you all he wanted you to do. Old Staff's pretty thorough, once he decides to undertake something."

Yes, indeed he was. Ian's appearance was not a simple visit to see how she progressed, but a warning. Stafford was reminding her of what he had told her to do. "Then he has told you what he told me," she said, carefully probing. If Ian knew and had been instructed to see that she carried it out, she would have a serious dilemma facing her, even more serious than it was now.

"No," Ian said cheerfully. "He just asked me to remind you of his instructions and your duty."

She flinched, just the tiniest bit, but she feared Nate saw it. "I remember," she told Ian coolly. "You may go back and tell him so."

Ian's gaze darted to Nate. "Am I not welcome to stay to dinner?"

"Of course," said Nate at the same moment Angelique said, "No." Nate glanced at her, then inclined his head. "Perhaps I should leave you to discuss that privately," he said. He turned and walked out of the room, closing the door behind him.

"I see Staff's fears were justified," said Ian after a moment.

"What fears?" she snapped. "What did he tell you about this mess, Ian?"

Startled, he threw up his hands at her aggressive tone. "Easy! He told me almost nothing, except that he wished he'd been able to prevent the American from coming along. I guess he thought the chap would slow you down—although not, perhaps, in quite this way."

"He has not slowed me down," Angelique said.

"What do you mean by 'quite this way'?"

"An exotic knife as gift? Ready to kill a man in your bedroom?" Ian shook his head. "That's a man guarding what he views as his. Has he tried to get in your bed yet?"

The blood rushed from her head and she felt light-headed with outrage. "You forget yourself, Ian," she said tightly. "What do you suggest?"

He looked puzzled as he searched her face. "That he wants you—not that he'd be the first, of course. What's afoot here?"

He didn't know; it wasn't written on her face, or apparent from the way she and Nate looked at each other. Angelique sighed and pressed her fingers to her temple, where a dull ache was taking hold. "We have been looking for this man Dixon," she murmured. "I do not like it, though."

"Let me persuade Avery to let you handle the rest alone," said Ian, rising to his feet. He laid one hand on her shoulder. "Or better yet, with my help. Are you well?"

Better than she'd ever been in her life, in some ways. And at the same time, terribly, terribly unwell in other ways. "He will not go. He is determined to see this through, for personal as well as patriotic reasons."

"I can be awfully persuasive when I set my mind to it."

"No," she said sharply. "Just . . . leave him be, Ian. He is not the source of my unease."

It was quiet for a moment. "What is, then?" he asked.

She heard the wariness in his tone, and gave a

hopeless laugh. "Nothing I can tell you. I need to think."

"You can always confide in me."

Could she? She didn't know anymore. Ian said Stafford hadn't told him much about what she was to do, but if Stafford really feared she wasn't up to the task, he might have instructed Ian to keep silent about it. She thought of Ian as a friend, but he was in Stafford's pay as well, and she would be an idiot to trust his affection for her over whatever loyalty he had to his employer. Everyone who worked for Stafford had his own reasons, and she didn't know what Ian's were. Angelique smiled bleakly and rubbed her temple again. Now she couldn't trust anyone, it seemed—except Nate. And she was lying to him already.

"Thank you," she said, shaking off her thoughts. "I will keep it in mind."

He nodded. "Do. And keep your eye on that American. He doesn't look like the trusting type."

When Nate closed the connecting door between his bedroom and Angelique's, all was quiet for a moment. Then the murmur of voices started again, just as he had heard before slipping into her room to see who had been lying in wait for her. As then, he stood very still for a moment. If he stepped right up to the door, he could probably hear every word they were saying . . .

With a disgusted huff he tossed his dirk onto the bureau, then went to the bed and sat down to pull his boots back on. He wasn't going to eavesdrop on her conversation, even if he didn't trust that Scot one bit. Ian Wallace turned out to be a giant of a man, with flaming red hair and arms like a butcher's. No wonder Stafford hadn't wanted to send Ian on this case; Dixon would have taken one look and run for his life. But Ian was here now, and Nate didn't know what to make of that.

He left his room and went downstairs, no longer bothering to move silently. In the hall below he encountered Lisette. The older woman had made no secret of her loyalty and service to Angelique alone, which Nate respected. Normally he let her go about her way with a polite nod, but today he stopped her. "Mr. Wallace is here, up in Madame's room," he told her.

She sniffed. "I know."

"Er . . . right." He paused. "Is he a trustworthy fellow?"

Her eyes narrowed. "Madame trusts him."

"Do you think she should?" he pressed.

Lisette could hide her thoughts almost as well as her mistress could. "It's not my place to say, Monsieur."

Nate sighed. "Of course not. I hope Mr. Stafford hasn't sent him to cause trouble."

"That is his specialty," Lisette said under her breath. "Do not worry. Madame is capable of dealing with a great deal of trouble."

He knew that. It was why he'd let her walk into her room alone; he greatly respected Angelique's capabilities. Of course, when Ian drew her knife as if he meant to use it, Nate felt it was better to be safe than sorry. He was vastly relieved to see that Ian was truly her friend, and not just another agent come to do Stafford's still-unknown bidding.

The trouble was, he could see that Ian's visit unsettled her. He couldn't forget what she had said the other day, that she kept secrets for good reason. Why would Ian's visit make her uneasy, since the man himself clearly did not? She had wanted to know what Stafford told him, and if there were additional instructions. Ian had been so focused on watching Nate he might have missed her response to his replies, but Nate saw. Angelique was troubled by something, and she wasn't telling him about it. He devoutly hoped it was because she saw it as not worth telling him, and not something she feared telling him.

"I know," Nate belatedly replied to Lisette's assurance. "But she shouldn't have to do it alone."

Angelique sent Ian off after persuading him to tell Stafford she had everything in hand. She wasn't sure he believed her, from the narrow-eyed look he gave her, but he didn't protest. Lisette fed him and poured him two large mugs of ale, which salved a good deal of his ruffled temper. He had taken his time eating, but now Angelique was almost shoving him out the door.

"How long do you need me to put him off?" he asked, tugging his cap back on his head.

"A week at least," she said. "We are at a crucial moment, and I would prefer not to be distracted by his impatience."

Ian laughed. "Right. Wouldn't we all? Well, best of luck to you, my dear." He kissed her cheek. "And mind what I said," he murmured near her ear.

"Off with you."

He left, closing the kitchen door behind him. For

a moment she stood by the door, thinking. Lisette was cleaning the dishes at the sink. "Lisette," Angelique said. "Has Mr. Avery gone out?"

"*Oui*, Madame."

She nodded, and came to stand next to her maid. "What do you think of him?"

Lisette's brow dipped as she thought. "He is no fool. He is a gentleman, as far as I can see, although loud and much too merry much of the time. He and that man of his are both tidy as well. They left the attics as neat as a pin, even blacked the grate. I admire that in a man, Madame."

She smiled. "Who does not?" Then she sighed. "But can I trust him?"

Lisette placed her hands on her hips and looked at her. Angelique noticed her maid's hands were red and cracked from the hot water, and she felt a pang for dragging Lisette into this life with her. A normal lady's maid didn't scrub and wash and worry about blacking the grates. "Monsieur Avery cares for you, Madame," said Lisette quietly. "I have seen the way he looks at you, like a man who has just found a priceless jewel where he expected to see paste. He worries for you, and he does not trust Monsieur Stafford."

"He told you that?" Angelique was surprised, almost as surprised as she was to hear Lisette speak Stafford's name.

Lisette nodded. "*Oui*. He worried about Mr. Wallace today, and if he is trustworthy. I do not think he fears Monsieur Wallace for himself."

"No, he does not." Not at all, to guess from the way he'd put a dirk to Ian's neck.

"And if you'll forgive me, Madame," Lisette went

on, "I think he's delayed on finding this man you seek because he wishes to be with you." Angelique frowned at her, and Lisette shrugged. "Lying in bed all day? Walking in the park and returning home without doing anything else? I asked Monsieur Chesterfield how long they expected to be in London; a week, he told me, and that was a fortnight ago. And I notice you do not press him to act. I am not judging, Madame, only remarking. If you are happy with him . . . I am happy for you."

She closed her eyes for a moment. It fed that ember of hope and happiness in her heart to hear that Lisette had noticed. "Lisette," she asked, "when I retire from this, what will you do?"

Lisette's dark eyes brightened. "Ah, we are to be done with this? No more will you wait on the devil?"

She had to smile. "Yes. I am done with this work, after this. But I do not know what I will do next. You might think for yourself what you will do."

The maid drew herself up in affront. "I won't abandon you, Madame."

"Not abandon. Perhaps you wish to retire also. I will provide you an annuity."

Lisette sniffed. "Perhaps not. But I will think, Madame, since you wish it."

"Do." Angelique turned to go. "I think the time to decide will be upon us very soon."

The change Nate had sensed in Angelique, beginning with Ian's arrival, lingered through that evening and night. The question he had wanted to answer all along was looming ever larger in Nate's mind: What the devil had Stafford told her to do?

Find Dixon, was all she had ever told him, but there was no need for that to make her anxious, especially not now, when they were closer than ever. If Stafford was just driving her to find the man, she should be at ease and confident. Instead she was tense and short-tempered, and Nate caught her staring at the fire after dinner with an expression of such ferocious concentration he couldn't take it any longer.

"Why are you upset about Wallace's visit?" he finally asked.

She started out of her reverie and blinked at him. "Ian? I am not upset at Ian."

"Not *at* Ian," he said carefully, seeing how she had picked a way through his words. "At his visit. At Stafford, perhaps, for sending him."

She closed her eyes for a moment. "There was no need for him to send Ian. We have been working diligently, and he is still impatient. It irks me to be poked and prodded to work faster, faster, faster."

Of course it would . . . "But that's not the whole problem, is it?" he tried again. "That alone would be irritating, but . . . I think there is something else." She just stared at him, the flickering flames atop the candles reflected in her dark eyes. "I hope you can trust me by now," he added with a crooked grin.

That was the wrong thing to say, though; she jumped up from the table and paced away, gripping her hands before her. Nate followed, feeling as though she'd stabbed him. "What's the matter?" he demanded.

She twisted out of his reach. "It is nothing," she snapped. "Only that I wish I had not agreed to do this. If only it were ended already . . ." She closed her eyes and drew herself up stiffly. "We should make every effort to capture Mr. Dixon tomorrow, or the day after. Stafford has grown restive, and if he is not soon satisfied, he will send others in who will not care for your goals at all."

"What, then?" All Nate's instincts were screaming in alarm. "What goal does Stafford have besides finding Dixon, Angelique? What does he want you to do?"

The color fled her face, and for a moment he thought she might faint. He reached for her and this time she let him pull her into his arms. "What is wrong?" he asked again, desperately. What could Stafford want? Did Dixon have some other secrets the Crown wanted to discover? Were they not planning to allow him to take Dixon back to New York as planned? Were they planning to keep him from returning to New York at all? "Whatever it is, tell me. I swear on my honor I won't be unreasonable."

She tipped back her head to look up at him. Her beautiful face was somber. "When this is over, and you have gone back to New York, how will you remember me?"

As the woman I love. As the woman I would cross an ocean to find. As the woman I cannot live without. But not as a woman who trusted him completely. "As the most exceptional woman I have ever been fortunate enough to know." She laid her cheek against his shoulder, and Nate held her to him. "Why?"

"I merely wondered." Her shoulders rose and fell in a silent sigh that spoke more eloquently than any words of the weight bearing down on her— whatever that weight was.

He wondered what terrible thing Stafford had told her to do. Kill him? Kill Dixon? Help him find Dixon, and then steal the money for the British Crown? He was tired of worrying over it, tired of trying to get her to tell him. Suddenly he, too, wanted this over. Let Stafford's secret plan proceed, at least so it would be out in the open and not chipping away at the bond between them. "I agree," he murmured, still stroking her back. "We should take Dixon as soon as we can manage it." He pressed her away from him, so he could see her face. "But promise me one thing: when this is over, there will be no more games and secrets between us. Ever."

She smiled, but it was a sad thing. "I promise."

He nodded once, and pulled her close again, hoping he had asked for the right promise.

Chapter 19

They elected a bold strike instead of stealth. The next afternoon Nate and Angelique strolled right into the Pulteney Hotel and asked to see Mr. Chartley. There was some delay as the porter went up to see if Mr. Chartley would receive them, and then again after he came back down to ask who they were and why they wished to see him. Angelique just waved her fan, acting the bored society lady again, while Nate pressed a ten-pound note and one of his cards into the porter's hand. "Tell him Davis Hurst sent us," he said with arrogant condescension.

The porter hurried away, and came back almost a quarter of an hour later to say Mr. Chartley would see them in one of the private parlors beyond the dining room. He led them there, then vanished with an assurance they would not be disturbed, another ten-pound note from Nate in his pocket.

"I don't think he's much interested," said Angelique listlessly. "We've waited an eternity."

"He's interested, my love." Nate also kept up his pose. He dropped into a chair and crossed his legs. "Mr. Hurst assured us he would be."

"Well. I hope you are right." She lowered her head and examined her fan.

The door opened, and Nate had to force himself not to whirl about at once. Deliberately he got to his feet and turned, almost holding his breath. If any of their information had been wrong . . .

It was not. Jacob Dixon was a perfectly ordinary-looking man of medium height and build. His brown hair was combed back from his face, and he moved with confidence and ease. He had grown a small beard, but otherwise was exactly as Nate remembered him. Only his eyes betrayed any kind of anxiety, flitting back and forth as he walked, never lingering but always surveying. No doubt he wished he could see behind him as well.

"I am Mr. Chartley," he said. "You wished to see me?" He hadn't quite gotten the last trace of servility out of his manner.

"Avery, Nathaniel Avery," Nate said, sweeping one hand toward Angelique. "My wife, Mrs. Avery. A great pleasure to meet you, sir."

Dixon had frozen in place at Nate's voice. "You are Americans?" he asked, his eyes sweeping from one to the other and back again.

Nate laughed. "Everyone can tell! Right you are— from Boston. Although my lovely wife is originally from Paris, of course."

"*Bonjour*," said Angelique, her voice a throaty purr heavily tinged with French, when Dixon looked at her. "How delightful to make your acquaintance, Monsieur Chartley." She dipped a curtsey, and finally Dixon's eyes settled in one place, right on her bosom. The gown she wore didn't look immodest, but when she curtsied, her breasts swelled up almost out of the neckline. Nate couldn't resist looking for a moment, too, before forcing his attention back to Dixon.

"Yes," said Dixon, still distracted by her bosom. "Er . . . Hurst sent you, did he?"

"Not willingly." Nate grinned proudly. "We met Mr. Hurst through the aid of Mr. Smythe, of Sewell and Smythe, jewelers in Bond Street. There was mention of a fine diamond parure you might consider parting with, for a decent price."

"Yes," said Dixon again. "I confess myself surprised. Mr. Hurst assured me of his discretion—"

"So he did!" Nate winked. "But when promised his usual commission, and upon my insistence on meeting the owner of such a set, he gave in."

"I see." Dixon's eyes had resumed their survey of the room, passing often over Angelique's bosom. "But you must understand, I asked Mr. Hurst to handle all the details himself, so I would not be inconvenienced . . ."

"But I insisted on seeing the diamonds before purchasing them. I'll not have paste around my wife's neck."

That caught the other man's attention. He drew himself up in affront. "It isn't paste—on the contrary, sir. In fact, given its size and quality, I shan't part with the set except on exceptional terms."

"But you do wish to sell it?" Nate gestured at Angelique. "Fetch some wine, my love." There was a decanter on the table near the door. With a flicker of her lashes she went, passing right by Dixon so that her skirts swished across the back of his legs. Dixon watched her from the corner of his eye. Nate could have laughed at how easy this was going to be. His heart thumped hard in anticipation. "Hurst said you might have some other jewels as well. I can't help but pamper my wife—is she not a lovely creature? A woman like that deserves diamonds and rubies, don't you agree?"

"Er . . . yes." Dixon had been watching Angelique pour the wine, but now he focused on Nate, a glint of greed in his eyes. "Rubies, you say?"

"Indeed, although she looks ravishing in blue as well." Nate chuckled, watching Angelique. She had poured a glass, and was tugging at her sleeve. "Have you any sapphires?"

"A few," said Dixon, and then he choked and gasped. Angelique had thrown her black rope around his neck and twisted. Had she been alone, Dixon might have gotten away from her, flailing about as he did, but Nate had leaped on him at the same moment. Angelique whisked out of the way, and the two men rolled to the floor. Dixon fought desperately, but Nate had the element of surprise on his side. He held off his opponent's wild punches with one hand and pressed the other hand over Dixon's nose and mouth until the man went limp.

For a moment Nate stayed where he was. His blood coursed hot and fast through his veins, making him want to roar in triumph. Instead he staggered to his feet, regarding his unconscious victim with relish. Then he turned to Angelique, who was coiling her rope.

"We got him!" he said in a fierce whisper. "We've got him, my darling!" She laughed, and he grabbed her to press a hard kiss of exultation on her mouth.

"There is no doubt he is your man, I take it."

Nate smiled grimly. "None at all! He looks just as I remember, and I would never forget that voice. Now let's get him out of here."

She was already nodding. She took out a flask from her reticule and dribbled gin all over Dixon's face and chest, until he reeked of it. They hoisted Dixon to his feet, and Nate draped the man's arm around his own shoulders. Angelique checked the corridor outside the room, and when it was clear they walked quickly out through the side door, where deliveries were made. At the end of the alley stood the hackney they had hired.

"Here, need a hand?" exclaimed the startled driver as they bundled Dixon inside.

"Thank you, good man. My brother, poor soul," Nate said sadly. "Much the worse for drink even at this hour; my mother bade me save him from his ruinous habits, but . . ." He shook his head. "We'll try to save him yet."

"'Tis hard when the drink gets you," agreed the driver. Nate clapped one hand on his shoulder and gave him the direction before swinging into the cab himself.

Inside, his eyes met Angelique's across Dixon's slumped figure. "Thank you," he said simply.

And she smiled, that real smile of honest feeling. "It was my pleasure."

In Varden Street, the driver helped them get Dixon up the steps. Angelique thanked him before closing the door. Nate hauled Jacob Dixon up the stairs into the attic room where Prince had recently had his laboratory. They had removed everything from it in preparation, and now Nate dragged his limp burden to the hearth. He ran a chain through a ring fixed in the brick there, then through the manacles he placed around Dixon's wrists, and padlocked it. Then he took off his coat and sat down to wait for Dixon to wake.

Dixon had begun stirring a few times during the drive, and Nate had put his hand back over his face each time, keeping him unconscious. But within a few minutes of being locked up, he started coming around. Nate fetched a glass of water and tossed it in his face. Dixon jerked and scrambled away, swiping at his face. The chains brought him up short, and he went still. As he blinked awake, his eyes darted about the room and finally settled on Nate.

"How dare you," he began shrilly. "This— You— You have no authority to hold me like this. I am an English citizen! This is illegal imprisonment."

"I have a good enough authority," Nate told him. "That iron chain around your wrists, for one. Be glad it's only imprisonment—for now."

Dixon shook himself like a wet bird. "I know who you are! You're one of those bloody Americans."

"Of course I am. No secret there. But unless you're even more worthless than I thought, not every American is out to get you, Dixon." He leaned forward to hang the lantern on a nail above Dixon's head. "So, make a guess why exactly I've got you here."

Dixon managed to look highly affronted, even though he had flinched at the sound of his true name. "Thievery, no doubt! You and your wife intend to steal my jewel collection. I knew there was something wrong about you both, the instant I saw you. You're no better than common ruffians!"

Nate gave him a dark smile. "You weren't alarmed enough to keep away from the chance to turn a pretty profit—or from peering down my wife's gown."

"Why should I ignore a fine pair of titties when I see them?" Dixon wrestled with the chain again. "Tell me what you want, you brigand."

"All," said Nate softly.

Dixon's eyes darted from side to side, but when he looked up, his face wore an impatient scowl. "All of what?"

"All the money you embezzled from the Port of New York," said Nate, savoring every trace of guilt that flashed over the other man's face. He'd waited weeks for this moment. He leaned back in the chair, folding his arms across his chest. "You played a nasty trick on some people. You stole a great deal of money, Mr. Dixon. That is a sin, and a crime."

"How dare you say that?" Dixon tilted his chin defiantly. "Slander is also a crime."

"True enough, but slander is only slander if one tells lies. The law defends the truth."

"Truth," sniffed Dixon. "The law demands proof."

"I have all that," Nate assured him. "Or rather, the prosecutor in New York has it."

"You can't take me to New York," cried Dixon, but his color faded. "I am an Englishman!"

"The English don't mind letting you go. Did you think I was fool enough to waltz into a foreign country and track you down without permission?" He would have done it, if necessary, but as it happened, he hadn't. Nate was feeling much better about that decision now that he had his quarry bagged and trussed like a hog bound for market. "The Foreign Office as well as the Home Office knows what I'm about; Lord Selwyn himself sent me to the . . . er . . . ruffians you were railing against. You've no friends here, Dixon."

"Selwyn?" Suddenly Dixon's outraged tantrum ended. His eyes grew round and his mouth sagged open in surprise. "Ross Selwyn?"

"That's the one."

Dixon was quiet for several minutes. Nate could almost hear him thinking, and from the tense expression on his face, it was a stark reevaluation of his situation. "How did you come across him?" he asked, trying too obviously to keep any trace of tension from his voice.

"He's deputy to the colonial secretary. An old friend of yours?" Nate asked with a smirk. Selwyn hadn't shown any hesitation in unleashing Stafford and his agents on Dixon, beyond a desire to keep this distasteful affair quiet.

"Rather the opposite, I imagine," Dixon murmured, and lapsed back into silence. Nate glanced at him curiously, then shrugged. He didn't really care what Selwyn's motives were. He had his man and he was getting out of England, as soon as possible.

"Where is the woman—your alleged wife?" Dixon asked politely. "She is not from America, I believe, yet she helped you bring me here."

"She's nearby."

"Yes, yes," Dixon murmured. "But then *she* was the one sent by the English—by Selwyn. Am I right?"

He considered, but it didn't matter. Jacob Dixon

wasn't freely walking the streets of London again. "Yes."

"Ah." The man in chains sounded relieved. "When will she be back?"

"At any moment, I expect." Nate was beginning to wonder about that himself. He'd thought she would have followed him upstairs already.

"Then we really must talk, before she arrives. You see, I believe you've been fooled—if she is from Selwyn, she quite likely has no intention of letting you take me back to New York."

Nate turned a bland smile on the man even as foreboding flickered in his mind. Angelique had been keeping something from him . . . "We shall have to ask her."

Dixon rattled his chains in agitation. "No, no! Please, Mr. Avery, I beg you to listen to me. I want to go back to New York now. I am eager to cooperate. I confess! I stole the money!" Nate looked at him in astonishment. Dixon nodded hard. "Indeed! I did it, and I am willing to help you get it back."

Nate's eyes narrowed. This was quite a turn-around, and not an expected one. Why did the name Selwyn—just some stuffy lord in the Foreign Office, very officious and full of himself—have such an effect on Dixon? How the hell did Dixon know him? "Well, where is it?" he asked in a neutral tone.

Dixon's gaze darted to the door and then back. "Nearby. I can get it."

"All right, let's go." Nate reached for his coat.

"No!" Dixon scrambled backward until the chain brought him up short. "I must have some security, some guarantee . . ."

"Of what? You're not in much position to bargain at the moment."

The thief licked his lips. Nate could almost see the thoughts stampeding through the man's head. "Of my safety. If you kill me, you'll never find the money, nor prove your case."

"It would give me some satisfaction," Nate told him, but he put the coat back on the hook. "You're safe enough, though. I never meant to kill you."

But Angelique . . . he wasn't quite so sure of.

Chapter 20

Angelique climbed the stairs to the attic room as quietly as she could. It had been several hours since they'd brought Jacob Dixon back to Varden Street, and she had fled the house, leaving Nate alone with him to extract as much information as possible about the missing funds. She would have preferred to wait a few days, but felt hemmed in. What if Stafford had set someone to following them, and already knew that they'd caught Dixon? Ian had said he would delay as long as he could, but if Stafford grew impatient, he might turn to his network of informers, just to be certain. And so for *her* to be certain, she had to act sooner rather than later. If she delayed, Stafford might well decide all of them—Dixon, Nate, Angelique herself—had grown too troublesome and unreliable, and task another of his spies with eliminating them. For Dixon, she didn't care; for herself, she had brought this risk upon herself when she started with Stafford; but Nate had done nothing but try to right a terrible wrong . . . and shown her the meaning of love. For his sake alone she must not wait any longer.

The door at the top of the stairs was locked, but the key hung on a hook nearby. She let herself in. It was cool in the room, since no fire burned. There was still enough light to see Dixon, huddled against the wall, his mouth open as he snored softly. She set her lamp on the mantel and drew her knife. It was not the Wyandot knife Nate had given her, but the one of fine French steel with the weighted handle, good for every sort of purpose from throwing to close attacks. She kicked Dixon's ankle.

His face wrinkled as he blinked awake, then he sucked in his breath as he saw her standing over him. For a moment he just stared, his mouth hanging open.

"Where is it, you stinking pig?"

"Wh-What?" he stammered. "I d-d-don't know what . . ."

"Tell me where the money is," she said in the same detached voice, "before I cut your throat."

Dixon began babbling incoherently. She kicked his ankle again, and he whimpered. "Is that what Selwyn wants from me?" he panted, trying to pull his feet beneath him. "The money? I'll give it to you, I swear, he can have it all—"

"No. That is not what he wants."

He wheezed. His face was white. "I told—Avery. I told Avery, I'll get the jewels back, and the money, all of it, but *you have to let me go back to New York*—"

"I do not take orders from you," she said softly.

"But he—he—" Dixon was almost choking on his own breath. "Who are you, that he can just order you to kill me?"

This time she smiled, darkly. "You do not want to know who I am."

He squeaked, and the sharp stink of urine fouled the air. Angelique went down on one knee and put the tip of her knife at his throat. He tried to jerk away, but she batted his hand aside and the man shrank on himself. "Our Father who art in heaven," he gasped. "Hallowed be thy name . . ."

"What did you do," she asked softly, "that he wants you dead? It's not the money."

"No," Dixon whimpered.

"What, then?" she prodded when he seemed incapable of saying more. A dot of blood welled up under the point of her blade, and tears began rolling down Dixon's face as he shook with fear. "I want to know."

She *had* to know. She needed to know what Dixon had done that made Selwyn press Stafford to have the man killed. She was here, her knife ready, prepared to complete her assignment and damn herself forever in Nate's eyes, but first she had to know why.

Dixon's eyes drifted past her, and he began gesturing urgently with his hands. "Help me," he cried. "Help!"

She knew who was behind her before she turned her head.

Nate couldn't say a word, even when Dixon cried out for help. He was frozen in place, appalled by the sight of Angelique with her knife poised at Dixon's throat. A trickle of blood ran down his collar, indicating she was not merely threatening. She meant to kill him—had probably meant to kill him all along—and she knew it was because of Selwyn. Nate had tried to work it out of Dixon why he feared

Selwyn, but the man had refused to talk, wanting guarantees and promises Nate couldn't give.

But this was what she had kept from him, Stafford's mysterious secret orders. Now he saw it all, why she had been so upset when Ian arrived, why she had been so sad the previous evening when she asked how he would remember her. All along she had planned to upset his plans, to deny him the justice he sought. For a moment it felt like she had gutted him, betraying him like this. Was this the woman he had lost his heart to?

She looked over her shoulder at him with absolutely no expression. "Go away," she said. "You are a distraction."

"He promised you wouldn't kill me!" Dixon cried. "He promised!"

"It was not his promise to make," she told him. Nate was unnerved by her voice, eerily calm and devoid of feeling. "Answer my questions."

"He—he knows!" Dixon croaked, flopping his hands desperately toward Nate. "I told him earlier that Selwyn was dangerous! I told him not to trust you!"

"Well?" she asked Nate, her voice more frightening for being so even and soft. "Does he lie?" Dixon yelped as she moved the knife. More blood welled up, almost black against his skin.

"No," he said, shaking himself. "He was frightened from the moment I said Selwyn's name. And he feared you as well."

For a moment she didn't move a muscle, not even when the man pinned beneath her knife began thrashing about with renewed energy, weeping loudly in relief.

Then with a curse Angelique raised her arm. The blade glinted for a moment before she backhanded Dixon with her fist, still holding the dagger. His eyes rolled back and his head hit the wall with a thump. His arms and legs fell limp.

She rose to her feet and turned to face him.

"You lied to me," he said numbly.

She raised her chin, still the cold and deadly spy. "I never said I would not kill him."

"You led me to believe you would return him to New York as I expected!"

She flinched, ever so slightly. "I never said that, either. You said it, and I did not demur."

He looked past her to Dixon, slumped against the wall. "This is what you planned all along—what Stafford planned all along. To kill him, in spite of assurances that you were to help me, not thwart my ultimate intention!"

"It is what Stafford wanted," she agreed.

Nate was about to tear into her; his heart felt carved to pieces, and he wanted to roar in rage and hurt. She had betrayed him, and he wanted to punish her and make her feel the same pain that he felt. But at the last second, he realized what she had said, and managed to hold back his temper a moment longer. "You didn't plan to kill him all along?" he asked tightly.

She hesitated. Her mouth softened. "In the beginning, I did. I was ordered to do so, and I would have done it, no matter how distasteful."

"You didn't want to?" He started toward her, one careful step at a time. She didn't move.

"No. It is my least favorite job, and this one was particularly unpleasant. But still"—she flicked her fingers—"those were my orders."

"And now?" Unconsciously he braced himself. She could shrug and say now was no different. She could throw her dagger right at him; he remembered how she had flung it at him and nearly taken off his ear the first night they made love. If that night and all the others had just been part of her orders, he almost wished she would throw the knife and put a quick end to the misery yawning before him.

"Now . . ." She glanced at Dixon. "Now I want to know why those were my orders."

"Why?" He was barely a few feet away from her, close enough to see the rapid flutter of her pulse.

"Because . . ." Finally her facade cracked, and her lip trembled. "Because I want to see you succeed. Because I suspect all is not right with Stafford's reasons. Because I could not bear to cheat you so grievously, but I feared what Stafford might do to you if I did not follow his orders."

"Angelique, do you trust me?" he asked quietly. Slowly she nodded. "Enough to put the knife away and not kill him, but wait to see what he has to say?"

Her head bowed. For a moment he wondered if she would do it, but then she laid the knife on the mantel behind her. "Yes," she whispered, and Nate stepped forward, closing the last space between them and putting his arms around her.

He must decide, here and now, if he trusted her. The wrong choice could bring disaster on him and everyone connected with this. Nate closed his eyes and tried not to be influenced by the faint lavender scent of her hair and the feel of her in his arms. She had fooled other men before . . .

He took a deep breath and made his choice. "Let's

see what Dixon has to say for himself. Perhaps he can cast some light on this tangled web."

She raised her head and looked at him warily. "Even after what I told you?"

He rested his forehead against hers. "I must trust you. You are right—you never lied to me and said you wouldn't kill him. No one seems to know just what this mess is really about, so it's best to be patient."

"I will explain," she said. "I swear to you."

Nate smiled. "I'm counting on it."

Putting it off seemed to help them both regain their equilibrium. Angelique went downstairs to put away her knife and to fetch another lamp. Nate leaned down to check on Dixon. The cut on his neck was a small thing, barely a scratch. As he inspected it, the man's eyes fluttered open. Dixon had had a hard day; not only the pricking of his throat, but now a bruise growing at his temple. Nate didn't want him beaten or scared to death, so he helped the man sit up and gave him a cup of water from the bucket in the corner.

"Where is she?" whispered Dixon after he drank, his eyes roaming the room. "Has she gone?"

"For the moment."

Dixon sagged in relief, then bolted upright. "We made a bargain, you and I—I help get back your money, and you take me safely out of England."

"You proposed that bargain, yes."

Dixon kept looking at the door in apprehension. "But you agree, do you not? All I ask is that you guarantee my safety from *her*."

Nate considered the benefits to leaving Dixon in fear of Angelique. It had made the man more voluble than before, and if he thought she might pull out her knife again at any moment . . . Yes, it could be useful.

"She is your security," he told Dixon. "If she doesn't return . . ." He smiled again, very gently, and shrugged. "The English already want you dead."

Dixon seemed to catch his breath. "Yes, perhaps that's it," he said hopefully. "All you have to do is tell Selwyn I'm dead."

"Perhaps." Nate paused. Selwyn was the key, somehow, to whatever had spooked Dixon. "I don't expect to see him again, to tell him that or anything else."

This agitated the man anew. He grew still and quiet, only his eyes moving, darting from side to side as he thought. "She can," he finally said. Nate made a face and held up his hands; maybe, maybe not. "She must," added Dixon more forcefully. "Isn't that why she's here at all?"

"She's here to kill you," Nate corrected him—rather calmly, especially given how he'd discovered the fact himself—"not to tell Lord Selwyn lies about your death."

"But you have to stop her," the man squealed in alarm. Now that he was caught and frightened, Dixon's legendary calm and competent manner had vanished.

"I already did. But if you aren't more forthcoming, this instant, I might not do so again."

The color washed from Dixon's face. He opened his mouth to reply, then snapped it closed again as Angelique came in with a lamp in each hand. Nate went to close the door behind her, then pulled up two chairs to face Dixon.

Chapter 21

"Why would Lord Selwyn want you dead?" Nate got right to the point.

Dixon glanced again at Angelique. "I would prefer not to say in front of her. I don't trust her."

"I do," said Nate. He felt Angelique start in surprise, but he kept his eyes on Dixon. "Talk, or be silent and take your chances."

After some fidgeting, Dixon sighed. "Very well. But remember what I said before." He nodded meaningfully. Nate waved one hand; Dixon meant the part about helping them find the money, or not. At the moment he didn't care about that. He wanted to know what he was missing about this story. Was Dixon making a desperate bid for escape and lying to him—or was Selwyn? Nate fully expected the first, and was on guard against it. But if it were the second . . . A chill of unease slithered over his skin as he glanced at Angelique, her expression composed and remote again. He did trust her. Completely. The men she worked for, however . . .

"I must begin by saying Lord Selwyn—or Mr. Ross Selwyn, as he was once known—is a man of great cunning and diplomatic skill, and considerable charm when he wishes to exhibit it. He was the nephew of the Earl Selwyn, before his uncle and cousin died and he became the new lord. I don't think he expected to inherit, as the previous earl and his son were both still young men, hale and hearty. It was a boating accident, I believe; quite shocking to all the family."

"How do you know all this?" Angelique asked, her eyes narrowed on him.

Dixon edged away from her. "I was his private secretary at the time. I ran everything and knew every minute of his days."

The words seem to hang in the air, like the puff of smoke from a pistol. Nate almost felt the reverberation in the air around him. Selwyn hadn't mentioned that, not at all. He'd acted as if he'd never heard the name Jacob Dixon in his life. The chill grew more pronounced. "When?" Nate asked quietly.

"Near twelve years ago now. He had inherited a sizable fortune from his mother, and married a local squire's daughter. He was a gentleman of property and leisure, respectable but not the highest society. The English, you know, are very conscious of their class at all times, and Mr. Selwyn was a mere gentleman. But when the earl died, he changed. It was as if a feast of ambition and power were opened to him, and he meant to taste all of it."

Angelique put up one hand. "I suspect you are about to accuse the Earl Selwyn of something dreadful, even criminal. You do know this tale you tell had better be true in every particular?"

"I most assuredly do," he retorted. "But I am not wrong. Perhaps you will acknowledge that I am not doing this lightly or even happily."

"Talk," Nate growled at him with an impatient gesture. "We'll decide how to punish you for any lies or omissions later."

A nervous scowl knit Dixon's brows, and his gaze swung between the two of them. "I am not lying," he said in a low, furious voice. "Lord Selwyn has reason to want me dead. For all I know, you are both aware of this and have simply come to do his bidding!"

Angelique leaned forward. "If we had, would you still be alive now?"

Dixon paled. He looked to Nate, who put his hand on Angelique's arm. She sat back without looking at him, but laid her own hand over his for a moment. Nate saw how the thief's eyes fixed on that touch, but he didn't shrug her off. "Why does Selwyn want you dead?"

"His lordship had a son at the time of his ascension to the title," said Dixon. For all his nervousness, he was clearly determined to tell his story in his own way, at his own pace. "There was something wrong with the child. He was kept mostly away in the nursery, but I saw him enough to know he was . . . abnormal." Nate frowned and raised one hand in uncomprehending impatience. "The boy always walked on his toes, pitched forward like a ship into the wind," Dixon went on more quickly. "He flapped his hands like a bird, and would do the same thing for hours on end. He didn't talk at all, but made strange grunts and noises. The lightest touch by some people would send him into a shrieking fit. Mr. Selwyn—who became Lord Selwyn—was distressed by it and sought the opinion of several doctors, all very quietly. He didn't want anyone to know of his son's condition. But the doctors said there was no cure and recommended the child be put away in an asylum for his own protection."

Nate recalled a child in Boston who had exhibited odd behavior like Dixon described. People there had whispered about demon possession, and the boy disappeared; sent to relatives in the country, according to rumor. Somehow he doubted the people of England were much different—particularly not proud men like Selwyn. Dixon's next words didn't surprise him at all.

"In cases such as these, it is common for the child to suffer an unfortunate accident," said Dixon with a significant look. "No one wishes to have an idiot in his family, especially when there is a title in question. This boy would have been the next earl, unless he predeceased his father."

Nate and Angelique shared a glance. "Then . . . Selwyn wants you dead because he doesn't want you to reveal the truth about his son?" Nate asked. "How can he hide it, if the boy is as affected as you say?"

Dixon's face grew cunning. "No, no. You mistake me."

"Ah." Nate looked at him in disgust. "You know he killed the boy."

This time the thief's smile was triumphant. "On the contrary. Selwyn wants me dead because he did no such thing."

For a moment Nate and Angelique stared at him. "If you're going to tell lies," Nate said, "better be certain they at least make sense."

Dixon shook his head. "Then listen, if you will

know. Selwyn wished the child dead, it's true; but Lady Selwyn loved her son. For all his . . . infirmities, he was a sweet, good-natured child. They argued passionately about it."

"In front of you?" Angelique asked in astonishment.

"Madame, I was a very efficient secretary," Dixon said with some affront. "I knew everything. It was my idea, in fact, which carried the day. His lordship would not countenance the child as his heir; his wife would not permit him to be harmed. It would have been quite messy, until I suggested an alternative. Lady Selwyn and the child could go away together. Lord Selwyn would pay for their support and maintenance, anywhere but in England, on the condition that she never return or reveal her true identity. To England and to him, they would be dead. I helped them slip out of the country unnoticed and set up the bank transfers to fund their new life. I . . . er . . . procured a young woman's body—a common prostitute, I believe—similar in stature and coloring to Lady Selwyn—"

"Procured," Angelique said in a cold voice.

Dixon cleared his throat. "Anything can be procured, for the right price. As one might expect, Lord Selwyn was prepared to spend freely." She tightened her lips but said nothing. Dixon glanced nervously at Nate, who just stared flatly back. "Yes. As I was saying, I arranged for the body to be found washed up on the rocks near the Selwyn estate with a broken boat. Selwyn identified her as his wife, declared the child swept out to sea, and publicly mourned them both. The body was buried in the vault as Lady

Selwyn." He paused, then added delicately, "At that point, Lord Selwyn and I agreed it was best that I seek my further good fortune in America."

Nate's head began to throb. He pinched the bridge of his nose and exhaled wearily. "So you committed fraud—among other things—and Selwyn paid you to go away and keep the secret."

Dixon hesitated. "Yes, I suppose one might look at it that way."

"Good God," muttered Nate.

"It could be worse," Dixon went on with a bit of glee. "Without an heir apparent, Selwyn may have been tempted to remarry."

Angelique sucked in her breath. "He would be a bigamist," she said, "his children bastards."

Dixon spread his hands. "Perhaps he has been more disciplined than that. Perhaps. But the title made him arrogant and vain. If his deception has not been uncovered in so long, the man I know would take what he wanted."

"And no one but you would have known of this?"

"Not a soul," Dixon replied indignantly. "It wouldn't have been so effective if they had. Lady Selwyn agreed never to contact her family again. Indeed, Selwyn swore he'd kill her in truth if she returned, with or without the boy."

"Not ship captains? Bankers? Servants? *Nobody?*" Nate queried sharply.

"I created an entirely new identity for her. Perhaps if you had made inquiries at the time, you could have located someone who might have identified Lady Selwyn, but after ten years . . ." Dixon lifted one shoulder. "She may be so changed, even Selwyn wouldn't recognize her."

Nate met Angelique's eyes. Without a word they both rose and turned toward the door.

"Wait!" cried Dixon. "It's all true, I swear it!"

Angelique glanced back at him, kneeling in his chains on the floor, his face now white with alarm. "We shall see," was all she said. Then she closed the door behind them and locked it.

Chapter 22

She followed Nate down the stairs and into his bedchamber. This time he shut the door behind them, reinforcing her feeling of being increasingly closed in by this wretched assignment. She went to the fireplace, where a blaze crackled in the grate, wishing it could burn away her rampaging unease.

"We have to verify it," she said, staring at the flickering flames. "You have told me many times he is a skillful liar."

"Of course we have to verify it," said Nate, his voice right at her shoulder. She couldn't stop her flinch when he ran his finger down the side of her neck. "I wouldn't be surprised to learn every word he said is a lie." He paused. His lips brushed the skin below her ear, and in spite of her anxiety, Angelique quivered at the pleasures of his touch. "However," he murmured, "I also wouldn't be surprised to learn every word is true."

She closed her eyes. Unfortunately, her feeling was the same. She had worked for John Stafford for almost a decade, trusting in the rightness of his objectives even if not always in his methods. But twice this year alone she had seen him proved deceptive and willing to use his spies for petty, if not outright ignoble, purposes. It had shaken her far more than she wanted to admit, even to herself. If he had lied to her this year, how many times had it happened in the past? If he had sent her to do something—to kill someone—completely unrelated to maintaining England's law and order, how many times had he done so in the past, when she never knew?

Angelique was good at what she did, and she made no excuses for it; some people did not deserve to live. But no one should be killed to hide someone else's secrets. If what Dixon said was true, then Angelique faced two terrible possibilities: either Selwyn had lied to Stafford, accusing Jacob Dixon of sins so egregious that Stafford had no hesitation in ordering him killed; or Selwyn had not lied but simply said to kill him, and Stafford did so just because Lord Selwyn asked. Either way, she couldn't kill Dixon, but if the first possibility was correct, she would have to tell Stafford, knowing full well he might next send her after Selwyn himself. For all his own lies and deceptions, Stafford did not like being lied to and made a fool. That would be bad enough. But if the second was correct . . . It would be much, much worse.

Nate was still stroking her neck, pressing his strong, capable fingers into the taut muscles there, letting her think, trying to soothe at least part of the strain. How she loved that about him, that he could see when she was thinking and not feel the need to tell her what to do. He had been honest with her, and now she would have to be unflinchingly honest in turn. Her heart felt torn in half; whatever he might suspect, she feared to acknowledge openly what she really was.

Her face was blistering from the fire. She turned, and his arm came very naturally around her shoulder, his palm still cupping her nape. "I will find out," she said quietly, "if what he said could be true. It will likely be impossible to be absolutely sure."

"It shouldn't be impossible to find out if Selwyn had a wife and child who came up missing years ago. It shouldn't be hard to discover if he has a new wife and children now." He pressed his lips to her forehead. "It should even be possible to learn who Selwyn's secretary was back then."

"That won't be proof," she murmured against his chest.

"It will be damning coincidence."

"I can't act on coincidence."

"I certainly don't expect you to," he shot back, his brows flattening at her sharp tone. "It's Stafford who does. Why does he want you to kill Dixon, Angelique? What did he say to persuade you to it?"

She held herself very still but couldn't stop the tremble that ran through her. "Nothing. He said nothing." Nate stared at her, uncomprehending. "He never does," she went on, the words like ashes in her mouth. "He simply tells me to do it, and I do."

For a long moment they stood facing each other, one rigid with anxiety, the other motionless with surprise. "You're not just his spy," Nate whispered. His green eyes were as dark as the sea. "You're his assassin."

Somehow that word, so harsh and blunt, replenished Angelique's courage, at least momentarily. She lifted her chin. "Yes."

Slowly he nodded. His arms fell away from her. "Ah. Of course. Now I see."

She clenched her teeth and waited. This was what she had expected from anyone who discovered the truth about her: shock and horror, disgust and fear. She told herself she could endure it. It would be good for her, actually, to see how he reacted to her true self. It would make it easier to forget him when he left, and not spend the rest of her life regretting what had never been possible in the first place.

Suddenly Nate turned on his heel and paced away, raking one hand through his hair. "How long?" he demanded, his words clipped and angry.

"Almost ten years." She said it defiantly.

Nate blinked. "Ten years? Christ, you must have been a child! How in the name of God did you fall in with him then?"

"I was eighteen, hardly a child."

"Hardly a seasoned killer," he retorted. "Why?"

"I didn't start with him as a killer," she said, fighting to keep her tone even. "First I was merely to spy and report back. Then to follow people, from time to time. Then . . ." She sighed. "It just . . . crept in."

"Ten years," he repeated, sounding dazed still. "How does an eighteen-year-old young lady get involved with the likes of him?"

She laughed bitterly. "Lady? I am not a lady. One needs money to be a lady, and family, and a name. I was a dressmaker's assistant, raised by my mother's maid who was too afraid to use my real name for fear French partisans might come after us, even years after they killed my parents. The Terror, Monsieur, had a strong effect on Mellie."

Some of the anger and shock faded from him. "Have you no family at all?"

Angelique shrugged. "Only distant," she said.

"My mother's cousin married an Englishman, and she gave us money for a few years, very quietly. I believe she still had family in France and did not wish to endanger any of them by her actions. Then she died, and her husband had no desire to continue paying. We had some hard years, Melanie and I. I had to work as soon as I could, and the dressmaker took me young because I spoke French and Russian."

"Where did you learn Russian?" he exclaimed, looking startled again. "And why?"

"There was a servant boy who lived near us, in the home of a Russian émigré." She smiled, remembering dragging her feet through chores until she saw Kostya's pale, narrow face, pinched with strain from the loads of wood he had to carry up and down the stairs to heat the house. Despite that, he was always ready to laugh. "He was my friend. I was good with languages. Kostya taught me his language, and I taught him mine. Our English we learned together." She shrugged, the smile fading. "By then, Russia was a French ally, and the English were nervous the two would turn on them. I was recruited to spy on several Russian ladies, wives of diplomats, who patronized the dressmaker shop where I worked. It was nothing much in the beginning, just listening while I fitted them and reporting what they talked of. Then . . ." She spread her hands. "It just grew. I did more and more." Nate said nothing, just looked at her with dark, somber eyes. "I needed money, if you must know," she added sharply. "Mellie had met Mr. Carswell by then and wished to marry him, but she would not do so as long as I lived with her. Mellie gave up everything for me—for my mother—

and I would not keep her from her own happiness."

"No," he murmured. "Of course not."

"The British paid me well, and they kept revolution and war away from England. Not that England was untouched, but there were no armies marching in the streets and in the fields. After Napoleon was no longer a threat, there were others, within London itself, malcontents who wanted to overthrow the government and start anew. Faugh!" She swept out one hand. "They had forgotten how easily that could become a bloodbath. My parents and thousands of others died because malcontents ran unchecked over a country, killing everyone in their path who opposed them. Even killing a king was not enough for them. I could not stop that, but I could keep it from happening again."

"You stopped a revolution from a dressmaker's shop," he repeated. "With the gossip of ladies."

She breathed deeply, hardening herself against what was to come. "No. By then I worked only for Stafford. He is the spymaster, you see; his people are everywhere. He and his master Sidmouth trust no one, and they make certain nothing is left to chance. If they deem someone a danger, that person will be sure to suffer some terrible, deadly accident. I am good at causing accidents."

"How is a cut throat an accident?"

She shrugged again. "Footpads. Thieves. Leave a body in the right place, and people will ascribe all manner of sins and perversions to him. They will think he reaped his proper reward. London is not a kind and gentle city."

He gave her a keen glance. "Well, neither is New York, to be honest." His shock seemed to be wearing off. "But why would you prefer a knife, when a pistol would be so much more to your advantage?"

"It makes too much noise. I have killed a man in a hackney carriage and removed his body without the driver ever suspecting."

"Why?" Nate's eyes glittered. "What did he do?"

"Conspired to assassinate Lord Bathurst, who directed the governor of St. Helena," she said shortly. "He was a Frenchman still loyal to Napoleon and felt Bathurst was responsible for his emperor's ill treatment."

Again he looked thunderstruck. "And you just reached out and slashed him?" he demanded incredulously. "No; that would not kill him. It must be a hard, deep cut to kill before he could fight back."

"No," she said, a little surprised he knew that. "I let him open my bodice, and while he was feeling my breasts I put my knife into his throat." She touched the hollow at the base of her throat where her pulse beat a tocsin. "Place the tip of the knife here and drive forward. It pierces the throat fatally, and requires little strength."

The silence was deafening. Angelique waited calmly, hiding behind a placid face. He looked as shocked as if she'd kicked him in the groin, disemboweled him, betrayed him, and abandoned him. Her stomach roiled and twisted until she tasted bile in the back of her throat. This was why she had tried to avoid becoming entangled with him; this was why she had tried to push him away. She had known this was inevitable, but oh God, how it *hurt*.

"Good Lord," said Nate quietly, his face pale. "At least the fellow died happy."

It was so incongruous, so unexpected, her mouth dropped open.

"And then you probably just dragged him out of the carriage by holding his arms around your neck," he went on, as if thinking it through. "On a dark night, in an unlit street, the driver would see a man embracing a pretty girl and never notice the blood."

She swallowed. "He had a long cloak," she whispered. "That, and a generous douse of gin, concealed a great deal."

He crossed the room, lifting her chin until she looked at him. "He was the first, wasn't he?" She gave a jerky nod. "And a Frenchman. Ah, damn. My deadly darling." He pulled her into his arms, resting his cheek against her temple. Angelique clutched at him, unnerved by how much she wanted his comfort. Her hands shook with remembered terror of that first kill; she had drunk almost as much gin as she splashed on her victim, to keep her nerve propped up. He'd been French and handsome, a slim, clever fellow who wanted to kill an earl and rescue Bonaparte to lead a vengeful sack of London. She'd only agreed to kill him after she became convinced he might succeed, terrorizing the city and leading to hundreds, even thousands, of needless deaths. He'd been so easily persuaded she wanted the same revenge on the English, the same anarchy and upheaval, because she was a Frenchwoman, in blood although not in spirit. After she had shoved his body into the river, she'd thrown up all that gin and not eaten again for two days.

"So," Nate mused, "Stafford chose you because he wants Dixon dead—with presumably no trace left of him. I always wondered . . . But that means he lied to me as well. How did he plan to trundle me out of England without Jacob Dixon, since I was perfectly explicit that my orders were to bring him home for trial?"

Angelique could hear the thump of his heart beneath her cheek. His arms were still around her, one hand looping a stray lock of her hair between his fingers. To answer his question would require her to sever the last connection to Stafford. Nate had discovered her true assignment piecemeal so far, and only by guesswork or when she had no choice but to reveal it. Stafford could forgive all that, as long as she succeeded in the end, but not if she completely broke his confidence and told Nate everything he had charged her with. She had long since decided to quit Stafford's service, but not like this; she had expected to collect her last fee, tell him of her decision, then quietly pack up her things and leave town. Move to a quiet place in the country—near Mellie, hopefully, but anywhere far from this life.

But it seemed too late for that now. Her instincts had been right, that there was something very wrong about this assignment, and her allegiance had been subtly shifting ever since that first day, when Nate flirted and teased and challenged all her presumptions about him. Whatever she had done or said, he stayed right beside her, undaunted. Now he was still holding her after what he had seen upstairs and even after what she had told him, and she realized her lot had already been cast, for better or for worse.

With Nate.

"I was to pack you off on your ship," she said.

"One way or another. He didn't care whether you got your money or not, although he was perfectly willing that you should try. It would make you more likely to go without a fuss, you see. You were only permitted any part in this because he could not locate Dixon without your help—and, I suspect, you would not help without being deeply involved."

"No," he said very quietly. "I would not." He hadn't moved a muscle except to breathe. "And you agreed with his plan."

"I did not want to."

"I remember," he admitted. "But you did."

She made herself ease free of his embrace and lifted one shoulder. "It was not so different from what he had asked me to do before." The faint scorn in her voice was for herself, but Nate's face darkened at it. "Why should I not? You even followed me, you were so sure I would agree."

"I followed you," he repeated. "Yes, I did. You were only one of several surprises. That was the first day I met Stafford; not only was he anxious to assist in my quest, he had already sent for you. I couldn't help but wonder at that, and then you made no secret of your disinclination to agree. Why would he persist in getting this particular woman, I asked myself—and there was no answer. I followed you because this *matters* to me. I am not just here because President Monroe sent me; I don't work for the government at all. Jacob Dixon ruined a good man, my godfather, the man who saved my father's life. If I hadn't been satisfied you were equal to the task, I would have gone back to John Stafford and told him in no uncertain terms to find someone else, or I would do it all myself."

"He wanted me because I am good at killing people," she said flatly. "It is my main talent."

Nate's face grew ominous and dark. "If we're confessing all our sins, then I should admit to my own."

"I don't want to know," she said quickly. "It will serve nothing."

For a long moment he just stared at her, his brows drawn in and his eyes as hard as glass. "You don't want to know," he repeated, and managed to make it sound like an accusation.

"You don't have to tell me," she tried to explain. "I did not admit my sins in order to extract a confession in kind. What can you have done, at home in your shipping office and paying calls on a president, that could compare to what I have done?"

An odd, funny smile crossed his face. "Angelique, I'm not a shipping merchant. I grew up working in my father's business because he needed help; I sailed with him as a cabin lad, and as he acquired more ships, we all worked in the offices, not just me and my brother but my mother and even my sister at times. He expects me to take it over eventually, and I will, eventually. I went west as soon as I was grown, though. I've spent more time on the frontier in the last ten years than in any city."

"Frontier?" she repeated blankly, trying to remember what she'd heard of America. "With the savages?"

He made a scoffing sound in his throat. "Some of them are savages. But no more so than many people in Washington or Boston."

"You are at ease in London. You speak proper English."

"My mother is from Hertfordshire, near Baldock. And I was raised in a city." He grinned. "Besides, there's quite as much gossip and social ambition in Boston as there is in London. It just doesn't aim as high."

That gave her pause. The son of an English-woman and a seafaring merchant, who lived with the savages. She never would have guessed. "Nevertheless," she began, then remembered stories in the newspapers about the natives of America: scalpings, torture, raiding. A place where people used scalping knives. She looked at Nate with new eyes, and for a moment he looked utterly alien to her. Perhaps this explained some of his odd habits, and the way he had caught Ian completely by surprise. Then she blinked, and the man she loved was back. He was the same. And she realized they had neither of them fully shown their true selves before tonight. Perhaps he had been as apprehensive as she had been about revealing it. And yet they were both still standing here. A small kernel of hope glowed in her heart.

"Nevertheless," she repeated, her voice stronger, "you do not want to tangle with Stafford. He does not know the meaning of fighting honorably."

"As I see it, he is tangling with me," Nate replied, and this time there was steel in his tone. "The man lied to me. He received my honest and frank introduction with a viper's smile, and never intended to fulfill the promises he implicitly made to help me achieve my ends. That, my darling, renders my conscience completely at peace in thwarting him. I came to right a great wrong, and he is not going to stop me."

She laughed a little sadly. "No? What will you do, then?"

"I'm thinking," he said. "Give me some time. But first we need more accurate intelligence: Is Dixon telling the truth about Selwyn? And if so, does Stafford know it as well?"

"Does it even matter?" Angelique lowered herself into a chair, feeling overwhelmed. "If he knew, he sent me out to kill a man to hide Selwyn's crimes. If he didn't, then he sent me to kill a man without even knowing the reason why he did so."

"It matters a great deal." Nate had begun pacing again, rubbing his hands together and flexing his fingers. It was like watching a musician limber his fingers before taking up his instrument. "If Stafford knew, then he has deliberately used his power—and the trust of his government—to exact a personal vengeance. That tends to cause scandal when it becomes known. If he didn't know, he will have no choice but to turn on Selwyn, or else he will be exposed as unfit and corrupt. If he can be misled by one fire-breathing aristocrat seeking personal ends, he might be misled by others, with less personal ends. He will be a danger to the Crown itself, and they won't like that."

Slowly she nodded. That all made sense. Nate stopped pacing and went down on one knee before her. "Can you find out which it is?" he asked, meeting her gaze steadily. "Is there any way we can discover without confronting him directly?"

"I asked Ian to see if he could discover anything," she said. "He is not the most subtle, but that may work to our advantage. Stafford will think nothing of it if Ian just asks."

"I suppose that will have to do." Nate sighed. "Now that we have Dixon, time runs fast and short. I had thought to bundle him on the ship and leave with the next tide. But now . . ." He shook his head. "We can keep it secret that we've got him for a short while. I'll go back to the Pulteney with a note from him, indicating that he's moving to a different hotel and I'm to fetch his things. We can put Hurst off the same way if he kicks up a fuss looking for Dixon."

Angelique studied him. His eyes were so clear and green, as deep as the ocean. None of the shock and anger of earlier remained. He had heard her confession, absorbed it, and now was focused on the more pressing task they must tackle—together. For a moment she could hardly breathe, from the force of hope and relief. "Will Dixon cooperate with that?" she said, trying to keep up with him even though she wanted nothing more than to throw her arms around him once more, for just a moment, and hold him to her in gratitude and joy that he was still there, working to solve the problem with her. It wasn't a promise, but it was better than disgust and rejection.

"I don't think his other choices are very appealing. He's scared witless of you, for some reason." She gave an involuntary smile, and Nate grinned. "But I am not," he added in a soft whisper. "Not at all." He took her hand and bent his head, seemingly absorbed in tracing every contour of her fingers with his thumb. "You must know I care for you."

Her fingers trembled in his grasp. "I am glad," she murmured. It was inadequate to what she really felt, but what more could she say? It was not a declaration of love or devotion. She wasn't even sure how she would react to one of those, if he were to make it. "I care for you as well."

She caught just a corner of his smile at that. He now held her hands in both of his, gently and reverently. It made her feel peaceful and contented. But she was unprepared for the determination blazing in his eyes when he finally raised his head and looked at her. "Do you want to continue working with Stafford after this?" he asked her.

She was shaking her head before he even finished speaking. "No. I knew before we began that this would be my last assignment." Nate said nothing. His unflinching gaze loosened her tongue. "He has lied to me and to other agents of his, men I respected and trusted. Because of him, two of them were almost killed. It makes me sick to think of the part I played in those circumstances, unwitting but direct. I came to him thinking I was making a noble sacrifice, for peace and justice." She sniffed as some of her ire at Stafford returned. "I am sure some of that was gained, but at what cost? I have slept easily because it was the wicked and amoral we targeted; now I am not sure, and I will not risk a mistake."

"That's why you didn't just kill Dixon."

"No," she said with a grimace. "It is a great and terrible price to pay, to be killed. Always I have tried to make certain there was no hope of dissuading a man from his wicked intent. Always I have tried to be sure he deserved it. This is the first time I have doubted, but it is not why I am done with Stafford." She drew in a deep breath and let it out in a sigh. "I am tired of this," she confessed. "My life has not been my own. I want to be free to do what I please, without the weight of his direction on my shoulders.

I am tired of pretending to be what I am not. I am done lying."

He gave a very small nod. "You are," he said quietly, a slight smile on his lips. "Let us finish this business, and then . . ." He hesitated. "You could come to Boston with us."

"To America?" she said in surprise, even as the idea took root and flourished. America, an ocean away from Stafford and her old life . . . and near Nate. "With you?"

He gave her that charming, crooked smile she loved so dearly. "That was my hope, but if you'd rather go with Prince . . ." She laughed out loud at that, and he shrugged, still grinning. "I wasn't sure you'd prefer me to him but thought I should ask all the same." He sobered. "Yes, with me."

"To see the savages?" For some reason she found the idea fascinating.

He laughed. "If you like, my dear, although you won't find them as savage as you might think."

"The unexpected can be very savage," she said, although his humor had lifted her own. "I shall cling to your side at all times in fear."

"I can't see you cowering in fear of anything, but I'm very happy to have you cling to me." He winked, and she laughed again. "So. We must try to find out Stafford's true motive, keep Dixon quiet and his disappearance a secret, and make plans to leave England as soon as possible."

Angelique's amusement fled. They were going to defy Stafford, in one way or another. He had let his other agents walk away, but for his own reasons. Harry Sinclair had married an earl's daughter, elevating himself above Stafford's reach. Alec Brandon had proved himself innocent of the accusations of treason that had been attached to his name since Waterloo, and no longer needed Stafford's protection. But she . . . She was nobody. She had no relatives, no family, no circle of powerful friends to shield her from anything Stafford might do to her. She also carried more of his secrets than either Harry or Alec had, and she very much doubted he would just bid her a polite farewell if she said she was leaving, especially if she left without finishing Dixon. That would make him worry about her, what she intended to do and how discreet she might be. John Stafford didn't like loose ends, as she knew all too well. After all, she was the one who often tied them off for him.

Nate noticed her sudden tension. "What?" he asked, no longer teasing and smiling. "What's wrong?"

"Stafford," she said. "He will not let me walk away so easily if I do not complete this assignment. I am a danger to his secrets."

"Right," said Nate with that closed, focused look she had learned meant he was thinking hard.

"We could persuade him Dixon is dead," she said. "Then he will not be so upset to see me go."

"Right," said Nate again. "I don't suppose he'll be satisfied if you simply tell him it's done."

"He might," she said slowly. "If you came along and made a great scene that I had done it against your wishes."

"He'd discover the truth if the New York newspapers cover the trial, which they're sure to do."

"Yes," she murmured. "He does not read the foreign papers, but Phipps might."

"The New York papers are no different than London ones," Nate said. "They love a scandal, and they've been full of the story since the theft was discovered. But you'd be across the ocean by then."

"Selwyn will fear what Dixon might say at his trial, and Stafford will know I lied to him." She pressed her fingertips to her temples. "Is America out of their reach? I don't know."

Nate got to his feet and laid his hands on her shoulders until she looked up at him. "Let that question wait a while. First we need to know if Dixon is spinning tales. If he's lying about Selwyn, it alters the situation." *Not enough*, thought Angelique with a pang. "How shall we put his claims to the test?"

She dabbed a handkerchief to her eyes, then folded it in one hand. "I know only one person who moves in the same society as Selwyn, and who won't quibble about telling me what he knows. I shall have to ask Harry."

Chapter 23

Nate was not at all certain he liked having to ask Harry Sinclair for help. For one thing, the man turned out to live in a big, white stone house in the finer section of town; the streets were wide and well swept, bright with gaslight, and quiet. It was the home of a man with money, and even though Angelique said it was all from his wife's family, Nate was well aware that money had a powerful impact on a person's point of view. This Sinclair might have been as common as Nate was, at one point, but now he had clearly moved up in the world, with aims to move even higher.

"You go first," Angelique murmured after she stepped down from the hackney behind him. She had dressed as a man for this visit. With her hair hidden under a blond wig and her chest bound under a padded coat, she somehow managed to look enough like a young man that Nate had blinked in astonishment at first. Her eyes would never be mistaken for a man's and her mouth was too lush, but hopefully it was too dark for anyone to see either of them that well. Nate didn't know what would happen if word somehow got back to Stafford what they were up to.

The hackney rattled away, leaving them alone on the wide pavement in front of the house. The windows were lit, but there was no noise of a party within. He hoped that meant Mr. Sinclair was at home; the more times they had to call, the greater the chance Stafford would discover it. With more than a little foreboding, he strode up the steps and rapped the knocker of the door, Angelique a subservient step behind him.

"Edwin Greenwood to see Mr. Sinclair," he told the footman who let them in.

The servant took the card Nate gave him and went to see if Mr. Sinclair would see them. In grim silence they waited, until the butler came and showed them into a drawing room. It was a handsome room, very fashionably furnished, but Nate could barely see it, and prowled restlessly about the room. It made his skin itch to approach this fellow, no matter what Angelique said about him. For her part, she perched mutely on the edge of a sofa, a sure sign that she was as tense as he was. Too late Nate thought of more arguments against coming here; what if Sinclair suspected they had come from Stafford and wouldn't see them at all? What if he missed whatever message Angelique had sent with the spurious card, and turned them away? What if he was acquainted with Selwyn—friendly, even—and warned the man people were making inquiries?

The door clicked behind him. Angelique sprang to her feet. Nate turned to see a tall, well-dressed man about his own age with dark hair and sharp hazel eyes in a lean face. For a moment they all stood in silence, Mr. Sinclair looking from Angelique to Nate and back again. Nate realized the muscles of his back had tightened in anticipation of an attack—of what sort he couldn't imagine—and consciously tried to breathe normally. Angelique had said this man would understand . . .

"I was once Edwin Greenwood," said Sinclair. He had the calling card in his hand, and now held it at arm's length, studying the name printed on it. "For only a day or so; it took me a moment to remember, but I see you kept the cards. How have you been, Angelique?"

A smile—of relief as well as pleasure—broke across her face as he turned to her. "Well, Harry," she said. "And you?"

One corner of his mouth crooked upward, bringing a sudden flash of humor and easiness to his expression. "Blissful. Please, won't you be seated?" He extended one hand.

Warily Nate came to sit beside Angelique on the small sofa. Mr. Sinclair took a chair opposite them, drawing it close. "I need your help, Harry," said Angelique quietly.

Sinclair's eyes flickered toward Nate. "You, Angelique, or your companion?"

"Both of us. This is . . . Nathaniel." Nate said nothing, just returned Sinclair's nod. "I cannot tell you more, except that you can trust him as you do me."

From the inscrutable expression on Sinclair's face, Nate wondered how much trust that involved. Angelique had told him very little about this man, and it was stretching his nerves as tight as a bowstring to sit here and depend on him. She didn't seem bothered by it, although she did add, "You mustn't tell anyone we were here, Harry."

"Ah," said their host. "That sort of help. What is the matter?" Nate did like that; at least he got right to the point.

"I need information," she said. "*We* need information—with no questions asked. I will understand if you say no, but I swear to you it is urgent."

"It's that important?" Again Sinclair's eyes flicked to Nate, who still hadn't said a word. Angelique could feel the tension between the two of them. She had worked with Harry only a few times, but he was as clever as the devil and even more perceptive. She was fairly sure he would take her word for it that Nate could be trusted, but it was not absolute certainty; once Harry had trusted her every word, but he had moved on with his life. He was married to an earl's daughter now, and planning to stand for Parliament. She didn't want to cause trouble for him by dragging out a part of his life he doubtless wished to leave behind, but she knew of no one else able to find out what she needed to know as quickly as Harry could.

"Vital," she replied to his question. To her relief, if seemed to be enough for Harry.

"All right," he said. He shot another unreadable glance at Nate before turning back to her. "What do you need to know?"

"Gossip," she told him. "Old gossip. You are the only one I know who might be able to discover it without drawing too much attention to the search."

"I cannot promise without knowing more. My entry to the *ton* is quite recent, as you know; it's very likely I've never heard of the people or events in question."

"Selwyn," Angelique whispered. "Do you know the Earl Selwyn?"

Harry's expression grew alert. "We've met. Why?"

"Is he married?"

"I think so. I seem to recall hearing about Lady Selwyn in some context, but I could be mistaken."

Beside her, Nate didn't make a sound. She dared a quick look at him; he was staring fixedly at the floor, his mouth set. "Does he have any children?" she asked, forging on with what they needed to know.

"I don't know." Harry's gaze had locked on Nate now, thoughtful and sharp.

"I need to know who his wife is, and when he wed her. If he had another wife, perhaps years ago, and what happened to her."

"Is this for Stafford?" Harry asked. By unspoken agreement, both had lowered their voices to almost inaudible levels. "I don't work for him anymore, and if you were to ask my advice—which I know you have not—you should consider resigning as well."

That wiped the expression right off Angelique's face, even though she had been thinking much the same thing. "Why do you say that?"

Harry sighed. "My grandfather, Lord Camden, is in the Home Office. He works with Sidmouth from time to time. Initially he was very much in favor of this little enterprise of Stafford's; hell, he gave them my name when they were recruiting. But I've heard things, Angelique. However they may have begun, they've grown reckless. Dangerous. Even Camden doesn't trust them anymore, and he's a ruthless old bugger. Whatever Stafford's asked you to do, be very, very careful how you proceed, especially with regard to someone like Selwyn, who is not only one of them, but *like* them."

She let out her breath slowly. "I am trying to be," she murmured. "That is why I came to you—and why you mustn't tell anyone I did."

"You know I never would." He glanced at Nate again. "I suppose I don't want to know who you really are."

Nate looked up, his eyes glittering. "Probably not," he replied.

If Harry was surprised by the foreign accent, he didn't show it. "I'll do my best. How should I get the information to you?"

"St. Margaret's," she said. "In Westminster." Stafford had people scattered through half the pubs and taverns in London, and she didn't dare come to Harry's home again. "Two days from now, in the morning."

Harry gave a curt nod, and Angelique rose. Nate was right beside her, as quiet as a ghost but clearly ready to leave. Angelique thanked her former fellow agent again, and they left.

She didn't say a word to Nate for some time. They walked instead of hailing a hackney, partly because there weren't many hackneys standing near Harry's home. It had taken her aback to see how lush his life was now, far better than when they had been Stafford's spies together, running in and out of rented houses, collecting information and changing disguises. Harry seemed the same as he ever was, but she felt a prickle of worry that he wouldn't be so eager to tell her all she wanted to know. What if he suspected why she wanted to know about Selwyn and balked at answering her question? She didn't think Harry had been explicitly told she was Stafford's assassin, but he might suspect. Unfortunately there was no one else she could ask, and it would take too long to go out to Selwyn's estate to poke around, not to mention call too much attention to themselves. Not only could she not ask Nate to wait that long, every delay was a greater chance Stafford discovered she had turned on him. And that, she shuddered to think, could be fatal to them all.

"Will he help us?" Nate asked, breaking the silence between them.

"I believe so," she said. "He is our best hope of discovering the truth quickly and easily, since he moves in the same circles as Selwyn."

Nate nodded. He walked with his head down, his brow lowered in concentration. "Then we have to wait until the day after tomorrow. What shall we do with Dixon until then?"

She sighed. "What we have been doing, I suppose. Perhaps Ian will have discovered something."

He grunted. They lapsed back into silence again, walking until finally Nate hailed a hackney. It was late, and not all the streets were as well lit and safe as the one Harry lived on. Not until they had climbed aboard and were rumbling back toward the house did Nate speak again, slowly and deliberately, as if choosing each word with care. "If Sinclair does confirm, in some manner, Dixon's story, and Wallace provides any insight into Stafford's motivation that suggests the worst, what are you prepared to do?"

Angelique thought about it. Stafford had been utterly wrong to deceive Nate, who had dealt honestly with him from the beginning. She refused to kill Dixon, no matter what. The sense that he had ordered her to kill a man out of personal, petty vengeance, or for political gain, wove guilt and doubt into everything she had ever done for him. If what Dixon claimed turned out to be true, she didn't just want to quit Stafford's service; she wanted him stopped. "Anything," she replied softly. "He has made me a killer, and he has yet to reap the consequences."

"No, no!" Nate shook his head. "You're not killing anyone again, not him, not *for* him. That's not what I meant. What are *you* prepared for?"

The way he lingered on the word "you" made her look up in confusion. "What do you mean?"

He said nothing for a moment. "It's just an idea I had. But it would require a great sacrifice on your part, and perhaps that is unnecessary."

She frowned. "Sacrifice of what?"

"Of . . . a great many things." Nate shook his head. "Never mind. Perhaps it won't come to it."

"What do you mean? Tell me," she said softly.

In reply he put his arm around her and drew her close beside him. "You don't need my wild ideas when you've got enough to worry about."

"Not all of your wild ideas alarm me." She touched his cheek. "Some I rather like."

He didn't smile. Instead he caught her hand and raised it to his lips. "This one isn't so pleasurable—not that I don't have many pleasurable ideas about you, of course."

"I can tell it is serious, from the way it has made you so somber."

He sighed. "You don't miss a trick, do you?"

"I prefer to think it is because I am coming to know you well," she replied.

This time he chuckled. "That you are." He pressed a kiss to her temple. "But I promise to tell you if circumstances warrant."

"How?" she asked immediately. "What circumstances?"

"Ones I hope we never see," he said firmly, and refused to say another word about it.

Chapter 24

Jacob Dixon didn't take it well that they would be waiting to see if his story stood up to verification. "I told you the truth!" he shrilled, throwing out his hands.

"Perhaps," Nate told him. "Perhaps not. You've got an unfortunate history with truth."

"What are you going to do until you get this proof?" He rattled the chains at his wrists in agitation. "Am I supposed to sit here like an animal?"

"Madame still has her knife, if you prefer a more immediate judgment."

Dixon recoiled, eyes widening. "You swore to me you wouldn't allow her—"

Nate smiled grimly. "You're mistaken if you think she obeys my orders."

A sly look came over the man's face. "Oh, I think she listens to you most attentively. I am not a blind man, you know."

"No, but you're not the most clever man, either. Keep your mouth closed, lest you wear out her patience and mine." Nate took out some papers and held them out to his prisoner. "For now, sign these."

Dixon's eyes flitted over the papers, then away. "Oh, this is too much . . . You haven't given me any sort of security, yet you want to collect all my worldly goods and dupe my only friend into thinking I'm not in any danger . . ."

"I'll get your baggage whether you sign or not, and Davis Hurst is no one's friend," Nate replied. "You have two choices here: You can preserve the illusion that you're not about to have your throat cut, which one might think would help keep your spirits up, and curry my good favor at the same time by making it easier for me to recover the United States' money. Or you can refuse, and be treated as any uncooperative thief might be."

Dixon's mouth flattened, and he glared at Nate with bitter hatred, but he put out his hand for the pen and silently signed the notes Nate had written, one to the manager at the Pulteney and the other to Hurst.

"Excellent choice." Nate folded the notes into his pocket and collected the ink and pen. The room was utterly bare, except for a thin pallet and blanket. He checked the chains that kept Dixon manacled to the wall, then let himself out of the room and locked the door behind him.

Ian Wallace was in the hall below, obviously just arrived. Dressed like a gentleman today, he was handing his coat and hat to Lisette as Nate came down the stairs. The big Scot glanced up and gave him that curious half smile he always seemed to wear. Nate wondered what that look meant, but Angelique came out of the drawing room then.

"Well?" she demanded of their visitor.

Wallace grimaced. "'Tis wet and rainy out, a raw

London day. I'm chilled right through to my bones."

"I thought a Scotsman wasn't bothered by anything less than a hurricane," she retorted. "That is not what I meant."

"Can you not even offer your guest a hot cup of tea?" Wallace said instead, giving her a broad smile. "With perhaps a wee bit of whiskey?"

Nate knew what Wallace was doing. He went down into the hall and put on his coat. "I'm going out," he told Angelique. He cast an oblique look at Wallace, still grinning merrily and not saying a single word about why he had actually come. "Good luck."

"Fetch some tea, without whiskey," she told Lisette, who nodded and bustled off through the hall. "Ian, I will join you in a moment in the drawing room."

"You slay me, lass," Wallace said as he headed toward the drawing room. "Just a drop . . ."

Angelique followed Nate across the hall to the door. "Where are you going?" she asked.

"To get Dixon's things. I'll be back soon." He picked up an umbrella standing by the door. "I may go have a word with Prince as well."

She reached up and did the top buttons on his coat, smoothing the lapels in a very wifely manner. Nate saw the signs of strain around her eyes and felt like hurting someone, just to ease his own frustrations and his worry for her. "Be careful," she said.

He smiled. "I shan't do anything dangerous at all. I might say the same to you, with that cagey fox in there waiting for you."

"Ian is no danger," she said reprovingly. "Not to me."

"He'd probably like to take my scalp," Nate agreed. "Which is why I am leaving the field to you, my dear." He tipped up her chin and kissed her, lightly, then deeply, as if he feared wasting a single kiss. Perhaps he did; there were a legion of problems facing them, and he didn't see a safe path through the thorny tangle. And if any of those thorns caught them . . . He didn't want to waste a single kiss.

She still wore a slightly dreamy smile when he left, shutting the door firmly behind him to keep the cold and rain out. Nate turned up his coat collar and raised the umbrella, turning his mind back to the problems at hand and away from the feel of her mouth against his. Hopefully Wallace would have something useful to say, even if he didn't want to say it in front of Nate, but Nate was glad to leave the house anyway. He needed to think, to stretch his legs as well as his mind, and he should check in with Prince as well as get Jacob Dixon's baggage. Perhaps there would be something in Dixon's belongings that would ease their current quandary, although Nate couldn't think of what that might be. The most he hoped for now was a large stash of jewels hidden in the bottom of Dixon's trunk. But sadly, recovering the stolen funds had become the least of his worries.

The manager of the Pulteney was very accommodating. Nate used his most polite smile and best English on the man, along with full payment for Dixon's bill, and in no time at all he was being ushered up to Jacob Dixon's—or Mr. Chartley's, as he was known at the hotel—rooms, allegedly to pack everything and send it on to Mr. Chartley at his new rented home, as directed by the note Dixon had signed. Nate did indeed pack everything, after a thorough search. Aside from a plump purse, there was no sign of the jewels. He found only one letter from Davis Hurst—the others presumably had been burned, to judge from a postscript reminding Dixon to dispose of their correspondence. Nate smiled dourly at that hypocrisy, remembering the stack of letters from Dixon in Hurst's locked cabinet. He put that letter in his pocket, and carried a small valise with diaries and ledgers with him, but dumped everything else into Dixon's trunk. He hailed a carriage and had the porter load the trunk into it, then drove down to the docks.

Prince had just returned to the *Water Asp*, a small wooden box under one arm and a newspaper held over his head against the rain. He grinned when he saw Nate unloading the hackney. "Ah, the pretty lady has finally tired of you, I see. I am not to be the only one sleeping on the ship."

"I have his things," said Nate grimly, setting the valise atop the trunk. "And a delicate question."

Prince raised his eyebrows, but said nothing. He helped Nate carry Dixon's belongings on board, then sent a boy for some ale. "What is your trouble?"

Nate shrugged off his wet coat and dropped into the chair at the table where Prince's equipment was spread once more. "Asking for Stafford's help may have been a mistake."

"The president told you to go through the proper channels," Prince pointed out. "What else could you do? Not that I am surprised to hear this, you understand."

"I know," Nate said. "But Monroe didn't know what sort of man we'd be dealing with." He sighed. "Nor what sort of woman."

Prince's teeth gleamed in his dark face. "I knew it! Our pretty mademoiselle is behind it after all."

"Our pretty mademoiselle is a dangerous woman," Nate said. "But even she's in danger because of this—more so than we are, to be honest."

Prince sat back in his chair, arms folded over his chest. He was still grinning, but his eyes were serious and alert. "Are you going to explain yourself or not?"

Instead of answering, Nate reached out and fiddled with some of Prince's experiments. There were vials of colored liquids, leather pouches tied with hemp cords, tall glass bottles of powders and crystals, and a mortar and pestle. He had never understood Prince's fascination with brewing odd potions and searching out exotic plants and substances, but today he was deeply appreciative and grateful for his friend's expertise. He picked up one glass jar with what looked like harmless white flowers sealed inside, and Prince reached out to take it from him. "That is poisonous," he said with a sharp look.

"I thought as much," said Nate. "In fact, that's why I'm here. Tell me about all your poisons."

Angelique didn't wait for Lisette to bring Ian's tea, with or without whiskey. "What did you learn?" she asked as soon as she had closed the drawing room door.

Ian grimaced. He was standing in front of the fireplace, warming his backside. "Nothing good. I asked right out, and got a freezing look for my trouble. All he would say to me was that you knew what needed doing, and I should remind you to get to it. He was quite keen to know if you were having troubles, and queried me for some time about how you were getting on." Ian shrugged. "I brushed him off and said I knew nothing, just that you hadn't found your man yet. Not even when I said I'd be glad to help, if only someone would tell me what we're doing, did he pry open his lips."

Angelique sighed and sank onto the sofa. "I did not expect otherwise, but it does not help. Thank you, Ian."

"Now Phipps . . . Phipps was a different story," he went on in the same vein, as if she hadn't spoken. "Phipps is no great admirer of yours, and when I let slip you were having difficulty in completing your mission . . . Well, the man's not cut out to be other than a clerk, and God help Stafford if anyone else realizes that. Phipps also tried to pry out of me what you had already done and what the trouble appeared to be, but I'd sooner swive an Irish whore with the pox than tell him anything. But while he was grumbling about sending a woman to do an important job—"

"Over ale, I assume," she muttered.

"It lubricates the throat," Ian replied equably. "And the tongue. Especially the tongue. Phipps can drink a lot more than one might think, to look at him."

"What did he say?"

"Ah, right. It's not just Staff who's anxiously awaiting the conclusion of this sorry business. Phipps indicated the old fox is being prodded and pricked to get this done, and by people other than Sidmouth—

hence my invitation to the scene." Ian gave a mocking bow. "How flattering it is that they send me in to succeed where you cannot, but without telling me a bloody thing about what's supposed to be done."

Angelique buried her face in her hands. She had feared as much; it must be Selwyn urging Stafford on. Or someone else, if Selwyn was innocent of Dixon's charges—but who could that be? If only she knew. If only she could divine where Stafford himself stood. Once again she hoped Harry would discover something.

The sofa creaked as Ian came to sit beside her. "Now that I've played my part as a wide-eyed messenger boy, will you tell me what the problem is?"

For a long moment she said nothing, then gave in. She trusted Ian as much as she trusted Harry—Ian was still in the game, after all. And at this point, she needed his help too badly not to trust him. "I suspect I have been sent to do something terrible," she said quietly. "Nate came to England to find a man named Jacob Dixon. His president instructed him to apply to the appropriate channels for help, and he did so, ending up in Stafford's office. But after assuring Nate he would give all assistance possible, Stafford told me to help find the man, then to kill him—without Nate or anyone else discovering it, preferably."

"Why?" Ian was frowning.

She lifted her hands. "I do not know. He would not tell me, even when I asked. But I agreed. Only after we apprehended Dixon—"

"You've already got him?" Ian exclaimed. "Ah . . . Now I see . . ."

"What?" For a moment her heart surged in panic,

and her hand made an involuntary movement toward her knife. "What do you see?"

"That's why you seem so flustered. I'm not used to seeing that, you know. The calm, cold Angelique is never without a plan." He grinned again, but only for a moment. "So you've got him and don't know what to do with him."

"No. Can you guess why?"

"I'd wager it has something to do with the American."

"In a way," she said slowly, "but not as you think. Nate did not change my mind, even though I thought it was very wrong of Stafford to treat him so ill; he allowed Nate to believe I was here to help him in every way, not to use him. It was Dixon himself who managed to make me doubt."

Ian let his astonishment show. "How?"

She knew it was completely unlike her, to be swayed by the arguments of the person she was supposed to pursue. Perhaps she had misspoken; if not for Nate, and her sense of the injustice Stafford did him, she never would have hesitated long enough to hear Dixon's story. "He told a story," she said. "I am still trying to discover if it might be true, but, if so, it calls into question everything about Stafford and what he wishes me to do."

"And if this man told you a lie?" Ian asked skeptically. "Then what?"

"Then . . ." If Dixon lied, then what was she to do? Kill him after all, for the trouble he'd caused her? Or let Nate take him back to New York for trial in defiance of Stafford's orders, because killing him made even less sense? Harry had better find something definite about Selwyn, because she didn't know what she would do if Dixon's story proved to be false, or demonstrably impossible. "I don't know. I will deal with that if I must."

"How will you know? Seems to me you've already started believing him, else you'd not have delayed so long, nor sent me out to quiz Stafford."

"I am trying to confirm certain details of Dixon's tale." She hesitated. "I have asked Harry, although he does not know why I want to know."

"You should have sent him to Staff," Ian said. "He could bring along his demon-faced grandfather and leave Staff on his knees groveling for pity."

"Demon-faced?" asked Angelique, diverted. She knew Harry's grandfather was a viscount, but little more.

"I saw him once, around Bow Street. I'd not want to cross that one. All of Sinclair's cunning and none of his charm."

She remembered again what Harry had told her: even his grandfather didn't trust Stafford anymore. A knot of tension twinged in her back, right between her shoulder blades. "Stafford cannot know I am hesitating," she said, returning to the main point. "If I had sent Harry, Stafford would have been suspicious at once. But I hope he can tell me if Dixon's primary claim is true."

Ian was quiet for a long moment. "You think he will." It was not a question.

Angelique nodded. "I suspect he will." There was too much in Dixon's story that made sense. A man rising to unexpected power and prominence becoming drunk on ambition and pride. A child suddenly not meeting his father's new expectations. A mother's fierce determination to protect her child at any cost . . . yes, that resonated deeply in Angelique's heart. And Dixon seemed just the sort of man to conceive of such a plan, carry it off with callous flair—finding a dead prostitute who resembled the countess was a morbidly dramatic touch—and then go on to other deceptions in a new land. It was all too easy to imagine the panic Selwyn would have felt upon learning of Dixon's return and how he might have acted to eliminate the threat once and for all, relying on the power and position he had sacrificed so much to achieve and defend. She could see it and believe it all . . . assuming it was true.

Therein lay the problem. She could believe it—but how could she *know* it was true? Even if Harry came back and said Selwyn had been married before, did it prove he had sent the wife away? If Selwyn had not remarried, did that cast doubt on Dixon's claim that the earl would still want him dead? And ever looming in her mind was the question of Stafford. If Dixon's story were true, and if Selwyn had acted as Dixon charged, where did Stafford stand? The tension had crept up her neck into her head, and she rubbed her temples wearily.

"When will you talk to Harry again?" Ian broke the silence to ask.

"Soon. Tomorrow, I hope."

Ian nodded. "And what's your American's part in all this?"

"My American?" She laughed a little. "He is not mine."

"Only if you don't want him. You said Stafford deceived him; I assume he feels the same way. Is he a danger?"

Angelique ignored the flare of longing that Ian's

remark about Nate ignited. If only it was true, or could ever be true . . . "He wishes to do what is right, but he is not pleased to have been used and manipulated. His duty is to his country, not to Stafford. But he will not act without telling me."

Ian's smile was grim as he patted her hand. "I hope not, love. For your sake."

Chapter 25

When Nate returned hours later, Angelique almost wilted in relief. She hadn't thought he would just leave, even if he had discovered the missing fortune tucked neatly in Jacob Dixon's desk drawer, but his absence had been more wearing than expected. The house had been eerily quiet and still after Ian left, and even Lisette had made herself scarce. Feeling as though she would go mad without something to do, but not wanting to be away from the house when Nate came back, Angelique had begun packing. One way or another, her work here was nearly done. As always happened on a job, things had gotten into a terrific mess, and she spent some time sorting and wrapping various dresses and disguises. To her surprise she found the magenta gown in her wardrobe. Lisette had cleverly repaired the long rent she had made, stealing some of the fullness of the skirt from the back and draping it around the front to hide the tight, flat seam mending the tear. Angelique brushed her hand over the cool silk, and remembered Nate's hands inside it, moving on her skin. A breath of want rippled over her skin, raising the hairs on her arms, and she was in the process of folding the gown when she heard the door.

Nate was in the hall, peeling off his dripping coat when she hurried down the stairs. "You're soaked," she exclaimed.

"It's still raining." He hung up his coat and hat, ignoring the drips of water falling from them. A puddle had already collected under the umbrella leaning beside the door. With a gusty sigh, he pulled off his boots, stained dark from the rain, and trudged up the stairs. Angelique hurried ahead of him to stir the fire in his room. The whole day had been dark and chilly, so she had told Lisette to lay fires in all the hearths. Within minutes it was blazing, and Nate gratefully held out his hands to it.

"Did you have any trouble?" she asked.

Nate shook his head, sending droplets of water flying from his hair. "None. I collected a large trunk full of personal effects, and some diaries and a ledger—there—that will hopefully prove illuminating."

She looked around, spotting a flat bundle wrapped in oilskin on the table. "Have you looked at them yet?"

"Briefly. Our Mr. Dixon thinks very highly of himself, judging from what I read so far. He was clever enough to secrete the jewels somewhere outside his hotel, though, and not write the whereabouts in his journal." He glanced at her over his shoulder. "I don't suppose Wallace had anything helpful to say?"

She came to stand beside him, even though the fire was too hot. After a day alone with her thoughts, she craved his presence. As if he knew all that, Nate turned his back to the fire and drew her into his arms, sheltering her from the blasting heat. He laid his cheek against her temple, his skin cold and clammy against hers.

"Not much," she replied to his question, leaning into him. Angelique had never known a man she wanted so simply and physically before; just standing here in Nate's embrace eased some of her worries and fears, and made her feel stronger and steadier. Nothing had changed except her, she realized. Always before she had worked essentially alone, even with other people around her. She had been the director, responsible for the safety of others and she had acted with commensurate reserve and cold-eyed calculation. With Nate, it was different. She was not alone; he was every bit her equal.

"Ian said someone is driving Stafford to finish this," she went on, "someone highly placed, although he could not learn who. Stafford is sufficiently moved by this person's concerns that he sent Ian to speed us along, even though he would not tell Ian any details of what is to be done."

"That's not terribly reassuring," Nate said. His voice was muffled against her hair.

"It is bad," she agreed. "But still does not answer the main question."

He was stroking her back, drawing soothing circles right over that tight, anxious spot. "It may be impossible to know for certain," he said, echoing what she had said the other night.

"I am believing in damning circumstances more and more," she replied.

"If any circumstances deserved to be damned, it would be these."

She sighed and closed her eyes. She could feel the

wet of his clothing soaking into hers, a creeping, insidious chill. He should get out of those wet clothes at once. "Ian asked what I shall do if Dixon's story turns out to be a lie."

For a moment Nate didn't respond. "I suppose that's what he believes."

"I do not know," she said. "But it is a valid question."

"Of course it is." He released her and turned back to the fire. Without his body pressed to hers, Angelique felt abruptly cold and wet. "And it neatly avoids facing the question of Stafford, which must be uncomfortable for both of you."

"If Dixon's story is a lie, it does not matter why Stafford acted as he did."

"Yes, because then I'd be the only one disappointed." Nate stripped off his jacket and dropped it on the hearth with a wet plop. "I have no doubt Wallace would prefer that outcome above all others."

"You are wrong about Ian."

He gave her a wry look. "Of course I am. He believes I'm in good faith. That's why he won't say a damned word in front of me and looks as though he'd like to pummel my face in."

Angelique's temper, already strained by the secrecy and unease that had weighed on her for several days, began to fray. "That is because you put a knife to his neck."

"I put a knife to his neck because he snuck into your room and then drew a blade on you." He was fumbling at the buttons of his waistcoat, his fingers stiff and clumsy, probably from the cold.

"I can take care of myself," she said evenly. "I am not your property to defend."

A dull flush rose in his face. "Then there was no cause for concern, when one of Stafford's men showed up unexpectedly, alarming even you, and snuck into your room to lie in wait for you."

He was right, of course, but somehow she seemed unable to calm down and admit it. "There was no danger from Ian," she said before she could stop herself.

Nate cursed under his breath and ripped the waistcoat open, sending a pair of buttons bouncing along the floor. He peeled off the garment and tossed it aside, and Angelique saw that he was soaked right down to his skin; the white linen of his shirt clung to his arms and chest. "Forgive me if I don't share your trust in him." He dropped into the chair facing the fire and sighed, running one hand over his face. "I spent the day worrying that you might not be here when I got home."

She jerked. "Why?"

He threw out his hands. "Because Wallace was here, most likely trying to persuade you not to trust me, perhaps with some new directive from Stafford—and you clearly value Wallace's opinion and trust him a great deal—"

"So you thought I would just *leave*?"

"And maybe take Dixon with you, if Wallace could talk you into it. That's what Stafford would want him to do, isn't it?"

Angelique felt her patience snapping, one thread at a time. She didn't want to fight with Nate, but the strain of the day had decimated her usual control. She felt trapped and tense and now even Nate questioned her. "If I wanted to leave, I would leave," she retorted. "With Dixon or without him, no matter what Stafford preferred. If this is how much you trust me, perhaps I *should* go, now that your true feelings are clear."

"The hell you will," Nate growled, lunging after her as she whirled toward the door. His weight crashed against the door a moment before she could fling it open. "That is not what I said!"

"No?" She arched her brow in contempt. "I have defied my employer because I want to help you, and this is how well you trust me—to think I would just walk away with your prisoner?"

"I said *Wallace*—" he began, his teeth gritted.

"And I said I trust Ian," she shot back. "Do you believe my word or not?"

Nate stared at her furiously. "Goddamn it," he muttered. "What a waste of time." She opened her mouth, drawing an outraged breath to lash out at his dismissal of her words, and he kissed her. Nate had kissed her many times before—with gentle yearning, with playful affection, with hungry seduction. None of those kisses compared to this one; his mouth claimed hers forcefully, almost harshly. She started to twist away and he grabbed her arms, dragging them above her head and pinning her wrists to the wall. In spite of her anger, she found herself kissing him back, her body arching toward his. She didn't want to think those wretched thoughts, let alone fight with Nate about them. Without him at her side, she would be lost, caught in an impossible situation with no idea which way to turn. As long as she had him, at least her ultimate goal was clear.

"I don't want to argue with you." He kissed his way down the side of her neck with sharp little nips of his teeth that stung with erotic pleasure.

"Then don't," she said, her voice gone husky with desire. He was still holding her hands, so she hooked one leg around his, pulling him closer.

He shuddered against her, and released her wrists. He dragged up her skirts as she reached for his shirt, yanking on the wet linen to pull it free of his trousers, sliding her hands up his cool, damp skin. His cravat was still tied, preventing her from removing his shirt, and she hissed her disappointment in profane French. Nate laughed under his breath as he slid both his hands under the bunched-up fabric of her dress, and then Angelique gave a little scream as he cupped her bottom with one hand and stroked her with the other.

"Your hands are like ice," she gasped, even as his wicked, freezing fingers ignited a fire inside her.

"You'll warm them up." He pushed two fingers up inside her, and she moaned, digging her nails into his shoulders to keep her balance. The cold of his flesh inside her heightened every sensation. She let her head fall back and pushed her hips forward, moving against the every stroke and thrust of his fingers. "God, yes," Nate muttered roughly. "That— just like that . . ."

Shaking with desire, she pulled blindly at his trousers until they gave way, and she could stroke him. This part of him wasn't cold at all, and a moment later he knocked her hands away and crowded closer, lifting her thighs to curl around him. He kissed her, stroking her at the same time until she teetered on the brink of ecstasy, and then finally he thrust high inside her. Angelique came apart as he entered her; she gave a low, keening cry, her body moving instinctively as Nate surged into her again and again until finally he climaxed with an almost feral growl.

They stayed where they were, wrapped around each other, for several minutes. Angelique didn't want to move. This was what she needed—not just this contentment flooding her, but Nate in her arms, holding her, loving her. Now she didn't feel alone, and that made all the difference. Nate must have felt the same way, for he didn't move for several minutes, either, and when he spoke, his voice almost startled her.

"I'm sorry," he whispered. "For losing my temper."

She stirred, remembering the terrible things she had said to him. "No, I was at fault as well. I am sorry." She sighed. "You are not wrong to keep a wary eye on Ian; he works for Stafford. I know there is a chance I am wrong about him, but still I trust him."

His lips brushed the curve of her shoulder. "Apology accepted." He heaved a sigh and raised his head. "And now I've gotten your dress all wet."

She smiled. "It is nothing. I shall just take it off."

Even his grin looked weary. "Let me help."

They undressed each other, and Nate threw another log on the fire before tucking her into bed beside him. His skin was still cool, but Angelique curled herself against him anyway. He held her close and dropped his head on her shoulder as if exhausted.

She ran her fingers through his still-damp hair. The tension in her back and neck had melted away under the heat of their lovemaking, leaving her mind refreshed and clear but not sleepy. She watched the firelight cast shadows on the ceiling, and listened to the slow rhythm of Nate's breathing, and thought.

She would do anything to keep this. Whatever she had to do to stay with Nate, she would do it and count it worth the sacrifice.

"What are you thinking?" he murmured without moving.

She laughed. "How do you know I am thinking?"

"I can tell by the way you hold very still and barely breathe," he said, a smile lurking in his voice. "I can practically hear the air vibrate when your mind is working on something. And since my own mind seems unable to function at the moment, I thought I would like to hear what you are thinking."

She turned her head and pressed her lips against his forehead. "I was thinking," she said softly, "that I would like to stay like this with you forever."

Nate rolled onto his back. The arm that had been draped over her waist fell away. "Ah," he said.

She felt a sudden chill. "Nothing lasts forever, of course," she said stiffly. "I did not mean—"

"You said you didn't know my true feelings." His eyes were wide open now, staring at the bed canopy above them. "The truth is . . . I love you."

Mouth still open indignantly, Angelique gaped at him. Finally he looked at her, his eyes as clear and sparkling as emeralds. "I have been too afraid to say it," Nate confessed, "but I love you, Angelique. Since the night you threw a damned knife at me. Since you promised to cut my throat that first day when I followed you from Bow Street, perhaps. You have fascinated me and confounded me from the moment I saw you, and I would go quietly mad if I had to leave you behind. That's why I want you to come to America with me." He shrugged, looking somewhat helpless. "But this grows more tangled by the day, and more dangerous for you. I can't ever forget that."

"And so you think I would just *leave* you—"

"Not think—fear." She could only stare at him. Nate sat up and took her hand, a faint frown touching his brow as he examined her fingers. "I know you trust Ian—enough that he might persuade you to take Dixon to Stafford, or just to leave and disappear. And the hell of it is . . . I would rather you just disappeared, than have to see you endangered by anything you've done to help me, or done at my suggestion. I would rather lose you, and know you were safe, than see that Dixon—or Selwyn or Stafford, for that matter—reaps his just reward. Even if I would be lost without you."

"Do you know," she said in a low, halting voice, "that before I agreed to this job, I had planned to quit. I am not so young, and I thought to retire before any chance of a quiet, happy life was gone for me. I thought I would have to persuade Ian to marry me, for no one else, I believed, would be able to overlook what I am and what I have done."

"You want to marry *Wallace*?"

"Because he knows the worst about me." She paused, smoothing her fingertip over his horrified expression. "Not because he loves me—for he does not—or because I love him—for I do not. Because I never thought another man would be able to know and still want me." She looked at him in wonder. "I still do not see how you can accept that I have been an assassin and a spy."

"It just is," he simply said.

Her smile was a little sad. "It is not easy, or wise,

for someone in my position to fall in love. I have never told anyone but Mellie, truthfully, that I loved them. Except you."

He lifted her chin and kissed her. She was lost, turning and reaching for him until they were caught tight in each other's embrace. "I will never leave you," she whispered.

Nate smiled. "I will never doubt you again."

Angelique laughed. "Doubt, I can live with."

"No. It would strangle both of us. I make you two promises. First and foremost, that I shall never doubt you, nor give you reason to doubt me."

"You have not," she said softly. "Even when you must have doubted every word I said."

"We're done with that now." He kissed her again. "My second promise is to get you safely out of England, no matter what."

"You cannot promise that—it is not in your control—"

His embrace tightened. "No matter what," he repeated firmly. "Whatever I have to do."

St. Margaret's church was warm and quiet after the chilly rain of the previous day. Pale morning sunlight filtered through the tall stained glass windows onto the polished floor. A couple dressed in deep mourning sat in the back, heads bowed in silence. From time to time the lady would press her hands beneath her veil, covering her eyes as she broke down in a fit of quiet weeping. Her companion patted her arm when she did so. They had come in early that morning, murmuring to the rector about a suddenly deceased father—carried off in the middle of dinner, right before their eyes—and the rector nodded in consolation and left them to their prayers.

After an hour or so, another man slipped into the church. He saw the couple at once and approached with respectful gravity, touching the woman's shoulder lightly. "I am deeply grieved to hear of your loss," he said softly.

She made a sound like a strangled sob, and got to her feet to clasp his hands. "Thank you," she said with a slight hiccup in her voice. "He was such a good man—"

The newcomer nodded. "I know. He will be missed." He reached into his pocket, searching, then offered his handkerchief. She took it and reached under her veil to dab her eyes. "If there is anything else I can do for you, for any of your family, you have only to ask," the man told her gently.

She raised her face, still shrouded in the black net of her veil. "You cannot know what that means to us," she said. "Thank you for all you have done. You are a true friend."

He bowed his head. "I owe you so much . . ." He looked past her to the man behind her. "My condolences," he said, putting out one hand.

"Thank you," murmured the gentleman, clasping his hand briefly. "How kind of you to come." He touched the woman's arm. "My dear, we should go."

The lady nodded, still drying her eyes. "In a moment."

The second man nodded again. "I will leave you, then."

"Thank you," whispered the lady as he bowed and walked off. The mourning pair sat again and stayed where they were for several more minutes, then rose and slowly left the church as well. The lady leaned heavily on her companion's arm until they were outside the church, where he hailed a hackney and helped her inside.

Once Nate had closed the carriage door, Angelique tore off her veil. She laid the handkerchief Harry had given her on her lap and unfolded it to reveal the small square of paper folded inside. With unnaturally steady fingers she unfolded it and held it up so they could both read at once.

It was brief but damning. *Ross, Earl Selwyn, Undersecretary of State for War and the Colonies. The first Lady Selwyn drowned along with her young son in a tragic accident; Selwyn mourned them for almost a decade. Married ten months ago to Millicent Beaumont, second daughter of the Duke of Ramsey. The new Countess Selwyn retired to the country in anticipation of the birth of her first child a month previous. Selwyn widely seen as a growing political force based on his connections.*

For several moments neither spoke. The carriage swayed as they jolted over the cobbles heading through London, surrounded by the sounds of a city in full hum.

"He could have read it in the newspapers," said Nate at last.

"Ten years is a long time to remember a tragic boating accident, and then connect it so quickly to the name Selwyn when you mentioned it."

"He could bear Selwyn a grudge for some other reason."

"He could." Angelique folded the note and slipped it into her reticule, along with Harry's handkerchief. "He could be the most brilliant liar I've ever seen.

But short of finding this missing Lady Selwyn and presenting her in the House of Lords like Banquo's ghost, I do not think we will find better proof."

"No," he agreed quietly. "I don't think we will."

"It is what I expected," she said. "I have not decided what to do next, but I was prepared for this."

Nate rapped on the carriage roof to signal the driver to stop. His fingers closed around hers. "I'm glad to hear that." He helped her down from the hackney and paid the driver. They were on the edge of St. James's Park, still some distance from Varden Street. Angelique tucked the veil from her bonnet into her reticule, glad to feel the sun on her face for a few minutes. "Let's walk a bit," he said, tucking her hand around his arm. It was still early, so the park was not busy.

"What I do not know is how to handle Stafford," she said. "He is the real concern, not Selwyn."

Nate smiled grimly. "I completely agree. And I have an idea how to do it."

Chapter 26

Ian sized up Jacob Dixon with a long glance. "So," he said, "you're the one who's stirred up such a fuss."

Dixon stared back at Ian with mingled horror and indignation. "I certainly have not done," he said, even though he flinched every time Ian moved. "I was s-simply going about my business . . ."

"Stealing, lying, fleeing the country, then more lying," interjected Nate. "We know what you've been up to. But in spite of it all, we've come to make you an offer of clemency."

Dixon kept his eyes fixed fearfully on Ian, still standing over him in menace. Today Ian wore all black, from the tall leather boots that shook the floor when he walked to the greatcoat that swirled around him like a shroud. It only made his red hair more alarming, especially all ruffled and spiky as it was now from having shoved his hands through it so many times. Angelique wondered what had gotten into him, showing up dressed that way in response to her summons. She suspected it had been Nate he expected to cow—as if that would happen. But she had to admit Jacob Dixon was more tractable in a state of perpetual terror, so she said nothing as Ian paced in front of the man several times before finally dropping into one of the chairs they had brought up to the attic.

From where he lounged in another chair, Nate watched only Dixon's face. His eyes cool and shuttered, he looked to Angelique even more dangerous than Ian. Ian was a growling dog, hair on end and back arched. Nate was a viper, coiled and silent but waiting to strike.

Jacob Dixon looked between the three of them and didn't seem to know where his best chance lay. "My good man," he said at last, appealing to Nate. "Perhaps we could have this discussion privately."

"No," said Nate evenly. "Because this is not just my idea." Even though it was, almost entirely. Angelique never would have come up with it herself, and it wasn't something Ian would do, either. But she had agreed to it, so she kept her face impassive and let Nate guide things his way.

"I came to England in search of justice," Nate said, still watching the thief like a hawk would a field mouse. "My charge, and only goal, was to find you, sir, and return you to face the man you ruined and the country you swindled. And before you accuse me of lawlessness myself"—he smiled thinly, for Dixon had opened his mouth—"let me add that I carried a letter of introduction from President Monroe himself, setting out exactly what I've just told you. General Davies is a decent, heroic man, and Monroe is aware of what our country owes him. He approved wholeheartedly of what I meant to do.

"Now, I would have been perfectly content to track you down like an animal and drag you back to New York in chains, but the president asked me to use diplomatic channels—discreetly, of course. That led me to Lord Selwyn, who was deeply outraged and most solicitous upon hearing my story. Of course this vile criminal must be apprehended, he told me. He sent me to another man, who in turn promised to provide assistance in capturing you. Unfortunately, it appears Lord Selwyn also gave him another charge."

"To kill me!" cried Dixon. His face had grown alternately red and then pale. "He wants you to kill me—we've already discussed this!" He thrust out his chained hands, pointing at Angelique. "You swore you wouldn't let her do it, and in return I promised to cooperate with you!"

"True." Nate's voice hadn't altered; it remained flat and relentless. "And so far you have done precious little in that regard."

Sweat beaded on Dixon's lip. "What do you want?" he protested. "You knew about Hurst; you have my baggage. Unless you plan to unchain me, I don't see what else I can do!" Nate just looked at him until Dixon swallowed, a loud gulping sound in the quiet attic. "What?" he cried. "Tell me what you want!"

Slowly Nate leaned forward. The old wooden chair creaked loudly, and Dixon flinched. "I want to propose a bargain to you," Nate said quietly. He rested one elbow on his knee and cocked his head. "Are you interested?"

Without a sound Dixon nodded.

"Good. As I see it, I have three choices. The first choice: I do as I meant to do originally and carry you back to New York to stand trial, publicly clearing General Davies of guilt for your theft. You'll go to prison for a very long time, of course, but that's no more than you deserve.

"The second choice: Prison might be too good for you. I could cut my losses, recover as much of the stolen money as I can, and sail back to New York. It turns out there are some Englishmen who take a particular interest in you, and I think I could hand you over to them and be wished Godspeed on my way home. New York will be disappointed not to have your blood, but they will have the money, which is far more valuable. I assure you, my conscience wouldn't suffer for your fate at all."

"What is the third?" Dixon whispered when Nate lapsed into silence. "I must say I prefer the first choice, though, by a generous margin. Selwyn will not be merciful, sir, you know what I told you about him!"

"The third choice," Nate went on, "is the most difficult. I shall have to relent on something very important to me, my companions shall have to sacrifice a great deal, and you . . . you shall be better off than under either of the previous choices . . . in some ways."

Hope—and calculation—sprang into Dixon's eyes. "Well, then I am sure we can negotiate, to ensure a better outcome for you," he murmured.

Nate's mouth curled into a deadly smile. "Oh yes. You're going to return the money, but not for my benefit. You're going to return it all to President Monroe. If even ten dollars is missing, the bargain is void."

"Er . . . all?" said Dixon cautiously. "But it was not a trifle to come to England. Surely you cannot expect—"

"All of it," repeated Nate in a silky tone. "Do what you must to cobble the sum together in any way you can, or the bargain is void." He waited as Dixon opened his mouth to argue, thought again, and subsided. "And in return, I shall not tell Selwyn you are here. I shall not tell him you are still alive. I will even take you out of England and not put you on trial for embezzlement. I shall help you to a new life, and a new name, and in return you will never return to any of the states, or to England—although I presume I need not urge you on that course, given what Lord Selwyn might feel on discovering you had fallen into his grasp once more. And if I should find you in my country . . ." He shrugged. "Well, the authorities there will already think you long dead."

"That's all?" Dixon looked as though he could hardly believe his ears.

Nate inclined his head. "That's all."

Dixon looked at Angelique, then at Ian. He seemed to regret the last, for his eyes widened until a rim of white showed all around the brown. He looked at Nate again and nodded so hard his disheveled hair tumbled over his brow. "I accept."

Nate smiled at him again, and Dixon shrank away. "You never had a choice."

When they had left Dixon to his fears and gone back down the stairs, Angelique let out her breath. "Do you think he will fulfill his part?"

"I suspect he'll try as if the devil himself is driving him."

Ian was staring at Nate. "You're that devil, aren't you? Not only coming up with this bloody daft idea but actually trying it. What'll you do if it doesn't work?"

"It will work," said Nate. He hadn't lost that cool, focused look that put Angelique in mind of a snake gliding quietly through the grass behind its prey. "And I haven't heard any other ideas from you, better or worse."

Ian glowered at him. "I've had a few ideas," he muttered before turning to Angelique. "And you—you, I expected more of. What are you thinking, lass?"

"Perhaps this is not the best way, Ian," she replied quietly, "but we do not have many options. I do not know what Stafford knows about this. I do not even know for certain Selwyn committed the acts Mr. Dixon accuses him of. But I am uneasy over it all, and I don't know how to discover the truth."

"This isn't meant to discover the truth, this is meant to confront Stafford!" Ian was staring at her in frustration, but now he lowered his voice and turned his shoulder to Nate, as if to exclude him. "Whatever you think of him, remember that he's not a fool and he's not unwilling to take chances. He's unpredictable, Angelique, and this could go wrong in so many ways."

"That is always possible, no matter what course we choose."

Ian swore, his brogue so thick she couldn't even tell what curses he used. "But the consequences—"

"I have chanced them before," she reminded him.

"Not because you created them to begin with!" he shouted at her.

The words seem to hang in the air. Angelique felt the sting of them, the implicit accusation that she was being reckless and worse, careless. Ian towered

over her with the fiery anger of his Highland fore-
bears flushing his face, his hands twitching at his
sides as if he'd like to grab her and shake some sense
into her. Nate said nothing, just watched the two of
them with hooded eyes. He hadn't moved from his
position, leaning against the door with his arms
folded across his chest. She was squarely between
them, caught between the cold sense of Ian's warning and the bright hope that she could finally be free
of her past.

"Ian," said Angelique softly. "I will understand if
you won't help me."

Ian raked his hands through his copper hair. "I
want to help you. I fear this idiotic plan puts you
in danger and only helps *him*." He jerked his head
at Nate. "Why should I plot against Stafford so a
conniving thief won't get a knife in the back like he
deserves?"

"Help me," Nate repeated, a hint of anger breaking into his voice. "Did you listen to anything I said?
I came to catch a thief and make him face justice,
and now I can't do it without putting Angelique
in an impossible—perhaps fatal—position. I'd be
happy enough to run Dixon through, I assure you,
except that it would be exactly what Stafford and
Selwyn want. Now the best I can do is return the
money, which I grant is significant and will spare
General Davies from destitution and shame, but
you're utterly insane if you think Dixon is going to
walk away from this a free man. I'll hand him over
to the navy, or a merchant sailing for China, or the
first bloody pirate who crosses my path."

Ian grunted. "That's better than nothing, I
suppose."

"You've never been to sea for months at a time, I see," Nate snapped

"Stop," Angelique snapped as they eyed each other like bristling pugilists. "There is one more thing we must add to the plan. If all else fails . . ."

"As it's likely to," Ian muttered.

"Good, then you will have no objection," she told him. "Because it is something you must do." She drew herself up, knowing neither man would like what she was about to say. "I support Nate's plan. It is daring, yes, and it forces a confrontation with Stafford, as Ian says; but it is necessary. If Lord Selwyn has been abusing his influence by ordering Stafford to have people killed, it matters. If Stafford has neglected his duty of care in exercising his power, it matters. If either proposition is true, it blackens all that you and I have done for Stafford, Ian, and the burden falls on us to restore things to rights."

"You've got a thief's tale and your own inclination as evidence."

"And Harry's warning that Stafford and Sidmouth have grown reckless," she reminded Ian. "I told him nothing of what we were doing, and he still warned me to be very, very careful how I proceeded in their employ. I have looked and looked for a reason to believe all is as it should be, and have not found it—nor have you."

Ian closed his eyes and sighed, but nodded for her to go on.

"If it happens that Stafford knew what Selwyn wished and why, he will not be pleased by our actions. I suspect he will not allow me simply to resign and walk away. I will forever wonder if he might

suffer an attack of anxiety and send someone to silence me forever. I know too many of his secrets."
Nate's eyes had narrowed, but she raised one hand
to keep him quiet until she could finish. "If this
should be true, I think it will be best if John Stafford
is assured I am no threat to him." She paused. "If he
sees me die."

"You— If— What— Sees you *die*?" choked Ian.

"Not in truth," Nate growled. "Angelique, I understand what you say, but—"

"You do not know him as I do," she said quietly.
"He will not hesitate to do it. Many times he has
asked me to act without telling anyone—not even
Phipps knows all I have done for him. If I were to
reveal publicly all his undertakings, it would cause
a tremendous uproar. And I am just a woman, an
assassin and a spy, hardly someone society will
mourn."

For a long minute all was silent. Ian gripped hand-
fuls of hair and opened his mouth several times to
speak, but never did. Nate just watched her, his gaze
frustrated but measuring. "How do you propose to
do it?" he asked at last.

"A knife to the chest. A bladder of blood, sewn
into my dress, will provide enough proof." Both
men gaped at her for a long moment. "Ian?" she
prodded.

"It's damned lunacy," said Ian heavily, "but I reluctantly agree."

"Good, because you will have to wield the knife."
Ian and Nate jerked in identical surprise at her
words. "If Nate does it, Stafford will have him arrested at once. If I do it, he will wonder why I took
my own life. And I would prefer to have someone I

trust holding the knife, rather than take the chance Phipps can be manipulated."

Ian's face had gone gray. "Bloody Christ, I can't stab you!"

"Let me," said Nate. "We can argue, you can attack me first . . ."

Angelique shook her head. "It must be Ian. Will you, Ian?"

After a long pause, Ian dipped his head. "I'm going to hell for this," he muttered. "But I'll do it. *Only* if absolutely necessary."

"Of course."

Ian grabbed his cap and gave her a tormented glance. "I'll be back in the morning. You can tell me what to do then. I can't think any more of it tonight." And he was gone, banging the door behind him.

"I don't like this," Nate said.

"Neither do I. But I want to be free, once and for all. I cannot go with you if I must spend the rest of my life in fear."

Nate scowled and folded his arms. "You won't. I won't let it come to that."

She came across the room to him and touched his face. "You are not in control of that." His expression darkened. "Thank you," she said softly.

He looked at her a long time. "You don't have to thank me. I would do it even if not for . . ." He stopped and turned away. "If you change your mind about coming with me, you can say so at any time. Then we would not need to go through this . . . this masquerade."

Her lips parted in shock. "You think I will change my mind?"

"I wouldn't blame you," he said with a sort of

philosophical detachment. "It is an enormous sacrifice, even before asking Wallace to stab you in the chest."

"Debilitating," she agreed. "I will lose my home, my employment, the country I have lived in almost all my life, even Melanie . . . Everything, really."

Nate jerked his head in a nod. "Everything."

"Except you," she whispered. "And that makes it infinitely worthwhile."

He didn't say a word; he didn't have to. Nate looked at her with his heart in his eyes, tormented and fearful and bright with love. She stepped into his arms and they clung to each other.

"I can't believe I'm agreeing to this plan," he whispered. "You know that if something goes wrong—"

"Nothing will go wrong," she said, stroking his back.

"I hope." But his arms didn't loosen.

"Trust me," she said. He sighed and pressed his lips to her temple. "What Ian said earlier—about Dixon walking away free—"

"If I thought letting Dixon go free would ensure your safety, I'd do it," he murmured, his breath warm against her skin. "Without hesitation."

"I know you wanted to take him home for trial."

"No, I wanted to clear Ben's name," Nate replied quietly. "A confession from Dixon will do that, and repaying the money will put an end to it."

Despite what he said, Angelique knew what he was giving up—for her. Her heart swelled. "Trust me," she whispered again.

After a moment he nodded. "I do." Then he released her. "I have to see Prince. I'll be back before dark."

She nodded, and he left. Angelique felt weak and shaky; unsurprising, after she had just faced down Nate and Ian both and persuaded them to help stage her death. Perhaps she had gone too far . . . But she thought of the deeds Stafford had had her commit and knew she was right to fear him. Harry had once compared Stafford to a spider, sitting in the center of his web waiting to see what got caught. She had seen how Stafford dealt with those he feared, and she knew how wide his web spread. But with Nate and Ian working with her, she was sure the three of them could outwit the spider.

But to do it, they must be prepared for everything; there was no time to lose. She hurried up to her room, threw open the wardrobe doors, and began digging through her dresses, looking for a pale colored one.

"Lisette," she called. "Lisette!"

The maid came running. "*Oui*, Madame?"

Angelique pulled a dress from the wardrobe. It was light blue, a soft comfortable dress that was a little worn and loose. She wore it about the house mostly. "You must alter this tonight," she said, "from the inside only." She turned it inside out, running her fingers along the bodice seams. "And you must go to the butcher in Whitechapel."

"The butcher?" Lisette blinked in astonishment.

"Yes. We require blood."

Chapter 27

She rose at dawn. Nate stirred and rolled over as she slipped out of bed, but she tucked the blankets around him and left. He'd made love to her last night, not with the driving hunger of before but more leisurely, his hands lingering on her as if he meant to spend the entire night memorizing her body and letting her memorize his. Angelique had luxuriated in every moment. In many ways he was her first true lover—the one man she had loved, fully and completely. If something went wrong today, this might be the last night they had, and she didn't want it to end.

But the sun would not be held back. Before the first rays of light penetrated the windows, she was awake, clinging to the last moments of warm happiness in bed with Nate's lean body relaxed and easy against hers. No matter how she might wish to delay, the day was upon her. Her time to be easy and relaxed and happy was over. Today she must be at her best, sharp and clear and on guard at all times, and lying in bed wouldn't accomplish that. Success today would mean many more nights in bed with Nate. Failure . . . was unacceptable.

She performed her full range of exercises, working her muscles until they burned. When Nate finally appeared in the doorway between their bedrooms, she was keenly awake and alert, her skin taut and warm with exertion. "You should have stayed in bed longer," he said, his voice still scratchy with sleep.

She stretched her arms above her head, feeling sleek and strong. "I needed to be awake."

"Then you should have woken me." He came across the room and hefted her iron bar. "Your weapon?"

"For training only." She laughed as he swung it through the air as she did. "It is heavy for me."

"Oh, it's heavy for me, too," he assured her, still wielding it with an ease that belied his words. "I just can't admit weakness in front of a woman. See, my arm trembles from the strain already." He raised the bar as if it were a fencing foil, pointed at her. "Do you yield?"

She folded her arms and cocked an eyebrow. "To a man who cannot lift a mere bar?"

He grinned, then flicked the bar around, hooking it behind her back and drawing her to him until she had to tip back her head to look into his face. "It's not *that* heavy," he whispered, and kissed her.

Angelique wound her arms around his neck and pressed against him. The iron bar clanked loudly as it hit the floor, and his arms were around her. "Are you nervous?" he whispered, feathering kisses along her cheek.

"No more than usual."

He gave a rueful huff of laughter. "I forget this is normal for you."

She shrugged. "Today will not be. But this . . . the preparation is normal."

"Perhaps it's a good thing." Nate squeezed her closer. "I'm nervous enough for two people."

His heartbeat was strong and steady beneath her cheek. No tremor shook his body, not even his hands. Angelique smiled. "I do not believe it."

"I am," he said. "And fearful that I've led you into something dangerous."

"You have not led me." She laid her palm on his cheek and kissed him once more. "You have been beside me all the way, but I couldn't say either one of us led the other astray."

His eyes closed. "I bloody well hope not."

"All will end well." She stepped out of his embrace. "But first I must bathe, and you have things to do as well. Out with you."

"A bath!" His eyes gleamed. "I can help you . . ."

She laughed. "Tomorrow. And the day after, and all the days to come after that."

He grimaced, but kissed her again and left.

Nate went downstairs to the dining room. Lisette jumped to her feet with a guilty look. Prince rose more deliberately. A plate heaped with food sat in front of him, a cup of tea in front of Lisette. "Good morning," he said.

"Good morning, Nathaniel," said Prince.

"I shall bring you breakfast, Monsieur," Lisette murmured, hurrying out.

Nate looked at Prince. "Finally friends, I see."

"You are not the only one who can charm a lady out of her prickly mood," Prince replied with a grin. "Although I believe her opinion of me improved greatly after we removed the laboratory and its foul smells." He paused. "She reminds me of your mother."

"Well, that may come in handy today." He prowled about the room, and after a moment Prince sat down and began eating again. "You brought the trunk?"

"It's in the drawing room."

Nate nodded. It was a bright clear day, but with clouds gathering on the horizon. "Is everything else ready?"

"Only your belongings are still here. Once we remove them and Mr. Dixon, we will be ready to sail." Prince pushed back his plate and watched Nate with a steady gaze. "You agreed to this plan; you authored parts of it. Are you changing your mind?"

"No," said Nate, still staring out the window. Those clouds drew his eye. A gentle rain to wash away the grime, or a storm to endanger them all? "But there is a last-minute change to the plan."

"What?" Prince lowered his voice, too.

Nate looked over his shoulder. Lisette could return at any moment. "I'll tell you later. It doesn't involve Lisette or Angelique; just a minor adjustment on my part, to allow for more possibilities."

The door swung open then, Lisette with a plate of food. Nate made himself eat, though he didn't taste a bite. Then he and Prince carried the empty trunk, the largest they had brought with them, up to the attic.

Jacob Dixon eyed the trunk in distaste. "Surely there's an easier way," he muttered.

"Absolutely. We could get a coffin," Nate told him, unlocking the manacles. "And send it directly to Lord Selwyn with my compliments."

Dixon glowered at him, but climbed into the trunk, rubbing his wrists. "Am I not to be fed first? After I was up so late creating that journal for you . . ."

"No. You can eat later." Nate closed the lid on the man's scowling face, and locked the trunk. He gave the key to Prince, and grimly they carted their load down the stairs. As they passed Angelique's door, Nate heard a splash and knew she was in her bath. She was going about her day as usual: her strengthening exercises, her bath . . . He knew when he returned, he would find her as beautiful and as calm as always, and ready to defy the man she had worked under for ten years, the man who might want her dead once he realized what she was doing. Nate gripped the trunk handle more tightly, and tried to push his fears for her aside.

They loaded the trunk with Dixon onto the cart Prince had brought. Nate bounded back up the stairs and finished packing his own trunk, dumping everything inside without care. He could sort it out later. He set it at the top of the stairs for Prince to take down, and tapped on Angelique's door.

She sat at her mirror, wrapped in a dressing gown. Lisette was combing out her wet hair. At his entrance, she put up a hand to the maid. "What is it?"

"Prince and I are taking our things to the ship, then Dixon and I will collect whatever is left of the stolen funds. I'll be back in a few hours."

She nodded, her dark eyes steady. "I will wait for you."

Nate nodded once. "Right." He hesitated. "Do not do anything until I return."

She arched her brow. "You think now I will strike

out on my own? I will be right here, regretting I cannot be with you to help chain him like a goat belowdecks."

He grinned in relief. "Very good. I'll see you soon." He crossed the room and kissed her, softly. She broke it off, reminding him they needed every moment of the day. Reluctantly Nate left, but as soon as he closed her door, his steps quickened. They did need every moment of this day. And as they drove to the docks, he explained to Prince how he was changing the plan.

It took a little longer than expected, but the results were also better than Nate had hoped. Jacob Dixon had deposited jewels and funds in a handful of banks around the City, and he didn't seem interested in quick and speedy visits. Dixon wanted to enjoy the flattery of the bankers who regretfully relinquished jewel cases and, in one case, a stack of gold coins. Nate did what he could, but the value of the recovered items kept his temper at bay somewhat. As jewels and gold piled up in his valise, Nate realized Dixon hadn't spent much of his stolen hoard; there would be a great deal of money to return to President Monroe, probably enough to fully redeem the pledges Ben had made. At least Dixon had put his head for money to some good use. That, along with the signed confession from the thief, should be enough to clear Ben's name.

"I trust you've remarked my considerable cooperation," Dixon said when they were on their way back to the ship.

Nate nodded. "Yes. I appreciate how you've spared me the trouble of shooting you."

Dixon inched away from him in the hackney. "Always *violence* . . ."

"It wasn't how I intended to proceed, but given altered circumstances, I believe I've gone to remarkable effort to protect you." Nate gave him a cold smile. "It may have made me a trifle testy at times, for which I do apologize."

He returned Dixon to the ship's brig and had a last word with the captain and Prince before returning to Varden Street, where he found Angelique at her desk.

"Did all go well? Is everything in readiness?" she asked when he came in. Nate nodded, and she sighed in relief. "I was just about to have Lisette take it." She held out the note she had written.

Nate glanced at the note, promising Lord Selwyn news of a most urgent nature relating to Mr. Jacob Dixon if he replied to Mr. Stafford at Bow Street at his earliest convenience. "What if he does not go at once?"

"Lisette will wait to see if he does and send word to all of us."

He handed back the letter. "You are ready, then." Her dress didn't look different than usual, but it was the same light blue one he had seen laid out on her bed when he left with Dixon.

She laid one hand against her bodice, just below her left breast. "It was cold at first, but I barely feel it now."

His eyes fixed on the spot. It didn't look remarkable in any way—thank goodness. "We could just shoot Stafford and Selwyn, then run."

"Do not be ridiculous." She rose. "We would never make it out of England alive."

She was right and he knew it. "Send the note," he told her. "Let's be done with this."

Angelique rang the bell at the narrow boarding-house, keeping her eyes fixed on the door. The land-lady rented rooms by the hour, mostly to whores whose customers wanted a bit more privacy than an alley off Covent Garden offered. Angelique knew her well, having often found herself in need of a private room for an hour here and there. When the woman opened the door, Angelique simply said, "A shilling an hour, if the room overlooks the street," and the landlady nodded curtly, showing her up to a small dingy room. The bed was barely wide enough for one, and the windows were grimy with dirt, but they did overlook the street.

She laid her cloak across the bed and drew the shabby curtains almost closed, opening one window a few inches to allow her to hear as well as see. From this angle, she had a clear view of the front of the Bow Street Magistrates office.

Now she only had to wait.

She tried not to let herself think of Nate much. His role in this was almost concluded. This morn-ing he had collected whatever remained of the stolen funds. Everything of his was secure on his ship, including Dixon, safely hidden away on board. At a moment's notice, Nate was ready to sail. She was glad for that, even though it would mean she didn't see him again for some time. He had gotten far more than he bargained for in London, but he hadn't flinched from a single challenge—including those she threw at him herself. In spite of herself,

Angelique's thoughts drifted to the sensual memory of Nate's lips on hers, his hands on her skin, her name on his tongue.

Until a glossy black carriage stopped in front of Bow Street, and a tall dark man with a long nose stepped down.

Nate was waiting by the kitchen door when the knock came. "Half an hour, sir," said the ragged street boy who stood there.

"Good work." Nate flipped him a pair of shillings, and the lad was gone the instant his fingers closed on the coins. Nate pulled on his coat, the same unfashionable brown coat he'd worn to Stafford's office that first time, just a few weeks ago. He glanced around the Varden Street kitchen for the last time, checking off things in his mind to ensure nothing had been forgotten. Then he slipped a small glass bottle and a wooden tube into his pocket before he let himself out and closed the door.

Ian had just poured another tot of whiskey into Phipps's glass when the sound of the outer door reached his ears. Slowly he closed his flask and set it aside, listening. "Someone's come to make a report," he said, gesturing to the door. "I'll leave you to it."

"That would be best," Phipps agreed, gulping down the whiskey and hiding the glass in a drawer of his desk. "Off with you, Wallace."

Ian took his time getting to his feet and collecting his coat. He'd been sitting here with Phipps for over an hour, freely sharing his whiskey, but now dawdled until the footsteps passed the door. "Eh, must have been mistaken," he said with a wink at Phipps. "Or someone's not reporting to you."

The pale little man scowled. "Everyone reports to me."

"Ah, everyone except her." Ian had opened the door and stuck his head out to look. "Madame Martand."

Phipps crowded past him to look. The hood of her cloak was down, revealing her glossy dark hair and unmistakable profile as she reached the stairs and turned to climb them. "Her," Phipps muttered in a petulant tone. "Too proud for her own good, that one."

"Aye, but good enough to earn some pride. She must have caught that American swindler," Ian said, still lounging in the doorway. "Miserable doings there, I gather."

Phipps's ears all but quivered. "Indeed. I . . . er . . . can't recall all the details of that assignment . . ."

Because he hadn't been told them, thought Ian. "Old Staff sent me out to check on her a week ago," he said. "I think she and the American—not the swindler, the one she was meant to work with— weren't getting on all that well. No surprise there, he's an excitable, unreliable fellow, the sort who only cares for his own affairs."

"Do tell," murmured Phipps.

"Well, she must have got around it one way or another." Ian paused. "I wonder you don't know all about it. They told me next to nothing, you know. But the old fox was quite eager to see that matter settled; perhaps we'll all reap a reward, eh?"

Phipps's mouth pinched. "I am hardly about to divulge what he tells me."

Ian laughed. "Nor I! Guess we'll just have to stifle our curiosity, then."

"Yes. Er . . . well, if she's completed a job, I shall be wanted," Phipps murmured, almost to himself. "To take the notes and send any notifications and such. I had better be prepared."

Ian shrugged. "Might as well go wait, aye?"

Chapter 28

The Earl Selwyn was a tall man, dark in hair and skin. He must have some foreign blood in him, Angelique thought. She guessed he was about forty years of age, and had gone a little soft around the middle as men of his years tended to do. But there was nothing soft about his cold, arrogant expression as he turned and glared down his long, sharp nose at her when she opened the door, interrupting what sounded like a tense argument.

"Get out," he said. Behind him, she saw John Stafford's eyes fasten on her.

Angelique closed the door behind her. "I wish to speak to you."

"In a moment, Madame," said Stafford, in a far more polite tone than Selwyn's simultaneous, "Go!"

There was a moment of silence. Angelique returned Selwyn's angry stare without flinching. "My lord," said Stafford reluctantly, "this is Madame Martand, my top agent. I engaged her on the matter we spoke of."

Selwyn's expression didn't alter, but a vein began

pulsing in his forehead. "Indeed," he said in a frosty voice. "What do you want? Have you come to report success?"

"I have brought you some news." She drew out a small, battered journal and held it out. "And a gift."

Selwyn scowled. He barely glanced at the journal. "What the devil is that? Have you done your job or not, girl?"

"My lord," said Stafford, giving the man a warning look. He came to take the journal from her. "What is your news?" he asked, laying the journal on his desk.

"I have done what you asked." Selwyn inhaled and glanced at Stafford, who gave a tiny nod.

"Excellent work, my dear," Stafford said. "If you would excuse us a moment—"

"But you must read the journal." She raised one eyebrow. "It will tell quite a story, one I believe you will wish to hear now."

Stafford paused. "Whose journal is it?"

"That of Jacob Dixon. I discovered it in his belongings while Mr. Avery was retrieving the stolen funds."

Selwyn's pleased expression faltered. Stafford was looking at the journal. "Perhaps you should tell us."

Angelique kept her eyes on Selwyn. "It begins many years ago, with a young husband and father who suddenly, unexpectedly, rose to an earldom." It was very quiet in the office. Selwyn looked stunned. "Unfortunately, his young son suffered a mysterious affliction the doctors could not cure. How distressing for a man to think of his new title and estates descending into the hands of an idiot. If only there were some way to remove the child from the succession . . ."

"Is this how you spend the government's money, Stafford?" interrupted Selwyn. He looked at Angelique with murder in his eyes.

"I assume you are telling this story for a reason," said Stafford slowly. He didn't look at Selwyn, but his face had gone hard.

Angelique smiled coolly. "Of course. It was a shocking story. As this earl was searching for a way to secure his posterity, free of whatever taint had infected his first child, his secretary proposed a plan. It was insupportable that a title so old and illustrious should pass to this child, who was not normal. Naturally one could not stoop to interfering in God's plan, but perhaps a quiet solution to the problem could be found." She paused. Selwyn's face was flushed and ominous. He still glared at her. Angelique felt in her bones then that Dixon had spoken the truth, that every word he said about Selwyn was accurate. This man wouldn't hesitate to do away with his own child, not to mention an indiscreet former employee. This man had forced his wife to flee into anonymous solitude to save her child, and Angelique could have killed him just for that. She stared back at him as she continued her story.

"The countess did not wish her child harmed, but she knew her husband shared no such tenderness and delicacy. The secretary proposed that the countess and her child could simply . . . disappear. After a short time, the earl could proclaim them dead, and no one would ever know the truth. The countess and her son would be well provided for by the earl, in secret bank accounts, and the earl would be free to proceed with his life. Perhaps marry again, for a lord of his stature must be a very eligible match even for a duke's daughter. Perhaps sire other, normal, children. And if any trace of this secretary, who knew the earl's terrible secret, ever came to light, why, who would believe a secretary over an earl? Particularly if that secretary happened to be under suspicion of stealing a fortune from a foreign government as well. Why, it would be simple enough to warn certain people that this secretary posed a danger to the Crown. The Crown, of course, would zealously defend itself."

Nobody spoke. Stafford reached out and flipped open the journal with one finger.

"What a bunch of rot." Selwyn was almost choking on his own words; he might have been breathing fire. "But you said you had done what you were ordered to do, yes?"

Stafford looked up at Angelique, then at Selwyn. "Is it rot, sir?" he murmured. "I wonder . . ."

There was a commotion in the hall, and then the door flew open. Nate stood in the doorway, his hair ruffled, his coat askew. He raised his hand and pointed at Angelique. "Arrest that woman, sir!" he demanded, breathing heavily. "She has killed a man."

"Be silent," commanded Stafford. "And close the bloody door! Phipps!"

Nate stumbled into the room, pushed by Mr. Phipps behind him. Ian ducked through the door, too, his expression alive and alert. He closed the door as Stafford tried to quiet Nate.

"She cut his throat, without warning," he was

saying loudly. "We agreed that he was to be bound back to New York for trial, sir!" Then he looked at Selwyn, still standing silently, and exclaimed in relief, "Lord Selwyn! Add your voice to mine; you know how this could adversely affect relations between our governments. I demand an explanation on behalf of my President why your agent killed the man I worked so diligently, and within your requirements, to apprehend."

Selwyn shifted his weight. "I cannot speak on matters of British sovereignty," he said stiffly.

"Mr. Avery, I beg you to retire to another room and compose yourself," Stafford said. "We will be happy to address your concerns, if events have not unfolded as planned."

"Yes, he should be told," said Angelique. "They should all be told, once and for all. Did you command me to kill that man to hide Lord Selwyn's crime for all eternity?"

Phipps's jaw dropped open. Ian started. "What?" he demanded.

"Madame, we should discuss this privately." Stafford's eyes were cold with warning.

She shook her head. "No, I think not," she said gently. "Monsieur Avery deserves to know, as he was honest with you in every way. Ian and Phipps deserve to know that you have not abused your office to curry favor with a man of Lord Selwyn's position. And I deserve to know if I have stained my hands with blood not in defense of Britain and her people, but in defense of one man's secret shame. Did you know Lord Selwyn's reasons when he told you Jacob Dixon was a danger to the Crown and must be killed?"

Stafford's gaze drifted to the journal again and rested there a moment. Then he looked at Lord Selwyn. "No, I did not."

His admission, quietly spoken though it was, crackled in the air like a lightning bolt. "You ordered Mr. Stafford to have Dixon killed?" Nate asked the earl, as though he could hardly believe his ears.

Selwyn's eyes darted around the room. "I am not going to discuss government affairs in these circumstances."

"And you acted on it without proof or even explanation?" Nate asked Stafford, even more incredulously. Without waiting for an answer, he turned on Angelique. "And you simply obeyed? What of a woman's tender heart?"

She looked at him without expression. "It was my duty." She turned back to Stafford. "But no more. I am done."

"Wallace," said Stafford in a deadly quiet voice. "Remove her."

"I tender my resignation from this moment on," Angelique said. "I will go my way, and you shall go yours."

Stafford hesitated. "My dear, I cannot let you do that."

Her heart skipped a beat. Slowly she slid her knife from its sheath and faced Ian. "Do not try it," she said to him. Ian hesitated. His gaze shot to Stafford.

Nate threw out his hands in alarm. "Christ! There's no need for that!"

"Mr. Avery, I believe you should leave," Stafford told him.

"You've got a madwoman on your hands," Nate charged, thrusting out his finger at her. "I saw her work, sir; the man was butchered, his throat cut from ear to ear." Selwyn let out an audible gulp, inching away from where Angelique stood, knife in hand.

"Mr. Avery, leave," said Stafford again. "Wallace, take her to Mr. Phipps's office."

"Ian," she said softly, keeping her eyes fixed on the big Scot.

Ian's face twisted with concern. "Come, lass," he said gently. "Put the knife away. You know I won't hurt you."

"I am not going with you, not on his orders," she replied. "I am done with this. He has used us, Ian, do you not see? On the word of men such as him"—she jerked her head toward Selwyn—"he has sent us out to spy upon, to follow, to incriminate, to murder. It does not matter why to him; we are just weapons for the government to use. For all we know, this has all been to his profit. Lord Selwyn has proven he will go to great lengths to keep his secret. I am sure he would be glad to pay a few thousand pounds for peace of mind."

"Madame Martand," said Stafford sharply. "Be silent. Wallace, take her downstairs, or I will have you taken with her."

Slowly she shook her head. "I have killed a man because I took your word that it was necessary. How many other men in the Home Office or the Parliament or the nobility would like to have someone conveniently killed, not by their own hand but by the anonymous hand of a government assassin? They would have no guilt, yet they would reap the benefit. And all they have to do is ask you."

"That is not what I do." A vein was throbbing in

Stafford's temple. "Have you really believed yourself to be killing innocent men and settling private scores?"

"No," she whispered. "I believed I did the right thing. And that is what haunts me."

Stafford said nothing. Phipps was white-faced but with the bright light of glee in his eyes. Angelique felt a moment of black humor that at least she could finally fulfill Phipps's expectations of her.

"Wait a moment," said Nate loudly. "You've done this before?"

She flicked him a cold glance. "Yes."

Nate turned to Selwyn. "Did you know about this?" he demanded. "Did you know, sir, that you were sending me into an assassination ring? That is not at all what we discussed—I wanted to take him to New York for trial! This must constitute a serious breach of protocol, sir, and an open affront to my country."

Selwyn's eyes darted to Stafford. "Of course not," he said stiffly. "You have been seriously misled, Mr. Avery."

"Mr. Phipps," said Stafford ominously, "show Mr. Avery out. He must catch his ship back to America, I am sure. Mr. Wallace, take Madame Martand belowstairs. I will deal with her shortly."

"No." Angelique moved toward the door. "I am done speaking. I shall leave. If I have your word that you will deal with Lord Selwyn's deception appropriately, you will have nothing to fear from me. I am ready for a new life."

"That won't be necessary." Stafford turned to Lord Selwyn. "We have worked together well for many years, Madame Martand. Surely you see that I still have need of you . . . and you have need of me."

"No. You must deal without me from now on."

"Don't be hasty, Angelique," said Ian quietly.

"Wallace," warned Stafford.

Ian held up one hand to him. "Wait a bit and think," he said to Angelique. "Let's go have a drink. Tomorrow we'll talk it over, and sort it all out."

Slowly, she shook her head, backing away from him. "No, Ian. I am no longer in his employ."

Ian glanced at Stafford, who made an impatient motion. "Remember who you work for," the spymaster said to him. "Remember all we must protect."

Ian turned to her, his face set. Angelique's heart pounded. Ian advanced on her, hands still upraised. For a moment he looked at her, his blue eyes clouded. "Do you really want it to come to this?" he said quietly—pleadingly.

This was the part of the plan Ian had hated most, and not unreasonably. She hadn't liked it herself, but knew it was her last defense against living the rest of her life under the shadow of Stafford's reach. She had thought it through, persuaded Nate and Ian both to accept it, and told them and herself she was prepared for it. But now it was upon her; Ian was offering one more chance before she crossed her Rubicon. Her heart climbed into her throat. She forced it back down, stiffened her spine, and raised her knife. "Remember your promise," she breathed, then spoke normally. "What choice have I?"

His face twisted in sorrow for a moment, then he lunged. Angelique made a wild swipe with her knife, without much force. Her blade flashed, drawing blood from his arm in a shallow cut. Nate began cursing like mad, shoving Selwyn down behind Stafford's desk and managing to knock over several chairs in the process. Phipps was shouting at both of them, even as he scurried behind a bookcase. Stafford barked something at Phipps, who shouted back. Angelique heard it all as Ian caught her wrist, the one holding the knife, and twisted. He backed her to the wall, his tall frame looming over her and blocking out the chaos in the rest of the room from her view. She struggled against his grip, appreciating for the first time how strong Ian was. He could hold her like this all day and she would be powerless to stop him. "Ian," she cried, looking up at him. "Please . . ."

"Madame, you have gone too far," shouted Stafford at the same time. "Wallace! Take care of her!"

Anguish flashed in his blue eyes. "Hold still," he murmured, and then he turned her wrist, pointing the knife at her ribs. Angelique froze, and the tip of the knife pierced her bodice.

Blood welled up at once. It stained the front of her pale blue dress with a garish purple-red blotch that seeped and spread. Angelique stared at it, touching the rip in her bodice as the blood poured forth. Ian pulled the knife from her fingers, and stepped back.

Selwyn made a sound that would have been a scream from a woman. Phipps's eyes were popping out in slack-jawed shock. Stafford stared blankly. Angelique pressed her hands to her chest, and more blood bubbled up; the stain had spread down her dress and was soaking her skirt. Her hands were covered in it. She trembled at the sight of her red-slicked hands, holding them up. The whole room seemed frozen in place, mesmerized by the sight.

With a curse Ian threw down her knife, and the spell was broken. Angelique swayed on her feet, stumbling a step forward before falling to her knees.

"Good God," said Nate in a stunned voice. "He's killed her."

"Mr. Phipps, escort Mr. Avery out, now," snapped Stafford. "*Now*, Mr. Phipps!" Nate made little protest as Mr. Phipps seized his arm and hustled him out of the room. He stared at her until the door banged closed behind him, and then she heard his voice, shocked and upset, echoing in the corridor outside. "Stay where you are, sir," Stafford said coldly to Lord Selwyn, who had started to rise and was eyeing the door with obvious intent. At Stafford's command, he froze, then stood back against the wall, his face pale and alarmed.

John Stafford walked around his desk. He was coming toward her. She sat down heavily, her skirts twisting around her, and stared up at him without a word.

His eyes fixed on the tear in her bodice, where blood flowed in a steady trickle. "Oh, my dear," he said almost inaudibly. "Why did it have to come to this?"

"You lied to me," she whispered. "You lied to us all."

Something like regret etched his face. "Perhaps," he conceded. "But it was all for a good cause."

"Not all," she wheezed. "Not all . . . Not what *he* wanted."

Stafford barely acknowledged her gesture at

Selwyn. "He will pay for that, you may depend on it."

She swallowed, her head drooping forward. "Good," she murmured. She groped for him. "But promise me . . . no more killing. It's not right . . ."

He recoiled from her bloody hand, but not in time to avoid her entirely. Her fingers left dark red stripes down the front of his gray jacket. "No more," he said kindly. "None but you could do them."

Angelique rolled to the floor and let her eyes drift closed.

Chapter 29

Nate strode down the street, his heart thundering. He clenched his hands into fists to hide how they shook. She was fine. Wallace would sooner stab himself than hurt Angelique. It was all part of the plan. He should be relieved it was over, and seemed to have worked, even though they'd had to resort to the most drastic part of it.

But he kept seeing her slumping to the floor, drenched in blood. His hands shook as if he had the palsy.

He walked to the dock at a rapid clip, unwilling to sit even for a hackney ride. Down the street from where the *Water Asp* was moored, he turned into a public house, a dingy little pub with a good view of the ship. Several members of his crew looked up from their ale as he threw open the door. "On board, all of you," he barked, loud enough to draw the attention of every man in the room. The crew leaped to their feet and began rushing around. "Where's the rest?"

"Back there, sir." One of the men pointed to a narrow hallway.

Muttering curses, Nate walked to the end of the

corridor, and pounded loudly on the door there. "The *Water Asp* sails tonight!" he shouted. "All out now, or be left behind." He pushed the door open.

Five men, including Prince, were hurriedly collecting their winnings from a table covered with cards and coins. "Make haste, make haste," Nate growled, glancing over his shoulder. No one had followed him down the corridor, but his crew was making quite a racket in the pub as they settled their bills. He turned around and glared at Prince. "Everything is ready?"

Prince nodded, sweeping the cards into his pocket. "Yes, sir. Just as you instructed."

"Good." Nate grabbed one man by the scruff of his neck and hauled him out of his chair. "Drunk already, I see."

"Not by choice," mumbled Jacob Dixon, swaying on his feet. "Drink or get shot . . ."

"Now walk or get shot," Nate muttered back, shoving Dixon ahead of him down the hall, Prince at his heels. The other men from the back room clustered around them, helping keep Dixon on his feet and moving.

It was a terrible risk he took. If by chance someone who would recognize Dixon had followed him, there could be trouble. He had no idea what would happen to him if he were caught out in the lie he had just told to Lord Selwyn and one very dangerous spymaster, but even more he had feared what might happen to Angelique. Wallace was supposed to get her safely away, but if something went wrong . . . If Stafford suspected anything odd . . . If anyone checked to see that Wallace's knife really had gone between Angelique's ribs instead of just through the bladder of blood sewn into her dress . . .

The thought was unbearable. So Nate had changed his plan. Dixon wasn't safely hidden on the ship; Dixon was close at hand, ready to be produced at a moment's notice if any exchange had been required. If things had gone wrong, and Nate's hand had been forced, he would have handed Dixon right into Selwyn's embrace without hesitation. If he must trade the man he sought for the woman he loved, Nate would have done it in a heartbeat and not wasted one moment of regret for Dixon or for Selwyn or even for Ben Davies. Ben especially would have expected no less of him.

Thankfully it hadn't come to that—yet. He made a bit more of a scene in the main taproom, shouting at his crew to get moving, and they rushed out around him. He thought Dixon would be well concealed in a pack of sailors, dressed as one of them, as drunk as any of them, but he kept his grip on the back of Dixon's jacket as they went down the narrow street to the dock. To his immense relief no one stopped them, and they made it aboard the *Water Asp* unimpeded. The captain, already alerted to be ready to sail, immediately sent the men scurrying about the deck to their stations.

Nate dragged Dixon, now stumbling badly, down belowdecks to the brig, a small iron cage furnished with nothing but a bucket. He shoved him through the door. Dixon collapsed onto his knees, then retched into the bucket. Without even wiping his mouth, he slowly toppled over onto the blanket lying beside it. A moment later, a loud snore drifted out of his open mouth. Just like any sailor.

Nate locked the cage and tucked the key into his pocket, giving the door a hard rattle to make sure it was secure. His hands were shaking again. It was dim down here, lit by infrequent lanterns despite the bright daylight streaming through the hatches. It smelled of pine tar and the rank stink of vomit and sour gin.

Prince laid a hand on his shoulder. "Everything went well?" he asked quietly.

"There must have been a gallon of blood in that bladder." His stomach revolted as the image flashed across his mind again, scoring into his memory. Nate had to bend over, resting his hands on his knees as he fought back the rising bile. "Good God, it was everywhere . . ."

"But she is well," Prince said.

"I hope. Wallace is supposed to send word as soon as he can." He dug in his pocket, and extracted the wooden tube and bottle of poisoned darts Prince had given him the day before. "I didn't need these after all." Although he almost wished he had used them anyway. He could have slapped a dart into Selwyn's neck in the mayhem when Angelique drew her knife, and blown another into Stafford, just to be sure no one would follow them. Now he had to spend the night wondering if things had gone wrong, and if he should have taken no chances.

Prince took the darts and nodded. "Come, Nathaniel. You should sit down. Get some air."

"I don't want to sit down," he growled.

"But you can't go to her," Prince reminded him gently. "And you mustn't give up the masquerade now."

Nate closed his eyes. Goddamn it. He couldn't do

anything for Angelique. Prince was right. He cast one more black look at Dixon, the author of all this trouble, and followed Prince up to the deck.

It was impossible to play at dying for very long. Angelique was able to let her mind drift for several minutes at a time, letting her breathing grow shallow and slow. She had seen men linger for days after being stabbed in the gut, before succumbing to slow, painful death. It was not a pleasant thought. The blood soaking though her dress was growing cold, and she couldn't stop a shiver from time to time, mostly of revulsion.

Above her she could hear Selwyn talking; arguing, cursing, pleading. The earl seemed to know his life hung in the balance and he was not going quietly. Stafford was saying little, and Angelique wondered if Lord Selwyn knew that was a bad sign. He might not believe everything Angelique and Nate had said, but he didn't disbelieve; he would send someone to investigate, to question, to dig up whatever remained of the truth. Angelique wasn't sure what proof he could find with Dixon apparently dead, but then, Stafford didn't always require definitive proof before he acted.

Ian was hunkered down on his haunches a few feet away from her, his head in his hands. After cutting into the bladder of pig's blood, Ian had said nothing. From time to time he would shoot an agonized look at her, as if to check that she was still carrying on with this. She could see his desperation to get out of that office in his face. It mirrored her own, but she had to stay limp. She closed her eyes and thought about Nate. Had he made it to the ship yet?

Everything should have been all ready to sail, with Dixon securely locked belowdecks. Nate and Prince had perfected all those arrangements without her; they couldn't risk anyone seeing her near the ship. She hoped Phipps had just released him at the door, but the little weasel hadn't returned yet.

The door creaked. Phipps. Angelique had to bite her tongue to keep from sighing aloud in relief. If he was here, he couldn't be following Nate.

She heard Phipps's inhalation of disgust. She had slumped back against the wall, leaving her bloodied front on display. "Sir," he said, "should I take care of . . . *this*?"

"I'll do it," Ian growled, springing to his feet. "Don't touch her."

Angelique opened her eyes to give Phipps one last freezing glare. The man leaped backward when he saw. "Bless my soul, she's still alive!" he cried.

"Not for long," said Ian harshly. "There's no help for a knife in the chest."

"Phipps, fetch a carriage," said Stafford. "Mr. Wallace will attend to Madame Martand. And when you have done with that . . ." He paused. "Send for Lord Sidmouth. Immediately."

Selwyn started arguing again in a low, fierce tone. Ian bent over Angelique and gathered her into his arms as gently as he would a newborn lamb, folding her cloak around her. She coughed as he moved her, making her breathing loud and labored. Ian flinched, but didn't pause. "A few more minutes," he breathed, then got to his feet, shifting her weight easily in his arms. "Hold the door, Phipps."

There was a shuffle. "Oh, really," snapped Phipps.

"Hold the door, or I'll be coming back for you," said Ian in a deadly voice. "The knife's already soiled."

The door creaked open, then Ian was walking. They were out of the room. Now down the stairs. Now moving through the barren corridor that led to the back entry. Now in the alley, being bundled into a carriage. Angelique's heart battered against her ribs, as much from anxiety as from the effort of wheezing and coughing on every breath. She was out of Bow Street. A clink of coins, the carriage dipped as Ian climbed in beside her and cradled her in his arm once more.

"Easy there, just a moment," he whispered, reaching out to snap the curtains closed as the carriage rocked forward, then lurched into motion. Angelique let her head rest against Ian's arm, and breathed a sigh—of gladness, of sadness, of relief.

It was done.

Chapter 30

~~~~~~~~~~~ ᎧᎧ ~~~~~~~~~~~

Two weeks later

So this is Scotland."

"Aye." Ian's voice was quiet with pride and wistfulness. Only a thin line of what should have been a glorious sunset was visible, a stripe of bright orange along the distant horizon. Thick gray clouds had begun rolling across the sky almost as soon as they set out that morning, and when Ian had pointed to the east and indicated Edinburgh, it had been nothing but an indistinct smudge. Wispy fog curled around their feet now as if to shroud even the streets of Leith from their view.

Behind Angelique, Lisette sniffed loudly into her handkerchief. "Damp," she muttered.

Ian grinned. "Damp, but beautiful."

"Damp and dark" was her retort. Lisette had found fault with everything since they left London, from the food to the weather to the way Ian loaded their belongings into the coach. Angelique had offered to release her, if she wished, but the maid had refused. The complaints were just her way of dealing with the upheaval in her life, and in that vein Angelique could take them with a measure of amusement.

Angelique said nothing now, just closed her eyes and filled her lungs with salty sea air. She could hear the water lapping at the docks and the creak of wood against wood as ships rocked themselves to sleep in the muffling fog. She liked Scotland. It was cold and damp and even dark, but she liked the mystical quiet of the place. Or maybe it was just this moment, so still and yet so taut. The end, and the beginning, of everything for her.

"A farthing for your thoughts," Ian said beside her.

She smiled. "You overpay. I was not thinking anything, merely feeling."

He cleared his throat. "Not regret, I hope. It's not too late to change your mind."

"But my mind has not changed," she whispered. The port was a forest of masts, creaking as they swayed ever so slightly, as if in a breeze. Men scurried along the decks and cross spars, small agile figures hopping along like birds. Skiffs slithered across the water around the hulls, in some cases visible through the fog only by the winking lanterns in their sterns.

"Good." Ian rocked on his heels for a moment. "If I ever disappointed you, or led you to believe . . ." His stumbling, muttered words trailed off as she looked at him in expectation.

"You wish to apologize for flirting with me?" she asked after a moment of silence.

"Yes!" The word burst out with obvious relief. "I never meant to let you think . . . or to suggest . . . That is, I've always held you in the greatest respect . . ."

She smiled. Ian was lying; he had gone too far for her to think he never meant a word of his flirting. Strangely, she did believe he had never been truly interested in her, and she wondered what game he'd been playing. But now it no longer mattered. "You flirted with me as I flirted with you. Neither was serious, and neither, I think, is hurt."

He tilted back his face to the evening sky and heaved a deep sigh. "Thanks be to all the saints," he said fervently. "I didn't look forward to apologizing in front of him."

Angelique raised one eyebrow. "You fear someone more than me?"

He grinned at her, cocky again. "Not a bit, lass. But I always knew if I crossed you too far, I'd never see retribution coming; I'd just wake up dead or castrated, and that would be that."

She laughed. "Not you, Ian. I would have let someone else do it, out of respect for our camaraderie these several years."

" 'Tis more than my own mother would do," he assured her. "But less than he would, I think."

"Yes," she simply said in agreement. Much less.

By now one of the small boats had turned toward them, heading like a one-eyed beast through the fog. She could make out the shape of a man, his arms swooping wide and then pulling in as he rowed. As the skiff drew near, the lamplight gleamed on his face; the rest of him was muffled in darkness. With a scrape, the boat ran ashore. The rower tucked the oars inside, then jumped out and pulled his craft onto the thin rocky beach. Then he turned toward where they stood and raised his head in an attitude of waiting.

Angelique stepped off the edge of the quay and walked toward him. His teeth flashed white in the darkness, and her heart leaped. Part of her had wondered—feared, really—if he wouldn't be here, if something would go awry and disrupt their plan, if he wouldn't have second thoughts and be far across the ocean by now. But perhaps he had wondered the same about her. Perhaps his heart had leaped with the same joy and relief that hers had, when he saw her. Or perhaps her heart would always do that when he grinned at her like this.

She stopped in front of him. He wore a thick woolen coat, with an equally nondescript cap on his head; no more tailored coats and polished boots, for now anyway. But when she looked into his lean, angular face, she couldn't stop the smile that broke across her lips. He opened his arms, and she rushed into them, clinging to him almost as tightly as he clung to her.

"I thought you would never arrive," he whispered, and just the familiar sound of his voice made her heart feel lighter.

She lifted her head and smiled. "It takes a long time to travel slowly and unremarkably from London to Leith."

Nate chuckled. "Darling, after my last glimpse of you, an hour seemed an eternity, let alone two weeks. And that reminds me: I owe your friend Mr. Phipps a good knock on the head, for the way he shoved me out of that office."

She touched his cheek. "I will make it up to you."

"Oh!" Nate brightened. "That's good enough for me. I forgive him." And she laughed, until Nate's mouth met hers in a kiss ripe with longing and relief. And love—more love than she had ever imagined two people could share.

Footsteps crunched behind her on the narrow beach. "I see you're in a rush to be off, Avery," said Ian. "But I think you need a bigger boat. You knew it was a pair of women you'd be fetching, aye? They've three hefty trunks."

Nate kept her at his side, his arm curled securely around her beneath her long cloak. "Prince was right behind me. The lazy fellow's probably just taking his time." Another larger boat was nudging closer to the water's edge as he spoke, and a moment later Prince jumped out to pull it up.

"Lazy?" Prince said indignantly. "I just hadn't your motivation." Still breathing hard, he swept off his cap and bowed to her. "Madame, a pleasure to see you again."

Angelique bobbed in reply, hampered by Nate's grip on her waist. "I am glad to see you are well, Prince."

He laughed quietly. "Well enough for having lived with a caged bear for two weeks! We would have thrown him overboard if you did not come to calm him."

"Ungrateful wretch," Nate said without heat. He pressed a kiss to Angelique's temple. "Where are your things?"

Ian helped them carry the trunks down to the water's edge. Without her spy's wardrobe and wigs, Angelique traveled surprisingly lightly. She had told Lisette to pack only her favorite things, nothing at all of Stafford's. That had all been sent to the ragman when Lisette cleared out her house after her supposed death. Nothing of that life was coming with her to her new life. Except Lisette, of course; not wanting to presume, Angelique had told her of the generous sum named in her will, enough for the maid to live in comfort for the rest of her days, but Lisette didn't want to stay behind. "I've seen enough of England, *merci*," she'd said with a sniff, and told Ian to send her own trunk on with Angelique's.

The only regret Angelique had was Mellie. When Stafford notified her solicitor that Angelique Martand had unfortunately met her end in a tragic accident, Melanie would believe her truly dead. Mr. Dexter would execute her will, selling her house and possessions and forwarding the bulk of the money to Melanie. It was blood money anyway; let Mellie put it to good use, serving the poor. Angelique knew that somewhere in that quiet graveyard behind the rectory, Melanie would grieve for her as a mother for her child, and feel responsible for her death. It tore her heart in two, but she had to let things play out, on the chance someone might have connected them. When they reached America, she would find a way to let Melanie know the truth. And perhaps, in a few years, she would be able to visit Melanie again.

As Nate settled one trunk in his boat and helped Prince secure another in the other boat, Angelique turned to Ian. He was one of her few friends, the only person associated with Stafford she would truly miss. She had contemplated marrying him at one time, and he had risked his life and future to help her escape with the man she loved. "Good-bye, Ian," she said softly.

He was staring over the water again, squinting into the encroaching fog. "It was a noble thing you did," he muttered. "Staff went too far."

She laughed. "Noble? That goes too far as well." Her smile faded and she raised her hands in surrender. "But it had to be done, and who better? I am ready to be done with him. I was ready a while ago. I have no regrets."

Ian shot her a wry glance. "And look how miserable your last job was."

"It worked out well enough in the end," she said serenely, then ruined it by catching sight of Nate and smiling again.

Ian snorted with laughter. "Aye, well enough. Your face, when you look at him . . ." He hesitated. "I wish you much joy, Angelique."

"Thank you. I wish you the same."

"I expect I'll come out well enough," he said. "We Scots are used to making do."

"I wish you better than making do," she said softly, and went up on her toes to kiss his cheek. "*Bon chance*, Ian."

He just gave her a lopsided smile, then stepped back as footsteps came crunching close again.

"Are you ready?" Nate asked.

Angelique nodded, holding out her hand. He had put her trunk in one end of the punt, forcing her to sit directly in front of him. When he shoved away from the shore and stepped into the boat, aided by a strong push from Ian, she had to grab the sides to keep her seat. Nate sat down, his knees almost touching hers, and set the oars in the oarlocks. He had taken off his cap, and now took off the coat as well, revealing a white shirt rolled up to the elbows.

"I wondered how we would find you," she said as he dipped the oars into the water and slowly they drifted away from the shore. Ian had gone on to help Prince with the last trunk, and Lisette was muttering at both of them in angry French. Even just a few yards from shore, their figures had grown hazy. Angelique kept her eyes on Ian, raising her hand in one last farewell when she thought he turned her way. It was too dark and foggy to see if he made any reply, and she turned her gaze back to Nate, blinking away the moisture behind her eyelids.

Nate grinned. "I've been sitting on this shore every night for the last week. You would have been hard-pressed to avoid me."

She arched her eyebrow. "I am surprised you waited."

"Are you?" He leaned closer, his eyes keen on hers. "Are you really?"

Angelique had to retreat; no more games, she had promised him. "No," she breathed.

Nate smiled, that reckless pirate's smile. "I would have waited another day, then come after you."

"Would you?" He dug the oars into the water and the boat lurched forward. Angelique had to hold the side of the boat to keep from falling into him. "Where would you have gone searching?"

"Everywhere." Back on the shore, Lisette gave a loud squawk as Prince stepped into the other boat. The trunks were settled between them, a looming bulk in the center of the boat. Ian was nothing but a dark shadow now. He said something to Prince in unmistakable Scots brogue, and the black man's low laugh drifted across the inky water, followed by Lisette's scolding tones.

Angelique turned back to the man in front of her. "If I had not wanted you to find me—"

"It would have made no difference."

She watched him a moment. The wind ruffled his unbound hair as he rowed, and the lantern cast a golden glow over his face and bare forearms as it swayed from side to side. "You would have dragged me away against my wishes?"

"Never," he said indignantly. "I would have dragged you away to persuade you of your true desires and feelings."

"And you know them better than I do?"

"Yes, ma'am." Again his teeth shone in the darkness. "Once we reach the ship, I'll be glad to show you just what you desire."

She was counting on that, but gave him a severe look anyway, then turned to look over the water. The light of lanterns on the ships they passed sparkled on the rippling surface, then vanished in the fog. There was an eerie sort of peace out on the water, where sound and light just seemed to melt away. Angelique had the sense that they could simply vanish into the fog and no one would ever know where they had gone. But as long as she was with Nate, the prospect didn't bother her.

"Where are we going?" she asked.

"Boston."

She waited, but he just grinned. "And then?" she prompted with a laugh. "Will we explore the frontier and see the native peoples? You have piqued my interest, with your tales of adventure and knives from the ferocious Wyandot."

Slowly Nate shook his head. "You've quenched my thirst for adventure, my dear. Seeing you lying limp and soaked in blood on Stafford's floor—"

"Pig's blood," she murmured.

"*Blood*," he repeated. "Oceans of blood. And then I had to walk away and trust that Scottish scoundrel to get you out of there before anyone realized it wasn't your own blood."

"There was no other way," she began, but he put up his hand.

"Agreed. You were right, and it worked, and I am grateful, but holy God in heaven, it took years off my life, waiting through that day for your note to arrive that you were well, and all had gone according to plan."

"It was the only way," she said again.

"And thank the good Lord above that it's over and done." He pulled hard on the oars again, sending the little boat scudding across the water.

"It has not been a pleasant fortnight for me, either." She hesitated, steadying her voice. "I am sorry for what Melanie will have to go through."

"Write to her. There is no reason for her not to know." Nate shrugged as she stared at him in surprise. "Write to her as yourself, though, not as Angelique Martand."

"How did you know?" she asked when she had recovered her voice.

"You said something once, that Melanie was afraid to call you by your real name . . . But it stands to reason. You were never completely Stafford's. Why would you reveal to him what Melanie risked both your lives to conceal?"

She shook her head, then laughed under her breath. "I should have known you would guess. But truly, I have not thought of myself as anything but Angelique in so long . . ." She paused. He was just watching her with that understanding little smile on his lips. Rowing the boat, even weighed down with her trunk, didn't seem to have winded him. "Marie-Louise Genevieve du Marchais d'Orvelon," she said impulsively. "My parents were the Comte and Comtesse d'Orvelon. My mother was named Marie also, so I was always called Genevieve. One of the smugglers who took us out of France misheard, and Melanie kept it. Only on my birthday would she call me by my true name."

"Do you prefer it?" He pulled on the oars again. When Angelique glanced up, the bulk of a ship loomed over them in the darkness, speckled with pinpricks of lantern light high above them. "I should know what name to tell the captain," Nate added. "For the marriage record."

"Marriage?" She raised her chin and gave him a frown. "What of marriage?"

"Ours," said Nate, stowing the oars. They had reached the ship, drifting past the anchor chain to the tangle of ropes waiting to haul them and the boat back aboard. "You'd better not think of jilting me now," he said. "It's a long voyage ahead of us. Weeks at sea with little to do, unless we are newly-weds with the private cabin."

"You already have the private cabin!"

He shrugged and got to his feet. "Yes, but I won't share it with you if you won't marry me." Even though the boat rocked alarmingly from side to side, he didn't seem bothered or unbalanced as he reached for a rope trailing in the water along the hull and gave it a few hard tugs.

"That is coercion," she protested. "You did not even ask properly."

He laughed. "Marie-Louise Genevieve du Marchais d'Orvelon, will you do me the very great honor of becoming my wife, to live a very dull but happy life with me, far away from the frontier and spymasters, with only the excitement of building a family together?"

"I am sure we will find other excitements, in addition to that one," she told him, "but yes. I will."

Nate laughed again. "Somehow I don't think life with you could ever be dull. And that's why I can't live without you." He swept her into one arm, pulling her close for a deep kiss so passionate, she almost toppled out of the boat when he released her.

The crew of the ship had lowered a sort of sling from the deck, and now Nate reached out and grabbed it. Together they hefted her trunk into it, adjusting the ropes until it was secure. Nate called up to the crew, and slowly it was winched up, the ropes creaking above them. With a quiet splash, Prince pulled his boat alongside them, and when the sling came back down, he and Nate sent up one trunk, then the other from his boat. When Lisette climbed into the sling, Prince attached some trailing ropes to his boat, then winked at Angelique before grabbing another rope and climbing it right up to the deck.

Then it was just the two of them, sitting in the small punt and waiting for the sling to come back down to take her up. "Last chance," Nate told her. "Once you're on my ship, you're not getting off until Boston Harbor."

She raised her eyebrows at him. "Once I board the ship, you will never be rid of me. Perhaps it is *your* last chance."

He pulled her to him, resting his cheek against

her temple. "Angelique, my darling . . . I was lost weeks ago. I never had a chance at all. And I've never been happier."

She smiled at him as someone on the ship deck above them hooted and whistled. "Then we are equal. As always."

Next month, don't miss these exciting new love stories only from Avon Books

Mad About the Duke by Elizabeth Boyle

The Lady Elinor Standon needs to find a new husband, quickly. When she hires a solicitor to help her land a lofty lord, she never imagines she might fall for the man! James Tremont, the Duke of Parkerton, hadn't intended to let his little charade go this far, but now he just can't help but wonder if he can win the lovely widow without divulging his title.

An Accidental Seduction by Lois Greiman

When Savaana Hearnes agrees to impersonate newly wed Lady Clarette Tilmont, she imagines it will be an easy way to make money for a fortnight. Until Sean Gallagher, a ruggedly handsome Irishman with a secret of his own arrives, and Savaana's plans are shattered by desire.

The Dangerous Viscount by Miranda Neville

To escape the reputation of her noble but eccentric family, Lady Diana Fanshawe is determined to make an impeccable match—which is why she *will* marry Lord Blakeney, though she'll never love him. But when the brilliant but unconventional Viscount Iverly kisses her and then steals her heart, will Diana choose love or respectability?

Lord Lightning by Jenny Brown

Unrepentant rogue Lord Hartwood is infamous for his outrageous behavior, and amateur astrologer Miss Eliza Farrell is not at all the sort of woman he amuses himself with. But when demure Eliza becomes entangled in his latest prank, sparks fly with an electric passion that threatens to transform them both.

Visit www.AuthorTracker.com for exclusive information on your favorite HarperCollins authors.

REL 091C

Available wherever books are sold or please call 1-800-331-3761 to order.

Unforgettable, enthralling love stories, sparkling with passion and adventure from Romance's bestselling authors

SOLD TO A LAIRD *by Karen Ranney*
978-0-06-177175-0

DARK OF THE MOON *by Karen Robards*
978-0-380-75437-3

MY DARLING CAROLINE *by Adele Ashworth*
978-0-06-190587-2

UPON A WICKED TIME *by Karen Ranney*
978-0-380-79583-3

IN SCANDAL THEY WED *by Sophie Jordan*
978-0-06-157921-9

IN PURSUIT OF A SCANDALOUS LADY *by Gayle Callen*
978-0-06-178341-8

SEVEN SECRETS OF SEDUCTION *by Anne Mallory*
978-0-06-157915-8

I KISSED AN EARL *by Julie Anne Long*
978-0-06-188566-2

A HIGHLAND DUCHESS *by Karen Ranney*
978-0-06-177184-2

THE ECHO OF VIOLENCE *by Jordan Dane*
978-0-06-147414-9

Visit www.AuthorTracker.com for exclusive
information on your favorite HarperCollins authors.

RT 061

Available wherever books are sold or please call 1-800-331-3761 to order.

AVON

JEAN REYNOLDS PAGE

LEAVING BEFORE IT'S OVER

978-0-06-187692-9

the Language of Trees

978-0-06-189864-8

TATIANA AND ALEXANDER

PAULLINA SIMONS

978-0-06-198746-5

Our Red Hot Romance Is Leaving Me Blue

DIXIE ÷ CASH

978-0-06-143439-6

Life After Yes

Aidan Donnelley Rowley

978-0-06-189447-3

MORTAL FRIENDS

978-0-06-117371-4

Visit www.AuthorTracker.com for exclusive information on your favorite HarperCollins authors.

Available wherever books are sold, or call 1-800-331-3761 to order.

ATP 0910

At Avon Books, we know your passion for romance—once you finish one of our novels, you find yourself wanting more.

May we tempt you with . . .

- **Excerpts** from our upcoming releases.
- Entertaining **extras**, including authors' personal photo albums and book lists.
- Behind-the-scenes **scoop** on your favorite characters and series.
- **Sweepstakes** for the chance to win free books, romantic getaways, and other fun prizes.
- Writing **tips** from our authors and editors.
- **Blog** with our authors and find out why they love to write romance.
- **Exclusive content** that's not contained within the pages of our novels.

Join us at
www.avonbooks.com

AVON
An Imprint of HarperCollins*Publishers*
www.avonromance.com

Availabl 3761 to order.

3 1901 02272 4969

FTH 0708